TETHERED BY BLOOD

JANE BECKSTEAD

LavenderNorth
Press

TETHERED BY BLOOD

First edition. May 29, 2018.

Cover Design by Alyson Misseldine

CONTENTS

*For Mom, who showed me I could be
anything I wanted to be.
And for Dad, who taught me to follow my heart.*

Waldriffeh Sea

Outer
Kingdoms

Hutterland

Waldrin

Belanok

Faronna

Maltury

Bramford
Rever Hall

Pebble

Hampstone

Faronnan Sea

THE
THREE
KINGDOMS

ONE

I DIDN'T NOTICE THE boy until someone shouted his name. "Ivan! Ivan, dance for us!"

Other voices joined in too. "Dance for us, fool!" and "Speak, fool!"

He stood in the middle of the town square, shoulders slumped forward with his gaze fixed on the cobbled stones. He was younger than my seventeen years, maybe a malnourished fourteen. Dirt layered his face, hair grimy and matted.

Ivan. The word sounded much too close to Gavin, the name my brother bore before the wasting sickness took him. I looked again at the boy, trying to find traces of my Gavin in his face. Ivan's face was vacant, but I felt something, a pull I couldn't explain even to myself.

He grunted in pain as someone poked him with a stick. Delighted at his response, his tormentors followed up with more determined pokes. "Get him in the leg, John!" other boys yelled, encouraging the boy with the stick.

Ivan let out a feral cry. He rubbed his arm as tears streamed down his face, but the dirt stayed stubbornly in place.

I felt a quick burst of anger like I hadn't since my fighting days before I was an underwizard, days when I brawled with other children my age over insults, real or imagined. Back when I still wore the skirts that betrayed my gender and Mama spent her evenings bewailing my ever becoming a "respectable lady."

My thoughts turned to Master Hapthwaite. "Give in to emotion, and you are a slave," he was fond of saying. "Rule your emotions, and you are free."

I supposed I took my emotional tranquility for granted since I had passed the Wizarding Board's mastery-over-self trial, the fifth test in a series of twenty toward becoming a master wizard. Serenity was my constant companion.

There were other ways to become a magician, but for those who chose to become a master wizard, control over one's baser emotions was paramount. Frustration had become foreign to me.

I was calm. It was the one thing I knew for certain.

Somebody let loose a rock. It thunked into Ivan's leg, and the boy jumped.

"Dance, fool!" a boy near to my own age cried. "Dance and we'll feed you. I've got berries." A grin twisted his face as he retrieved another rock. Ivan lurched side to side in what I realized was his form of a dance.

That was when I understood. This was a common occurrence for Ivan, and the dirt on his face was not only dirt but bruises as well.

My fingers formed a fist, compelled by an instinct I'd forgotten I had. A few words were all it would take. A few muttered words and I would be through with the whole of them. I'd never performed a killing spell, but I knew the incantation to a handful of them. Performing one would violate the code of the Wizarding Board, since as an underwizard, I could perform strong magic only at the behest of my master. And so I checked myself and forced tranquility into my mind, unwilling to give up everything I had worked for so easily. My fist loosened, and the tension eased from my body. I averted my eyes and forced my steps away from the square.

Maybe it was a mistake to go to the village. A pain raged at the back of my head that I'd ignored for hours, as I refused to acknowledge it was an aching-head sort of day. Besides, forays into the outside world were rare since I was an apprenticed underwizard. Many underwizards disappeared from society altogether during their training, only to emerge a decade later as trained master wizards. But add Master Hapthwaite's illness to a shortage of potion ingredients, and there I was, wandering the streets of a village whose name I couldn't remember, looking for the storefront of William the Botanist.

By the time I found the shop, the noise had receded enough that the scene from the town square had faded from my mind. Smells wafted from the shop's entrance, intoxicating, mysterious scents. My calm had returned.

"Edgar's apprentice, are you?" William the Botanist boomed at me, and it took a moment to remember Master Hapthwaite's given name was not "Master." He clapped a meaty hand on my shoulder. "What's your name?"

"Avery, sir." I pulled the now-crumpled list from my pocket, written by my hand only that morning. "We are in need most especially of baneberry, if you've any to spare."

While William gathered ingredients, I focused my attention on the plants growing in the warm shop. A few I could identify by sight: sage, marigold, vervain, basil. Others were unknown but pleasing in an almost bewildering way.

I inhaled the scents of the shop, many intended to bring calm. In the distance, I imagined I heard a shout. My fingers reached for a rosemary plant, and an unbidden memory sprang to mind: those bad days and nights of brewing rosemary tea with the hope that it would cleanse my brother's diseased body.

Gavin as he was in the days before he died, worsening in his sickbed, the damp hair plastered to his forehead, the clammy skin, the weak grin that attempted to make me smile even as he neared death.

I couldn't shake the image of my brother Gavin and those false words I'd whispered to him that last night before he died. "You will not die, Gavin. You'll be well." And the biggest lie of all, "I won't let anything happen to you."

A few words and a twist of my fingers, and my hearing sharpened enough to listen to goings-on as far away as the town square. I took a moment to sift through the cacophony of other noises in my head—an argument at a nearby market, children playing, an old man mumbling to himself—but at last I singled out the sounds I sought.

Ivan the fool made a wild, grunting cry. Laughter rippled through the accumulated crowd.

"I didn't know fools could bleed," someone said. I heard the crowd's excitement behind that one voice.

My fist clenched, and it was moments before I realize I'd snapped the rosemary in half. I stared at the crushed plant in my hand and recognized that I teetered on the edge of something dangerous. My teeth clenched against the trembling of my body. I forced my eyes closed and pushed all sound and thought from my mind.

That wasn't Gavin. He had nothing to do with me. I was calm. I was in control.

I opened my eyes and placed the crushed rosemary back in its pot. My finger ran down the length. It knit and held, once more alive. I exhaled a breath of relief. That spell didn't always work for me.

"Can't seem to find the baneberry." William emerged from the back of the shop, his arms full of several plant varieties which he deposited on the counter. "I know I have some." He scratched his head and looked around. "Has John been in my stores again?"

"John?" I asked, showing an interest I didn't feel. In my head I planned a route out of the village that would avoid the square.

William rooted around shelves behind the counter but threw an apologetic glance my way. "My son. Gets into things occasionally. Not much younger than you. You know how boys are." He took in my underwizard robes and rubbed a dirty hand along his grizzled chin. "Or perhaps you don't."

For a moment my heart picked up speed, slamming against my ribcage, and I wondered if he'd guessed my secret. Could he tell I was a girl? After all the pains I had taken to conceal it?

I looked down at myself, but all I could see was a shapeless mass of robes, as always. When I looked up again, he had gone back to foraging among the shelves. To himself he muttered, "I told him to stay away from the poisonous plants, though."

My eyes widened. *John.* I wasn't thinking at all when I bolted out the door. I paid no heed to William's voice behind me. For several brief seconds it was just me, robes lifted to my knees, legs pumping, shoes slapping the cobblestoned streets. I charged into the town square and stopped to gasp for breath, hands on my knees.

Crumpled and pathetic, Ivan sobbed into his palms. A boy stood over him, hand extended.

"Are you hungry, Ivan? I have some berries. Do you want one?"

Ivan's trembling hand reached for the glistening white baneberry the boy held out to him.

I tackled the boy around the knees. He was bigger and stronger, but I was faster. My speed had been the deciding factor in most of my fistfights. Still, I could strangle him with a flick of my finger and some muttered words if I so desired. But I didn't. I swung a fist and connected with flesh. He grunted, and we rolled and grappled. Pain lit up my senses.

Anger sung through my veins; outrage throbbed in my chest. He was the wasting sickness that took my brother, the father who abandoned me, the Wizard's Council which demanded of me my emotions. I felt awake for the first time in a long time. "This is me, Gavin. This is me, Ivan," I wanted to say. I didn't know which one I was talking to or if it mattered.

I tasted metallic blood: nauseating, thick. My pulse pounded and my sight blurred. I spat red and swung again.

A blow from behind hit me between the shoulder blades, and I went down, face-first. My brawling partner jumped aside, and a new someone leaned on me, a weight on my back pressing me into the ground. I fought, but hands pulled my arms backward until I wanted to scream.

"Who do you think you are, underwizard?" the voice at my back bellowed.

I wriggled, but my arms felt like they might pop out of their sockets. Rage filled me, and I twisted my head to the side to glimpse my new attacker.

"Don't imagine you can behave as you wish just because you're an underwizard," he growled. You're under Bramford's authority now."

All I could see of the man were bulging tendons in his neck and the cut of his jerkin. Then my cheek met the cobblestones, already slick with blood from my face.

My fingers curled to prepare for the magic I was about to perform, the strong magic which would send this man to the next life and prevent me from completing my master wizard training, though I was too enraged to care.

Somewhere, a voice of quiet reason warned me to *stay calm, Avery*, and *stay in control*, but I was too far gone to listen. And then my eyes fell on the one thing I could see with my narrowed vision—Ivan. He was crouched and sobbing, his hands covering his head for protection. Baneberries lay scattered around him. The boy I had fought with cuffed Ivan on the ear, and he sprawled.

I had failed to protect Ivan the fool, just as I had failed to protect my brother. The fight went out of me, and I sagged against the cobblestones.

My captor, sensing my capitulation, loosened his grip. His feet stepped into my view.

"Send for Master Wendyn," his voice said above my head. Then his booted foot came toward me, the last thing I saw before pain and light exploded behind my eyes. I welcomed the darkness when it pulled me under.

MY HEAD THROBBED a sickening beat when I awoke. There was no denying that the aching-head day I didn't want to acknowledge earlier had turned into a full-fledged crawl-under-the-comforter-and-shut-out-the-light sort of ache. A weight dug at my neck, and somebody sniffled nearby.

I rolled to my knees. My surroundings, bleary as I squinted into the painful light, showed that I was in a small cell, surrounded by bars on three sides and a chinked wall on the fourth. The sniffling paused at my movement, and I looked to find the reason.

In the cell next to mine, Ivan the fool huddled against the bars nearest me. Blood that wasn't there earlier smeared his face. He had been beaten while I was unconscious.

I crawled nearer.

He watched me, his face cautious and fearful. He scrambled backward when he noted my progress toward him.

I swallowed against the bile rising in my throat as it threatened to push its way out. "It's all right, Ivan." My voice came out hoarse and thick. I swallowed again. "I won't hurt you. I won't let them hurt you."

But I knew it was a lie, even as I said it, just as much of a lie as I told my brother. I already comprehended without looking that the weight around my neck was a trammel, used to prevent the use of magic, which left only my wits and strength to save us both. And hurt as I was, how could I help Ivan, let alone myself?

"He doesn't understand," a deep voice said, and I started back, surprised we weren't alone. "Not very sharp, our Ivan. Although your concern is touching."

The man stood under the window where the light was so bright it turned my stomach to look at him. My first impression was of dark eyes beneath heavy brows, but my assessment of him stopped there as I realized he wore the robes of a master wizard.

My stomach dropped. I scrambled to my feet and wavered there while my skull pounded and spots blinked through my vision. Would I be sick?

I wore a trammel. My magic and all spells I had cast on myself had fallen. This meant my voice-modulating spell—the magic that made my voice deep as a boy's—was no longer in place. How high had I spoken just now? Did I sound like a girl?

"Well?" His voice sounded impatient and cold, and he moved around to the front of my cell so the distance between us was an arm's length. I wondered if he was from the Wizard's Council, come to end my apprenticeship. If so, I didn't recognize him from the trials.

"Well?" I repeated stupidly, more concerned with reaching a deep enough pitch in my voice than sounding intelligent. "Well what?" There. That was husky enough.

The man's eyes bored into me, *through* me, with more scrutiny than Master Hapthwaite ever managed. If I wasn't careful, here was a man who would find out my secret.

"Your master has heard of your doings in my village, under-wizard. He's washed his hands of you. You're no longer apprenticed."

Disapprenticed? It was only natural, but it was still a blow. I looked away from the man's fierce eyes, which saw too much, and looked at Ivan instead. I had given everything up for a boy who couldn't understand what I'd done. Which of us was the real fool?

"You've violated your apprentice oath. You will be stripped of your levels and punished for public brawling."

I nodded, still watching Ivan. "I understand."

He continued after a brief pause. "But only if I report you."

My gaze swung to him. His smile, when it came, was not pleasant. I wanted nothing to do with this man.

"I think you can be of some use, underwizard. Until I find out if I'm right, I'm taking you home with me."

I stared at him, uncomprehending.

His frown deepened when I didn't move. "Well, what are you waiting for? Bow to your benefactor."

I trembled, wavering where I stood, and then bent at the waist and vomited at his feet.

TWO

MAMA USED TO SAY a mind distracted can't sew a straight seam, her way of telling me to pay no mind to diversions. With her it always came back to sewing.

I could still see her as she was in the years she was bedridden, leaned backward onto misshapen pillows, the husk of some brilliant flower faded to the crumbled browns of autumn. I remembered the sunless day we buried her on the hill, Papa and Gavin and me.

Gavin. My brother. Dead and buried next to Mama, two crude markers reaching toward the sky.

Focus, Avery. Sew a straight seam.

I knew that I was concussed. Master Hapthwaite had a copy of *Rudimentary Medicine* I devoured, along with most of the rest of his library. If the headache and nausea weren't indication enough, the way my thoughts were running through the cracks in my brain like water, too slippery to hold onto, verified it.

Across from me, the master wizard—whose name I had somehow forgotten—slumped forward, his fingers shoved into his inky black hair. His face wasn't as lined and weathered as I expected, which meant he was younger than I first thought.

Beard growth of a few days rambled over the lower half of his face like lichen on a log. As the carriage continued its jolting and swaying and rolling forward, he looked up, caught my gaze on him, and frowned. His unpleasant expression turned my stomach more than the swaying conveyance.

"You will not soil my carriage, underwizard." His voice sounded hard as granite, and he tucked his shoes beneath his robes.

"Yes," I said, nodding. "I mean, no."

He sniffed in clear disgust, and his gaze shifted to the fool. I was still not clear why the boy was here, but I knew the new master wasn't happy about it.

There was a conversation in the jail of the vile little town, which it turned out was called Bramford, between the new master and the man from the town square, the one who knocked me to the ground and kneed me in the back. I caught snatches of it while still behind bars, trying to control my nausea and the spinning room.

"The fool is not my responsibility," the master said.

"Your apprentice fought on his behalf. The town council wants the fool out. He's always causing trouble," the bigger man replied.

The master's voice grew fiercer. "He is not my apprentice, and the fool is none of my concern. Take care of him yourself."

And yet here we sat, the three of us.

There was no conceivable reason for me to be here. What did this man want from me?

I rubbed my neck. The trammel was gone, but the memory of its weight against my neck remained. I didn't like feeling so powerless. At least I'd had a chance to recast my voice modulating spell, making my voice deep once again.

Next to me, the fool—Ivan—made a guttural noise. He was trying to shrink into the corner, shrink himself into nothingness.

The vulnerable innocence on his face made me want to reassure him, but I knew it was a weakness, this tender feeling I couldn't seem to shake.

This was not my brother.

"What level are you?" the wizard asked, glaring at the rolling hills and trees pushing past the carriage window. We had been a quarter of an hour on this road.

He couldn't make his dislike of me any more obvious, so why was I here? Could he know I was a girl? Did he have designs on me in the way that my mother warned a man could have designs on a woman?

"Your level, underwizard," he snapped at the window. "By the red of your robes, I see you're at least a novitiate."

I blinked and swallowed and tried to force my brain to focus. "Five. I passed the mastery-over-self trial at the beginning of the year."

His eyes swiveled to me. "Devil's dawn, is that what you were doing today? Showing your mastery over self?" He shook his head and continued, "You've gained some abominable habits from Master Hapthwaite, the great baboon. With such a poor example, it's no surprise."

My mouth opened to defend this unjust attack on my master until I realized—Edgar Hapthwaite was no longer my master. I had no master. My mouth snapped shut.

"I can only presume you had bandits for parents."

I forced my anger down. One explosion was enough for today. "Mama died when I was eleven. Papa's still alive, at least as far as I know. Given the time of day, he's probably drinking himself into a stupor at this very moment."

He raised an eyebrow, but then the fool caught his eye by trying to hide behind the window curtains. "Stop it, Ivan," he barked. "We'll be there soon enough."

Ivan cringed against the wall but became still.

"You know his name?" I asked, unable to hide the surprise in my tone. "I mean—"

His eyes flashed back to me. "Everyone in Bramford knows Ivan. I see him often on my visits to town."

"And you let them torment him?"

He raised a brow. "I *let* them? What makes you imagine that I control the townsfolk of Bramford?"

"But . . . you're a master wizard."

"And you would prefer I force my will on them? As you tried to force yours today?"

My mouth opened. "That's not fair. They were—"

"They were doing the same thing they always do. It's because of you that I am forced to take Ivan in. Had I left him there, they would have taken their anger at you out on him." His knee jiggled up and down, up and down. "You have something to learn about fighting. Never start a conflict unless you can remove the threat completely, or else it will come back with even more ferocity the next time. In Ivan's case, your actions could have cost him his life."

I blinked and turned to the opposite window, unable to come up with a rebuttal. He was more than likely right.

The carriage pulled to a stop, the red curtains swaying to and fro before its windows. We had halted before a looming house, all shutters and stone and unwelcoming. It rose larger than Master Hapthwaite's manor. Nerves tickled my stomach, and a glance at the fool showed that he seemed to be trying to make himself part of the conveyance's inside wall.

With one last distasteful glance at the carriage's occupants, and without even waiting for the footman, the man unlatched the door and leaped to the ground. His robes billowed around him like a giant winged creature launching into flight. He strode into the house without looking back.

Seconds passed while the fool—no, his name was Ivan, and I

would call him that—and I looked at each other. His eyes darted toward the road we'd just covered, back toward Bramford. He was thinking about running, and the thought had occurred to me too. I could step out of this carriage and take to the road, free from this man and his unknown intentions.

Free from my dream of becoming a master wizard.

The footman had the door stretched wide, and he peered inside at Ivan and me. Whatever he saw made an eyebrow raise. Neither of us moved toward the door.

"Are you coming out—" he glanced at Ivan and paused before finishing, "—sirs?"

I took a breath, steeling myself for what was coming, and stepped out of the carriage.

Green lawn and fields stretched around the estate, meeting with a thick wood in the distance. A fine fog of dust hung in the air, kicked up by the carriage wheels. It was late in the day, and the sun hung on the horizon. Movement whispered behind me, and Ivan scrambled out of the carriage, ignoring the footman's proffered hand. I expected that he would disappear, perhaps run toward the road without looking back, but he didn't. Instead he sniffed, wiped the back of his hand across the crusted blood on his upper lip, and slunk closer to the carriage's wheel.

A woman bustled out the front door, her black dress swishing around her ankles.

"So it's true." She stopped with her hands on her hips, frowning at me. Her bun pulled so tight I suspected without it, her face would transform into a mass of wrinkles. "He's brought home an apprentice. And what a mess you are." She squinted at me in the sunlight and stepped closer, eyeing me up and down. Her glance lingered on my face, and for the barest breath of a moment, I was nervous that she'd see my true gender, the feminine cut of my chin, the soft curl of my brownish hair against my face. I had only been around Master

Hapthwaite for three years, and he was the least observant man I knew.

Females were banned from practicing magic in Faronna, as well as the entire three kingdoms. Small spells and charms were tolerated, but anything more complicated than that could get a female hauled before the Wizard's Council for a slap on the wrist. The Council reserved their biggest sanction of all, death, for females who persisted in performing complicated magic. That included any female foolish enough to disguise herself as a boy in order to train to become a master wizard.

Gavin and I used to play at being master wizards when we were children, before we knew any better, before we knew I never could be one. When we got older, Gavin hung around the street magicians to learn spells that he later showed to me. I caught on to the spells quicker, but his spells were always bigger. He made me promise before he died that I would learn as much magic as I could. He asked me to do it for him, since he would never be able to. And I'd promised.

The bun-wearing woman made a clucking noise. "You're nothing but a common ruffian. Has Master Wendyn lost his senses?"

"If he has, that's his own business."

Her eyebrows drew downward. "Don't take that tone with me, boy."

Getting along with this woman would take finesse, something I had little of, if I was honest. But at least I had gotten the name of my new master out of her. Master Wendyn. The name knocked out of my head with the kick of that great oaf in the town square.

I inhaled and gathered myself. "I meant no disrespect, ma'am."

Her frown lessened a minuscule amount. "See that you don't forget your place. Master doesn't put up with much here at Ryker Hall." Her gaze swung around, taking in the area behind me. "And where's the other one? Master said he brought that fool."

Ivan was no longer huddled against the carriage wheel. I took a stride in that direction before I realized I was doing it again, caring about him when he was none of my concern.

A noise to my left drew my glance. Ivan crouched behind a thicket growing against the house. A bush loomed over him, almost obscuring him from view.

"Here he is."

Her frown deepened. "Well, come along, then." She whirled and headed into the house, muttering all the while. "Two boys to clean up after. What can he be thinking?"

I stood and stared at the bush. A part of me felt that if I left now, I would never see Ivan again. He would disappear back to Bramford, to daily humiliation and beatings and, if Master Wendyn was right, to possible death because of my interference.

"I suppose they'll want to feed us," I said to the bush. Maybe he couldn't understand me, but judging by the skin and bones of him, it had been a long time since he ate a regular meal. "The food will go to waste if you don't come along, as I have no appetite."

No movement from the foliage. Perhaps his ears were incapable of hearing. Or maybe, as the wizard said in Bramford, he wasn't bright enough to comprehend words. Still, I couldn't stop myself from trying to make him understand.

"Food," I said again, with emphasis. I hoped if he could hear me that it was a word he knew. "All those gravies and fine cuts of meat and stewed vegetables and pastries . . . it would be a shame for them to go uneaten." I didn't know what food this wizard's kitchen would provide, but I was certain they wouldn't starve us. I headed toward the entrance, with its line of unfriendly columns, giving the boy his space to decide what to do.

There was activity in the entrance hall, but once I got there, I was too distracted by the architecture to pay much attention. Colored light filtered through stained glass windows, ceilings arched high above, and complicated patterns crawled across the stonework of the floor, etched in place. A staircase rose from the middle of the room, carved with detailed animals.

"But Mrs. Pitts, ma'am," a young housemaid was saying to the crotchety, bun-wearing woman. "The east wing? Those rooms are all dusty and musty." The girl's arms teetered with linens.

"Thank you, Edie," Mrs. Pitts said, her voice cold as morning frost. "I well know that." She caught sight of me and dismissed the maid with a glance. "There are no rooms ready." Her expression made it clear this was my fault. "You must wait while they're made up. Come along, both of you."

I was surprised and pleased to discover that Ivan had trailed in behind me, keeping a safe distance. He continued to follow as Mrs. Pitts showed us to a sitting room.

"Touch nothing," she advised, with a sharp look at both of us, "and get nothing dirty. I know every detail of this room, so don't imagine you can get away with thievery." She left with a backward glance that said she found it doubtful we'd be able to follow such advice.

I longed to lie down and sleep, but sitting would have to suffice. I picked the nearest chair and arranged myself in it, looking over my ripped and dirtied robes in dismay. The thumping in my head had only gotten worse since I woke up in the jail.

Ivan stood just inside the doorway, looking lost. "You may as well sit," I said, but he didn't move.

In truth, he looked nothing like my brother. Gavin looked a

lot like me: Wavy brown hair, skin that freckled, bright blue eyes, and a lopsided smile. But Ivan the fool had hair that, even when dirty, was the palest blond I'd ever seen. His eyes were a shade of gray identical to the sky on a stormy afternoon. His ears seemed large, sticking out of his small head.

It was the similarities, though, that sickened me. His slight build, bony shoulders, and thin frame. The apprehension in his eyes. It was too much like Gavin in the advanced stages of wasting sickness. It was painful to look at. I changed my gaze to the fireplace and scrutinized the well-shined grate.

The minutes lengthened along with the shadows, and my eyes drooped while I strove to stay awake. To keep myself alert, I pulled a scrap of rope from my pocket which I had developed the habit of carrying these three years now. Unknotting a rope was the first spell Gavin and I had learned, and ever since then, I did it in times of boredom—and to keep my skills sharp. Sometimes the spell came easier than others. Today, after tying the rope, I couldn't budge the knot, though I stared and mumbled the spell multiple times. My head ached too much to think.

I blinked and nodded and tried not to sleep.

"Beg pardon. Didn't mean to disturb you."

My eyes snapped open, and I sat up straighter. It was the young maid, Edie, her apron stiff and straight and her gaze interested. "Wasn't there another—er—gentleman?" she asked, looking around the darkened sitting room.

Friar's bones, I'd lost him again. But it didn't take too long to locate Ivan. He was huddled in a corner, sitting against the wall with his legs pulled into his chest. His knees were visible through the holes in his trousers. He watched both of us.

Edie was carrying a tray and set it down upon a table nearby. The scents coming from it might have been intoxicating, but at the moment, they turned my stomach.

"Will the master be long?" I asked.

Edie looked startled at the question. "Young master has retired for the evening."

"What?" I sat up straighter. "Retired?"

"Yes, he—oh my." She stepped back as Ivan launched to his feet and pushed past her to get at the tray. He stuffed a pastry in his mouth and followed it up with a sandwich—meat, from the looks of it—and a wedge of cheese. His cheeks bulged while his jaws worked.

"Young master?" I prompted. "Is there an old master?"

Edie looked away from Ivan. "To be sure, old Master Wendyn. He's the young master's grandfather." She smiled and red flushed her cheeks. "I'm Edie."

"Er—yes," I said. "I gathered that."

She bustled around the room, lighting lamps. "Mama makes a paste of comfrey that will help with those cuts." She gestured at my face. "I'd hate for you to have any scars."

"That won't be necessary." I didn't like all the notice she was giving me. "This face is used to cuts. Bruises too. But thank you for your concern."

"Or bilberry," she went on. "It's good for bruises—"

"That will be all, Edie." Mrs. Pitts stood at the sitting room door. "You may go."

"Oh. Yes, ma'am." Edie gave a curtsy and hurried out, pausing in the doorway to smile in my direction behind the housekeeper's back. I looked away.

Mrs. Pitts frowned. "Well, you've managed not to destroy this room. That's something. Come along, then. Your rooms are ready."

Her eyes moved to Ivan, who was stuffing sandwiches in whatever pockets would hold them. She made a noise of disgust but didn't stop him.

"Did the master leave instructions for tomorrow?" I asked as we walked up the grand staircase. "What time does he want to speak to me?"

There was a smile in her voice. This pleased her. "Master said he doesn't want to see either of you for a few days, at the very least."

I frowned. "But why—"

"When he wants to see you, he'll let you know. He doesn't want reminding of either one of you until you're cleaned up and smelling better. And maybe not even then, he said." She smiled, as happy about this news as I was annoyed by it. She added as an afterthought, "And you're to keep that fool out from underfoot."

I glanced at Ivan, who was cramming what looked to be a chocolate pastry into his mouth. Now I was a governess.

"Here we are." We stopped at two doorways on the same side of the hallway. "I've had baths drawn for both of you. See that you scrub well."

After Mrs. Pitts stalked away, Ivan and I stared at each other. His jaw worked up and down with chewing, and his clothes bulged in various areas with food.

Why had Master Wendyn brought me here? The question remained unanswered, and it didn't appear that it would be answered soon. I realized I was frowning and forced my face to relax into a more pleasant expression.

"Come along, Ivan," I said, opening one of the doors to wave him inside. "You'll be fine here for the night. I'll see you in the morning."

He was hesitant to go in the room at first, but once I walked in, he followed.

I had gained a second shadow.

"Good night," I said and slipped out the door, closing it behind me.

THREE

"SHAMEFUL, AN UNDERWIZARD SO lazy."

The voice penetrated the fog of my sleep, and then I was falling. There was no time to even get my legs under me. I tumbled out of bed onto the cold ground, sprawled on my side. Early morning light brightened the room.

Mrs. Pitts glared down at me. "Master will not be happy about this, you sleeping the very day away."

My shoulder-length hair, wet when I went to bed, was tied at the base of my neck most days, as was the standard for under-wizards. Now its dried waves tumbled around my face as I rolled to my knees and blinked down at the wooden-planked floor. The fog in my head lifted as I rubbed my ear and listened to Mrs. Pitts' footsteps and the whisk of curtains being pushed back.

I remembered soaking in the bath last night, my eyes and neck heavy. When my face dipped low enough to graze the water, I toweled off and dressed in sleeping clothes. Thank the heavens that included binding my chest, since I didn't know who might wake me in the morning.

When I first became an apprentice, I had gone through

dozens of spells to make myself appear more boyish. It took several voice-modulating spells before I found the one that would make my voice sound deep but not geriatric. Then there were spells to alter my appearance to make me taller, flat-chested, slimmer through the hips, broader of shoulders. I implemented them over the course of my first year as an apprentice so that Master Hapthwaite never noticed. I regretted every spell when I walked onto the testing dais for my first trial. Master wizards were notoriously tight-lipped about what went on at the trials, so it wasn't until I crossed the threshold of the dais and all my spells fell that I understood: Outside magic would not be allowed.

There I stood, exposed at the worst moment. I shortened by four inches, my chest leaped outward, and the deep baritone voice I'd magicked myself with disappeared. The shock of it destroyed my composure.

It was fortunate for me that my bosom was so small to begin with, because the test proctor and judges were so distracted by my sudden decrease in height and my higher voice that they didn't notice the most telltale sign I was a female. Instead, they snickered and coughed to hide it, and the test proctor said he hoped I'd learned my lesson about vanity.

The damage was done, at least to my self-possession. Every spell I'd studied, every skill I'd practiced . . . all of it fled. I failed.

Somehow I kept enough of my composure to not reveal my secret completely there on the dais. When I left the Conclave, head hung low in shame, I vowed to never rely on appearance-altering spells again. There were too many risks. Instead, I perfected my method for binding my chest and spent time around Larkspur House, watching the way various male servants moved. Even if I didn't have the exact shape of a male, at least I could imitate them well enough to pass for one.

Nowadays, the only two spells I relied on were a soiling

spell for the monthly bleeding and a voice modulating spell, though a less deep version than I once used.

"Peck told me you'd slept the whole morning," Mrs. Pitts continued. "Mark this, underwizard. Master won't countenance laziness. If you want to sleep the day away, crawl back to whatever backwoods village you came from and laze about there."

What did she mean, I'd 'slept the whole morning'? I sat back on the floor and looked at the window again. It faced east. I'd been thinking the sun was not yet high enough to shine in my window, but I was wrong. That wasn't early morning light filtering through the glass—it was the light of midafternoon. I had slept long and hard, the sleep of the concussed.

My long slumber had helped. I felt clear-headed in a way I didn't yesterday.

"I had hoped the bath would make you more presentable, but you're more a mess than ever." She shook her head as she took in my face. "Those bruises." She sniffed at me. "At least you smell better. Now, on your feet."

I stopped myself from pointing out that any stench clinging to me yesterday came from my short stay in the Bramford jail. I'd been in fine form before being beaten and jailed.

"On your feet, I said." Mrs. Pitts' sharp voice cut into my thoughts. "And you may as well know, the fool left. Climbed out his window and disappeared in the night."

"Gone?" I repeated, caught unawares. Dismay overwhelmed me, dismay I shouldn't be feeling for a boy I barely knew, and I didn't like it.

"Gone," she repeated. "His bed wasn't slept in, and his bathwater is untouched. A relief to us all, I assure you. Now, get off your lazy bones. Master wants you in his study."

Once she was gone, I stayed on the floor for longer than I cared to admit. When I rose, I crossed to the window, opened it, and leaned out to see what Ivan might have experienced while climbing down. His window was far to my right, several arm lengths away. The foliage beneath the window, a bush of some sort, appeared rather trampled. I ran a hand over the stone exterior next to my window. It presented several handholds all the way to the ground. It would be an easy climb for an experienced wall-scaler such as myself. During our poorest days in Waltney, Papa and I became thieves, scaling buildings in the dark of the night to get at the finer wares within. But I wondered how Ivan had managed that climb.

He had chosen Bramford. A pathetic existence at best.

No. I didn't care. Ivan wasn't my brother.

"Sweet carrot sticks!" a voice exclaimed in the distance.

My glance swung to the open meadow. A rotund man strode toward me, holding a mallet of some sort in one hand. Every few feet he stopped to hold his mallet high in the air while turning around in a circle. He wore short pants the color of old moss, dark socks that reached his knees, and boots. His shirt was plain and practical, the shirt a farmhand might wear. A wide-brimmed hat hid his face from view.

It was impolite to stare, but even so, I couldn't help myself, knowing that Master Hapthwaite would have rapped my knuckles with something painful if he'd seen. It was the most unusual sight to greet my eyes in a long time.

He looked at me and shouted, "Hullo there! If you're not busy, come help me find him!" He turned and trotted back toward the forest.

What sort of place was this Ryker Hall? Was it possible there was a nearby lunatic asylum?

I dressed, donning the new clothes I found in the wardrobe and found Master Wendyn's study by asking directions of the first servant I saw, which turned out to be Edie, the maid from last night.

After pointing the way, she reached into her pocket and

pulled out a small jar. "It was no trouble, sir." She held the jar out, the color high in her cheeks. "Comfrey, remember? For your face."

The prudent thing would be to turn it down. This gift represented something to the girl, something that would be a problem for me. But I couldn't bring myself to do it when I saw the hopeful look on her face.

"Thank you." I accepted the bottle, and Edie's face split in a smile. She was a beautiful girl. For a moment, I envied her the dresses and the length of her hair. As much as I wanted to be a master wizard, I also longed to be myself—a female.

But there was no use in thinking about that. I had made my choice.

"Rub it on those cuts once or twice a day. In no time you'll be all healed up."

I thanked her again, and when she continued to stand there, looking hopefully at me, I turned and walked away.

The door to the master's study was ajar. I stood there for a moment, peeking through the crack to see if I could glimpse the man and gauge his mood. My efforts were unsuccessful, and it only took a moment for me to realize how ridiculous I was being. If any of the servants should see me, I would resemble a frightened rabbit. I squared my shoulders and tapped on the door.

"Enter."

I did so and found myself confronted with a shelf-lined room holding a variety of books and knick-knacks. A tingle of excitement ran through me upon sight of the books. I had only learned to read three years ago when I entered Master Hapthwaite's tutelage, and it took about two years to work my way through his collection. To have fresh, unread books at my disposal filled me with delight.

Only they weren't at my disposal yet. First, I must learn why I was here.

"Don't stand there with your mouth hanging open. Sit down."

The man sat behind a large, tidy desk. A chair sat opposite him, ornate, just as everything in this house was. I sat in it and looked, for the first time with more than a passing glance, at my new master.

He was leaned back in his chair, arms crossed, dark hair hanging in his eyes. His master wizard robes—all black, whereas my novitiate robes were gray edged with red at the collar and cuffs—were neat enough, although there was a button missing near his throat, and the strings where it once sat hung loose. I was positive there was no Mrs. Master Wizard, who would have seen his hair trimmed and his clothes mended. He was much younger than I first thought, here in a well-lit room and without the lens of concussion clouding my vision. He couldn't be over ten years older than me.

"Your name?"

"Avery," I said. "Avery Mullins."

"Mullins. That's right. The baboon told me you're a borderline underwizard."

It took a moment to remember that by "baboon" he meant Master Hapthwaite, and that he'd just insulted me. A part of me wanted to fire a spell at him and prove just what I could do. The feeling reminded me of my brawling partners in the streets of Waltney, boys who had told me I was too stupid for learning. They usually took it back once I beat them into submission.

"Borderline?" I repeated. "Perhaps you misheard him. Mightn't he also have said my skills were divine? He told me so often enough." Master Hapthwaite had never said anything of the sort, but I had become very good at lying since I first disguised myself as a boy.

He rubbed a hand along his jaw, rubbing the whiskers there. "Or maybe he said asinine."

The smugness on his face irritated me. "Then why am I here?"

He shook his head as if even he didn't know the answer. "I suppose because I'm too soft-hearted. Too blasted soft-hearted for my own good."

Perhaps the concussion was still impairing my judgment, because I said, "Yes. You ooze benevolence."

Annoyance flitted across his face. "And hasty," he said. "I'm far too hasty. But never mind that. You will solve a problem for me, underwizard. I live here with my crazy—no, that's not right; let's call him my eccentric grandfather." He reached for a piece of paper, dipped his pen in the inkwell, and scrawled something messy and dark across the page. "Master Oscar Wendyn is his name. You may have heard of him."

The name rang familiar, and after a moment it clicked into place. "Wasn't he PMW?"

"That's right. He was Preeminent Master Wizard until about ten years ago when he retired due to age." He was still scrawling. "His mind wanders these days. What he needs is an occupation. Something to keep him sane. There." He picked the paper up and waved it in the air, drying the words he'd just written. I tried in vain to read what they said as he weaved the paper back and forth, back and forth.

"Everybody needs an occupation," I said, hardly aware of what I'd said. I couldn't decide what he was getting at.

"If you're agreeable to becoming apprenticed again, it's time for the apprentice oath." He set the paper down before me.

Relief washed over me. I would be apprenticed. There was still hope for my master wizard dream.

Every master-apprentice relationship began with an apprentice oath. My oath with Master Hapthwaite was so long ago, lost amid my beginning days as an underwizard, that remembering its details was like looking into a fogged mirror. My behavior in Bramford would have rendered that oath null—I knew that much.

I placed my hand on the paper, but Master Wendyn's words checked me. "You'll want to read it first. I want no claims you didn't understand what you were swearing."

The oath couldn't be that different from my last, but I removed my hand anyway and glanced over the messy writing, trying to make sense of its scrawls.

I, Avery Mullins, do hereby promise and swear to become the apprentice of Oscar Carden Wendyn —

My eyes darted upward. "I'm to be apprenticed to your grandfather?"

He blinked at me, eyebrows raised, as though surprised at the sharpness of my voice. "That's right."

"When you've as much as said the man is crazy?" My mouth gaped.

"Not crazy. He needs a purpose to keep him sane. An apprentice, say."

More clicked into place. "He's that man I saw out in the meadow, isn't he? With the mallet? Carrying on like a lunatic?"

His brow darkened. "I've said he needs an occupation. The man was a genius in his day. He can be again."

I couldn't believe I was ready to swear an oath to a man who probably couldn't remember his own name. I rubbed at my nose, just like Mama. She always rubbed at her nose when worried.

"Do you have a better offer?" he continued. "You're free to go if you think you can find another master, someone willing to take on an underwizard who's already broken one oath. I wish you luck in that case." He retrieved the paper and crumpled it into a ball.

I deflated. I was certain of two things in that moment. One, he was right. Finding and convincing another master to take me would be a difficult—maybe impossible—proposition. And two, I hated him for it.

"I will swear." It took effort to get the words out.

"Ah. I thought you might." He smoothed the crumpled paper out. "Let me read it to you in full." His deep voice commenced, and I found that I hated every nuance of the sound, every confident rise and fall in his tone, the smooth smugness underlying it. The general meaning of the oath was that I must promise to be a model underwizard and apply myself to my studies with dedication. I placed my hand on the crumpled paper when he finished. He did the same. We said the words, and the magic mixed between us, sparking off of our fingers and twining together. I glared at it.

I stood on the edge of a cliff, rage tugging me over the side.

"Forget everything the baboon taught you," he said, an afterthought as I turned to go. "Tomorrow your real training begins."

As I left, I couldn't help but worry I had just ruined my chance of ever becoming a master wizard.

FOUR

I DIDN'T CHOOSE A direction so much as look up and realize that I was outside. Mrs. Pitts' voice echoed in my memory. I felt as though she might have called something at my retreating back about supper.

A glance around showed that the meadow was empty but for a grazing cow in the distance. I started toward the trees with no destination in my head. But among the trees, at least there would be a place to think and walk undisturbed. The rage washed over me, and I let it. I needed to experience it and let it go before I did something stupid with it. That was another thing I'd learned about rage.

Halfway to the forest, a noise to my left drew my attention. I stumbled in surprise, because the hat-wearing fellow was beside me, his stride matched to my own. When I stuttered to a stop, so did he.

"So you're here to help?"

This was old Master Wendyn, former PMW—Preeminent Master Wizard, or in other words, the highest magical office a master wizard could hold. The PMW ruled all magic-wielders with the help of the Wizard's Council. Up close, I could see that his chin was grizzled with a patchy white beard, his face wrinkled and tan.

"Help?" I repeated.

"Just playing a game of scry and seek. Would you like to help?"

"I don't know what that is."

"Oh. You don't." He sounded disappointed but recovered quickly enough, removing his hat to crouch down and place an ear to the ground.

Seeing the man up close didn't increase my anger. Up close, it was plain he couldn't help what he'd become. Anger directed at him would be useless. It was the grandson I should be angry with.

I gave him a short bow. "I suppose I should introduce myself, Master Wendyn. Avery Mullins at your service."

"Oscar," he said, holding a hand out. I helped him up. Did I imagine I heard the creak of old bones? "Pleased to make your acquaintance. And don't call me master. Nobody calls me that anymore but the servants and people I don't like." He plopped his hat back on his head and gestured with one arm. "This is Forthwind."

"Er . . . who is Forthwind?" I asked, looking to the space he'd just gestured at.

"Don't be dimwitted, boy. The stick." He waved the arm around more, the one holding the mallet.

"You named your stick?"

"Of course. I name all of them." He gave me a look up and down, one eyebrow raised. "You're the new apprentice, eh? I thought you'd be smarter."

I chewed on my lip and didn't reply. How long could this master-apprentice relationship really last? He didn't look as though he'd live the period of an apprenticeship, which could sometimes exceed ten years. What happened if he died amid my studies? Would the grandson inherit me, like chattel?

He raised his mallet in the air and turned in a circle. At last he stopped, squinted into the distance, and took off across the meadow. I was unsure what to do until he called over his shoulder, "Well, come on, then. He won't just find himself!"

By the time I caught up, Oscar had come to a stop at the edge of the forest. The trees all ran together here, thick as berries at the height of summer. Dappled sunlight filtered through the branches.

"I saw that boy come out the window." Oscar wheezed as he looked over at me, his voice almost mournful. The brim of his hat flopped back and forward on a breeze. "He might have broken his neck, but I slowed his fall." His fingers twitched at a branch, and a leaf drifted to the ground at half the normal speed.

"'That boy'? You mean Ivan?"

He gestured into the trees. "The boy that came with you. Then he ran into the forest. Seems a shame to leave him. Wild animals come this far sometimes, you know."

I stared into the blackness between the trunks. "He's in the forest?"

Oscar leaned the mallet over one shoulder. "It'll be a day or two at the most before the big animals hunt him down. Do you want to help me find him?"

I already knew I wouldn't leave Ivan in the forest, though I couldn't understand why. That boy wasn't Gavin, but there was a part of my mind that didn't seem to care. "I suppose so."

Oscar scrubbed at his chin. "Well, don't sound so excited about it. Forthwind and I are just saving a life, that's all. You needn't feel obligated to join us."

I refrained from rolling my eyes. This broken shell of a mind —a man who named his mallet and spoke of it like a companion

—was a master wizard? "Yes, I'll join you and your stick. Lead on, Master W—I mean, Oscar. I'll follow where you lead." I let him pass me and then trailed after him into the forest, its needles and leaves and twigs crunching underfoot.

It was an hour or more before we found Ivan, an hour of listening to the ground and twisting the mallet in air and Oscar calling out meaningless incantations. But at last we found Ivan by dumb luck when I spied his pale hair glinting through the foliage. He huddled against a tree, eyes closed and head leaned back, snoring. Dirt streaked him up and down. He was twice as dirty as the last time I saw him.

"Impressive," Oscar said, nudging Ivan with his foot. "It isn't easy to accumulate so much filth. Is it a natural talent, or have you had to work to develop the skill?"

Ivan started and opened his eyes, taking in the two of us. He rubbed the sleep from his lids with one filthy hand. Did I imagine there was a flicker of recognition when his eyes lit on me?

"What were you doing out here in the middle of the night, anyway?" I asked Oscar.

He looked at me with surprise. "It's the best time to scry and seek, of course. Scrying at night is excellent practice." He helped Ivan to his feet.

"Well, don't expect me to join you, even if you are my master," I grumbled.

Oscar turned back and blinked at me several times. "I'm sure I must have heard you wrong. Did you just say I'm your master?"

THE JOURNEY back to the manor house was swift. Oscar stormed through the brush and stomped over detritus, single-minded in his purpose of returning to the house. I caught hold of Ivan's hand and dragged him behind in my haste to follow. Oscar whacked any branches unlucky enough to hang in our path with his mallet.

"I'm sorry . . . I . . . did you . . . was it something I said?" I huffed and puffed.

But Oscar said only one thing. "Miranda's cutlass! Who does he think he is?"

The cow took off at a gallop when it saw us coming. We were barely across the threshold of the house when Oscar bellowed, "Garrick! Garrick Wendyn, I'd like a word! Where are you? Where is he?" Oscar demanded, as he rounded a corner and came face to face with Mrs. Pitts.

"I—in his study," she stuttered, and Oscar pushed past her, muttering and swinging his mallet.

Mrs. Pitts stared after him before turning to us, and then she became all huffs and sniffs and harrumphs when she saw that Ivan was back. "Filthier than ever. I suppose I must have another bath drawn. And you've missed supper."

There was shouting coming from the study at the end of the hall. We all pretended we didn't hear it.

"You will scrub this time, believe you me," Mrs. Pitts warned Ivan, and his hand tightened in mine. I tried to slide my fingers from his grip, but he clung as though I was his lifeline in a vast ocean.

"You, underwizard!" Oscar shouted from the end of the hall. Only his head stuck out of the doorway to the study, that ridiculous hat with the floppy brim still on his head. "Get down here. You are going to explain all this." He turned to say something inaudible over his shoulder, and then bellowed at me, "NOW!"

I extracted my hand from Ivan's. He gave a strangled grunt before Mrs. Pitts dragged him off.

I hurried toward the study. The sound grew as I approached, angry words falling louder and faster, a rainstorm of rage.

". . . mean to tell me you assumed? That because I have more free time than I once had, of course I'd want an apprentice?"

The younger Master Wendyn stood facing the window, his back to the room. His hands clasped behind his back.

"I left your father's house for this very reason, and now you want to treat me the same way?" Oscar continued. "As though I'm a child who can't make his own decisions? Let me tell you, Garrick, I won't stand for it. I will happily evict my tenants and return to Hampstone."

Master Wendyn continued to stare out the window.

"You." Oscar turned. "What's your excuse? What makes you think you can just declare yourself someone's apprentice?"

My mouth opened. "We . . . swore an oath," I said stupidly, at long last.

Oscar thumped his mallet against the desk, and a sheet of parchment on top—the oath?—went up in flames.

"That's the value of your oath. You can't swear on another's behalf, underwizard. And you of all people should know that, Garrick. You did your Postulate on oaths, or have you forgotten that year of studying and preparing and defending yourself to the Council? Or is it that you didn't care?"

"You're being ridiculous," Master Wendyn said to the window. "And if you don't calm down, you will damage Forthwind."

Oscar dropped the mallet on the desk. "Ridiculous? Am I? You're the one who brought this boy here, most likely with promises of being apprenticed. What are you going to do about that now?"

Master Wendyn turned from the window. "It isn't my problem; it's yours. I brought him here for you."

Oscar's face had by now turned a shade of purple. "You know my age. I may not even be alive by the end of his apprenticeship. You'll have to make this right."

"Don't make this my problem, Grandfather."

"You're forgetting who you're dealing with here. I faced down the ambassador to Belanok without batting an eyelash. You'll not bully me into compliance."

"You need an occupation."

"As do you. All you ever do is mope around and feel sorry for yourself these days."

Master Wendyn scowled in my direction. "You may go, underwizard."

"No, stay," Oscar ordered me. "This concerns you."

"I said go."

"What's come over you, Garrick? Ever since Cailyn—"

"Get out!" the younger Master Wendyn thundered in my direction, and I hurried out the door. It slammed behind me, propelled by the force of hastily wrought magic.

I could still hear their raised voices through the door, and I wasted several minutes eavesdropping, though I learned nothing new. Oscar proclaimed his belief that his grandson was lazy, while the grandson told Oscar his brain had become unmoored. And most definitely, neither had an interest in becoming my master.

The oath forged mere hours ago was dissolved. I was masterless once again.

———

COLORED sunlight filtered through the stained glass as I ascended the staircase. The sun was on its way down.

The door to Ivan's room stood open, and I stopped to peer

in. He had collapsed in the middle of the room, crying with snorts and gulps. A robe several sizes too large enveloped him, and his hair dripped water. He looked like a drowned cat. A sobbing drowned cat. Two manservants were busy cleaning up the remains of the bath. Peck passed me, carrying a bucket of filthy water.

"Here are your clothes, you ungrateful wretch," Mrs. Pitts said. "*Clothes.*" She stood next to the bed and patted the garments laid out on the mattress. "To wear."

Ivan didn't move. He continued to sob, his wet hair and tears dripping down his face.

"Oh, great Hepzibah's fiddle, this is ridiculous. Help me, Donovan." She gestured for the manservant and strode to Ivan's side. He shied away, but she grabbed hold of his arm. "Clothes!" she shouted again, as though she could force him to understand by sheer volume. Donovan grabbed his other arm, and the two of them wrestled Ivan toward the bed. I imagined that getting him to bathe used much the same process.

But all at once it was too much. Too much meddling in my life, Ivan's life, too much being pushed around. I understood the look of helplessness on Ivan's face, because it was just how I felt about my apprenticeship. And I'd had enough. I stomped into the room and pulled Ivan out of their grasp.

"That is *enough*," I said, and my teeth might have been bared, I was so angry. "He doesn't understand. What right have you to treat him this way?"

"How dare you," Mrs. Pitts sputtered and reached for Ivan again.

I knocked her hand away. "No. You are not needed here any longer. I will see he sleeps in the bed. I will see he bathes. I will see he dresses. You are never to so much as think about pushing him about in any way again, do you understand? Now GET OUT."

My voice had risen, and even though I knew I was yelling at the wrong person, that I should yell at those two meddling master wizards downstairs, I couldn't seem to stop myself.

Mrs. Pitts backed off a step. Her neck was stiff, head high as she glowered down at me. "Well," she sniffed. "The master will regret taking you in, sooner rather than later, I'm certain. I wish you luck. Don't expect my help again." She motioned for Donovan, and the two left with a firm click of the door.

Ivan watched me, the tears still glittering on his cheeks. I had a hold of his wrist, and with a sigh, I released it and step back. He skittered to the side of the room and huddled in a corner.

Ah, friar's bones. Back to this again. At least he didn't seem to be crying any longer.

I sat on the edge of the bed and leaned forward, my elbows on my knees and my head in my hands. "It's been one day. *One.* Only yesterday I was an apprenticed underwizard. Today everything is in question. How can it all be gone?"

My nose caught a whiff of something. I realized a tray of food sat next to the table and that I was hungry.

"Have you eaten, Ivan?" I asked, getting up. Here I went talking to him again. But there was a part of me that just felt certain, though he'd never responded, that he heard me.

The soup bowl was half empty, and the roll had teeth marks in it. "Of course you have. You have no problem eating when you're hungry. I saw the way you stuffed yourself last night." I helped myself to a piece of bread and ham.

Ivan got up and crept closer to take the last piece of bread. He backed off a few paces and munched on it.

"We should get you dressed." I eyed the oversized robe coming off one skinny pale shoulder. "That thing could fall off at any moment, and I don't much want to see you naked."

There were sleep clothes laid out on the bed, pants and a

long shirt. I put down my half-eaten bread and held them up. "You need to put these on. You can do it by yourself, can't you?" In reality I didn't know what he could and couldn't do by himself, but I wasn't about to volunteer to dress him. I did that for Gavin during his last days when he was sick and weak as a kitten, but I wasn't prepared to do it for a stranger.

Ivan finished the bread. Then, with deliberate movements, his eyes on me the whole time, he took my half-finished piece of bread from the tray and finished that off too.

"Fine. You can have my bread. But in return, you have to get yourself dressed. Understand?" I held the clothes up again.

Ivan finished the bread and backed off to his corner.

I carried the clothes to him and set them on the floor. "You must know how to wear clothes. You weren't naked in Bramford."

He looked up at me, which I thought a fine beginning. I returned to the bed.

"Once you're dressed, this is where you're supposed to sleep. The bed." I sat on the bed and then laid down. "Like this, see?" A glance at Ivan showed he hadn't moved and was no longer even looking in my direction.

I stared at the ceiling and sighed. I wondered if he could even hear me. And if he heard me, could he understand? Would any of this even matter tomorrow? Tomorrow I would have to leave to find a new master.

During my first round of master-hunting, I showed up on Master Hapthwaite's doorstep and was refused entrance. But I begged and pleaded and cajoled until he at last agreed to give me one chance at becoming a master wizard.

If I could make my way to his doorstep again, could I persuade him to give me another chance?

I blinked drowsily at the rafters and thought of Master Hapthwaite. Of course I could.

FIVE

I WOKE IN THE night and realized that I lay in Ivan's bed. It had been stupid to lie down on it last night. Climbing into any man's bed invited risk, fool or not. Under normal circumstances, I never would have, but losing my master—twice over now—seemed to have affected my better judgment.

I was reluctant to leave the warmth of the bedclothes, but I pushed myself up and surveyed the room in the darkness. Where had Ivan gone to?

My eyes settled on him, still in the corner where I left him, his head lolling to the side in sleep. I got up and crept closer. The robe pooled around his feet, discarded in favor of the sleep clothes. He had dressed himself.

Moonlight from the window touched his hair and high-lighted his face. It was a mass of bruises, purple mingled with green and yellow and brown. He could be the survivor of some great and terrible war. He looked far too innocent.

My chest gave a strange pang I couldn't decipher, and something burned behind my eyes. If I could produce tears, I might just be blubbering like Papa when he came home drunk and remorseful. Disgusted at my reaction, I pulled the quilt from the bed and arranged it around him so he wouldn't get cold. But this was more out of concern for myself, since if he got cold, he'd wake and maybe try to climb out the window. Then he'd either fall and break his neck, or else I'd have to find him in the forest again. I was about to leave, when movement at the window caught my eye. I stepped closer to investigate.

Oscar stood out in the meadow again with his mallet—Forthwind. What kind of man named a stick? As I watched, he traipsed through the moonlight and then disappeared into shadow near the forest.

When did the man sleep?

I gave a sniff of disgust—to think I was nearly apprenticed to that lunatic—and I headed to my room.

IT HAD BEEN two years since I lost the ability to cry.

To be clear, I didn't so much lose the ability as curse myself with a spell I didn't know how to remove. It was my fault for reading a book Master Hapthwaite warned me not to. It was where all my knowledge of advanced magic came from—time manipulation, shape-shifting, fighting, and killing magic. Those were all big magics that underwizards were forbidden to try without permission from their master. I used a spell called dry as desert, a liquid-stopping spell useful for things such as bleeding wounds and leaky roofs. It seemed to be less advanced magic than the others in the book, although still above my abilities.

But that didn't stop me.

After my third time taking the first trial, I was a mess, standing there in the Wizard's Conclave great room packed tight with underwizards and masters. When the proctor announced I had passed, I couldn't help it. I forgot I was supposed to be a boy, forgot I was stoic and strong and silent, forgot everything but that I had passed. At last. Tears of relief poured down my cheeks.

I was nothing but mortified that I was in tears, certain that everyone present would see at once I was a girl. So I stood there frozen, willing the tears back into my head, while underwizards gathered around to congratulate me.

The panic of the moment lent me unintended power. Without even thinking, I clasped my hands together and whispered words I had read in the prohibited book only a few days earlier. In the next breath, the tears rolled back into my head, and I smiled and thanked those around me, my face dry as dust.

That was the last time I cried, and mostly I was glad of it. But every once in a while, when I got to thinking about Mama or Gavin, I got an ache behind my eyes, and I wished I knew how to reverse the magic.

I RECEIVED word the next morning to come to the study.

Master Wendyn was concerned about my welfare, he told me. He said it with his back to me in his usual style, speaking to the windows that looked out over the meadow rather than speaking to my face. It was the same view I saw from my bedroom. His profile, when he turned his head to catch my response, seemed more annoyed than concerned.

"If you're worried I won't find another master, you needn't concern yourself."

"What makes you say that?"

"Because I will."

He turned to face me, his brows pushing downward in a scowl. "You seem uncommonly certain, which means you're either conceited or naïve."

"Neither. I'm stubborn."

"If tenacity were the only thing that mattered, half the street magicians in Faronna would be master wizards by now."

I shrugged. "It may not get me all the way, but the rest I'll make up for with hard work."

"I see. And if stubbornness and hard work are not enough?"

"It will be enough."

"And if it isn't?"

"It will be." My voice had grown tense, and I forced myself to relax. I was calm. I was in control.

"You're thinking of going back to Hapthwaite, aren't you?"

The question made me defensive. "And if I am? It's not as though you have any say in what I do."

He shook his head. "A piece of advice, underwizard. If you're as dedicated to this road as you say, you would do well to stay far, far away from that baboon of a master wizard."

"His name," I said with mounting irritation, "is Master Hapthwaite. And he's not as bad as you make him out to be. He was a good master."

He frowned. "Were I you, I'd count myself lucky that I was out of his control. There are plenty of fine wizards out there. If you're truly devoted, you won't have difficulty finding another master. I'll give you a week to do so."

And with that, he waved me from the room.

I TOOK several days composing a letter for Master Hapthwaite, the perfect letter which I proofread and reworded and rewrote a hundred times at least. In sum, I apologized for my momentary lapse in judgment in Bramford and promised it would never happen again if only he'd give me another chance. I peppered it liberally with flowery words of flattery. When it was just right, I prepared to send it off the next day with one of the servants.

The next morning, I descended the staircase for breakfast and saw that Mrs. Pitts stood at the front entrance, holding a low conversation with an unknown someone behind the half-closed door.

". . . won't be staying. Master's discharged him." She caught sight of me, and her frown deepened. "Here he is. You can talk to him yourself." She opened the door wider, and my mouth fell open.

Callum stood there, Master Hapthwaite's footman.

My heart jumped into my throat as I realized he'd come here for me. Master Hapthwaite wanted me back!

And then my eyes fell to the ground where my traveling trunk, which held all my belongings, lay at Callum's feet.

"I've brought your trunk, sir." He gestured.

My heart finished falling back to its usual position in my chest, and I reined in my disappointment. Master didn't want me back.

Yet.

I gathered myself. "Thank you, Callum. If you'll wait just a moment, I have a letter for the master." I turned and dashed up the stairs. The letter lay on my desk, just where I had left it. But before I grabbed it, a new thought occurred to me, and I stopped.

Why shouldn't I return with Callum and deliver my message in person? I knew Master Hapthwaite would take me back.

I left the letter on the desk.

Ivan came out of his room just as I left mine, still in his sleep clothes and rubbing his eyes.

"Not this again. You must dress first," Peck said behind him, his voice impatient. This conversation had happened before.

"Come, put on your clothes before you leave." He grabbed Ivan by the collar and hauled him back into the room.

I couldn't just leave Ivan here. Once Master Hapthwaite took me back, Ivan would be at the mercy of the tyrants in this household. I couldn't think what Master Wendyn wanted with the boy, but whatever it was, it couldn't be good.

I stepped into the room. "You there. You're dismissed." I jerked my head at the door and held the man's gaze. He looked me over before he shrugged and left the room, muttering.

When he was gone, I closed the door and grabbed the clothes laid out for Ivan on the bed. "Here. Put these on. I'll wait."

I stood facing the door with my back to Ivan. There was no sound. I dared a look over my shoulder. Ivan stood there staring down at the clothes in his hands, as though mystified how they got there.

Sounds of exasperation escaped my throat. "I'm in a hurry, all right? I'm about to leave for good. If you want to come with me, get dressed. Otherwise you can stay here. By yourself. And be bullied and pushed around for the rest of your life." I turned back to the door.

The faint rustle of clothing brought a smile to my lips. While I waited for him to dress, I pondered the possibility that Ivan was smarter than everyone seemed to believe. If he could dress himself, and if he could hear, then what else was he capable of?

An elbow bumped mine. Ivan stood by my side. His tunic was laced unevenly, leaving gaps to the milky white skin of his chest beneath. My fingers twitched of their own accord, that was how badly I wanted to fix it, but I stopped myself.

"Much better," I told him. "Now, then, shall we go?"

CALLUM'S PROTESTS put me in mind of Master Hapthwaite and his fussy disposition. I smiled, listening to him gripe that Master never said to bring me back with him.

"But he never said not to either, did he?" I asked.

Callum tilted his head to the side in scrutiny of me. At long last he shrugged and said, "If you're that determined, I don't suppose I can stop you."

It was that kind of ambivalence I was hoping would convince Master Hapthwaite to take me back.

I wasted time trying to convince Callum to take my trunk with us, but he stood firm on that point, saying he was sent to deliver the trunk and he always did as the master ordered. I was only trying to save him a trip later, but I gave up, as I could see it was an argument I wouldn't win.

It took at least an hour to travel to Larkspur House. I didn't engage Callum in conversation, and as speaking to Ivan was useless, it was a quiet ride. Instead, I planned out what I would say to Master Hapthwaite.

As we pulled up the familiar circular drive, relief settled over me. I was coming home. Excitement zinged through me, so much so that I launched myself over the side of the buggy the moment we stopped moving. Ivan followed a moment later and huddled into my side. I didn't like this new familiarity, and I pushed him to arm's length. "That far," I said. "I want you at least that far away from me, understood?"

As usual, he didn't respond. He trailed after me as I headed up the wide staircase to the entrance. At one of the upper floor windows, a face paused and looked down at us. I recognized Master Hapthwaite's doughy face through the warped glass. He was too far away to read his expression, but seeing my master's face again lent me confidence. I squared my shoulders, lifted my chin, and marched up the stairs.

Only when I was at the top did I realize I'd lost Ivan. I looked backward to discover he was running in the opposite direction. As I watched, he disappeared around the side of the house.

Coward. I needed to train him to stop doing that.

The housekeeper, with whom I'd always had a friendly acquaintance, smiled and showed me to a sitting room before going to fetch the master. I practiced my speech as I waited and wondered if Master would still allow me to sit for the mastery-over-fear trial in the spring, as he mentioned a week ago. I didn't think we'd lost too much time yet.

"Underwizard Mullins."

I looked up from my hands, which I'd been staring at in extreme concentration, and rose. Hapthwaite stood before me, his expression curious, perhaps even concerned. His dark hair, shot through here and there with gray, curled against his forehead.

"Master Hapthwaite." I dropped into a bow.

"What are you doing here?" Surprise filled his tone, but nothing much beyond that—no anger or animosity at my presence. That was good, I supposed, although I'd hoped for some emotional reaction, some sign he felt a connection toward me.

I rose from my bow. "I asked Callum to bring me back with him. I was hoping to have a word with you."

"About?" He tilted his head, and the pudgy, loose skin around his jowls wobbled. He seated his portly self across from me. "If you're having a problem, you should discuss it with your new master. Wendyn, is it?"

"That man is not my new master. He never wanted me. He only—took me in briefly."

His eyebrows shot up. "He never wanted you? So he's still waffling, is he? How like him."

I forged ahead. "My behavior in Bramford was wrong. I'm

more sorry than I can say that I disgraced you. I'm here to ask you to take me back."

His expression didn't change. "I can't help you."

"Please, just listen. Five minutes of your time."

He shook his head. "You've disgraced me once already. I should think that was more than enough."

"I was showing kindness to a—a fool," I explained, because once he understood how it all happened, I knew he would forgive me. "Honor in all things, remember? It is the most important." I was repeating back to him words he said himself dozens of times, part of the apprentice oath.

With a shake of his head and a deep sigh, he said, "Don't throw that phrase in my face as though its meaning escapes me, Mullins. I am the master wizard here. I knew the meaning of honor in all things before you were a babe in your mother's arms. And what it does *not* mean is assaulting a young boy and brawling in the streets like a common scoundrel."

"You're right," I said, trying to look more humble. "It wasn't honorable. It was weak and shameful."

He leaned forward to pat me on the knee. "Which is why there's nothing I can do for you. Run along to . . . wherever you're going."

"But I've come so far with your help. You know how much I've learned. Look, I'm getting better at holding fire." I held my hand out and summoned the magic. It sparked and tickled along my palm, a fire almost catching but not quite.

Bones. I'd hoped to make a better showing than that.

"Ah, Mullins. This is why. Your fire is barely passable. It's a first level underwizard's trick, and you, a level five novitiate, cannot manage it. I thought you were just a slow learner, but it's more than that. You're not cut out to be a master wizard, boy."

I was stung. He'd never been so blunt with me. "But . . . I passed the trials. Isn't that what matters?"

"You passed the trials," he agreed. "It's the only reason I kept you on. But you only passed by a narrow margin each time, and you've had to take each trial more than once. Even with those under your belt, you still have difficulty with the most basic of underwizard skills."

Had he been skirting the truth all this time, afraid to hurt my pride?

"Look, take some advice, will you, Mullins?" he said, his voice kinder. "You've got the makings of a fair magician. You know, the amateur sort. Master wizardry isn't for everyone, and there's no shame in admitting that."

An amateur magician? He thought I had the makings of a common street magician?

At last I found my voice. "You—you're mistaken. I have what it takes. I'll work harder, I'll study more. Whatever you ask of me." My voice sounded panicked to my ears.

He stood. "You don't have the skill required. Your behavior in Bramford only confirms it. If you're still determined to become a master wizard, I suggest you go to Wendyn and beg him to take you. You two deserve each other."

The flaccid skin of his jaw wobbled as he turned his back. He was going. I needed to say something, to plead my case further. But the words were gone, my confidence pulled out from under me.

"I—no—wait," I managed in a strangled voice. The door closed. I stared at it with bewilderment.

My eyes pulsed and burned and throbbed, but not a tear came out.

SIX

SOMEHOW I ENDED UP outside of Larkspur House. Ivan came back. We walked the road, in what direction I couldn't say. There was a heavy feeling in my insides I didn't want to put a name to.

I had been so certain that Master Hapthwaite would take me back. I knew the man better than he knew himself; of course he would take me back. That's what I had been thinking. But perhaps I didn't know him so well as I thought.

I tried to gather myself. What would be my next step? I always had a next step. I fingered the knotted rope in my pocket and tried to pull strength from it.

When that didn't work, I pulled it from my pocket and practiced my customary unknotting spell on it, hoping the action would clear my brain and give me my next step. The rope unknotted, but still nothing came to me. I shoved it in my pocket and pulled Ivan after me. I was too befuddled to do anything but put one foot in front of the other and keep moving down the road away from the only place I had called home since my family fell apart.

Lost, that was the heavy feeling inside me. I was lost.

A carriage rattled past, and I had to haul Ivan out of the way to keep him from being run down. "Open your eyes," I growled. "You could have been killed."

He scratched the side of his head and stared at me.

"You're a great coward, you know? You run off every time you're scared of something. It's humiliating. Make use of your backbone, why don't you."

We stood in the middle of the highway while I glared at him and he toed the ground. Light caught at the bruises on his face as he looked up at me, his expression almost frightened.

Shame filled me, and I gave a great sigh. "Never mind. I'm sorry." I rubbed my eyes and wished I could cry and feel better. "Sorry. Come on; let's keep going." I walked on. When I turned to look, he was following.

I'd been too cocky. I was so sure that things would work out the way I wanted, just because I wanted it enough. And now I needed to do what I wanted Ivan to do: have courage. Step into the dark of a new path and hope the light found me.

The only options left were to find a new master or become a street magician. And I would only accept one of those two options.

I would go to Hampstone, to the Wizard's Conclave. I could make inquiry there about master wizards seeking apprentices, as I had when I first sought a master. If I had to, I'd take work until I found a new master.

For the first time, I took stock of the direction we were headed. I smiled when I discovered we were going toward the dreadful village of Bramford. That wasn't the part that pleased me, but the fact that we were already headed toward Hampstone was helpful.

More importantly, we were headed toward Ryker Hall. My trunk was still there, and while I didn't mind losing some of its contents, there were other things inside I considered irreplaceable. Mama's hairbrush, for one. My brother's old tin mug, for another. We could collect our belongings and spend the night at the hall before continuing on to Hampstone in the morning.

"Come along, Ivan." My smile deepened when his hand slid into the crook of my arm.

IT WAS A LONG WALK. I babbled to pass the time, which was unlike me. But then again, it had been a long time since I had someone by my side to talk to, so perhaps it *was* like me and I didn't remember it.

The late afternoon sun had wilted me inside my robes like a steamed vegetable served up for supper by the time we turned down the lane to Ryker Hall. Ivan didn't look much better.

A buggy stood in front of the house, meaning that one of the Masters Wendyn had company. I took Ivan around to the kitchen entrance, and we went up the back staircase to our rooms. I deposited Ivan in his bedroom, telling him to rest since we'd have another long day of walking ahead of us tomorrow. Before I went into my room, however, I paused at the voices drifting up the grand staircase. I drew closer out of curiosity.

". . . explosion at the Conclave last week? It destroyed a portion of the basement wing." It was a man's voice speaking. He must be in the entrance hall below.

". . . theories on causation?" That was Master Wendyn's voice.

"It originated in an alchemy lab beneath the library. Somebody mixing things they oughtn't, I suppose."

"Imbecile."

"Agreed," said the stranger. "Oh, and in case you haven't heard, there's rumors the Council will soon take action on the low matriculation rate."

"What sort of action?"

"The rumor is they may mandate able-bodied wizards to take on an apprentice every ten years. Faronna is at an all-time low for masters and apprentices."

"I can't imagine you with an apprentice, Matt. Please don't teach the boy to fight."

"Murk and shadow, have a little faith in me. I haven't fought in years. Besides, you know the rules. I can't have an apprentice while I work for the Council. No time."

I tiptoed closer to the banister to peek downward, filled with curiosity. Without meaning to, a noise of surprise escaped me as I looked down on the scene below. I knew this visitor. I'd seen him with some regularity at the trials. He was several years older than me and had a beautiful face. More than once he'd flashed his strong white teeth at me in a smile that made my knees go weak. And then I had to remind myself that I was a boy and things such as beautiful faces and handsome smiles didn't affect me.

Master Wendyn looked up the staircase. "Oh, it's you, boy. You may as well come down and meet Master Kurke."

I descended the stairs, cursing my unfortunate luck. I didn't want Master Wendyn's handsome visitor to see me in my current hot and wilted, unkempt state. Until it occurred to me that seeming slovenly would only make me more boy-like. I squared my shoulders with resolve and marched the rest of the way down.

"This is the boy, Underwizard Mullins." Master Wendyn shifted a sheaf of papers under one arm to gesture at me. "He's had a—er—disagreement with his last master . . . which is why I'm considering taking him on as my apprentice." His tone was all business.

Confused by the unexpected words, my feet forgot where they were on the steps and tangled in one another. Master

Kurke swooped forward and righted me at the bottom of the stairs.

"I—thank—sorry—pardon me?" I said. Master Kurke's arm rested around my waist, while his other hand steadied my elbow. I was tilted backward, gazing up into his celestial blue eyes, while my heart thumped and I went hot and cold. This was terrible. I might do something idiotic at any moment, such as swoon. Must he be so handsome?

He laughed, making his face soft and warm and inviting. "Look at you, Garrick, one step ahead of the Council. So that's why you wanted the file. But didn't you prepare the boy at all? You nearly knocked him off his feet." He righted me and stepped away.

"Master Kurke is an old friend," Wendyn said. "He works for the Wizard's Council."

The blue eyes smiled at me again. "Your face looks familiar. I'm sure I've seen you at the trials."

"Yes. I believe I've seen you as well," I said with perfect composure, though I was disappointed he didn't remember the various—if fleeting—moments we'd had together. The time he grinned at me and said, "Best of luck, underwizard. I'm sure you'll pass with ease," for example. Or the time he patted me on the back as I left the fourth trial, exhausted, and told me I'd done all I could do; no use worrying anymore. The smile we exchanged across the great room as I waited for my turn at the fifth trial.

"Sounds as though you two have things to discuss. I'll be off." Master Kurke set a wide-brimmed hat on his head and doffed it at me. "Good luck in your training, underwizard. If you can convince Garrick to take you on, you won't regret it."

I smiled and nodded and bowed. Master Wendyn followed his friend a little down the main hallway, and they spoke in low voices. I breathed deep and regulated my pounding heart.

So Master Wendyn was now considering me as an apprentice, was he? After tossing me out on my ear?

A part of me wanted to turn my nose up at him and tell him I'd find someone else. But another part, the part where reason lay, told me that Wendyn was the only offer I had. The longer I waited, the more behind I would become in my studies, and the less likely it was I'd be able to find another master. Regardless of his temper, there was only one choice. I'd have to become his apprentice. And I should be grateful.

"Well," said Master Wendyn, turning back once Kurke had left. "Don't just stand there with that vacant expression on your face. Come into my study. You and I need to talk."

THE FIRST THING WENDYN DID, after seating himself in the ornate chair behind his desk and gesturing for me to sit across from him, was produce a piece of parchment which he waved in front of my face. After a questioning glance at him, I took hold of it and read. Magic crackled along the edges of the parchment. It was a new oath.

"I'll be honest," he said. "It galls me to take Hapthwaite's castoffs. But the mere fact it's him that's cast you off should earn you a second chance. He couldn't teach water to run downhill."

The words set my teeth on edge.

Wendyn gestured at the sheaf of papers he'd set on the desk. "Matt was good enough to bring me your record. I must say it's . . . disappointing."

I flushed.

"You took the first trial three times, and every trial after that at least twice."

"But I'm a hard worker. I don't give up." I hated that it felt like I was begging.

"Stubborn, you mean. I've seen that already. That's not always a good thing."

"And I love learning," I went on, as though he hadn't spoken. "I read every book I could get my hands on at Larkspur House. Most of them twice."

Master Wendyn shook his head. "Whether you can learn is not the issue. The question is whether you have an aptitude for magic."

I blinked and stared, stiffening. *You don't have the skill required, Mullins.* The words Hapthwaite had spoken mere hours ago. Since I was a child, I'd known I was meant to do magic. But why was it so hard for me? I rubbed at my eyes and wished I knew the answer.

"Devil's dawn," Wendyn said, watching me. "You're not going to cry, are you?"

"Of course not," I said hotly, without thinking. "I can't."

"You can't?" he repeated. "Can't cry? Explain."

I hadn't meant to say that. But he was watching me, and if there ever was a bad time to lie to him, it was when I was trying to convince him I would make a reliable and trustworthy apprentice.

"I cast a spell a few years back. Accidentally. And I . . . don't know how to undo it." I hurried on, "To be fair, I haven't tried much. Master Hapthwaite took away the book I got the spell out of, so I never learned how to remove it."

His brow furrowed. "What spell was it?"

"It's called dry as desert. I found it in a book—"

Master Wendyn came to his feet, looming over me. "You cast a desert spell on yourself?" His voice climbed. "And Hapthwaite did nothing about it?"

"I—didn't tell him." My voice faltered. Why was he angry? "It was stupid, I know—"

"Stupid doesn't even begin to describe it." He shoved a hand into his hair and shook his head in clear disbelief. "Stupid is too kind. Colossally idiotic is more like it. Do you know what kind of spell that is?"

"Of course," I said with surprise. "It's a liquid-stopping spell."

"It's a killing spell. You're lucky you only dried up your tears. That spell is meant to suck the moisture out of an entire body. To leave a desiccated husk of flesh."

My mouth opened and closed as I tried to form words. "But . . . but . . ."

"And Hapthwaite just left this book lying around for you to find? What other spells were in it?"

I was too stunned to lie and make myself, or Hapthwaite, look better. "Advanced magic. Defense spells. Killing spells. Shape-shifting."

He shook his head. "The carelessness of the man is shocking. He's a menace. I don't know how he's still a wizard."

But I couldn't let Hapthwaite take all the blame. "He warned me not to read the book. I . . . disobeyed him."

Wendyn sat back in his chair, massaging his temple, jaw ticking in frustration. "Devil's dawn," he muttered. "I don't know what to do with you. You're lucky you didn't kill yourself. You should never use a spell without understanding its full power! Didn't that baboon ever teach you that?"

I kept my mouth shut. It seemed prudent in this situation.

The man wasn't done talking, anyway. "On the one hand, you're a dreadful underwizard, but on the other, you're good enough to at least cast a partial desert spell. That's advanced magic, very advanced. If you're not trained further, you may be a menace to Faronna."

Not the most flattering words ever spoken about me. "So . . . can you remove the spell?"

The annoyance faded from his face. "I'll need to research.

Probably. Maybe. But I don't know the incantation." He closed his eyes, breathed deep, and then opened them to stare at me with those deep, dark eyes. "I suppose it's not your fault you ended up with Hapthwaite for a master. You couldn't have known any better." He drummed his fingers. "Pity Uphammer already has an apprentice."

"Who?"

"My master. The best there is." More drumming of his fingers. "Devil's dawn. I can't believe I'm even considering this. But left to your own devices, who knows what you'll do with those advanced spells? For your own protection and the safety of Faronna, something has to be done."

I watched him. I might even have been holding my breath.

He fiddled with the sheaf of papers. "Underwizard," he said, "I—I offer . . ."

Would he choke on the words?

"I offer myself as your master. I wish for you to be my apprentice." He pushed the words out with effort.

I breathed in, long and slow. He wasn't the man I would have chosen for a master, but at least it meant I still had a chance of becoming a master wizard. And wasn't that what mattered? "I accept."

We swore the oath much the same as the last time, laying hands on the parchment and speaking words that left magic crackling and twining around our fingers.

"There. That's done," he said, tucking the parchment into a drawer of his desk. "Now I'd like to test you. If you could endeavor to be brilliant, that would prevent me from regretting what I've just done."

I nodded and murmured, "I'll do my best."

"Superb."

We launched into the tests. First, I showed holding fire, although I only made something the size of a flickering candle in my palm. Next, it was on to reparations, and I repaired a broken vase—or tried to. I put two pieces back together which held, but the rest of the vase remained shattered where it lay on the floor.

After that, he told me to make the plant on his desk grow, the third trial. I made a new leaf pop out on one side—a brittle, undersized new leaf, but a new leaf nonetheless. And then it was on to water magic, and I created a swampy area in the center of his study floor, although I meant for it to be a babbling spring, not muddy quicksand. At last it was time for hearing magic, and I told him what Oscar was doing and saying in a room several doors down, though I had to guess at some of it.

Overall it was a pathetic showing, and I knew it. If it weren't for all the times I had successfully performed magic, I'd almost doubt my own abilities. But I remembered too vividly the first time I uttered the words to the unknotting spell and how the rope unfolded before me. I remembered when I realized for the first time that if I concentrated hard enough, I could see lines of woven spells invisible to others. I remembered when I understood the sparking glow of magic was almost always around me, touching my skin or hovering in the spaces of any room. Gavin had been so jealous that I could see magic when he couldn't.

But I still didn't know how to control my magic fully. Sometimes it behaved as I expected, but more often it didn't.

Master Wendyn walked to the window, staring out at the hot afternoon.

I felt as though I should say something more, give more explanation, but the angry set of his back convinced me that words wouldn't help. I stood silently, waiting.

He spoke to the window. "There is no choice left, underwizard. You haven't completed a single task to my satisfaction. Therefore, I'm stripping you of all levels and starting you over from the beginning." A ripple of magic ran through the room.

"If you are able to regain them within three months, then I will consider keeping you on as my apprentice."

"Stripping me—" I sputtered.

"—of all levels," he confirmed and turned from the window to face me. "And don't bother arguing with me. It's done."

"You're giving me three months?" Friar's bones. It took three *years* to get to where I was, years of study, hard work, and, far too often, disappointment. Most of those trials I almost didn't pass. And now he wanted me to do it all over again? And in just three months?

"If you have the abilities, that should be enough time to show it. We'll start your studies in the morning after breakfast. For now, you're dismissed."

I opened my mouth. "You can't just—but that's not fair!"

"You may leave."

He sat down at his desk and pulled out a pen which he dipped in an inkwell and scratched across a piece of paper. It was as though I wasn't even there. I stood there stupidly for a minute or two, trying to think of something to say. But at last I realized it was no use and stumbled out of the room to stand outside the door. My mouth opened and shut. I was so bewildered I couldn't even think what to say or do.

Three years of hard work, gone. I was a first level underwizard again.

SEVEN

IT WAS AFTER MIDNIGHT, and I stood in front of my open window, dressed in a tunic and trousers and looking down on the meadow. I would have put a dress on if I owned one any longer. My belongings lay next to me on the ground, stuffed into a knapsack.

I'd reached my limit.

The feeling took me back to the night my brother died. I was wrung out with emotion, teetering on the edge of despair. But I was resolved to take charge of the only thing I could still control: my future.

What would I do? I couldn't decide. Should I go back to sewing or washing or—no, not thieving. It broke Mama's heart when she discovered it before. I couldn't do that to her memory.

I'd become a street magician, an illusionist maybe. But I wouldn't stay here to have further humiliation showered on me.

It was too bad I had to leave Ivan in the care of this loon, but I didn't even know if I'd be able to provide for myself, let alone a helpless boy. At least here he'd have food and clothing. His existence couldn't be any worse than it was in Bramford, could it?

I couldn't worry about him anymore.

There were no words to my fury. It took three years to pass those levels, and Wendyn discarded all my progress in the space of less than three minutes. That man was not a rational human being. He was as crazy as his grandfather.

I wished I'd gotten him to remove the desert spell from me before I left. Although it was no matter. I'd find a copy of the spell somewhere and learn how to reverse it.

It was quick work to tie the knapsack across my chest so it wouldn't flop about on my back as I shimmied down the side of the building. I could have left via the front door, except I watched Mrs. Pitts lock the door and stick the key in her apron pocket. Besides, leaving out the window struck me as so much more defiant. It made me feel as though I was thumbing my nose at Master Wendyn, doing things my way. And that pleased me very much.

The activity of climbing down the exterior of the building felt good. It had been a long time since I scaled anything.

I was halfway down when a noise drew my notice. It seemed to be coming from Ivan's window. As I squinted through the darkness, I realized it was open. A leg appeared over the side of the sill.

"Get back inside," I hissed. If he heard me, he didn't show it. The other leg appeared, and then Ivan slid out over the side onto his belly. He glanced down at me.

What was he doing? Had he lost his mind?

That was a stupid question.

My fingers dug into the stone, holding on tight with one hand, while I gestured at the window with my other. "Go inside!" I hissed again in as loud a voice as I dared under the circumstances. I was making so much noise, I might as well have left through the front door of the house after shouting I was leaving.

Ivan didn't go back. Instead, he scooted out further until he held onto the sill with just his forearms.

If he let go now, he'd fall two stories and land in the bushes. Perhaps he'd break bones. Perhaps he'd be fine.

Or perhaps he'd be dead.

He pushed himself further, fingers gripping the ledge of the window. He was moments from falling.

I couldn't decide which way to go. Down, where I could try to catch him? But what good would that do? He'd kill us both.

Or up?

I was already climbing. "Don't move. I'm coming. Stay where you are." I climbed diagonally, angling myself toward him. He could fall at any moment, but I wouldn't think about that.

When I looked again, he was in the same place, gripping the sill with his face turned toward me. I couldn't see his eyes in the darkness, and I wished I could. It was the only way to know if he was listening.

"Don't move," I told him again. I was even with his feet now. I found a handhold in the stone and pulled myself up. Another handhold and I pulled myself up until I was next to him, the window sill above us both. I climbed onto it, and he wriggled, trying to crawl up. I hauled him in the window. He trembled like a frightened animal.

I was ready to yell at him, but now I stood close enough to see his face through the darkness. His skin had transformed into splotchy patches of red, and tears trickled down in a steady stream.

"Are you hurt?" I looked him over to make sure, but I couldn't find any injuries. He was just scared. I gave him a shake, hoping to snap him out of it. He wiped at his face with the back of his hand and then reached out for me.

"Whoa now." I backed off a few steps, as he seemed to be

trying to embrace me. I couldn't very well hug him; my chest wasn't bound. At this moment, I was supposed to be starting down the road in whatever direction appealed to me, reclaiming my life as a girl. He advanced on me again, reaching arms and hands out.

"None of that." I sidestepped him again.

But he was still reaching, so finally I looked down at myself and realized he was trying to grab the knot of the knapsack tied on the front of my chest.

Did he understand? Did he know I was leaving?

I unknotted the knapsack and let it fall to the floor with a clank of belongings. "You have got to stop climbing out windows, you. What happens when I'm not here? You'll die, that's what. Or is that what you want? Are you trying to kill yourself?"

A hiccup reverberated through him, and more tears trickled down his cheeks.

"You'll make yourself sick," I told him. I was trying to sound angry but with little success. My voice sounded soft to my own ears. My eyes ached, and I rubbed my nose.

Had he grown so attached? If so, this was terrible. I couldn't afford to have him tagging after me. I couldn't take care of him; I was leaving.

But I didn't leave. I walked him over to his bed and made him lie down. He only did that once I showed I was going nowhere, by pulling up a chair and sitting next to him. He continued to clutch my hand.

To fill the charged silence, I talked, my voice far more tender than it should be. I told stories, the ones my parents told me when I was a child, Faronnish folktales: The Lonely Mouse, Fairfax and the Fourteen Figs, and Miss Violet Goes to Market. Eventually he fell asleep.

Even after that, I stayed, brushed the hair off his forehead, and tucked the quilt around him.

I couldn't help but feel we'd turned a corner. But I didn't know what the corner meant or where we were.

I AWOKE STILL in the chair, my top half leaned over on the bed. Ivan was still asleep, and my neck was sore. Even worse, a dull thumping had settled in at the top of my head, a sign it would be one of *those* days. A headache day.

The sun peeked in the open window. It had cooled off overnight, and the room had a chill. I rose to close and latch the window. The dingy white of my makeshift knapsack, made of a stolen bedsheet from my room, reminded me how I ended up here. The sheet wasn't dirty when I started out with it last night. I scooped it up and considered the thing.

I had lost my chance to slip away unnoticed.

In the cold light of day, my decision to give up master wizardry seemed rash and ill-advised. I had almost given up everything I'd worked for, on a whim of anger. A sick feeling formed in the pit of my stomach when I considered all I would have lost.

I had promised myself. I had promised my brother.

If I was meant to be a master wizard—and I felt I was—then this small setback was just that, a setback. I would overcome this.

Besides, I could only think of one reason Master Wendyn would have forced me to begin again as a level one underwizard. The man wanted me to quit. He never wanted me for his apprentice to begin with. Nothing would make him happier than if I were to give up and run away.

A firm resolved entered me, and I was suddenly glad Ivan had distracted me from leaving last night. I would not turn and run as the master expected. Proving him and Hapthwaite wrong would be so much more satisfying. I'd regain my levels, and since Master Wendyn didn't want me around, I'd torture him with my presence every day until I became a master wizard.

"COME ALONG, MULLINS." Master Wendyn jerked on the back of my robes, pulling me off balance. I stumbled backwards before righting myself and then hurried to catch up to him. We were at the Conclave, headquarters of the Wizard's Council, to file the parchmentwork that would make our apprenticeship of record. Master Wendyn's long stride was impossible to match, and I had to take several smaller steps to keep pace with him.

"Is it necessary we rush through this place at a gallop? The Secretary of Apprenticeships will still be there if we arrive five minutes later."

"Yes, but filing this paperwork is delaying your studies," he tossed over his shoulder. "You have a lot of work to do."

If I had work to do, it was his fault for stripping me of my levels. I opened my mouth to tell him so, when I realized we'd gained a follower, even in our mad rushing through the hallways.

"Ex—excuse—me," puffed a girl, struggling to keep up. A girl, here in an enclave of men. I stuttered to a halt as I stared at her and then realized it was just the librarian's daughter. She was always poking around in the library. I'd even spoken to her before. What was her name? Oh, yes—Orly.

"Erm . . . can I help you?" I looked her over as though maybe her appearance could give me a clue why she was chasing me down the hall.

Wrinkles crisscrossed her ill-fitting dress. A long dark braid hung over one shoulder, dark against the olive skin of her neck. She couldn't be over fourteen. She clutched a book in her hands and smiled at me. "You have a new master?" she asked.

I looked up just as Master Wendyn disappeared around a corner, making no effort to wait for me. "If you can call him a master. Seems like I should call him Tyrant Wendyn."

"I'm glad." She grasped the book to her chest and looked up at me. "I heard about what happened to you. How you defended that boy."

My mouth opened in surprise. "You heard about that? Here in the Conclave? But how?"

She shrugged. "Some wizards were talking. I heard you got disapprenticed. Remember, you borrowed a couple books just before—"

"Mullins, what're you doing? I said we're in a hurry, didn't I?" The master stomped back into view, his frown causing lines to appear on his forehead and between his eyes.

"I'm having a conversation, all right? There's no need to snap at me; I'll be right there." Turning back I said, "Sorry, Orly. I'd forgotten I borrowed those books from the library. Master Hapthwaite must still have them. You'll need to contact him if you want them back."

Her mouth opened to say something, but I would never know what, because I scurried after Master Wendyn, whose scowl had deepened. He grasped me by the nape of the neck until we were within the walls of the secretary's office.

"Mm-hmm, mm-hmm," the pruny secretary said, paging through the parchment the master and I had filled out earlier. It listed our names and wizard rank—his of master wizard and mine of underwizard level nought—while the second page was the oath we swore. It would go in the master's file, while a record of apprenticeship would be placed in mine, along with the other documents which should still reside there, thanks to my previous apprenticeship: documentation of my place of origin, identifying information such as my parents' names, my eye and hair color, and proof of gender. I had to bribe three men from Waltney to sign that last one. And then, to be safe, I cast a spell of forgetfulness on them. A weak spell, given I had no magical training at the time and learned it from a passing magician.

I hoped the spells still held. Someday soon I'd go back and cast an oblivion spell on those men. The oblivion was much stronger and more reliable than a mere forgetfulness spell. I had read about it in Master Hapthwaite's forbidden book.

"Very well," said the secretary, stacking the parchment he'd just finished signing and stamping. "Your apprenticeship is official. If you'd like to stop in the office of the trial coordinator, you can schedule the boy's first trial, if you've a mind to. The next trials are just two weeks away. You can schedule them up to six months out." He rose from the chair and took the parchment with him, disappearing among rows upon rows of files.

"Two weeks?" The master's dark gaze turned on me. "What say you, Mullins? You've three months to pass five trials. When do you want to take the first one?"

My chin rose. I refused to let him know I was nervous just at the thought. "Two weeks is plenty of time to prepare. I'll take the first trial then."

He gave a faint smile and nodded. I couldn't quite tell if he believed me full of the bravado I was trying to portray or not.

You're supposed to be torturing him with your presence, I reminded myself. But I had a sudden sinking feeling the torture was already flowing in the opposite direction, from the master to me.

AFTER RETURNING TO RYKER HALL, the master told me to bring Ivan and meet him in the library, a cavernous room off the main hallway. Books and magical artifacts lined the walls and shelves while the fore of the room was filled with a handful of tables and chairs.

I didn't know why Ivan was to join us. But master said he didn't want him getting into trouble, so he might as well come along.

The library was empty when we arrived, and it was just as well, because the place took me off guard. I thought the collection in Master Wendyn's study was enormous, but his library didn't even compare. The only place I'd seen a larger collection was the Wizard's Library at the Conclave, kept and maintained for use by master wizards and underwizards in training. But this . . . the amount of money and time necessary to amass this collection must have been enormous. I looked around with eyes I knew were shining. I browsed through the rows of books while I waited for Master Wendyn to arrive.

I didn't realize how much time had passed until I looked up with a start at the master's voice and noted the changed light of the room.

"Sit," he ordered and then fiddled with some magical items along a shelf. I chose the seat nearest me and lined up my parchment, ink, and pen in preparation to write notes, should my new master say anything noteworthy. I doubted this would happen, but it was important to be prepared. Ivan had ignored the tables altogether and crouched in a corner.

The master walked the length of the room to stop in front of me. He held something in his hands.

Bones, the man was holding a trammel. I regarded the hinged, neck-sized device with loathing and slid to the back of my chair.

"Starting today," he announced, "this trammel will be your closest friend." He fidgeted with the device, opening and closing its metal hinge. It gave a small squeak. "You will wear it at all times, waking and sleeping." He frowned. "And I don't want to hear any whining that it's uncomfortable."

"If that's what you want." I knew I would regret this, but I took the trammel from him anyway and fixed it around my throat. Its metal was cold against my skin, and I shivered. It shut with a precise click. Master Wendyn came around to insert a key from his pocket, which he turned several times. When the key turned the last time, my magic had fled, leaving me bereft, cold, and nauseated.

He slipped the key into his pocket and retrieved a handful of books from a nearby shelf. "I've a collection of spell books here. I want you to start at the beginning and practice each spell until you know it from memory."

"I—excuse me? Every spell from memory?" I pitched my voice deeper to compensate for the loss of my voice modulating spell.

"You heard me." He stopped in front of my table and deposited the books with a heavy, solid thud. I believed the man resented being questioned. "When you're done with all these, we'll talk about taking the trammel off."

I looked at the stack. "It will take days. Weeks, maybe."

"Don't be dramatic. There's maybe a hundred spells there, all told. I suggest you get started." He glanced at Ivan and frowned. "And see you keep Ivan out from underfoot." With that, he left the room.

Five books sat on the table in front of me. Several of them were fat, as tall as the mug I drank my milk out of this morning.

I would kill the man.

No. I breathed deep of the musty, bookish smell around me,

and closed my eyes. I'd been looking for a friend in my master, and I wasn't going to find it. It would seem he was incapable of close relationships.

I leaned forward and opened the first book.

———

"SIR? YOU'VE A VISITOR."

I jumped, I was so startled by the voice. It was Edie, the maid, her face filled with pity as she regarded me, trussed up in the trammel.

"A visitor?" My voice sounded thick with distraction. I'd been so involved with my reading I couldn't even say how much time had passed since the master left.

"It's Master Kurke," Edie said.

I sat up straighter. "To see me?" I clarified.

"Young master is out," Edie said. "So he asked to see you instead."

Friar's bones, I didn't want anyone to see me like this, wearing a trammel. How humiliating. I wanted to tell her I wouldn't see him. There was no good reason for the man to want to talk to me, after all. But there was also a traitorous, pleased flush suffusing my face at the mere notion of spending more time in his company.

Before I could say anything in protest—or worse, celebration —Master Kurke's lanky form filled the door frame, and I rose to my feet.

Edie leaned in closer. "I think it's terrible mean of the master to make you wear that," she whispered and then turned and slipped out of the room, her cheeks a rosy pink.

Then it was just the two of us staring at one another. Master Kurke stood tall and elegant as usual, with a bit of the wickedness I'd come to know him for lingering about his mouth. And me: a slim "boy" with a freckled, crooked nose and a metal bracelet fixed around his neck.

Master Kurke gave me a slow bow. "Underwizard Mullins."

"Master Wendyn is away," I said.

"I know." His robes swished around him as he moved toward my table. "I wouldn't have come otherwise."

"Wouldn't have . . ." The deep blue of his eyes distracted me. No, focus, Avery. Pay attention. "What may I help you with?"

He pulled out a chair and seated himself next to me, turned so he was facing me while leaned forward, his elbows resting on his knees. It was a distractingly intimate pose. I sank into my chair, my heart thudding against my ribs.

"A trammel, eh?" he observed. "You must be in need of some hefty rehabilitation."

"I suppose you are right. But my master knows best." I somehow managed the words without gritting my teeth.

He clasped his hands together and rested his chin on them. "You seem quick-witted, Mullins. I imagine you'll have it off in a few days. I don't envy you the sleep you'll lose in the meantime, however."

My heart might leap out of my chest with his nearness. He smelled like vanilla, cigars, magic, and . . . something else. "Thank you for your concern. What is it you need from me?" I tried to keep my voice even.

"Does it bother you?"

My fingers ran over the trammel. "If you're asking does it hurt, no. It's just heavy and inconvenient."

"I don't mean the trammel." He leaned back and regarded me with one eyebrow raised. "I mean the lying."

"Lying? I'm . . . not sure what you mean."

He smiled and opened his mouth to say words that sent my world tilting. "Oh, I think you do. You are lying about being a boy, aren't you?"

EIGHT

"LYING? ABOUT BEING A boy?" I echoed, my features frozen in place. A girlish squeak ran through my voice, thanks to the trammel's cancelation of my voice modulating spell. I cleared my throat and aimed for a more husky tone. "Of course I'm a boy."

He continued, undeterred. "I'd be a sorry excuse for a man if I failed to notice you're a girl, after having you in my arms yesterday."

I moved my frozen features into the vestige of a smile. "If my mother were alive, she'd thank you, sir. Mama wanted me to be a girl."

He tilted his head, his gaze curious. It would be adorable if it weren't for the turn the conversation had taken. "It's clear Garrick doesn't know. He'd never allow it. Nauseatingly virtuous, that's Garrick."

"You are persistent, aren't you? But you're wrong. I'm *not* a girl." My voice held firm. "Underwizards are boys, and I have three affidavits of gender on file to prove it."

A grin moved across his mouth, slow and lazy. "There are

ways around that, as I'm sure you've discovered. But you are a good little liar, and I can use that."

I came to my feet, and my chair tilted backward, meeting the floor with a clatter of wood on wood. "I'm sorry to disappoint you, sir, but you are very, *very* mistaken. Now, I have a lot of studying to do. If you wouldn't mind leaving." I scowled and pointed at the library door. My heart was beating so fast and thumping so hard, I'd be surprised if he couldn't hear it.

He flicked a finger, and the chair righted itself and pushed at the back of my legs. I was forced to sit down.

"I couldn't have asked for a better arrangement than this." He flicked a finger at me, and with a mutter of a spell, I was pinned in my chair by unseen magic, unable to rise.

"Wha—let me up!" At least I still had control of my voice.

"No."

"What is it you want from me, Master Kurke?" I asked through gritted teeth. I wanted to argue, but I saw little point in it when he wasn't listening.

"First off, call me Matt. You, my dear girl, are going to help me destroy the Wendyn family."

Of course I will not call him Matt was my first ridiculous thought. As if that were the issue.

And second: Destroy the Wendyn family? But they're old friends.

And third: Bones! With this contraption around my neck, I won't be able to perform an oblivion spell.

I had never performed an oblivion spell, but I had read about them in Master Hapthwaite's forbidden book. It had been my in-case-of-disaster plan ever since. I couldn't have foreseen that on the day I'd need to use the spell I'd have a trammel locked around my neck.

Some said that Ladarius the Heroic, great mage of the

Oceanic Wars, wore a trammel during the final battle. He'd been captured by the enemy and the trammel placed around his neck to keep him from aiding Faronna and the Three Kingdoms. But his powers were so great the device couldn't contain his magic.

After several minutes of intense mental strain, I realized Ladarius and I did not share the same talent.

"Stop whatever it is you think you're doing," Master Kurke said. He had been scouting the shelves, examining the magical items and devices perched among the books. Now he held a long flat metal object with a crank on one side. I didn't know what its purpose was. "Get used to the idea that not only do I know more magic than you, but I'm stronger and cleverer. If you try to defy me in any way, I *will* make you regret it."

This was what came of mooning after a man I knew nothing more about than the deep blue of his eyes. I was so absorbed in Master Kurke's pretty face that I had left myself open to his schemings.

"I'm not a girl," I insisted. Perhaps it was naïve of me, but I felt it was worth one more try.

He put down the object and strode closer to grasp my jaw. His hand squeezed, and for a moment I wondered if he meant to force words of agreement out of my mouth. But then he tilted my face first one way, then the other, eyeing me.

"Not handsome, but definitely girlish," he declared, stepping back. "Now, let's come to an accord, you and I, so we can work together on this. Never fear. I offer something in return for your help." He pulled parchment from inside his robes. "Here, read."

The parchment dropped into my lap, and filled with trepidation, I picked it up. It was an oath. *That the undersigned, Apprentice-Underwizard Mullins, will assist Master Wizard Matthias Kurke in any way required to permanently dispose of Master Wizard Oscar Wendyn and any other souls who impede the carrying out of said task before the winter solstice. In return, Master Kurke will not reveal the true state of Underwizard Mullins' gender.*

"I think it's a fair trade," he said, "but please don't feel compelled. I'll warn you, however, that if you refuse me, it'd be best if you head for hiding as soon as you can. Remember what happened to Underwizard Ingerman when it came out that he was a she? They only found pieces of her after she underwent the Punishment."

Not surprising. The Punishment involved being rolled down a mountain inside a barrel filled with spikes. Once it stopped moving, the barrel was ensorcelled to explode. So if you didn't die from the spikes, you'd die from the explosion. It had been in use in Faronna for centuries under a variety of circumstances.

"'Permanently dispose'?" I looked across the table at him where he had just pulled out a chair and seated himself so that we faced one another across the wide wooden expanse. "You mean to kill him?"

"Let's not quibble over terms. If you want to be vulgar about it, I suppose yes. Kill."

I put the parchment down and stared at him. "But he's just a crazy old man. Surely he hasn't harmed you enough to warrant your killing him."

"Murk and shadow, what do you know about what he's done?" Kurke sounded almost petulant. "Not to mention the harm he's done Faronna."

"What harm?" I asked, but perhaps I shouldn't have, because he fixed me with a look so forbidding that I remembered I was at his mercy, pinned in a chair by his magic. "I mean . . . I'm just curious."

After staring at me for a moment or two in silence, he pushed to his feet.

"Perhaps you need persuading," he said. "And here I thought the threat of Punishment—" he cut himself off.

Footsteps *tip-tapped* across the room. I craned my neck to look behind me at the doorway.

Mrs. Pitts made her way toward us, a tray in her arms. She nodded to Master Kurke and frowned at me.

Friar's bones, had she heard anything?

"Tea," she announced, setting the tray down on the table before me. The aroma of steamed leaves wafted on the air. "I thought you might like some refreshment, Master Kurke, although it's beyond me why you'd want to speak to the apprentice. Perhaps while you're here, you can introduce him to the importance of behaving oneself."

"Yes, perhaps I can," Kurke said.

I focused more precious seconds on attempting to remove the trammel using only my magic skills. But I could no longer feel the surrounding magic. I knew it must be there—I could almost always feel the tingle of magic along my skin—but now I felt nothing around me at all. Nothing but the heavy weight of metal against my neck and the jitter of nerves through my body.

If only I dared raise my hands to the trammel. Perhaps if I could tug at its locking mechanism, I would know if my attempts at loosening it were having any effect.

Mrs. Pitts turned to go, and I gave a quick glance from her retreating back to Master Kurke's deliberative expression.

I didn't know why, but her presence was almost comforting. It was insulation against Kurke. Maybe if she remained, he wouldn't do anything stupid.

"Wait," I blurted, hoping my voice didn't sound as desperate to her ears as it did to my own. "Er—would you mind pouring the tea?"

Mrs. Pitts paused and gave me a withering stare. "*And* he's lazy," she said to Kurke. "Poor Master Wendyn has a lot of hard work and frustration ahead of him." She turned to the tray and set to work pouring the steaming beverage.

"Indeed he does." Kurke accepted the cup from Mrs. Pitts and, while staring her straight in the face, began to say the words of a spell.

I watched, my dread growing, as I tried to identify the incantation. But I recognized it when the cocoon of silence fell around us. It was a privacy spell, meant to keep this conversation private, no matter how loud it became.

Confusion quirked Mrs. Pitts' brow. "Pardon, what was that?"

Kurke ignored her question, going straight into another spell which I couldn't identify. Whatever it was, moments later Mrs. Pitts crumbled to the floor with a yelp. Beneath her skirts, her leg turned at an odd angle.

"What are you doing?" I tried to free myself from the spell holding me in the chair. "Leave the poor woman alone!" There was no love lost between myself and the housekeeper, but not even *she* deserved this.

"I'd like to hear you say the words, underwizard," he said, his voice unperturbed. "Tell this woman your true gender."

My mouth opened. All this to get me to admit I was a girl? "I—you—"

Kurke raised a brow and then muttered more words. With a flick of his finger, a sickening crack and a long wail filled the room. Mrs. Pitts' ankle hung oddly from her foot.

"Fine! I'm a girl, all right? I'm a girl."

Mrs. Pitts sobbed so loud I doubt she could hear me or even cared what gender I was.

"Now tell her what you'll help me do." He gestured at the oath.

"Why?" I shouted, anger pushing its way through the fear

washing over me. "What does any of this prove? Let the woman alone!"

A lazy smile made its way across his face. "I will kill her, Mullins, if you don't do as I say. Tell her what you're going to help me do."

"Fine! I'll help you . . . dispose of . . . Oscar Wendyn." I gulped, almost choking on the words.

Another spell and a flick of his fingers. On the floor, Mrs. Pitts stilled.

For a moment, it felt as though my heart had stopped. "You —you said if I—"

"She's not dead. Only unconscious. Now, if you don't mind, it's time to swear the oath."

My breath came again and relief coursed through me. I felt as limp as old lettuce. She wasn't dead. "Very well. Let's swear." I scarcely knew what I said, only that I was in the presence of a true madman. What else did one do in such a situation but agree?

"I'm so pleased to hear you say that." He caressed my chin in a manner I would have found swoon-worthy only an hour ago. But it wasn't an hour ago, and I had to force myself not to jerk away. Who knew if such an act of defiance might set him off on another tirade?

"Er—how do you suggest we swear this oath? I'm wearing a trammel." Oaths were sworn using magic. With the trammel on, I had none.

He reached for his hip and produced a knife. "Not a problem. Your hand, underwizard."

Friar's bones, what would he do?

He grew impatient and reached for my hand himself. Fighting with a knife-wielding man while pinned in a chair seemed the height of stupidity, so I surrendered the limb and watched his movements. He held the blade to the pad of my thumb and pressed downward. There was a quick prick of pain, and then he put the knife down and squeezed the finger. Blood trickled down my thumb, and it commenced a dull throbbing. He performed the same deed on his own thumb and then placed the parchment between the two of us.

"Press here." He left a smudge of his own blood at the bottom of the oath, and I did the same. Hope—a dim hope, but all I had to hold onto—grew within me. None of this bound me in any way. Blood magic didn't exist, not anymore. Master Hapthwaite had told me so himself. Kurke was trying to frighten me into following the oath, by making it seem solemn and realistic. But the truth was no binding magic could be sworn while I wore a trammel.

I wasn't the gullible schoolgirl he seemed to think me.

"I don't suppose you'd be willing to tell me what you have against Oscar Wendyn." My tone was so careful my own mother wouldn't have recognized it.

"My reasons are my own." His voice was terse. "Give me your hands."

Much as it made my skin crawl, I leaned forward and grasped his hands as he seemed to want me to. The parchment containing the oath sat between us now, in the circle of our arms. He said a long, loud word in a language I had never heard before.

"Now," he said, "You say it."

I repeated the word, and something happened to the room.

No, it was me. Something had happened to *me*. I felt a shift inside of me. There was a pull, a yank behind my breastbone, lining me up with Master Kurke. An invisible something pulled between us. I couldn't see it, but I knew it was there. A tether of sorts. Meanwhile, a crimson pattern crawled its way across the parchment, overlaying the words with something that looked like blood.

No apprentice oath ever did *that*.

He let go of my hands and stood, dusting his palms on his trousers. "Well, that's finished. Don't be alarmed. The pulling sensation is normal. We're connected now, you and I. My heart's blood to your heart's blood. Working together toward a mutual goal." He retrieved the parchment and rolled it up before sliding it into his sleeve. "You'll find yourself unable to speak of any of this to anyone other than me, so save yourself the trouble and don't attempt it. I'd best be off now. Garrick's on his way here."

I looked from the still form on the floor back to the wizard. "But . . . Mrs. Pitts—"

"Oh, yes." He flicked a hand in her direction and went into several healing spells, some of which I had seen Master Hapthwaite perform before. The breaks in her legs righted themselves, and even the tears on her cheeks dried up and disappeared.

Then another spell, and this time I recognized the words as soon as he spoke them. They were the words I'd been straining to remember as I sat here, the words of the oblivion. He was taking her memories.

I supposed I should be relieved. She wouldn't remember the horrible things that had happened to her here, including that I admitted I was a girl. Then one last flick of his wrist in my direction, and the spell holding me in my chair released.

"The housekeeper will wake in a few hours. Tell Garrick I came by to talk him out of some betony from that herb garden of his. You'll hear from me soon, Mullins. But in the meantime, I'd like you to keep an eye on Oscar Wendyn. Become the man's shadow. I want to know everything about him. Everything. His daily schedule, the food he eats most often, how he spends his time, what side of the bed he sleeps on. If he does it, I want to know it."

I mumbled something in response. It must have been words

of acquiescence, because he nodded. "Good. I'll be in touch." And with that, the library door swung wide, and he had gone.

Confusion held me captive. I remained in my chair, staring from the still form of Mrs. Pitts to the doorway Kurke had just vacated, trying to comprehend what had just happened.

But the unpleasant truth made its way through my foggy consciousness at last, and I faced it.

I had pledged myself to kill a man.

NINE

MY EYES FELT GRITTY and dry the next morning as I made my way to the breakfast room. Turned out Kurke was right; the trammel was impossible to sleep in. The metal dug into my neck no matter how I lay my head. I wasted an hour trying to find a comfortable position until I realized I would have to sleep upright.

But the trammel wasn't even the worst of my problems. I couldn't stop thinking about Kurke or poor Mrs. Pitts crumpled on the floor in pain or the strange pull I felt behind my breastbone, twinging and pulsing now and then.

How I'd promised to help murder Oscar Wendyn.

Nor could I seem to forget what a useless underwizard I had turned out to be. Even with all my training, I was helpless when confronted by a stronger, more experienced master wizard.

I never wanted to be at the mercy of Kurke again. Or any other person, for that matter. I hated that feeling of helplessness. It reminded me too much of the past.

The few times I fell asleep, my dreams danced with images of exploding barrels and angry wizards that looked like Masters

Kurke and Wendyn, and a screaming woman with legs bent at wrong angles.

It came to me in the middle of a long night of fitful sleep that I had to find out how to get around that oath we swore. Was it possible to nullify a blood oath? And where would one find such information? Master Hapthwaite had never been eager to talk about blood magic, having mentioned it only that one time. I imagined Master Wendyn's reaction would be much the same.

I knuckled my eyes and found a seat at the long rectangular table. My neck felt heavy and sore, but I endeavored to hold it upright and keep my thoughts from straying toward the nightmares that still wanted to haunt my thoughts. I poured myself a mug of water and drank it. Master Wendyn showed up a few minutes later, late for breakfast as usual. I poured myself a second mug.

"You look tired, underwizard," Master Wendyn said. He sounded annoyed, as though I'd contrived my weariness as a ruse to annoy him.

"Yes." Oscar squinted at me. "Is it absolutely necessary for you to wear that contraption at the breakfast table? I can feel it stifling the flow of magic." He fanned his face. His patched sleeping robe, which seemed to be his usual breakfast attire, looked even rattier than normal. His white hair pointed in several directions at once. I couldn't help wondering, not for the first time, why Kurke wanted him dead when he seemed so harmless.

Master Wendyn answered for me. "I warned you, Grandfather. Don't question my methods."

"Oh, don't be so serious all the time, Garrick. Sweet carrot sticks, it's not as though you can't feel it. The magic in here is being suffocated by that thing."

I finished my water and poured a third mug.

"And are you always so thirsty? Save a little water for the

rest of us, will you?" Oscar frowned, bit into a sweet roll, and scratched his side.

There wasn't enough water on the table to fill my thirst, but I was used to that. I was a thirsty person. "Sorry." I put my mug down and ate a bite of fried egg.

Master Wendyn never came to breakfast in sleep attire, though he didn't always bother with his wizard's robes either. Today he had dressed in velvet pants and a fine leather jerkin. The man had an eye for expensive clothing. I noticed he was eyeing my mug with a raised brow and decided I'd better not drink so much water at breakfast.

Ivan settled into the seat next to me and pointed at the fried eggs in front of me. It was the first time he'd done that. Most days he sat there until food appeared in front of him.

We were learning to communicate, I supposed. I slid my plate in front of him, and he fell to shoveling it in with gusto.

"Erm, yesterday—" Something caught in my throat, and I coughed and *ahemed* several times. My voice suddenly seemed too high to my ears, without the aid of my modulating spell. I'd need to pitch it lower.

Master Wendyn looked up from his meal and raised an eyebrow. I didn't know what would happen when I said the words I had planned, but for the sake of trying everything possible, it had to be tried.

"That is, yesterday, when your friend Kurke was here—" Yes, that was the right amount of huskiness.

"That's *Master* Kurke."

"Master Kurke," I corrected, and something warmed in my chest, as though that strange connection in my chest—the tether —recognized who I was speaking of. I wondered if Kurke, wherever he was, could sense it as well. "Our conversation was unusual. He m—" I meant to say he made me swear a blood oath. At least, I thought I did. But then I blinked and couldn't remember what I had meant to say at all. What was I even talking about? I stared at my plate in confusion until Master Wendyn's voice prompted me.

"Unusual how? You said he wanted betony."

"I—" I struggled to remember what I had been talking about. Master Kurke. Yes. That was it. "Did I say unusual?"

"Yes. Unusual was your word. Now do you have something to say or don't you?" The impatience in his voice was clear.

The blood oath. That's what I was talking about. I had to tell them about what happened to Mrs. Pitts. I sat up straighter. "Yes, I do. Kurke—*Master* Kurke fo—" But I didn't even get the word "forced" out before I stumbled to a stop in confusion, though I forged ahead again desperately. "Mrs. Pitts, ask her. Ask Mrs. Pitts what happened with Ma—" And then confusion whirled my thoughts away again. What was I doing?

Oh, yes. My gaze took in the food on the table before me. Eating breakfast. I was eating breakfast. I was hungry. And thirsty.

"Are you all right, underwizard?" Oscar said. "Look at him. He can't even form a complete sentence, Garrick. He didn't get enough sleep. I'm telling you, it's unhealthy to make him wear that trammel."

"It's not the trammel," Master Wendyn said. "He's hardly eaten anything. Dish him up potatoes or something."

The two wizards muttered between themselves for a minute, and I closed my eyes, shutting out their words and trying to focus on clearing my thoughts. I hadn't felt so muddle-headed since I woke up in that jail in Bramford. I thought I was over the concussion, but perhaps I was wrong.

"Ah, Mrs. Pitts," Oscar said, his voice cutting into my thoughts. "The underwizard was just speaking of you. Do you have any idea what he's trying to say?"

I sat up straighter and blinked at Mrs. Pitts. She carried a tray of fruit, slowly making her way toward the table.

"The underwizard? Speaking of me?" Her voice was blank. "I'm sure I don't know why."

When did I mention Mrs. Pitts? I had no memory of it. "It was nothing," I said. "I suppose I'm hungry."

"Very well." Master Wendyn piled fried potatoes on the plate in front of me. "Eat something, then. I'd prefer it if you didn't die while under my authority. That looks bad to the Council."

"Yes. Of course." I took up my fork and noted trembling in my hand, and what was this faint pulsing behind my temples? Was I getting sick? I gripped the utensil tighter and picked at the potatoes.

Silence filled the room for a moment, but for the thump a-thump a-thump of Mrs. Pitts' footsteps. In the silence, as I stared at Mrs. Pitts' face, it came back: what I was trying to say to the master here, the truth about Kurke, everything that had happened yesterday.

Kurke said I wouldn't be able to speak of what happened between us. I couldn't even seem to hold onto my thoughts long enough to speak them aloud.

The tray *clanked* against the table as Mrs. Pitts set it down. After Kurke left yesterday, I had wasted ten minutes trying to remove the trammel with my mind and my bare hands, so that I could put into use a lifting spell to carry Mrs. Pitts, one of the new spells I'd memorized. In the end I'd given up and dragged the inert form of Mrs. Pitts down the hall to her room by myself. It had been no small feat to do so without attracting the attention of all the servants. I suppose it was lucky that I'd had experience lugging Papa to his bed on more than one occasion when he'd collapsed on the doorstep in a drunken stupor. After depositing her on her bed, I informed other staff members she wasn't feeling well. This was the first I had seen her since, and I was relieved that she seemed mostly normal.

"Ma'am," Oscar said to Mrs. Pitts. "You seem to have developed a limp. Are you well?"

She looked down at herself. "Have I? I don't recall having a limp. Perhaps I slept wrong."

"Yes," Oscar said. "I too often develop injuries while lying unconscious in bed."

"Comes with age, I suppose," Mrs. Pitts offered and limped out of the room. She hadn't even shot me one glare in the time she was present. How many of her memories had Kurke taken?

I tried a different tack. "I only wanted to ask, Oscar, how well you know Master Kurke."

Yes, that was good. If I couldn't get at the heart of the matter, perhaps I could skirt the periphery.

Oscar blinked. "Matthias? Since he was a boy. Perhaps even from the day he was born. Yes, I expect that's right. Why do you ask?"

"Only curiosity. Would you say he's a good friend?"

He shoveled in a forkful of food and chewed it before speaking. "We've been close, yes. Matthias used to be something of a rebel, but these days he's straightened up and become a close friend to the Wendyn family. I'd trust the boy with my life."

Now it was my turn to blink in surprise. "Your life?" I echoed.

Before he could answer, the master wiped his mouth on a napkin, leaned forward, and said, "How far did you get in the spell books yesterday, underwizard?"

"Partway through *Charms Without Number*." Not as far as I'd hoped, but Kurke's appearance had set the whole afternoon on its ear. "Don't worry. I've taken to heart your deadline. I'll regain all five levels within three months." The words came out with more confidence than I felt.

Oscar sat forward, interest splashed across his face. "You set a deadline, Garrick? You realize that if the underwizard passes all the trials at that rate, he'll be a full master wizard in a year? That would almost beat the fastest master wizard ever, Hammond Ecklebert. He passed all twenty trials in eleven months, and even his Postulate. Why don't you try to beat that?"

I choked on the water I was sipping.

"Don't be absurd," Master Wendyn said. "Hammond Ecklebert was an exceptional case and a good deal brighter than Underwizard Mullins."

The insult stung, even though my master might have meant nothing by it. I knew the story of Hammond Ecklebert. He'd been brilliant, raised in a master wizard household, and had performed his first spell accidentally at just over a year old. I didn't perform my first spell until I was fourteen, the same year I learned to read. I was no master wizard prodigy.

"Still." Oscar reached across the table to dish me up more potatoes, without my asking, as I had finished the food on my plate. "Just to try. What could it hurt?"

"A good deal if he fails. Too many appearances at the trials could bias the judges against him and affect his confidence. Let's have no more talk of Hammond Ecklebert."

At least Master Wendyn and I were in agreement on that.

For a moment or two quiet reigned, until Oscar broke it by asking, "So, Mullins, I understand you were disapprenticed for fighting in Bramford."

I sat up straighter, looking from Oscar to the master to Ivan, who had started on a piece of bread. He dipped it in the saucer of jelly whenever he thought no one was looking. The master gave him a pained glance and didn't look at me at all.

Oscar was still staring at me, sipping at his tea. "Is it true?" he asked. "Because if so, I can't help but wonder why you didn't use magic when you have it at your disposal. Why fists?"

I shrugged. "It felt fair. Besides, I'm good with my fists."

"A little too good," Master Wendyn inserted.

"Use what you have at your disposal, I suppose," Oscar mused. "What about your parents? You had some, I'm guessing."

"Father's a drunk," Master Wendyn supplied, and I shot him a glare. Trust him to remember the worst thing he could.

"Yes," I said, before Master Wendyn can insert anything else. "Papa drinks too much. And Mama—well, she died when I was younger."

"From what?"

"Overwork, I suspect." I shoveled a forkful of potatoes in my mouth, hoping he'd quit talking.

He didn't take the hint. "What about siblings? Are there any little Mullinses at home, eager to see their older brother become a master wizard?"

The potatoes in my mouth tasted like crumbled ash. I had to swallow twice to force the food down. "There was one," I admitted. "But he died too. From the wasting sickness."

Oscar nodded. "I suppose none of us are immune to tragedy. Losing my dear Anelina was a blow. And Garrick here—"

The master stood. "There's work waiting, underwizard." He nodded at the door. "If you're done eating, I suggest you get started on your studies."

"But we were getting to know one another," Oscar said, dismay in his voice.

"That trammel won't fall off on its own. You'd best get to studying." Master Wendyn pointed at the door. The subject was not open for discussion.

"Fine." I pushed myself to my feet, and Ivan scrambled to follow. I stopped long enough to grab a piece of fruit for each hand and headed to the library.

OVER THE NEXT FEW DAYS, I shared time between memorizing spells and studying out the new problems dropped in my lap. My goal to become a master wizard hadn't changed, but the obstacles blocking me had. There were two people in my way now—Masters Wendyn and Kurke. To keep Wendyn happy, I had to memorize spells and regain my five levels within three months. And to keep Kurke happy, I had to spy on Oscar Wendyn.

The truth was, there was more to the task than just spying on Oscar, but I wasn't prepared to confront that just yet—the part where Kurke wanted my help to dispose of my master's grandfather. I'd never killed a man before. The fact that he was nutty as a fruitcake and probably innocent didn't make me feel any better about it.

I'd let that problem simmer until I found a solution.

One evening when I was sick to death of memorizing spells, I pulled out parchment and ink and worked on another idea that had been developing in the back of my mind.

To Masters Garrick and Oscar Wendyn, I addressed the letter. It only made sense for me to address the letter to both. Oscar, because he was the one whose life hung in the balance, and Master Wendyn, because he was my master.

I'd written the letter's opening with no confusion or swimming thoughts, and that was a fine beginning. Perhaps there was a simple answer to my problem after all.

I am writing to inform you that a few days past, I

The next word I meant to write was *swore.* But though I put pen to paper and tried to make it write, something stopped my hand from moving. And then the confusion overtook me, pulling me under, so I blinked and stared at the paper before me. As I watched, the words I had written faded and disappeared altogether. Even the imprint of my quill disappeared.

I blinked and looked at the pen in my hand and the paper before me. What was I writing again?

A few minutes passed before I remembered and made another attempt. I readdressed the letter and began once more.

Everything repeated itself as before. A third attempt was no different. At last I wadded up the parchment and tossed it into the fire.

Kurke certainly did all he could to ensure I couldn't tell anyone the truth.

"AGAIN." Master Wendyn leaned forward, his head in his hands, staring at the floor. "Show me fire." He sat in an armchair in front of the library's fireplace while I stood before the south window, its light falling around me. A slight chill seeped through the glass, a sign that autumn had arrived. It soothed my skin. The vibrant colors of the Waldrin-woven rug beneath my feet gave me something else to look at besides my disgruntled master.

Today marked the end of the second week of my apprenticeship with Master Wendyn and four days before I was to take the first trial. In that time, I had focused my efforts on three things: memorizing spells, trying to learn things about Oscar, and preparing myself for the first trial.

The magic felt reluctant when I summoned it to my hand. There was not much left. We'd been at this all afternoon, and I was tired. A faint blue flame flickered in the palm of my hand and then went out. It was a half-hearted attempt.

"There." I had the grace to feel embarrassed by my poor showing.

He looked up and said, "Perhaps you haven't been listening. You must hold it longer than that."

"I heard you. And the last five times." I kept my voice polite.

"Then stop wasting my time and show me a flame." He rubbed at his eyes. "And without the impudence this time, unless you'd like to wear the trammel again."

I had worn that contraption until the previous day, when he released me after I recited all hundred and seven of the spells he required me to memorize. The recitation alone took the better part of an hour. He even paid me a sort of compliment after I was all finished, saying, "You're quick, Mullins, and that'll serve you well. Perhaps you ought to consider becoming the next Hammond Ecklebert after all." But from the quirk of his eyebrow, I knew he wasn't serious. And then he ruined it by saying, "I admit, it'll be a relief to have you out of that trammel. You're so theatrical in your supposed suffering—creeping around the house looking like a haunt, missing meals, staying up all hours—that the sight of you has been ruining my appetite."

That night I had my first full night's sleep in a long while.

With the master watching now, I pulled the magic to my hand again. The flame glowed and lit, and I held it in place with everything I had. It built to a respectable size and paused there, then sputtered out without warning. It was the biggest flame I'd produced all day, but if I was expecting a celebration, I was disappointed.

"Bigger."

I dropped my hand and paced back and forth in frustration. "I can't get it any bigger!"

"You can't, if that's what you believe. Stop thinking so much, Mullins. You must let go of your emotions. Empty yourself. Feel nothing."

"I'm *trying*."

"There's your problem. You can't just try. You must *know* it will work. If you spent as much time practicing this spell as you do following my grandfather around, you'd be an expert by now. Go again."

Kurke had ordered me to spy on Oscar, but I wasn't doing it to help him. I was following Oscar around out of curiosity mixed with a healthy amount of desperation. Maybe if I could figure out why Kurke hated Oscar so much, I could talk him out of this foolish plan. Besides, Oscar was in and out so often, constantly disappearing on things he termed "adventures" that I couldn't help being a little curious. Half the time he was just playing around with his scrying stick, but I knew for a fact that sometimes he left the Hall and the grounds altogether, even when he claimed not to. I'd searched the place up and down for him a few days before with no luck. I had yet to figure out where he went during these times.

I rubbed my hands on my trousers. Producing fire was hot work, and I had shed my robes an hour past. I brought my hand up in front of me, emptied my mind, and summoned the magic.

Flame flickered and disappeared.

"Devil's dawn, Mullins." Master Wendyn came to his feet, striding at me. "You can't get more basic than making fire. If you're unable to pass the first trial, there's no point in my keeping you here." He stopped in front of me, his hands on his hips, dark brows low over his eyes as he glared at me.

With only three months to become a fifth level underwizard again, and the tests given once a month, I should be taking more than just the first trial. But I'd given such a dismal showing at fire that my master had informed me I was incapable of more.

Even I was wondering if I was capable of more, though I'd never admit it to him.

I scowled. He'd like nothing more than for me to give up. "I will pass," I informed him.

"Then go again," he said.

He wasn't wearing robes today either. He seldom did around the house. Today's attire involved long droopy sleeves with frills at the wrists and a lacy tie of sorts at the neck. Pretty fussy, but then again, it suited his disposition.

I raised my hand and something warmed in my chest, reminding me of Kurke and the tether that bound us. It happened now and then, that warmth, and I didn't know what it meant. I hoped it was a chance occurrence, just the tether reminding me it was there and not that Kurke was off somewhere thinking about me and all the ways he could use me to his advantage.

What if every time I thought about him, he felt the same sensation on his end? It was an unsettling thought.

"Well?" Master Wendyn asked crisply. "Today, if you please."

I bit my lip and raised my hand, reaching out for any tendrils of magic I could find. The room felt devoid of it. I was pulling from a dry well and might as well be wearing the trammel.

"There's nothing left," I told him, dropping my hand. "I need to rest. I'm too tired."

"Too tired?" my master said. His jaw tightened. "Too tired? Do you think you're the first wizard asked to perform magic under demanding circumstances? The first to feel exhausted? Come here."

He grabbed my hand, not gently in the least, and flattened it against his two, palm up, the fingers splayed. I was taken aback by his touch, so I could only stare at him with what felt like consternation on my face. Friar's bones. This was a first. He'd never touched me before. Not on purpose. It was frightening.

"Don't you think I'm tired too after these irksome days of trying to force learning into your impenetrable head?" His voice was as hard as the stone that surrounded the fireplace behind him. "This is the sort of magic you must perform if you want to be a wizard, whether you're fresh or whether you're all done in. Now *observe*."

I didn't hear the words of the spell. All I saw was the fire that roared to life in our hands, blinding and hot in its intensity. I tried to wrench myself backward away from the flame, but his grip held me in place until the conflagration died down and then flickered out.

His face was sooty, and sweat glistened on his brow as he glowered down at me. "No matter how exhausted you are, you must find the magic, underwizard. It's never far. I don't want to hear you say that there's nothing left ever again." He dropped my hand and wiped his brow on his sleeve. "I'm going to Bramford. I want fifty more tries on that spell before supper. Understood?"

Bramford. That would mean official wizard's business, helping townsfolk who had requested his services. Master Hapthwaite sometimes took me along on such calls for practice. But Master Wendyn had never even mentioned taking me along. He just disappeared to do the work and returned, barely paying me a glance.

It was probably because I was so dreadful at magic. He thought I needed the practice here more than the hands-on practice. And he was right.

I swallowed and nodded. "Understood. Fifty tries."

"Good." He was halfway out the door when he turned back as an afterthought and said, "Oh, and you should do something about your hair. It's smoking."

TEN

FOR TWO DAYS I split my time between practicing the fire spell and following Oscar on his ridiculous jaunts through the woods. My fire spell didn't seem to be improving, and following Oscar yielded quirky but useless bits of information. He had a profound weakness for all things sweet and told me he was developing a "sweets box," as he called it, a container that magicked desserts into existence.

Additionally, he was under the impression that his mallet game, which he called scry and seek, had the ability to save the world, though he'd never elaborated on how. But he had informed me it was not a mallet—Forthwind was a scrying stick. Also, I was beginning to suspect he wore the same homespun farmer's shirt every day, just magicked into different colors. I'd seen it now in white, red, blue, yellow, and a brilliant orange, the color of a sunset.

The time spent with Oscar only emphasized the need to find a way out of the blood oath so I never had to harm him. I began a perusal of the master's library for books on blood magic, but after two days of searching, I still had no results. On the third afternoon, as I skimmed the titles, my finger running over the spines, I noticed a presence by my side.

Ivan stood next to me, engrossed in running his fingers over the books as I was, almost as though he was reading their titles.

I stared in consternation. Was he mimicking me? Or could he read?

He looked over at me and then back at the books. He pulled one out and opened it up, running his finger over the page as though he was reading and following the words. Then he turned to the next page.

The book was upside-down. I sighed. He *was* mimicking me.

Still, it was a start.

I reached out, took the book from him, and asked, "Ivan, do you want to learn how to read?"

He held his hand out toward me. His fingers touched the palm, and then he opened his hand again. Open and closed, open and closed.

Ivan and I had developed our own form of communication, one that involved pointing and guessing and nodding. But this was different. I'd seen him do this gesture before, but I had assumed it was just a—I didn't know, a twitch or idiosyncrasy or something.

"What does that mean?" I held my hand out and copied his gesture—open and closed, open and closed. "What are you trying to tell me?"

Then Ivan did something I'd never seen him do before—he smiled. He made the open-and-closed gesture several more times and seemed to be enjoying himself enormously. One last time and then he turned and went back to his usual crouched position behind the bookshelf nearest the corner.

My gaze moved away from Ivan's corner and back to the bookshelf. But this time, my eyes lit on the magical device perched at the end of the row of books I stood in front of—a trammel.

The master seemed to have a strange affinity for magical contraptions. Various magicked mechanical boxes and spheres and funny shapes with gears were all over this library and his study. Whenever the master or Oscar was in the room, I asked about the uses of each one.

I traced one finger over the trammel's cold, metallic edge, wondering what it would be like to clap this contraption around Kurke's neck. To see him as helpless as he had me in the library. My fingers tightened on the device, and Ivan made a guttural noise. I glanced up. He was on his feet, pointing. I followed the line of his finger, and my gaze stopped on a shimmery something wavering into existence in the middle of the library.

As I watched, a large rectangle appeared in the middle of the room.

It was a door. A wizard door.

They were the best method for wizards traveling between far distant locales. Master Hapthwaite had a wizard door hidden in several rooms in Larkspur House, one that led to the Conclave, another to Vickermond, and another to Mergendale, both remote cities he often visited for various wizardly duties.

The door's edges pulsed with magic. I didn't know whether to be frightened, on my guard, or if this was a normal occurrence here in the Wendyn household.

The golden wood of the door swung open, and a bright-eyed, beautiful young woman crossed the threshold into the room. She held a child in her arms. She paused in the middle of the room and looked around until her eyes fell on me.

"Oh, hello there," she called, waving, her gaze alight with interest. "Who are you? Are you an apprentice? You must be; I recognize the robes. When did Garrick take on an apprentice? Mother, did you know about this?"

"Rrrrk," said the baby in her arms.

A woman with brown hair streaked with gray crossed into the room on the heels of the younger woman, a small boy gripping her hand. "Don't be ridiculous, Marelda. How would I know anything about what Garrick does? Why should he tell his own mother anything?"

I nearly choked on my tongue. Mother? I rose to my feet and took several steps in their direction. Ivan, meanwhile, scampered off to hide in some corner somewhere.

"Can you make magic?" the boy asked, staring at me with large adoring eyes. He tugged his hand away from the master's mother.

"Er—sometimes," I answered. "What can you make?"

"Messes," Mother Wendyn answered for him.

"Here," said the beautiful woman, Marelda, the one holding the baby. I straightened and turned to her. "This is Maud. Be a dear and hold her, will you?" She deposited the baby in my arms before I could protest. "I'm going back for Carrington. Don't tell Garrick we're here till we all come through, all right? He loves a good surprise." She slipped back through the doorway while I was caught so unawares by, well, everything, that all I could do was stare after her.

The baby looked up at me, blinking large blue eyes. "Blrr-ba," she said.

I was holding a baby.

But I hardly had time to wonder over this because people began traipsing through the doorway two at a time, toddlers, children, adults. Several carried parcels, and two of the women had pots of something that smelled like sweet toffee.

"Who has Chauntel?"

"Stop wriggling, Phil! If you make a ruckus, won't Uncle Garrick be disappointed in you?"

"He's gotten more books since the last time we were here."

"Don't break anything!"

There must have been fifteen or twenty people milling about the library. Children ran races across the room. Unfamiliar men and women examined magical artifacts and chatted over them. A toddler pulled books from the shelves and tossed them every which way until she was stopped by an adult.

"Hullo! Who're you?" bellowed a portly gentleman in my direction. At least a dozen eyes swiveled my way, pinning me in place. I looked around, hopeful he was addressing someone other than me.

"Erm," I said, returning his gaze as I hefted the baby. "Hello. I'm the apprentice."

"Pleased to make your acquaintance. Be a good fellow and go get your master, would you? Tell him his family has come to visit."

"Sure." I edged toward the door. "I'll get him directly." Two more steps and I turned and fled the library.

In the hallway, I came upon Mrs. Pitts, who frowned upon sight of me. "The master doesn't allow babies, underwizard. Is this the result of some spell? Send it back." She limped closer.

I filled her in on the visitors in the library, and her eyebrows headed toward the ceiling. "Great Hepzibah's fiddle! Master Wendyn hates when his family drops in unannounced. I'd better let Cook know. Don't you do anything stupid." She headed off toward the kitchen.

The day had taken an unexpected turn, but it was more interesting than combing through every book in the library. I bounced the baby on my hip, reached up, and knocked on the study door.

"Enter," the master said.

I took a deep breath and looked down at the baby.

"Grrrb," she said.

"WHAT?" Master Wendyn exploded at me in his study when I announced the news. "My family? And you just—you just let them in?" He looked from me to the baby and back again. "It's not as though they asked my permission. Would you have preferred that I shoved them back through the wizard door?"

He pushed a hand through his hair, surged to his feet, and paced back and forth. "I had that door closed. Permanently. How in the three kingdoms did they get it restored?" He paced more and then stopped dead in the middle of the room and said a rather bad word. I had a ridiculous urge to cover the baby's ears. "It must have been Grandfather. Who else could have done it but him? But what are they—why are they here? What day is it? Can it be—" He rifled through papers on his desk and came up with one he stared at in concentration. Resignation colored his expression, and he sank back into the chair. "Oh no. It's my natalis."

"What?" I didn't mean to say anything, but it popped out on its own.

His shoulders slumped forward. "I suppose there's nothing for it."

"Really? Your natalis?" I digested that information for a moment or two. Today was the anniversary of the master's birth, his natal day. I didn't know why it surprised me. Having a natalis like any other person made him seem so . . . ordinary.

He heaved a sigh and stood. "Whose baby is that? Give her here. You look ridiculous." He took Maud out of my arms, and to my surprise, he seemed to know what he was about. At least, he didn't throw her over his shoulder like a sack of apples, as I expected him to. Instead he held her against his chest and looked down into her face, bouncing her.

"Her name is Maud. I think she's your niece," I said,

hovering close because I was still a little concerned at what he might do with her. Knowing him as I did, I expected him to undo her existence if the fancy took him. "Shouldn't you know who she is?"

He stared at the baby in concentration for a moment and then gave up with a shake of his head. "I haven't been in contact with those people in a few years, underwizard. In fact, I would have preferred it to stay that way." He looked at the baby again. "Maud, you say? Perhaps Wallace and Essie's child. She has the Fowler chin." After a minute of furrowed-brow thinking, he looked to the door. I could feel his hesitation. The man seemed afraid to leave the safety of his study.

"What are you frightened of? They're just your family." The crack in his armor disconcerted me. I couldn't help but poke at it a little more and see if I could widen it. "They have gifts. I'm certain I saw some. And maybe pudding. Oh! Do you think they will sing?"

Stiffness moved through him. "How would you feel if your drunk father showed up here unannounced, underwizard? My family arriving like this is not much different. Don't make light."

"If Papa showed up, he wouldn't bring gifts or pudding. He'd want money. I doubt that's why your family is here."

"Oh, believe me, they want something. Perhaps not money, but they want something. The question is what."

"Probably to eat pudding," I said. "The fiends."

His jaw worked, and his brows pushed downward. "Never mind. Not one word unless you're spoken to, and otherwise, I want you on your best behavior. Where's Ivan?"

"Hiding."

"Good." He ran a hand over his face. I'd never seen him at such a loss of composure. "Come along. They'll want to meet you. And then you are to return to your room and study until they leave." He stepped toward the door and hefted Maud higher.

I couldn't help but feel, as I followed him out of the study, that whatever was about to happen would be very entertaining.

———

THE FIRST THING that became clear was that some of the master's family were under the mistaken impression he was a friendly person.

"Uncle Garrick!" several voices shouted as we walked into the library, and boys crowded him. Even more surprising than the children's reaction was the master's. He ruffled the hair of several and didn't grimace or snarl once.

"There's Maud," a blond-haired woman with a rather pointy chin said, and she scurried to the master's side to lift the child from his arms. "Hello, Garrick. Lovely to see you again. Happy natalis."

"Essie." The master's guarded gaze swept the library, taking in the many bodies crowded there. He scooped the smallest boy at his knee up into his arms. It almost seemed that he did it for protection, now he'd lost the baby. I couldn't fathom what he was so afraid of.

The portly man came to his side and clapped him on the back with a bellow of "Happy natalis, boy!" Mother Wendyn was there, too, and kissed him on both cheeks.

Master Wendyn frowned and pulled away. "You shouldn't have come."

"Nonsense. Of course we should have," said his father.

"And you had to bring the whole—" Master Wendyn's voice became too quiet to hear. For a moment, the master and his parents whispered back and forth, and I only caught snatches of what was being said.

"... family ... not fair ..." Master Wendyn said.

"... being ridiculous," his mother said.

"... childish ... Bastian ..." his father said.

But the conversation culminated when Father Wendyn said loud enough for everyone in the library to hear, "I have a right to visit my own SON!"

An uncomfortable silence dampened the room. Even I wasn't sure where to look. But then the room exploded into a flurry of movement as Edie and Mrs. Pitts bustled into the room carrying trays of tea and dispensing them at random. Oscar arrived, eliciting several cries of "Grandpapa!" Last and worst of all, a final figure emerged from the wizard door: Master Matthias Kurke.

My stomach dropped to my toes.

Vaguely, I became aware of children clustering around Oscar, but my gaze fixed on Kurke. I felt shaky, my face hot with pumping blood. He stood just inside the door, chatting with a woman who must be the master's sister, judging by the shape of her mouth. Three children played at his feet, and he smiled at them. One of them was the little boy I met earlier. He tugged at Matthias's hand and tried to get him involved in whatever game he was playing.

Kurke's blue eyes and strong white smile remained as attractive as ever. Edie handed him a cup of tea as I watched, and I forced myself to turn away, hands clenched into fists.

Why was he here? Was this it? The revenge? Was he here to kill Oscar already?

I thought I had more time. I hadn't come up with any defense against him yet. It might as well be two weeks ago because I was still just as helpless.

What could I do?

Oscar was delighting the children by pulling candy out of the air and depositing it into each of their little hands, most likely another sweets spell he'd been working on. I glanced at the master and his parents. They were conversing in somewhat quieter tones now.

I needed help, but where was I going to get it?

"Er . . . Master Wendyn?" I edged as close as I dared to the master and his parents, not wanting to overhear a conversation they might consider private.

The master didn't even glance up. "Well, if Grandfather didn't open the wizard door, then who did?"

"Matthias, of course," said Father Wendyn.

"Yes," Mother Wendyn said, dabbing at her eyes. "At least he cares about our family enough to make contact once in a while."

"I suggest making Matt an official member of the family, then," the master said, his face serious. "He can take my place. Don't worry; I'll bow out gracefully."

"Don't say things like that." Mother Wendyn gestured at me. "The underwizard will think you're serious."

"I *am* serious—" The master broke off and looked at me. "Do you mind, Mullins? I won't abide eavesdropping."

"But I need to talk—"

"Go." He turned me about and gave me a push in the opposite direction. I took four steps before my momentum ran out, and I darted a resentful look back at him. He'd continued his conversation with his parents as though my interruption never happened.

But wait. I wasn't just as helpless as two weeks ago. I had a hundred or more spells under my belt now, thanks to the master's mandate. Could I put those to use?

After a few moments of deliberation, I decided that whatever happened, I'd be more useful closer to Oscar. I sidled nearer to where he had begun a conversation with an older and portlier version of the master about Faronnish literature. I didn't want to attract their attention, so I stood next to a bookshelf nearby and hoped it looked as though I was perusing the shelves.

I cataloged the spells I knew that might be of use in this situation. There was the armor spell, although it was only useful against actual weapons, not magic. A deflection spell could toss any magic sent Oscar's way back at the caster, although that one wasn't very precise and more often than not sent the spell careening off toward innocent parties, I'd heard. Then there was the freezing spell, a version of which Kurke used on me the day he forced me to swear the oath.

I loathed that spell.

Yes, it was the perfect irony. I would defeat Kurke using the same spell he had used on me.

Then again, the master hadn't allowed me to cast any of these spells yet. I'd memorized them, sure, but the trammel had only just been removed. I had no actual practice at these spells, so whatever I cast, it would be for the first time.

All at once I realized I had an audience. The little boy I had met earlier stood at the corner of the bookshelf peeping at me, one eye visible, as though he believed he might be invisible. From what I could see of his face, it bore the same adoring expression it had carried earlier.

Perhaps if I ignored him, he'd go away. Right now I had a grandfather to save.

"Hello, underwizard. I can't help but notice you've been looking at that shelf of books for ten minutes."

I started and glanced up at Master Kurke. He had been across the room talking to the sister last I checked. I wasn't paying close enough attention, which wasn't a good sign right before I may have to incapacitate the man. A nervous shudder passed through me, though I tried to hide it. "Master Wendyn asked me to stay out of the way."

"Yes, well, I can see you're taking that job quite seriously. This is a party, or hadn't you noticed?" His voice dropped to a murmur as he stepped closer. I had to force myself not to move away from him. "I hope you plan to obey my commands as thoroughly." His eyes flicked to Oscar and back to me again.

Was this it? Should I freeze him now?

I pulled magic toward me and muttered the words of the spell. Before I got it all out, Kurke held up a hand. At the moment my freezing spell should have hit him, instead it seemed to dissipate into nothing. When I felt for the magic, my woven spell had disappeared.

"Wordless magic and an absorption spell. Tricky but useful. I just absorbed all the magic from that badly cast freezing spell. No offense, Mullins, but you'll need to do better than that. That wouldn't even immobilize a beetle."

My jaw clenched in frustration. He was mocking me. Very well. I would try something else.

For some reason my mind jumped to the forgetting spell I cast in Waltney so long ago, the spell I used on the men I bribed to sign my affidavits of gender. It was a weak spell and only erased one specific memory—not like the oblivion, which took large chunks—but if I could get Kurke to forget he was here to kill Oscar, just for a little while, perhaps I could save a life tonight.

I uttered the words of the spell, and the woven magic left me. This time the spell didn't dissipate; it deflected. I felt the moment the magic rebounded on me and—I blinked in surprise.

What had just happened? Something felt different, although I couldn't put my finger on what. I was conversing with Master Kurke, a man I didn't like. A man who had forced me to swear to help him kill Oscar Wendyn. A man who was here to help the master celebrate his natalis.

Kurke looked smug. "A forgetting spell, eh? I'll presume

Garrick never taught you that one. You're lucky it was strong as wet paper."

I blinked and thought and pieced together what must have happened. He deflected my spell at me more precisely than I thought possible. I'd forgotten something—oh, yes. Now it was coming back through the haze of weak magic. He was here to kill Oscar.

"I won't help you," I hissed at him. "You may have forced me to swear, but you can't force me to do your bidding."

He frowned. "Now, your defiance I can do without. There are plenty of innocent people here I could threaten to get you to help me. I don't want to do it, but I will."

He was right. Upwards of twenty people filled the room, and a third of them were children.

"You don't want to hurt all these people," I told him. "But if you do this now, you'll have to."

"It's interesting you think I care. But there's one thing you don't seem to understand. They deserve it."

There was something behind his eyes, something like hesitation, and I knew he didn't mean it—at least, not entirely.

Use what you have at your disposal, that's what Oscar said about my fist fighting, rather than using magic. Maybe the answer was already in front of me. I'd seen Kurke had a soft spot for children.

My eyes lit on the little boy, and I stepped past Kurke. "Hello again. What's your name?" I crouched down so I was on his level.

"Vito." He peeked around the corner at me.

"Do you know Matthias too?" I gestured at Kurke.

That got him to come out from behind the bookcase. "'Course." He grabbed Kurke's hand and tugged him toward me. "We're friends."

"Indeed we are," Kurke said. He frowned at me. "But now I

must go say hello to your father." He dropped Vito's hand and veered across the room.

I watched him go. Would it be that easy? Would Kurke forget about his murderous plan, just for tonight?

"Can you make candy, like Grandpapa?" Vito asked me.

My gaze swung back to the little boy. "'Fraid not." I smiled at him. "That's your grandpapa's trick. But I can do this." I held my hand out and formed a spark of fire in my palm.

The little fire impressed him. "Wow! See what I can do?" He spun in a circle, kicking one leg out. I was sure in his childish mind it was the height of impressive.

"Unbelievable."

"Yeah, and I can do it the other way too!" He spun the other way, but this time he kicked into a pedestal at the end of the bookshelf. It tilted, and the carved stone sculpture atop teetered and fell. I realized in that instant that, one, I was too far away to catch it before it hit the ground, two, even if I were closer, the thing was heavy enough it would just crush me, and three, it would crush Vito instead.

I acted without thinking. The words of the lifting spell came out of my mouth without my even thinking about it. It was the same spell I had considered for moving Mrs. Pitts when she was unconscious. The sculpture's weight pulled at the magic that tried to hold it up, dragging the spell toward the ground. I would only be able to slow its fall, not stop it. I stepped closer and snatched the little boy out of the way. The sculpture crashed to the ground, cracking the marble floor beneath it and breaking itself into several pieces. The pedestal toppled over on top of it.

Adults and children surrounded us in the next moment, chattering voices all wanting to know "What happened?" and "Are you all right?" Vito ran past me. When I looked over my shoulder, I saw that he clung to Master Kurke's side. After a moment of deliberation, Kurke swung him up into his arms, and Vito threw arms around his neck in a viselike grip.

I crouched down to examine the sculpture, which lay in several indefinable shapes. Beneath it, the library's marble floor was a mess of spider-webbed cracks.

"He saved Vito," the boy's mother said breathlessly to the master as he strode closer.

Behind me, Vito wailed, "It's broken!"

"Nice work, underwizard," Oscar said, coming to a stop next to me where he stood staring down at the floor. "I never liked that sculpture."

I winced and looked at Master Wendyn who had come to a stop on my other side.

"Was that a lifting spell?" he asked, his eyes, too, on the floor.

"Yes."

"Glad you learned it now, aren't you?"

"I suppose."

Kurke joined us. "This is a replica of a sculpture at the Conclave, isn't it?" He nudged the broken remnants of the sculpture with his foot.

"It is," Oscar agreed. "Hideous. Good work, Vito. I've always wanted to smash it to bits."

Vito wailed louder.

"No one cares about the sculpture, Vito," Master Wendyn said sharply. And then, his voice gentler, he asked, "Is he hurt?"

Kurke pried Vito's arms from around his neck and handed him over to Essie, the mother. She looked him over and reassured that he wasn't harmed, only frightened.

"Don't listen to your mean old uncle, Vito," Kurke said. "This sculpture can be fixed."

Vito lifted his tear-stained face. "Truly?" he asked.

"'Mean old uncle'?" Master Wendyn repeated.

"Of course it can be fixed," Oscar boomed. "Don't worry yourself, Vito." To Master Wendyn he said, "Or you could just put a more tasteful sculpture in its place."

"We'll talk about it later," Master Wendyn said.

"That was quick thinking, Mullins," Oscar observed, turning his attention to me now. "You've got good reflexes. He's not as bad as you keep saying, Garrick."

I frowned.

"Bad?" Father Wendyn bellowed. He'd come up behind the three of us. "The boy saved my grandson. You're family now, underwizard." He clapped me on the shoulder.

The words warmed me. It had been a long time since I had anything resembling a family.

Then I remembered I had pledged myself to kill their patriarch. If they knew the truth about me, they would have no warm feelings toward me at all.

The family clustered around, and I was introduced to a dozen or more people by name, most of which I forgot. Carden, Eren, Chauntel, Wyman, and the list went on. I smiled and nodded and pretended to have committed every name to memory.

We adjourned to the sitting room, and the family stayed for hours, talking and eating, opening gifts, playing games. After an hour, Master Kurke announced he must leave, and relief sank into me, bone-deep. But from the dark glare he gave me as he went, I presumed his revenge had only been postponed for the moment. At least now I had more time to come up with a plan.

I remembered the master's words that I was to return to my room to study once he'd introduced me, but every time I tried to slip away, one of the family found an excuse for me to stay. At last the master cornered me in the hall outside the library, the farthest I'd made it yet, and told me to stop trying to leave, as his father said nothing he didn't mean. Whether or not I liked it, I was part of the Wendyn family now. With a frown and a hand on my shoulder, he led me back to the sitting room.

———

MUCH LATER I lay in bed, knotting and unknotting my length of rope and thinking about the events of the day. Every time I thought of my pitiful try at incapacitating Master Kurke, I flushed with embarrassment. I was no match for his magic.

I must work on my defense and attack spells. The next time Kurke showed up to kill Oscar, it would be unlikely I'd have little Vito around to deter him from his plan.

I was glad of that, though. I didn't want Vito or anyone else in the Wendyn family getting hurt if I could stop it. They had welcomed me into their ranks with open arms, and I couldn't deny it was nice to be part of a family again. I'd forgotten what it was like, and now that I'd had a taste of it again, it was obvious I'd missed it.

My mind wandered back to what I'd been doing when the master's family first appeared—searching for a blood magic book. The master didn't seem to have one in his collection, even as expansive as it was. I'd need to find a bigger library.

It came to me then: The Conclave. The library there overflowed with books on every topic imaginable. They must have a section on blood magic.

I'd go to the Wizard's Library and discover what I needed to do to break this wretched oath I'd sworn with Master Kurke. And I'd keep trying to tell Oscar and Master Wendyn about the oath. There must be some way I hadn't tried yet.

I muttered the unknotting spell, and the tie on my bit of rope slid open, leaving me pleased and triumphant. I settled down to sleep, its length clutched in my hand.

ELEVEN

IT HAD BEEN MONTHS since I sat for a trial—three, to be precise. The trials were offered the first Wednesday of every month, which made the day after the master's natalis a trial day. I awoke, with a sick feeling of nervousness snaking through my middle. It was a familiar feeling, accompanied by occasional bursts of terror and difficulty drawing breath when I imagined myself standing on the testing dais. Even when I was ninety, I would remember what trial-day nerves felt like.

I couldn't help but recognize the importance of doing well with this trial. Master Wendyn would see me in a testing situation. He would draw conclusions, forming his first and most lasting opinion of me and my abilities.

Failure was not an option. I rubbed at my nose.

"Oats or potatoes?" Edie asked me at breakfast and then leaned close to whisper, "I saw you save that boy from the falling sculpture. You're magnificent. Is there anything you can't do?"

She'd never leave me alone now.

Still, it was a nice boost to my confidence on trial morning. I couldn't stop myself from smiling, though I knew it would only encourage her. "Potatoes, please."

There was more to the trials than just performing magic. There was proving one's emotional maturity, which could be a difficult prospect when one felt as though a bag of butterflies had been freed in one's stomach.

I kept my composure throughout breakfast and accepted Oscar's well wishes, just before he ran out the door on another of his mysterious adventures. The master turned up late and clean-shaven, rather than his usual scruffy look, and brooded over his meal. I imagined he was pondering how he would use the extra space in my bedroom once I failed and moved out.

After breakfast, I followed him to his study. We donned our wizard robes, and then he paused, looking me over with an expression that almost seemed perplexed.

"You're not tired?" he asked. "You've not been doing too much magic this morning, have you? Headache?"

Was he worried I would disgrace him? "I'm fine. Why should I have a headache?"

His eyebrows rose. "I'd be a poor master if I didn't notice my underwizard gets headaches with some regularity, and that he sucks down water like a dry well."

My eyes flashed to his. "What do you mean?"

"It's another side effect from the desert spell. Don't tell me you haven't noticed."

"I—I thought I was just thirsty."

"You're dehydrated. The spell isn't just sucking water from your eyes; it's sucking it from your whole body. Which means you guzzle water and get headaches, among other things."

"Oh. Well, that makes sense, I suppose."

He sighed. "I haven't found how to undo it yet. Let's hope we can figure it out before you turn into a desiccated husk and blow away."

I rolled my eyes. "There's no danger of that happening." Was there?

He smiled. And then it was gone, fast enough for me to wonder if it even happened. "Maybe. But it made you forget your worry about the trial for just a moment, didn't it?"

"I guess."

He shrugged. "Stop looking so concerned. You've passed this trial before. You'll do well." He paused. "At least . . . probably."

How could I not feel inspired when my master so clearly believed in me?

He drew back the tapestry covering the wizard door and pulled it open, ushering me through. I slipped through ahead of him, lost at once in a sea of underwizards and masters who gave the door a wide berth. I looked back and watched Master Wendyn come through the doorway. He pulled it shut, and the outline of the door shimmered into nonexistence.

"Come along, underwizard," he said, taking me by the elbow and propelling me through the pushing crowd.

This was nothing like the cathedral hall we visited a couple weeks ago, empty but for a few passing wizards. This was a trial day, and the crowd pressed against me as we made our way across the room.

I used to fight with the boys in Waltney. Once a week when I went into town for goods on market day, they told me I was too stupid for book learning. I remembered the first boy, the smug expression on his face, and the satisfaction I found in blacking his eye. I remembered Papa telling me to forget all my silly ideas about magic. The memory of Master Hapthwaite was no better. I remembered how he urged me to give up underwizardry. Then there was Master Wendyn, telling me I had to do better, to try harder, and that there was only a *possibility* I would do well.

I stood beside my master in the testing room as time passed and underwizards both passed and failed, and I wondered which I would do today.

All at once my master jostled my elbow. "They're calling your name," he said, his voice more terse than usual. Catching a glimpse of the look on my face, he turned me to him. "Are you well?" His hands moved to my shoulders, and he gave me a little shake. "Pull yourself together, boy." His voice was low, and I could tell he was holding himself back because of the people milling about. "You will do well, do you hear me? You will not disgrace me in this forum. Nor will you disgrace yourself. You will do this."

"Mullins, Avery." The test proctor's voice was impatient, clipped. How many times had he called my name while I drifted in self-doubt? I was allowed a few minutes' grace period before he moved on to the next candidate. Had I used it all up?

"Move," the master hissed as he plunged into the crowd, pulling me behind him.

I already had all the skills I needed to pass this trial. But that didn't stop my heart thrumming against my ribs and the color rushing to my face.

"Underwizard Mullins is present," Master Wendyn called.

The three wizards who would judge the trial shifted in their line of seats along the raised edge of the dais and looked me over. Meanwhile, the proctor, seated to one side, perked up and sifted through the parchment on the desk before him. One hand clutched a seeing glass. He found what he was looking for and scanned over a sheet of parchment before glancing up. "Does Underwizard Mullins wish to sit for the first trial?"

"He does," my master announced.

"Then let him enter the testing arena." The proctor waved a hand. That would be for the privacy spell.

We took the steps, and then we stood on the dais, past the

threshold of the spell. Now the crowd could observe, but they couldn't hear. Master Wendyn left me at the mark on the floor and retreated to the edge of the dais. He stood within the privacy circle, as was his right as my master, but I still didn't like it. I knew the questions that were coming. But there wasn't much I could do about it at this point. The twenty trials were designed to bring humility. Thus they could be humiliating, and that was just the way of things. I stared at the floor and waited, preparing to pitch my voice deeper now that my voice modulating spell was inactive.

The first few questions were formalities, things such as my name, age, and village of origin. I gave Howchister as I always did, since it was the place I was born, though Mama and Papa were only passing through. I preferred not to announce to the Wizard's Council my hometown of Waltney, should anyone take it into their mind to conduct further research.

After those questions came a few more about the length of my training, the identity of my master, and any trials I had sat for in the past. The proctor made several long notes when I told him this was my fourth time taking the first trial.

"Underwizard Mullins will confess his most egregious wrongs." The proctor leaned back in his chair, a hand to his chin as he considered me. Confession of past wrongs—a topic I had never cared for. These personal questions had always been my least favorite part of any trial.

I had admitted these things every time I'd taken the first trial, and sometimes it was easier than others. Today, with a new master looking on, I was acutely aware I was about to acquaint him with all the worst parts of myself. Better if I did this without looking at him. I took a deep, steadying breath, my eyes trained on the proctor, and spoke.

"I have a short temper. This has led to many confrontations . . . fights . . . and has hurt many people. Usually I considered these altercations justified, but looking back, I was just angry. I wanted to fight."

It didn't do to hold back at the trials. The proctor and judges could sense, with the help of a scrying spell, if an underwizard withheld anything. I'd learned that my biggest lie, that of my gender, was also the simplest to hide. Because of my belief that there was no reason a female shouldn't be able to become a master wizard, my conscience was at ease regarding it. And since my conscience was untroubled, it had never been an issue at the trials. This seemed a rather large loophole in the trials, and one I believed accounted for unbalanced people such as Matthias Kurke becoming master wizards.

The proctor nodded. "Please continue."

"I fought with my father all the time. I shouted at him the last time I saw him. Awful things. We parted ways, and I haven't seen him since."

"Mmm," the proctor said, scribbling. "Go on."

My least favorite confession came next, not that the others had been that pleasant. But offering any excuse was a good way to fail a trial. I learned that the hard way during my second failure. "I—I used to steal things, though I knew it was wrong. My mother was never well. When she found out how far the thieving went, I think the knowledge that this was what I'd been doing to keep us alive . . . I think it was part of what killed her."

He scribbled more and then looked up at me. "Please continue."

I looked down at my toes. "That's all."

"I think not."

My head jerked up. I had confessed the same wrongs at every first trial, and being contradicted by the proctor was the first step toward failure.

"A recent incident in . . . Bramford, was it?" He squinted at me. "The underwizard lost his master over that flare of temper."

Bones. I forgot about Bramford. "You're right. I—I brawled in Bramford. I lost my temper and fought with a boy."

The proctor's head tilted as he watched me, his deep-set eyes more unreadable than I liked. "The underwizard lost his temper. *And* his master. Many people in Bramford felt that the underwizard wronged the boy badly on that day."

Blast that scrying spell. It was so unnerving to have a complete stranger know intimate details of past events that had occurred in one's life.

My head sank lower. This was my fourth time doing this, and I had left out something so simple. The judges would think I wasn't taking the process seriously or, worse, that I was trying to hide the truth.

I was going to fail.

But the proctor hadn't finished. "To make such a mistake while apprenticed and aware of the expectations of self-control placed on underwizards—it was an enormous misstep." He closed his eyes, and I stared at my feet. "The boy was . . . trying to poison a fool, was he? A fool tormented nearly beyond endurance." He scribbled on his parchment before looking back to me. "Why did the underwizard interfere in that instance?"

"I tried not to at first. I knew I shouldn't lose my temper. But he reminded me of my brother, and I lost all control when I saw they meant to poison him." I hung my head. "I have no excuse. It was wrong to beat that boy, and I knew it."

There was a long stretch of silence wherein I didn't look at anyone. Was this it for me? Had I used up my last chance?

The proctor drew a breath and spoke again. "It was wrong of the underwizard to let his temper rule his actions. However, it is my belief, after weighing the two things in the balance, that there is nothing to harbor any shame over."

I looked up at the proctor, surprised by this admission. But I heard the unspoken words in that sentence. *He* might believe I was guiltless in the exchange, but what would the judges think?

"For the rest of these acts, does the underwizard feel sorrow?"

"Yes," I said, nodding. "Every day." Or at least once in a while.

He pursed his lips. "What has the underwizard done to atone for these wrongs?"

"Not enough."

"What will the underwizard do in the future to atone for these wrongs?"

I bit my lip. "There's nothing I can do. I can only live my life every day, trying to be better."

"The underwizard is correct." He shuffled the papers again, and I gave a long, silent sigh of relief. We were past the questions. "Now," the proctor said. "The underwizard will make fire."

I already felt wrung out, and now we were at the moment I'd been dreading. I raised my hand in front of me. I didn't dare look at Master Wendyn. Instead, I stared at my hand with as much intensity as I could muster. It was shaking, though I tried to hold it steady.

Empty your mind, Avery. Think of nothing.

I said the spell for fire.

There was the faintest pop of noise, and the fire came to life in my hand, a flickering, sad, pathetic excuse for fire.

You must make it bigger, I imagined the master telling me. *You must know it will work.*

I tried to think of my past successes, of the unknotting spell, or the rosemary plant I'd fixed in Bramford, or the voice modulating spell, which had always worked for me. But I had failed at the fire spell so often that I didn't know it would work. In fact, I was sure it wouldn't. As I stared at the flame, it flickered into nothingness.

Ugh. This felt like my first attempt all over again. My face had become the flame now, alive with embarrassment.

The proctor looked only mildly concerned. "Try again," he encouraged. "I'm sure you can get it higher."

My hand still shook as I held it out and said the words again. A fire flickered to life, slightly taller than the last. But within seconds, it, too, simmered down to a small blue light and then flickered out altogether.

"Once more," the proctor encouraged. "I'm sure the judges would like to get a good sense of your abilities."

I was sure they had already.

No. No doubt. I looked at my hand one last time. This would work. I gathered the magic, as much as I could find lingering in the nooks and crannies around me. When I felt it warm and solid against my skin, I cleared my mind and said the spell one last time.

The flame went twice as high this time, which wasn't saying much. I struggled to hold it out, to make it last. How long was I supposed to hold it? Five seconds? Ten? I counted the thrums of my heart, and finally, shaky with exhaustion and nerves, I said the words that ended the spell. It flickered out, and I was left standing in a faint haze of smoke. I coughed, and the noise sounded loud in the silence of the dais.

Well. That had been unimpressive. But was it good enough to pass?

"The underwizard has made a decent showing." The statement was kinder than I deserved. He was patronizing me. I'd sat for enough trials to recognize when that was happening. "Now, if Master Wendyn and his apprentice will step down from the dais, the judges will confer."

My legs shook as I took the steps down, my master at my side. I looked up at him. He frowned at the ground before him.

The full noise of the throng hit me as we crossed the threshold of the privacy spell. Chatters and murmurs and whispers combined into a buzz that would have overwhelmed the testing dais if not for the spell. I stood next to my master at the front of the crowd, watching as the three judges huddled in conversation. Their exchange went longer than I would have liked.

Was that good or bad?

The proctor approached the judges upon their wave, and they held more conversation I couldn't hear. Then the proctor gestured, and the privacy spell fell. He held a hand up for silence, and it came at last. He cleared his throat. "After discussion, it is the judge's decision that on the occasion of sitting for the first trial, Underwizard Mullins has passed."

My breath came out in a whoosh. Every part of me felt limp. Passed.

It was nothing extraordinary. I was seventeen. Younger underwizards than I had passed the first trial, even today. My attempt at fire had been smaller than many of theirs.

But still, the brotherhood among underwizards included me, and apprentices surrounded me and congratulated me on my pass, jostling my shoulders and slapping me on the back.

Somehow, my pathetic attempt had gotten me past the first trial. So why did I feel like such a failure?

TWELVE

FOR SEVERAL DAYS, THE master descended into an inexplicable bad mood. He responded to any knocks on his study door with, "Go away. I'm busy." And if I dared to loiter, "Leave now, Mullins. Have you cast fifty unbroken spells yet? Then do fifty more."

Strange. I would think he'd be delighted. My dismal showing at the first trial meant he was that much closer to getting rid of me as his apprentice.

Nearly a full week passed before he showed up at mealtime again, walking into the breakfast room and assuming his usual place at the table as though the intervening days of his absence never happened.

This was good. I'd been waiting for my chance to ask his permission to visit the Wizard's Library at the Conclave. They must carry books about blood magic. Who knew when Kurke would show up unannounced again with murder on his mind?

"So," Oscar said, dabbing at the corners of his mouth with a napkin, "the self-imposed exile has concluded?"

"Been busy," Master Wendyn grunted, without looking up from the sweet roll he was buttering.

"Can I take your plate, Underwizard Mullins?" Edie asked. She'd been hovering all morning.

"No, thank you. I'm still eating."

"Yes, you've been busy," Oscar said. "It's just that your busyness coincides with the family's visit."

I blinked in surprise. I thought it coincided with my first trial.

Master Wendyn's eyes rested on me, and understanding came. He didn't want to have this conversation in front of Ivan and me. I pretended absorption in chewing my sausage and eggs and glanced sidelong at Ivan to ensure he was doing the same. He didn't even seem to realize there was a conversation going on around him. He carefully peeled the shell back on a hard-boiled egg, appearing delighted with himself. When he caught me looking at him, he sat up straighter and smiled.

"Coincidence." Master Wendyn ran a hand over the beard shadowing his chin. "Could we speak of this later?"

"Nothing to do with Bastian, then?"

Master Wendyn's jaw ticked.

Bones. Oscar seemed determined to bait Master Wendyn this morning.

"Can I pour you some juice?" Edie asked.

"I have enough to drink, thank you." How could I get her to leave me alone?

Mrs. Pitts limped in, carrying a bowl of apples which she set in the middle of the table. Her face crumpled into a scowl when her eyes fell on Ivan and me.

"I couldn't help but notice," Oscar said, "Bastian was your only sibling who didn't come to your natalis." He poured himself a cup of barley tea and took a delicate sip.

The master sighed. "Right. And I'd rather not talk about it." His gaze shifted. "Underwizard, you and I will repair that broken sculpture today."

"Me?" I asked around a mouthful of eggs, sitting up straighter.

"Swallow before you speak."

"I thought we agreed you were getting rid of that sculpture," Oscar said while I swallowed too much and had to gulp down water to keep from choking.

"No, *you* wanted to get rid of it. I like it."

"Why do you need my help?" I asked once I was in control of my voice again.

"I don't *need* your help." The master's eyebrow quirked up, his tone making it clear his needing anything from me was ridiculous. "But do you know any other underwizard in this household who is preparing to perform an unbroken spell?"

Oh. The second trial. "No."

"Which is why you'll be helping me today."

Oscar clapped his hands. "Splendid. And I'll help too."

Master Wendyn sighed and took a sip of his tea.

THE AFTERNOON SUN created a gauzy filter of light that fell across the library's variegated marble floor. I longed to go stand in its warmth, but instead, I sat at the only long table in the room, fragments of the broken sculpture scattered in front of me.

"Try again." The master, seated across from me, pinched the bridge of his nose as though trying to stave off an aching in his head. "Clear your thoughts this time."

I picked up the same piece of broken stone I'd been trying to affix to the main body of the sculpture for the last hour. Fitting it into place, I cleared my mind of all thought and pulled what magic I could find toward me. I said the words of the spell and let go of the stone.

The sculpture held. Hopeful, I leaned closer to see if the cracks and seams around the piece had knitted and held as the spell intended.

All at once, the fragment clattered to the table.

Nope. Not fixed. Not fixed at all.

"Clear your thoughts, I said!"

Oscar looked up from his book. He'd retreated to a chair in the sun three-quarters of an hour ago. "Perhaps try thinking of your biggest toe," he suggested. "I've heard for some underwizards this works the same as clearing their minds."

Master Wendyn made a noise of disgust. "If you have no helpful suggestions, would you mind keeping your thoughts to yourself?"

With a snap, the book closed, and Oscar came to his feet. "Miranda's cutlass, I thought that *was* helpful. It won't improve matters at all if you let your temper get the best of you. Perhaps a dessert would help lighten your mood?"

The master's jaw worked. Then all at once he threw his hands in the air. "Fine. We'll take a break for dessert. Make mine gingerbread pudding."

Oscar looked pleased. "And for you, underwizard?"

Dessert? It was the last thing I was thinking about at the moment. "Maybe an apple?"

An exaggerated sigh from Oscar. "I said *dessert*."

I bit my lip and tried to think of something. "Well . . . I wouldn't say no to some burnt toffee pie."

"That's better. Come along, Ivan. I'll need your help." Oscar waved, and Ivan came out of the corner he'd been hiding in.

Once they were gone, the master turned back. "There. Now we can focus without interruption for a little while, at least. Try again."

I sighed and picked up the stone fragment. White and gray striated its jagged edges. The broken pieces of this statue were just like me. My magic seemed broken half the time. If I didn't figure a way out of Kurke's heinous scheme, I'd never get a chance to try to put my magic back together.

"Well? Try again."

I put the piece down and stared at Master Wendyn. "I need to tell you something."

He rolled a chunk of stone around in his long fingers. "If it doesn't have anything to do with why you can't perform a simple unbroken spell, I don't want to hear it."

"Believe me, you'll want to hear this."

He blinked and his eyes flitted to mine. "Sounds important. What do you have to say?"

I took a deep breath. "First I have some questions, though."

He gave an exaggerated sigh. "And now you're stalling."

"I'm not," I assured him. The doubt didn't leave his face, but I launched into the questions anyway. "You know about oaths, right? Oscar said you did." In my chest, the tether stirred, and I swallowed against the unpleasant sensation.

"As much as any wizard who spent a year preparing his Postulate about them knows. Which is to say, more than the average master wizard. Why do you ask?"

I chewed on my lip and tried to think how to say this in a way that wouldn't cause me to lose my thoughts. I could already feel it hovering, that forgetfulness, a faint warning buzz of magic about to descend on me. "How does one end an oath?"

He frowned. "Don't you remember your one-hour apprenticeship to Grandfather? Destroy the written contract and the oath ends."

My thoughts turned to the blood oath parchment crisscrossed with a web of crimson. Something told me that even if I had access to it, destroying it would not be as simple as ripping it in half or sending it up in flames. "Isn't there some way to end it without destroying the parchment itself?"

"Use your brain, Mullins," he growled. "Your apprenticeship to Hapthwaite ended when you violated the terms." He shoved his chair back.

All I had to do was violate the terms. My face screwed up as I tried to remember the details of my oath with Kurke. I would help him kill Oscar, and he wouldn't tell I was a girl. So . . . if I just refused to help him, would that be enough to violate the terms of the oath? Could it be that simple?

Doubtful. Magic was never that simple.

"Is it the same for all oaths?" I asked, and looked up to find Master Wendyn leaned over the table, hands flat on the wooden surface, glowering at me.

"If you're already unhappy in this apprenticeship, Mullins, you don't need to go to the trouble of violating our contract. I'll happily release you."

"I—unhappy?" I stuttered. "Release me? No, you misunderstand."

"Do I?" He straightened and ran a hand through his hair. "Devil's dawn, after all I've done for you, this is how you thank me? You're ready to jump ship at the first obstacle in your path? If that's all the sticking power you have, then by all means, leave."

Now I was getting annoyed too. "Why would I want to leave? Haven't you realized yet how determined I am to become a master wizard? I was just curious. *Curious.* It was . . . a question I had after doing some studying."

He eyed me, his frown lessening a fraction. "Oh. Well. If that's so, then I apologize." He sank back into his chair and, after a moment, picked up another fragment. "What do you have to tell me, then?"

Friar's bones. I'd have to remember not to give the master reason to jump to conclusions again. He could be rather hotheaded. "You didn't answer my question. Is it the same for all oaths?"

"Mostly." He set down the fragment and straightened. "What kind of book were you reading, anyway? I don't even have any oath books in my library. I donated the darker ones to the Wizard's Library, and the rest I left with Uphammer."

Ah. So that's why he didn't have any oath books. They were all at the Conclave.

Then that was where I needed to go.

"I read it a while back," I invented. "It was . . . one I found at Hapthwaite's house."

He made a noise of disgust. "That baboon. It figures. You really were just stalling the whole time, weren't you? Come on. Show me another unbroken spell."

I thought about my big toe. It couldn't hurt to give Oscar's method a try, could it?

By the time Oscar and Ivan returned, arms laden with magicked desserts, I'd failed another six times at setting the piece into place.

"Now, now," Oscar scolded. "You said we could take a break, Garrick. Never mind the statue for now. Sometimes clearing your mind is all you need."

For a time there was silence as we all ate our respective desserts—gingerbread pudding and burnt toffee pie for the master and I, apple cake for Ivan, and melon tart for Oscar.

"You know," Oscar said after setting his empty dessert dish on the table in front of him and resting a hand on his stomach, "your father said Bastian wished to come to your natalis. But he feared angering you."

"This again?" The master set down his spoon. "Fine. You have something to say, Grandfather? Say it."

"He's your brother. Have you ever pondered the possibility that maybe you've carried this grudge a little too far?"

"Grudge?" Master Wendyn repeated, his expression darkening. "No. This is not a grudge. This is a natural consequence of betrayal. If you know nothing else about me, know this: I never, *never* forgive people who betray me."

I remembered the faces of the master's family. Little Maud, whom I held in my arms. The master's sister Marelda, his parents, his numerous nieces and nephews. They were all kind and respectful, even to a nobody apprentice. I thought of all of them coming to visit the master on his natalis, bringing gifts and desserts. I had spent my last four natal days without a single well-wish from anyone. Just because of a little spat with his brother, the master was willing to give all that up?

He didn't know how good he had it.

Oscar's thoughts must have been in line with mine, because he said, "You're ostracizing the whole family because of Bastian's behavior. They went to a lot of trouble for your natalis, too. You're acting like a spoiled child."

Master Wendyn shook his head and shoveled a spoonful of pudding into his mouth. Once he had swallowed, he said, "You know it's not just because of Bastian. There's much more to it than that. But if it will make you feel better—fine. My family made a nice effort for my natal day, even if I didn't want them there. But too many times in the past, it was easy for them to forget all about me."

"Let them make it up to you."

"No."

I must have made a sound. A snort or a puff of air through my nose, though I was trying hard to hide my disgust. Master Wendyn turned his gaze on me, his expression forbidding. "Do you have something to say, underwizard?"

I gulped. Stay out of it, Avery. That's what I was thinking.

And then my thoughts went back to the library, filled to over-flowing with people who just wanted to remind the master they cared for him. I sat forward. "When I was eleven, my mother died." I kept my voice even. "My only brother died a few years later. The one person left in the world to care about me is my father. But Papa? Well, on most nights he drinks himself to unthinkingness at any of the inns and taverns in Waltney. Any night. I don't believe the man even remembers he has a d—" I gulped back the word *daughter* and corrected myself, "a *son* besides my brother. Do you know who will show up on my natalis with gifts? No one. And who will care if I am ill or in danger or in need of help? Not a soul. I have nobody in the world who cares if I live or die. And you're complaining that twenty-some people bother enough about you to show up on your natal day to wish you well? I just—I think that's horrible."

I shoveled pie into my mouth, just to give myself something to do so I didn't explode at the master any further. But I'd said everything I wanted to say.

Quiet had fallen around the table. A glance at Oscar showed his face had turned thoughtful.

"I thought you were from Howchister," Master Wendyn said.

My eyes snapped to him. "I—I am." I glanced back down at my plate. "But Papa—he's in Waltney."

"I see."

I couldn't read the master's tone, and I didn't like it. The silence stretched out, and I couldn't stare at my pie forever. At last I looked back at him. His jaw was still ticking, so I knew he was angry.

He cleared his throat. "My personal life is none of your affair, underwizard. You may think you understand what I'm feeling, but you're wrong."

I opened my mouth to speak, but he held up a hand and cut

me off. "No. And now it's time to get back to the unbroken spell."

His refusal to even listen made me angrier than ever. It felt like the boys in Waltney, the ones who would point and laugh and refuse to acknowledge that a girl could even think intelligent thoughts, let alone speak one.

I let the feelings stew as I picked up the hated stone fragment. What was the point in trying to clear my mind? This wouldn't work, anyway. I held the stone in place against the body of the sculpture and thought about what a hard-headed idiot my master was, how impossible he was to work with, and how much I loathed him. I said the words of the spell and let go of the stone.

The sculpture held. It had all the other times too, at first. I sat back and waited for the piece to fall out. When it didn't, I leaned closer and squinted at it.

The cracks and seams of the triangle-shaped stone had disappeared. It appeared to have become one with the sculpture.

I gulped. "I think—I think it worked!"

"Why, I believe you're right." Master Wendyn leaned closer to look. "Don't sound so astonished." He sounded faintly surprised himself.

Ivan clapped his hands.

"Were you thinking of your biggest toe?" Oscar asked. "Did it make a difference?"

"Tried that," I informed him. "It didn't work. I was thinking —" I stopped. I couldn't tell them I was thinking about how much I loathed my master.

"Well?"

"I was thinking . . . that my hands are sticky. May I go wash them?"

Master Wendyn nodded and waved at the door. "Go ahead. But be quick about it. You have more practicing to do."

After I took my leave, their voices carried from the library. I stopped to listen.

"The boy has backbone," Oscar said. "You must give him that."

"He's too headstrong. He jumps to conclusions without all the facts."

A noise of impatience. "You're no fool, Garrick. It's ridiculous to punish the whole family because Bastian married your intended, and you know it. Besides, Cailyn played a part in it too."

"So, what, I should punish both of them?"

Cailyn. I knew the name. I had discovered in my time at the Hall she was a topic you didn't want to mention around the master. Now I knew why—she had jilted the master in favor of his brother.

Bones. And here I had been lecturing him about accepting his family, including the brother who had betrayed him.

I needed to learn to keep my mouth shut.

After a pause, Oscar said, "There'll be a baby soon. Cailyn is with child."

My eyes widened.

But Master Wendyn didn't explode as I expected him to. He heaved a heavy sigh instead. "That's to be expected."

"You're making this needlessly hard on yourself. The family too."

"You know what they did. I don't know whether I can ever forgive them." Silence. Then the master went on, "I'm grateful for your support, Grandfather. It means a lot that you've been there for me, even when no one else was."

Mrs. Pitts turned down the hall then, and I hurried upstairs to my room. If nothing else, this afternoon had given me a lot to think about.

That's when I remembered—I'd forgotten to ask for permission to visit the Conclave.

THIRTEEN

BY THE NEXT DAY, I had developed a new approach to the unbroken spell. Rather than trying to clear my mind, all I did was think about my loathing for the master. My results were, admittedly, sporadic, but I had more success than with trying to clear my mind. It seemed to work best when the loathing sang through my veins, as opposed to just thinking of his face and how I disliked him. But it was difficult to maintain that level of contempt, especially when the master wasn't constantly cruel.

I managed to put the same green glass bottle together twice in the morning, quicker the first time than the second. It made no sense why it worked. I had never read in any magic book that *one must always clear their mind, unless they hate their master, in which case they must always think about their hatred of their master.* And yet the method seemed to be working, at least until Mrs. Pitts showed up.

She limped into the library just after I'd assembled the bottle for the second time, holding a letter for the master from the letter box. Her mouth turned downward in a severe frown, as it had all morning. Her foul mood had come on suddenly and for no apparent reason, as many of her moods did.

"Thank you, Mrs. Pitts," the master said, after taking the proffered letter from her. The woman turned to go, but the master stopped her with a hand to her arm. "I think you're forgetting something."

"Oh?" She turned back.

Master Wendyn flourished a hand, and a pink flower appeared in his fingers, pulled from the air. He deposited it in her hand and turned back to his book.

Mrs. Pitts' cheeks flushed almost as pink as the flower, and she turned to go, the air about her decidedly lighter.

I almost wouldn't have believed it if I hadn't seen it.

My next attempt at the unbroken spell didn't go so well. I couldn't seem to hold onto my loathing of the master. After a few tries I sighed and gave up, approaching Master Wendyn at his reading table.

"I was hoping to study the sprouting spell further, now that the unbroken spell is coming along," I said. "You know, the third trial. Could I go to the Wizard's Library?"

Master Wendyn frowned and scratched at the short growth of beard that always covered his chin. "I suppose." He leaned back in his chair, legs stretched before him and jutting out beneath the front of the table. "You've worked hard today, and I've seen progress. An outing may be a good idea. Take the wizard door in my study."

I nodded.

"I've been meaning to tell you, I haven't had any luck with your desert spell. It looks like, for now, you're stuck with it."

The desert spell seemed like the least of my worries at the moment. "I've lived with it this long. I suppose I can live with it for a little longer."

"If you don't die of thirst first," he said with a raised brow. He held up a hand and pulled a glass of water out of air, which he handed to me. "Just in case."

I drank the water and left the cup with Master Wendyn. As I walked down the hall toward his study, I held my hand in front of me and tried to make fire. But my angry thoughts about the master held no conviction, and the fire fizzled in my palm.

Friar's bones, why did he have to start being nice now, just when I had found something that worked for me?

Down the hall, Edie exited the kitchen and moved toward me, bearing a tray of sweet rolls. She stopped to bob a short curtsy.

"Good morning, Underwizard Mullins. I wanted to congratulate you—" her tone turned bashful, "on passing the first trial. You must be a superb magician."

I frowned. "Not really. It was probably a fluke."

Her face turned earnest. "But you are! You must be! Not just any underwizard can pass the trials. There's a boy in Bramford, Eustace Kelly, and he became an underwizard with a master and everything. Only he could never pass a single trial. After a few years, he was disapprenticed and sent home in shame."

That wasn't so unusual. I'd heard it estimated that thirty percent of underwizards washed out of their apprenticeships within the first four years. But still . . .

"I didn't do well," I confessed. "Not at all. I almost didn't pass."

"But you did." If she weren't carrying a tray, I imagined she'd be holding my hand and gazing up at me adoringly while saying the words. "Passing matters. You're a much better underwizard than you give yourself credit for. And so handsome. You could be PMW someday."

Her words brought a faint smile to my lips, ridiculous though they were. "I appreciate the vote of confidence." But her words had perked me up.

"If you ever need anything—anything at all—come ask me. I want to be the woman you turn to when you're in pain."

Now that was taking things too far. I edged away. "Well. I'd better get going."

Her face split into a beautiful smile. "Goodbye, Avery." I turned to go, and she called after me, "Never forget—you can do anything you put your mind to!"

Edie excelled at confidence-building. She'd be a great friend, if she weren't so plainly taken with me. I should do something to dissuade her.

But I didn't know what.

MY FOOTFALLS ECHOED on the stone floor of the Conclave's cathedral hall. The room was almost empty, as was normal for a non-trial day. Light slanted in through high stained glass windows.

I'd been to the Conclave many times in the company of Master Hapthwaite, and twice now with Master Wendyn, but this was my first time without supervision. I should be grateful that my new master trusted me enough to send me on my own.

Or was it that he didn't care enough?

The nice thing about being here alone was now I could take time to nose around a little. The cathedral hall overflowed with portraits and glass cases along the walls, museum-like exhibits that memorialized master wizards of the past. Master Hapthwaite never took the time to stop, so I'd always looked at them from afar. But today I had more freedom, and curiosity brought me to a halt.

I browsed through portraits of past PMWs and glass cases containing items such as the dagger of Ladarius the Heroic and the sandals of King Baldarich the Miser. After that, I gave a cursory examination to an exhibit detailing the evolution of armor, from the early iron-plated models to the more modern magic-and-steel amalgams. Then I came to a stop in front of a glass case housing a heap of smashed wood.

It was a shrine of some sort. A metal plaque pinned to the front of the case bore words that crawled across it in an elaborate font. Beyond the words, stained and discolored shards of splintered boards leaned against one another in a heap. There seemed to be some sharp ends poking out of the wood. A chill crept across my skin, and almost against my will, I leaned closer to read the words.

Here lies the barrel used to Punish traitor Keturah Ingerman, a female who impersonated a male in an attempt to become a master wizard. Her lies to the Wizard's Council and her own master were discovered before she ascended to the honored position of master wizard, and she was thereafter tried and Punished.

A date followed.

I stared at the wooden remnants. Red and brown streaked them in a way I would dismiss as the natural grain of the wood if I didn't know better. More likely it was blood, as the barrel would have exploded once it stopped moving.

This was how the last female underwizard had died.

Of course I'd known Ingerman's fate, but confronted with the barrel up close . . . suddenly it seemed very real.

My heart sped up to an erratic thumping. If the Council found out about me, I'd be Punished too. That could just as easily be my blood staining the remains of that barrel.

Sickness crawled up my throat.

When Gavin made me promise to learn magic, I doubt he meant for me to risk the Punishment. Becoming an underwizard, the whole disguise, all of it had been my own idea, one that built in me slowly after Gavin's death. He might have lived if we'd had the money to hire a wizard to heal him. How many more people like him would die because they lacked money? It wasn't fair.

But I wasn't entirely a philanthropist, either. I loved magic and I wanted the freedom to practice it. In Faronna that meant I had to be a man and a master wizard. And so I had risked the Punishment for three years now. I'd told myself that maybe one day I would be caught and Punished, but at least until then I would be true to myself. If I did happen to be Punished, I could return to be with Mama and Gavin free of regrets.

Staring at Ingerman's barrel and the reality of my future if I were caught, I wasn't so sure I was willing to risk it anymore.

A shudder ran through me. Several underwizards moved past, and suddenly conscious of how I would look to anyone else who passed this way, I straightened my shoulders and forced my steps away from the cathedral hall.

The library resided in the north wing of the Conclave, a matter of a few turns off the main hallway. I rounded a corner, and the immense library opened before me, all floor-to-ceiling books and rows upon rows of shelves. The chill that had moved through me at Ingerman's monument receded as I looked over the room. It bustled with wizards and underwizards, and thick tomes climbed the walls. I took in the movement, the robes swishing around ankles, the milling bodies. Ranged at tables around the room, contemplative faces poised over open books. I pushed thoughts of Ingerman and the Punishment out of my mind.

Three wizards loitered at the librarian's desk in the center of the library, and when the largest of them stepped out of the way, I saw Maximo, the head librarian, chatting with one of them. I did my best to wait patiently as I stood at the back of the line. Master wizard custom dictated that underwizards must wait for their betters to be served, so it wouldn't do me any good to become restless.

The last wizard took ages to settle on what he wanted. I listened as he argued with Maximo about whether he could have access to the vault, whatever that was. "Not without a member of the Council," Maximo insisted.

"But I have permission." Frustration fueled the wizard's volume. "Look here, signed authorization from Robenhurst!" He waved a piece of parchment in the librarian's face.

"That's not enough. Perhaps you're unaware, but the rules state you can only enter when accompanied by a member of the Council."

At last the wizard gave up and stomped off in disgust, grumbling about coming back later. At last it was my turn. But before I could step forward, a hand to my arm stopped me.

"Well—hello! Underwizard Mullins, right?" A bright voice said at my side.

I turned. "Hello, Orly. Did you get those books back from Master Hapthwaite?"

She waved a hand. "Yes, don't worry your head about those. He brought them back last week. Are you in need of some assistance? Perhaps I could help you."

A glance at Maximo showed he was already at work on something else, not paying me any notice. "Yes, you can. I'm looking for books on blood magic. Or alternatively, blood oaths."

Her face turned from composed to aghast in about three seconds. "Lower your voice," she whispered, glancing around. "That's a dangerous question these days."

My brow crinkled in confusion, but I lowered my voice anyway. "Dangerous?"

She swallowed and then reached out and took me by the arm. "Come with me." She started across the library, pulling me along behind her.

We wove through mazes of tables and bookshelves, through narrow aisles with stacks of books looming on either side, and then stopped at a door which, when opened, revealed a room empty but for a table and chairs. Orly pulled me inside and closed the door.

"Er," I said, which was the most eloquent thing I could come up with at that moment. "Why are we here?"

"Sit." She pushed me into a chair and pulled out another for herself so that we sat across the table from one another. "You can't just come in here asking about blood magic like that. It's dangerous. Don't you know?"

"Know what?" Bewilderment filled me.

"About the explosion."

I searched my brain, wondering why that sounded familiar. At last it came to me. "Oh, in the Conclave's cellar? I heard something about that."

"In the vault," she corrected. "The place where the most important books are locked up. All books on blood magic are in there. I think the Council is noising it about that the explosion was just a stupid alchemist's mistake, but there is no alchemy lab down there. All that's down there is the vault, and somebody deliberately set an explosion to get inside."

So that was the vault I heard the wizard talking about earlier. "Was anything taken?"

She shrugged. "I'm not allowed down there, but Papa said it's difficult to tell. A large section of books ended up a pile of ashes and shredded pages. Pinpointing whether a book was stolen or disintegrated in the explosion is difficult."

I drummed my fingers on the table. I wasn't keen on blowing my way into the vault with explosives. "If an under-wizard such as myself wanted a harmless piece of information about blood magic, how would he get into the vault?"

She chewed on her lip, looking unhappy. "There's an order to things. You must get permission from the PMW, and then only with a Council member along would you be permitted to enter. But even just to ask about blood magic these days will get your name put on a special list that the Council watches. You of all people don't need that kind of scrutiny."

Her words stopped me. "I of all people? Why I of all people?"

She reached across the table and grasped my hand in both of hers. "You thought you could keep the secret forever, right? Papa says I'm unusually observant, though. Don't worry. I won't ever tell anyone you're a girl."

My stomach dropped. I pulled my hand away from her. "Girl? Have you gone mad?"

Her smile faltered. "I realize you have to act shocked. It wouldn't seem genuine otherwise. See, I first noticed you when I was about twelve. You must have still been working out your disguise. If it makes it any better, I doubt anybody else has noticed. You've become so good at your disguise, I doubt anybody ever will."

I'd gotten sloppy, with all these people that knew my secret. If I couldn't convince this girl otherwise, would she blackmail me too, like Kurke? But she looked far too innocent for that.

"Orly, you don't know what you're playing with here. The Punishment is real, and I don't much want to undergo it. Let's stop this talk of female underwizards."

She didn't give up. "If I were a boy, I'd be a wizard, and a fine one, too," she said stoutly. "Why, I did a time-slowing spell the other day, and do you know Papa never even noticed? That's why I was so glad to find out you're a girl. Avery Mullins, I want to be just like you." She said these last words so earnestly that tears glistened in her eyes as she leaned forward and looked up into my face.

Time manipulation was big magic, the kind girls were supposedly unable to do, the kind no man should do unless he was a master wizard or an apprenticed underwizard. Surprise took me off guard, so that I forgot all pretense of claiming to be a boy and blurted out, "Time manipulation? You did a time manipulation spell?"

She fumbled in her lap and came up with a book that she slid across the table. "I've seen you at the trials. You're struggling, and I can help. I grabbed this book the minute I saw you come in today. I wanted to give it to you that day you came in with your new master—do you remember?"

So that was why she'd been following me around that day. "Yes, I remember." I shouldn't encourage her, but I slid the book closer anyway. The leather binding creaked as I opened the ancient cover. "Magic and the Female Mind," I read from the title page.

Her hands clasped. "Go ahead, look at it. I found this one in the archaic section of the library a few years ago, written at a time when female magicians were still allowed in the three kingdoms. Enchantresses, they called them then. If Papa knew the books I've read here . . . but he's better off not knowing. I found this one more than enlightening."

I flipped through a few pages and then pushed the book back at her. "Thank you, but I can't risk being seen reading such a book. Take it back."

She looked wounded. "But . . . but it has loads of useful information."

"Summarize it for me, then."

"Well . . . all right." She sat forward, looking me in the eye. "Your masters have always told you to clear your mind, right? To think less? Not be so emotional? To remain in control no matter what?"

The statement startled me. "Of course. That's how you do magic."

"And yet you've never gotten very impressive results on the testing dais following those directions, have you?"

I reflected for a moment and then, my thoughts on Ingerman and the Punishment, admitted, "I rarely get impressive results anywhere. To tell the truth, I'm not even sure why I'm doing this anymore. I used to think I had what it takes to be a master wizard, but lately . . ."

Her mouth stretched in a grin, somehow pleased at my response. "You have what it takes. You're just going about it wrong. See, boys are far too logical to understand how emotions and magic can coexist. But we girls can't just tamp down our emotions and pretend they're not there. That's not how we work. We must work *with* our emotions. Feel them. Don't suppress them."

"Feel emotion?" I repeated, more interested now. That was the exact opposite of anything I'd ever been told, and yet, it made sense. I'd let my emotions run free when I thought of my dislike of Master Wendyn, and that had brought me some measure of success.

She smiled and hooked a loose lock of dark hair behind an ear. "Trust me. Do this, and I promise you'll pass your next trial —and every one after that."

I stared at her. It was true what they say, that hope drew from an endless well, because it filled me as I stared at her.

"Do a spell," she said. "Any spell. One of your worst spells, maybe."

The fire spell leaped to my mind. I held out my hand and pondered what Orly had said. Stop resisting your emotions. Feel emotion rather than suppress it. An emotion came to my mind, the closest one at hand—hope. I pictured the situation I had the most hope for, myself becoming a master wizard. I watched myself in imagination climb the dais steps after the ascension ceremony. Then I muttered the words of the spell. In my hand, a puny flame formed before flickering out. Predictable.

"Thinking too much," Orly announced.

"I did just what you said. I imagined hope."

"You can't imagine it. You must feel it. How does it make you feel?"

I shrugged. "How does it make anyone feel? Hopeful."

She rolled her eyes. "All right. But think about the secondary emotions. When you're hopeful, what other emotions fill you?"

I chewed my lip. "Excitement. Confidence. Happiness."

"Feel those things. Don't imagine anything that's not real. Feel what's real."

I stared down at my hand. This seemed silly, but if it meant my magic skills would improve, I was willing to try almost anything.

This time I decided against hope and went for an emotion I remembered more vividly: elation. The first time I did magic, it was like nothing else I'd ever experienced. I was so exhilarated, I imagined I was floating. Just thinking about it again filled me with a similar emotion. I almost wanted to smile. I filled my head with the emotion, closed my eyes, and said the words of the spell.

My voice seemed loud in the empty room. For a moment I thought it hadn't worked again, but the whoosh of heat and flame against my face made my eyes fly open. The fire in my hand blazed to life, stronger and brighter and more sustained than it had ever been before. I was so startled that I shoved my chair backward as though I could get away from my own hand, and the spell winked out. I stared down at my hand in astonishment.

"Not bad," Orly said. "But you can do better. Let's try it again."

I stared at her, and a slow grin moved across my face. I was going to like this.

FOURTEEN

IN THE DAYS THAT followed, I practiced letting my emotions free, as Orly explained. In the privacy of my room, I attempted the fire spell again and again, consistently reproducing the results I got in the library. Then I moved on to the unbroken spell and the sprouting spell. Each time, the magic surprised me. I performed the spells with ease. Not perfectly, but the magic was there, flowing through me in a way it hadn't before.

I couldn't wait to show Master Wendyn how much I'd improved.

But the more I thought about it, the more I wanted to keep my secret to myself. The thought of surprising Master Wendyn at the trials pleased me very much. I wanted to see the look on his face, there in front of the judges and the proctor and the crowds of underwizards and masters—the look of shock and pride when he realized for the first time that his underwizard wasn't half as bad as he thought.

Besides, the master could do with some good news. When I had returned from my visit to the Conclave, it was to discover that he'd had two uninvited visitors while I was away. The first was Matthias Kurke, and according to Edie, my source, they had quarreled. Apparently Master Wendyn was upset with Kurke for providing his family the avenue to visit him by reopening the wizard door he had removed.

The second visitor was his brother Bastian. His aim was to beg the master's forgiveness. It hadn't gone well and, from my understanding, ended with the master shouting at his brother to get out.

I was glad to have missed both visits—though I couldn't help but wonder what Kurke's real reason for visiting had been. Did he come to see me?

Ivan sneaked up on me one day as I was practicing magic in my bedroom before breakfast. I didn't even hear the door open, just the gasping intake of breath when he saw the fire whoosh up in my hand. I whirled, and the fire abated, dying down to nothing as I stared at him.

He pointed at my hand and made a gesture I couldn't interpret.

"I . . . I've figured out fire." I meant to warn him he couldn't tell anyone, and then I realized—this was Ivan. My secret was safe.

He gestured again. It was different from the last time he had gestured at me. This time he was moving his pointing finger in a circle. But still, it seemed to mean something to him.

"What does that mean? Are you trying to say something? Is it some kind of hand-speak?"

In reply, he made the gesture again.

I gave up trying to figure it out and summoned the fire to my hand. "How about fire? Do you have a gesture for that?"

He looked from me to the fire and back again.

"How about this?" I extinguished the fire and wiggled my fingers in the motion that licking flames made. For a moment, Ivan only watched and I thought it was too complicated for him to comprehend. Then he lifted his hand, mimicked the motion, and pointed at the fireplace.

Delight filled me at the notion we might have a way to communicate. We spent the rest of the morning inventing hand-speak gestures. We made up signs for everything I could find in my bedroom. Candle, book, bed, chair, door, tapestry, clothes, shoes, magic, and several body parts. I took a blank piece of parchment and recorded the gestures and their meaning, so I wouldn't forget them.

"What's so interesting that you two missed breakfast and lunch?" Oscar asked from the doorway. "Cook wants you to know there'll be no food until supper. However, if you're inter-ested, I could magic you a strawberry fizz or some almond pies."

He wore the same shirt as always, in an unusual mix of pink and green. The sight of him pricked at me. I'd been spending selfish hours perfecting my magic while his life hung in the balance. I should have been working on dissolving the blood oath.

"Strawberry fizz?" I asked. "What's that?"

Ivan pulled the parchment with its recorded gestures out of my hands and looked over the characters with fascination, although I knew he couldn't read them. He was so engrossed that I shrugged and stood.

"Drink of my own invention." Oscar grinned, clearly pleased that I had asked. "Come with me, and I'll get you one."

It would give me a chance to observe Oscar further. Not for Kurke, but for myself.

Oscar's bedroom was in the ballroom wing. I'd seen inside from the doorway a few times, enough to see he likely had the largest bedroom in the house. Now he invited me across the threshold, and I looked around with interest as we stepped inside.

An alcove with large windows contained a door leading to

a balcony. Purple drapes hung on either side. A bed stood against one wall, smaller than I would expect, and shoved almost into the corner like an afterthought. A fireplace had been built into one wall, above which hung a portrait of a young couple. After a moment of staring, I recognized the man.

"That's you," I said with some surprise. "You're so young! And—is that your wife?"

"Sweet Anelina. The world made more sense when she was alive." He stood for a moment, staring at her, his eyes liquid and warm. Then he gave himself a shake and continued to the table in the north corner. A carved box sat in the middle.

"How long ago did she die?" I hadn't meant to ask the question; it just sort of dragged from me, pulled by my own sympathies. Death I understood.

"Too long. We've been apart almost forty years. Her Time was in the summer."

It was a Faronnish phrase, calling one's day of death their Time. Forty years, and Oscar had somehow found a way to remain upbeat. After that many years, would I still miss Mama and Gavin as sharply as now? "Does it ever get easier?"

Oscar blinked and looked at me, really looked at me. "It's never easier to live without her. Mostly it's just . . . different. It helps to remember the good times we had together."

I stared at the box on the table without seeing it. Good times?

Yes, I suppose we had those—once. Before Mama was sick, Papa worked hard at farming. They used to laugh and tease one another. Gavin and Papa used to play at ball tossing with a round orb as big as a squash from the garden. Mama sewed it from leftover cloth and stuffed it with rushes. We'd had enough food and money to take care of all our needs.

Once we were happy. What changed?

"I'm sorry. Death and disappointment are two things I've seen too much of."

"Garrick too," Oscar said. "You have that in common."

I didn't know what he meant by that, but before I could ask, he bent over the box, pronounced a short incantation, and lifted the lid. "Strawberry fizz?" he asked, lifting out a tall cup of a pinkish beverage.

I accepted the cup, and took a sip. Strawberries and sweetness and cream with a tangy, fizzy flavor I couldn't pinpoint the origin of. I sipped the divine creation while he turned back to the sweets box. I glanced beyond him and saw several books spread out on his desk. For me every book was a new opportunity to learn, and I stepped closer while he fiddled with his box. *Death and Magic: Murder in Waldrin* read the spine of the first volume I picked up, a small black book. *Killing Curses of Belanok* lay beneath it. Four more books sat stacked to one side; a quick glance over the spines showed several more titles full of words such as demise, annihilation, and extermination. A final book lay open on the desk, turned to a diagram of person. Arrows pointed to various body parts, with an explanation of each part's weakness and how one might exploit its vulnerability.

"Friar's bones, what are you studying here, Oscar? How to become a killer?"

He swiveled toward me. In two strides he stood before me and yanked *Murder in Waldrin* from my hands. "Don't help yourself to other people's belongings, Mullins. These weren't meant for your eyes."

"But why do you—"

He closed the open book and stacked the rest into a pile which he deposited out of sight beneath the desk. "Retirement can be dull. Reading entertains me. The more interesting the subject, the better."

"Oh." I supposed I couldn't argue with that reasoning. "Still, it's dark reading, isn't it?"

"Believe me, I've seen darker." At my questioning glance, he continued, "One of my least favorite tasks as PMW was investigating deaths caused by spells gone wrong. Usually oaths."

"Oaths?" I asked, startled. "What kind of oaths?"

"Oh, every kind. Apprentice oaths, intermediary oaths, blood oaths, life bonds."

"Blood oaths?" I tried to say it as though it meant nothing to me, but my heart picked up speed just the same. "What's that?"

"Nasty sort of oath invented by blood magic users, and that's all I'll be saying on the topic." He put his drink down and gave me a sharp glance. "We shouldn't be talking about them at all. It's a taboo business these days. I'd advise you not to bring it up at your next trial."

I shook my head, disappointed. "Of course not. But . . . you saw deaths happen when oaths went wrong?"

Oscar perked up. "Some of them truly bizarre. Body parts detached or missing altogether, organs ripped out of chests, complete blood loss . . ."

Is this what was in store for him, courtesy of Kurke? The room suddenly seemed too close.

Oscar chuckled and went on, oblivious to my reaction. "Do you know, once we found an entire intestinal tract—"

I had to make him stop talking, because the more he spoke, the worse it got. My gaze moved past him to four mallets all clustered together in the corner behind the desk. "You have more than one scrying stick?" I blurted out. "I thought—you know—you only had the one. Forthwind."

He put his drink down and strode closer to retrieve one. "It would be impractical to have only one scrying stick. They're my specialty, and they aren't indestructible, you know. It never hurts to have extras on hand."

"And . . . have you named them all?"

He grinned and extended the stick. "What do you think?"

I took it, sliding my hands over the wood and examining its grain. "I suppose you call this one the Earl of Efraingate."

"Don't be ridiculous. I'd never give them a false title." He guffawed, as though giving a stick a title was infinitely more ridiculous than naming it in the first place.

"Oh. Of course not." Somehow I refrained from rolling my eyes. "What makes you say it can save the world, anyway?"

A smile slid over his face. "Back when Anelina and I were first married, back when I had just constructed my first scrying stick, she misplaced a pearl necklace. I'd given it to her as a gift when we wed. She was frantic, and there was no consoling her. Fortunately, I tracked it down with my scrying stick. The dog had buried it in back of the house." He lapsed into silence and retrieved his beverage to take another sip.

"And?" I swung the stick at my side. "What does that have to do with saving the world?"

"You don't understand women or you wouldn't ask that," he said. "Losing that pearl necklace was the end of the world for Anelina." He set his drink down to take the stick from me and patted my shoulder. "Don't worry. The female mind is something some men never understand."

I choked on the sip I'd just taken.

A brief tap tap tap sounded at the door.

"Yes?" Oscar called.

The door swung open, and Mrs. Pitts limped just inside the room. "You've a visitor, Master Wendyn."

He swiveled and thumped the stick into the opposite hand. "Not the arch-councilor? I wasn't expecting him so soon."

I blinked in surprise. Arch-councilor? That was a ceremonial title in Hutterland. Why was Oscar expecting a visit from a Hutterish governmental representative?

"It's the Preeminent Master Wizard. He's in the sitting room."

My stomach dropped. Stranger and stranger. Why was the PMW here? Could he have come about me? Had he found out my secret? Had Kurke or Orly talked?

"Is he? I'll be right down. See to the tea, will you?"

Mrs. Pitts bowed. "I already have." She backed out of the room.

About that time common sense took over. The PMW wouldn't have visited Oscar if he knew my secret. He'd have called on my master. Or more likely, he'd have sent Council guards to collect and trammel me. Besides, Mrs. Pitts and Oscar were so casual about the whole situation that such visits had to be common.

"Arch-councilor?" I tried to sound casual. "And the PMW? My, you attract some high-profile visitors, don't you?"

Oscar downed the rest of his drink in one gulp. "When I was PMW, I knitted to relax. Once Robenhurst took over the job of PMW, I stressed to him the importance of not overextending oneself. Somehow that led to my giving him knitting lessons. Now we get together to make socks and lap blankets and ear warmers." He set down his mallet and picked up a basket next to his desk.

"You're joking. You knit together?"

"I would never joke about knitting. Do you think he'll want a strawberry fizz?" He looked toward his sweets box. "No, I suppose not. His wife wouldn't approve. Bit of a stick in the sand, you know. He doesn't have the mettle to defy her, poor man."

I followed him to the door. "And why is the arch-councilor visiting? Are you teaching him to embroider?"

He guffawed. "Don't be ridiculous. We started a book club

many years ago. We discuss classic literature of our respective countries. Well, I'm off."

I watched as he headed to the sitting room. Once he was out of sight, I made for the library as quickly as possible. But when I positioned myself near the door and cast a listening spell, no sound came from the drawing room. I couldn't even hear the crackle of the fire, which I was sure Mrs. Pitts would have seen to. One of them, Oscar or Robenhurst, had to have cast a privacy spell to protect their conversation. Why, if they were only knitting? What could they be talking about in there?

FIFTEEN

THE NEXT TRIAL DAY coincided with an early snowfall. I looked out the window of the breakfast room into a world blanketed in white. Nerves fluttered through me, despite—or perhaps because of—the new power I'd discovered, thanks to Orly. I was still unused to the wide, deep ocean my magic had become, and it often behaved in ways I didn't expect. I felt almost as though anything could happen today at the trials.

Master Wendyn showed up halfway through the meal, clean-shaven once again. Maybe it was his usual trial day look, and all the other days he didn't care enough to use a razor. He was as silent as my last trial day, at least until he watched Ivan and I carry out a gesture-conversation about boiled eggs.

"What is that?" he asked, taking a bite of potatoes. "What are you two talking about?"

Ivan sat up straighter, apparently aware that the conversation concerned him.

"Eggs," I supplied. "The boiled kind. Ivan likes them better than fried."

"You said all that with just your fingers?"

"Just as you saw." I made the gesture for milk. "Guess what this one means."

Master Wendyn raised a brow. "No idea. Judging by your conversation, perhaps . . . chicken?"

Oscar leaned forward. "Or maybe another way to prepare eggs—poached? Scrambled? Over easy?"

Ivan pointed to the pitcher of milk while I made the gesture again. "Milk. It's simple. Go ahead; try it."

Oscar copied my gesture, while the master's eyes rested on Ivan for a long moment. "Good work, Ivan," he said at last.

"He's much smarter than people believe." I leaned forward across the table in my eagerness. "I bet he could even learn magic."

The master's face turned doubtful, and Oscar shook his head.

"Wordless magic requires skill, more than Ivan has at the moment," Master Wendyn said. "Beginners have to start with worded spells. Since Ivan can't speak, it's unlikely he'd manage it."

"Oh." I sank back into my chair, hopes dashed.

"To be clear," Oscar inserted into the conversation, looking up from a biscuit upon which he'd spread far too much jam, "it's not unprecedented, just unlikely."

Still, now that I'd put the idea into my head, I couldn't let it go. After breakfast, I pulled out my bit of rope and showed Ivan how to do an unknotting spell.

"And you say the words like so, and the tie comes undone. See?" I uttered the words, and the knot loosened and fell open. "Just try thinking the words, since you can't speak them." I tied another knot, this one looser, as was appropriate for a beginner. "I'm sure you can do it, no matter what the master said."

Ivan stared at the knot with intense concentration. After

several moments of nothing happening, he glanced back at me helplessly.

"It takes practice," I told him. "Even saying the spell aloud, it took months to master it. Here, you keep my rope."

He went back to staring at the knot, and I backed off a few steps, trying to behave as though I wasn't watching. After staring at the cord for a few moments, he put it in his pocket and fell to tracing invisible patterns on the breakfast table.

He would practice with it later. At least, I hoped so.

I made my way to the master's study, trying not to think about my empty pocket. It was strange not to have the bit of cord with me, to have passed it on to someone else. It had been my constant companion these three years.

The rope remained on my mind half an hour later as the master and I made our way through the push of the crowd to the testing dais. I didn't think I'd ever taken a trial before without that rope in my pocket. The superstitious part of me wondered if this was a bad idea. Then again, I had failed several trials with that rope in my pocket.

At last I heard, "Second trial. Candidate Avery Mullins." Master Wendyn and I ascended the steps, passed within the privacy spell, and I took my place in the middle of the dais.

The first questions related to forgiveness of self and others. The proctor grilled me about those to whom I owed forgiveness. It was a long, embarrassing list, and sometimes a bitter pill to swallow. We spoke of everyone from Master Hapthwaite to Bramford's jailer to my father. I pledged to let go of the hard feelings that still existed.

"Now," the proctor said, holding up a delicate statue of a woman with one hand on her hip and the other extended. She'd look better if both her hands were outstretched as though she were about to cast a spell. "Examine it closely." After an appropriate amount of time had passed—perhaps a minute—he tossed her to the ground, shattering the statue.

Having taken this trial multiple times, I knew how it worked. It was my task to put the statue back together with the unbroken spell.

I knelt before the shards, unease ribboning its way through me.

Focus on Orly's words. Stop resisting your emotions. That's what she'd said.

I looked down at my hands, held out before me toward the shards of glass. There existed one night in my past which I avoided thinking of where possible because of the raw emotion and pain involved. Thinking of it felt like slipping out of control. I didn't want to remember it, but Orly had said not to resist. My eyes slid closed.

Memories tickled my mind, dark and sorrowful.

Steady, Avery.

The past took hold of me, and I gave in.

The night my brother died, Papa wasn't there. Though I argued and Gavin coughed as rain dripped from holes in the thatch in a steady drip drip drip, Papa insisted he needed to hunt or we'd starve during the coming winter.

"You can hunt later." I hadn't said what I wanted to, that he was a coward for even suggesting such a thing. That he could hunt when his son's face was not so gray. That he might never see Gavin alive again.

My protests did no good. Papa left, but not before we shouted unforgivable things at each other and he clouted me in the head. Outside, rain came thick and fast, and dark took hold of our cottage on the edge of the Midnight Forest. I kept the fire stoked and brewed more rosemary tea for Gavin. Still, his labored breaths slowed. I raged against Papa, struck deals with God, wept.

Somewhere in the middle of the night, the painful rattle of my brother's breathing ceased. In the silence of the moment, I waited for his next breath . . . and realized that it would never come.

I left the next day after burying Gavin. Waiting around to tell my father anything—that Gavin had died, where I was going, even just goodbye—seemed like more than he deserved. Instead, I left the uprooted rosemary plant on the kitchen table.

There in the testing room, my eyes prickled with the pressure of tears that weren't there. Emotion crawled through me, the emotion of my last night with Gavin. I drew it in and out with my breath. It was me.

I opened my eyes and uttered the incantation for the unbroken spell.

Crystalline shards came together as though the statue had been smashed in reverse, a tornado of whirring sound and whirling glass. I held my position and didn't look at Master Wendyn, even though I wanted to know what he thought so badly it hurt. The spell held, and glass shards clinked together. The tiny glass woman took shape before me. Magic crackled throughout the dais until, at last, the statue stood before me, whole once again.

Or—not whole. A large chunk had failed to set itself in her head. Frustrated with myself for missing such a basic piece, I retrieved and put it in place, saying the words of the spell with such force that it shot across the dais and just missed impaling the test proctor. The man jerked backward in his chair, while the audience gave a collective twitch and the master made a choking sound. I pulled the shard back toward me and set it into its rightful place.

There. The woman stood complete.

Never had I reassembled a broken anything in just one go. Or almost one go. Never had I almost killed the test proctor, either. Had I gone too far, or was it enough?

"Well," said the proctor, his voice blank. And then he seemed to gather himself. "I mean, the underwizard has done well. Very well. The judges will now confer."

After a protracted discussion, they gave me a pass. I breathed a momentary sigh of relief—far too brief for my liking—and then it was on to the next trial.

During the third trial, I was asked to grow a seedling ivy plant from its pot on the desk down to the floor. But when I uttered the words of the spell, the vines shot out of the plant with a sudden velocity that took them to the opposite side of the dais before I could pull them back.

This had become a regular problem during my private practice sessions in the library. I untangled myself from the vines and glanced at the master for the first time. Dissatisfaction marred his face, and my stomach sank at the sight of his frown. In imagination my plan to impress him had gone better.

During the judges' discussions, the test proctor and judging panel took turns shaking their heads in animated discussion. I hoped this meant my powerful show of magic had impressed them, and not that they were happy to have escaped with their lives or, worse, disgusted at my lack of control. But when they announced my results, once again, I passed. "Although the underwizard would do well to control his powerful magic." The proctor eyed me with a frown.

Relief coursed through me. I looked at the master, hoping to see the pride on his face I had imagined so often when picturing this surprise. However, his frown had gotten fiercer, if possible.

"Fine show, Garrick. What a spectacle. The boy could entertain on the streets with those abilities," said a stooping, string-beaned man, clapping the master on the back. PMW Robenhurst. The PMW had watched my trials.

The master murmured some appropriate response, and

then the PMW moved on to talking of other things. "How's the family? Your father is still lecturing at the university, I assume?"

Hmmm. Whatever Oscar and Robenhurst had discussed in the drawing room the other day, apparently it hadn't been the family.

I felt limp and, despite the master's distemper, giddy. I left the conversation, pleading the need to sit down. In the hall outside the testing room, I paused, pondering the folly of finding Orly in the library and announcing to her I'd passed two more trials. I liked the thought that there was someone who cared to know the outcome of my trial. And there were two such some-ones, for I knew Ivan would be waiting at home to hear the results too.

But my steps didn't take me to the library. Without even knowing what I was about, my feet took me toward the cathe-dral hall. I walked down the line of exhibits and came to a slow stop in front of the glass case bearing the remains of Under-wizard Ingerman's broken barrel. Nothing had changed about the splintered, stained wood, the vicious rusted spikes, or the words engraved on the inscription. But I couldn't suppress the shudder that ran through me at sight of it.

"Congratulations, underwizard." I turned at the new voice behind me, ready to accept more well wishes. But my smile faltered and fell when my gaze fell on Master Kurke.

"What do you want?" Hostility threaded my tone.

"Now, now. There's no need to get nasty. You ought to thank me. I'm the one who's not letting your secret out, remember?"

I glanced around. "Lower your voice."

He looked past me. "I see you and Ingerman have found one another. Are you here paying your respects?"

"I appreciate your words of congratulation, Master Kurke.

Now I need to get back to my master." I gave a short bow, turned, and walked away.

Kurke fell into step beside me. "Impressive reassembling of that statue. I've only seen quicker once. Garrick must be delighted. As though he needed a reason to think more highly of himself."

When I didn't acknowledge him, he grabbed my arm and swung me around to face him, his fingers biting into the skin.

"Don't get too comfortable with the Wendyns, underwizard. They might seem harmless, but let them get close and they'll destroy everything important to you. Now, I think you owe me a report." He looked around and then darted down a dark hallway, dragging me behind.

"What—hey!" I protested, but I couldn't wrench my arm from his grip.

Shadow obscured his face as he recited a spell, and then it fell around us, a cocoon of silence.

A privacy spell.

He rounded on me. "Tell me what you've learned about Oscar Wendyn."

I squared my shoulders and raised my chin. Time for battle. "I've learned a lot of things, actually. Firstly, that this blood oath needs to end. I won't help you hurt Oscar."

He gave me a probing look. "This again? Look, you're not going to change my mind like you did at Garrick's natalis. I lost the perfect opportunity, there with the whole family present to witness the downfall of their patriarch. But you tricked me with little Vito. I couldn't terrorize him in that way." He rubbed his hands together with something like exhilaration on his face. "But no matter. I've come up with a better plan."

"Better?" I didn't like the sound of that. "Better how?"

"You'll know when the time is right."

"What does that mean?"

He blinked at me, his expression baleful. "Tell me what you've learned about Oscar."

I folded my arms. "You may have made me swear, but you can't make me talk. I won't help you."

His brows drew together. "Won't you? Not even when we have so much in common?"

"I—what do you mean?" I asked, in spite of myself.

"You imagine yourself principled and noble, working to change the world, as all underwizards think they will. But you'll understand soon enough that we're the same."

"You and I are nothing alike."

"Oh really." He stepped closer. I tried to move away, but found the wall at my back. "You find me greedy. Self-indulgent. Egocentric. And yet you don't see the same qualities in yourself. Don't you understand? Disguising yourself as a boy could bring the Punishment down on Garrick's head as much as your own. Every proctor of your exams. Your last master, whoever the poor fool was. Your family. Everyone associated with you is a prime candidate for Punishment."

Ice shot me through and my stomach flip-flopped. When I spoke, a quiver moved through my voice. "That isn't true. That's not what happened with Ingerman."

"Not officially. But if you read the records, you'll find that everyone associated with her met an early demise, most due to the Punishment, for various fabricated reasons."

A blow to the stomach would have surprised me less, but I strove to hide how the words had affected me. "You're lying." I couldn't force conviction into my words. My voice sounded hollow. It would be easy enough to check if he told the truth.

Sympathy slid across his face. I saw it in the liquidness of his eyes and the softness around his mouth. I thought his blinding smiles were attractive, but his expression now made me tingle all the way to my toes. "Avery, I wouldn't lie to you about this. I understand you. I *am* you."

I tried to step away, but he caught at my elbow. My nails dug into my palms. "Let me go."

A smile touched his mouth. "I'll admit, I've hurt a few people in my day, but only when they deserved it. But you—you know these people will be collateral, and you don't seem to care. Your goals are more important to you than anyone who stands in your way. I understand the kind of desperation that requires."

I couldn't hide my trembling any longer. It had taken me over. "That's not true. I want to help people. I only want to help."

"There's no shame in it. Some people would call the two of us heartless, but that's a short-sighted view. We're not afraid to go after what we want; that's all. We're determined."

Was I so callous? My composure scattered to the four winds at his assessment of me.

His voice dropped as he stepped closer. I felt his breath on my cheek. "After we destroy Oscar, I can show you how to become as powerful as I am. We can be a partnership of sorts, you and I." He touched my chin. "Now tell me what you've learned about Oscar."

I slipped sideways away from his grasp and swiveled. He swung around too. Frustration compelled me to speak, though I knew I should stay quiet. "But—I don't understand this. Why Oscar? He's nothing but an old man. He only wants to spend time with his family and eat sweets and live a quiet life!"

Kurke shook his head. "You're letting pity cloud your judgment. You don't need to feel protective of Oscar. He's not a good person."

"You're wrong. He's kind. I've seen it."

He ran a hand over his eyes. "Oh, yes. Oscar Wendyn is an upstanding and noble master wizard. How dare I say anything to the contrary? So noble that his tenure as Preeminent Master Wizard was riddled with scandal."

I didn't like his tone. "Scandal?" Did I dare ask, when I knew he would just spew lies and hatred? "What scandal?"

"Ah, he's never mentioned the business with the Belanokians, I see. Or the Waldrinish trade predicament? How about the fact he was the PMW who Punished Ingerman?"

My mouth opened. "That's not true."

His voice turned gentle. "It is, on my honor. He gave the word to send her down the mountain in the barrel."

"That's impossible. Ingerman died thirty years ago."

"Twenty. It happened at the beginning of old man Wendyn's appointment."

Sickness welled up in me. I didn't know what to think. How much of this was truth and how much lies? I felt a certain amount of kinship with poor, Punished Underwizard Ingerman. Her name brought a melancholy feeling of friendship ended before it could begin. Could Oscar have been involved? He didn't strike me as the most mentally balanced individual I'd ever run into, after all. He studied killing spells for fun, talked to sticks, and made up outlandish stories about knitting with Robenhurst. I doubted his tale of discussing literature with Hutterland's arch-councilor was any more true. Not to mention those mysterious outings he constantly disappeared on. What was he really up to?

I strove to keep my voice steady. "Oscar said nothing about any of that."

"Then I suppose it's safe to assume he hasn't mentioned my family either."

"Your family?" I swallowed back the uneasy feeling that rose in me. This was a bad story that wouldn't end. "Why should he mention your family?"

Kurke shrugged, a nonchalant movement that belied the words that followed. "Oscar murdered them; that's all."

I should dismiss his words. They were crazy. *He* was crazy.

But one could argue that Oscar was just as crazy. Bones, I'd seen it myself. So where did that leave any of us in the grand scheme of good and evil?

"How did they die?" I asked, wishing it didn't feel like a concession. I didn't believe his story. Not yet. But that didn't mean I shouldn't investigate it.

"I was only twelve, and had been apprenticed for less than six months. I got word that my entire family had died in a buggy accident when their horse was spooked. But it wasn't true. As I discovered later, much, much later, in truth Oscar killed my father himself. Then he sent the Council guards that murdered my mother and sister. If I'd been there, I probably would have died too."

I felt the sorrow beneath his words. For a brief moment I saw him for what he was—a grieving man broken by the tragedy of his childhood. "But you lived. In part thanks to Oscar, who's looked after you all these years. And now you want to kill him?"

"I lived thanks to him and they died thanks to him. One doesn't cancel the others out, Avery. Can't you see that? He has to pay."

My chin jutted out. "I won't let you kill him."

He sighed. Ran a hand over his face. "Murk and shadow, but you're stubborn. Fine. Fine, you want a concession from me? All right. I have a heart. If you can get Oscar to take responsibility for what he did and admit it to the Council, then I'll cancel our oath. Oscar will live."

Hope beat its way through my chest. But still . . . "How do I know you're telling the truth?" I demanded.

"Just watch." He muttered an incantation. "That's called a deception defense spell. If I tell a lie now, I'll get kicked in the head by powerful magic. It feels like being beaten with a brick." He folded his arms. "I promise that if Oscar takes responsibility for killing my family and admits it to the Council, he can live."

A tightness eased in my chest. "Thank you." My voice sounded stiff, but what was the correct response under circumstances like this?

"Now will you tell me what you've found out about Oscar?"

I sighed. "I'll tell you," I said at last. "But only because I think it'll prove to you that you need to forget this whole thing. Oscar is a pathetic figure these days."

I told him the things I'd learned—Oscar's love of sweets and plain clothing, his collection of scrying sticks, his hours in the meadow and forest playing scry and seek, his mention of Hutterland's arch-councilor and recent visit from the PMW.

"Robenhurst? What did he want?"

"According to him, to knit. I tried a listening spell, but they must have blocked it somehow. I couldn't hear any of their discussion."

His face turned thoughtful. "What are you up to, Oscar?" he said, halfway to himself. Then, "You've done a good job, Avery. I knew this was a good idea. You're a useful little partner."

The compliment felt more like a knife to the gut than a boost to my confidence. I frowned. "I don't suppose you're going to tell me when you plan to carry out this revenge?"

"When the time is right, and that's all you need to know."

I sighed deeply.

He rubbed the back of his neck. "I'm going to ask you to dig a little deeper now, Avery. Most of what you've given me is mere fluff—unimportant things I could have figured out on my own. I want to know his darkest secrets, what he's most ashamed of, and what he wants hidden from the world. Listen in on his private conversations wherever possible. Send anything you find in the messenger, care of Platten View. Questions?"

My eyes flashed to his face. Every master wizard house had a messenger, a receptacle used to send letters and packages to other wizard's houses across the three kingdoms. Master Wendyn's was an ornately decorated white and gold sphere that sat on a table in the front hallway. Master Hapthwaite's had been a plain black box.

"In the messenger?" I repeated. "Why? Are you going somewhere?"

"Soon, yes."

"Where?"

"Now, that's none of your concern. I'll be expecting to hear from you." With a wave of his fingers, he dismissed the privacy spell and strode out of the dark hallway.

It took several minutes for me to gather myself enough to move. My head felt foggy, my thoughts confused. I didn't know what to believe. In the main hallway I stood next to Ingerman's monument, running my gaze over the date listed there.

Twenty years ago. Kurke had told the truth.

My face reflected in the glass—a boy's face. A girl's face.

A liar's face.

Now how in the three kingdoms could I get Oscar to admit he murdered Kurke's family? Because if I didn't, he would die.

———

A HAND FELL on my shoulder, and I jumped, still skittish.

"Careful, Mullins. It's just me." Master Wendyn stood beside me, looking cross. "What're you so jumpy about?"

I rubbed my nose. "You caught me off guard, is all." An unreasonable wish came as powerful as it was ridiculous: I wished I could tell him the truth. I wished I didn't have to hide who I was any longer. I wished I could be honest with him.

He nodded and pinched at a spot between his brows. "Let's return home. We need to talk, you and I."

The words had an ominous ring. "Talk?" I struggled to keep up with him as he strode across the floor to the opposite side of the cathedral hall.

"Talk," he repeated, his voice terse. He muttered a revealing spell, and his wizard door appeared near the head of the room. At least the place had emptied so no daydreaming underwizard was in danger of walking full tilt into it.

"I can't believe," Master Wendyn went on in clipped tones, "the insolence of you. The brazenness, there in front of the Council and even the PMW."

I went hot, then cold. For a moment my steps faltered, but he kept up his brisk, stalking pace, and I had to jog to keep up.

"Insolence?" My voice sounded like a mouse's squeak to my ears. "What do you mean?"

We had almost reached the door by now. "Don't play the fool. It doesn't suit you. Get in there." He swung the door and pushed me through, and I ran face-first into the tapestry. By the time I untangled myself and pushed it back, he'd followed me through and closed the door behind him with more force than necessary. I stood there, holding the tapestry until he cleared it and turned on me again.

"Well? Explain yourself."

I dropped the tapestry and lifted my chin. I'd had just about enough of being groused at by angry master wizards. "Whatever it is you imagine I've done—" I began.

"It's clear as glass, underwizard. As clear as that statue you reassembled almost perfectly today—something you've never once been able to do in our practice sessions. You've been lying since the first day you walked into my house."

SIXTEEN

"LYING?" I REPEATED. SOMETHING panic-like rushed me. "Why should I lie to you?" My heart fluttered like the wings of a hummingbird.

"You tell me." He nodded at the still-swaying tapestry, shimmering lines of blue and green. "That performance back there on the dais was nothing like what you've been showing me in the library on any afternoon. 'Oh, Master Wendyn, I can't make fire.'" He fixed me with a look. "Is this all a joke to you?"

My mouth opened in surprise. "No. I've been working hard at my spells, hours upon hours. When I improved, I wanted to surprise you."

He stared at me hard, his gaze so fierce it was almost a glare. "You wanted to surprise me? What in the three kingdoms convinced you I would enjoy being surprised?"

He made a good point, and I felt my face flush as I realized how stupid my idea must sound to him. But I couldn't just simply admit defeat. "Oh, I don't know. I thought maybe you'd be proud of your apprentice for doing a fine job."

"Proud of you?"

I wished he would stop repeating everything I said, as

though it was the most preposterous thing he'd ever heard. "Yes, *proud*," I repeated with emphasis. "I passed, in case that somehow escaped your notice." I moved to push past him, ready to flounce out in an unwizard-like and unboy-like manner, but he grabbed my arm. His fingers dug into my flesh, and I had to stop myself from wincing. I had no choice but to look up at him, his clean-shaven face and dark eyes inches from my own.

"See you don't do it again." His glare subsided into an irritable frown. "If there's anything I hate, it's being surprised." He dropped my arm and strode toward his desk, unbuttoning his robes as he went.

I rubbed my arm. "I thought you'd be pleased. Everyone likes surprises."

"Not everyone." His face twisted sourly as he looked over his shoulder at me, shrugging out of his wizard robes in one swift movement. "All the worst things in my life have been surprises."

Cailyn, I realized. He was talking about his once-sweetheart.

"Oh," I said. "Ohhh, I see."

He rounded on me. "Don't imagine you know anything about me."

"Of course I know nothing about you. You never tell me anything, do you?" I folded my arms and glowered at him every bit as fiercely as he glared at me.

"What do you imagine I should tell you? If any part of my personal life becomes pertinent to you, I'll let you know. In the meantime, I don't appreciate being made to look a fool." He loosened the collar of his white shirt, one of those lacy ones he seemed fond of.

"You never looked like a fool. No one was even looking at you. They were looking at me."

He worked the sleeves at his wrists. "Sure they were. I was

tense. Nervous, and I don't like to be nervous. I'll admit, I thought you would fail, Mullins."

So much for his reassurance to the contrary. "Yes, well, I was nervous and tense too. It's normal."

"Not for me. And I don't appreciate your toying with my emotions like that."

This was ridiculous. He was mad at me because he got a little anxious? "Look," I said, "I meant no harm—"

He tugged at the bottom of his shirt, and it came free of his trousers. All at once I realized he wasn't just making himself more comfortable, the man was *undressing*.

"What are you doing?" My voice rose in alarm.

He tugged at the buttons. "Well, I can't keep it on, can I?" The shirt slid open, revealing a man's chest underneath—*a man's chest*—and I didn't know where to look, and then he slid his arms free of the sleeves and held the shirt in front of my face.

"Do you see the perspiration? The fabric is ruined. I may as well have just climbed the Sardath Mountains." He balled the shirt up and then fanned himself with one hand. "This is your fault, underwizard. You owe me a new shirt."

"I—er—" I tried to articulate something, anything, rather than stare at his chest. But my mind had gone blank, and his bare torso was right in front of me. I'd seen a man's chest before —there was Papa, of course, and Gavin—but this was not like that. What was this hot flush I could feel creeping up from my neck? I was not blushing, not over Master Wendyn. That would be ridiculous.

"Yes . . . well, I'm sorry," I stuttered, forcing my thoughts into place. "Give me the shirt, and I'll see it's cleaned." I held my hand out, but he swung it out of my reach.

"It's ruined, I tell you. Beyond saving. This is silk; can't you see that? Not even that overpriced laundress in Bramford could get this clean."

Laundry. There was a normal thought I could hold onto, and I grasped it like a drowning man thrown a rope. "Beyond saving? Don't be ridiculous. It's just a little sweat." I eyed the material, which was looking rather yellowed and damp. "Sure, this is trickier because it's silk, but I've gotten out much worse stains when I was taking in washing."

He raised an eyebrow. "O-ho. You took in washing? I didn't know I was speaking to a washerwoman."

My mouth opened and closed. "I didn't—I mean—" But I could think of no way to backtrack my statement. "All right. Yes, I took in washing. Mama was dying, and Papa drinking night and day. Gavin and I had to eat somehow, didn't we?" I snatched the shirt and pushed past him, stopping at the door long enough to toss back over my shoulder at him, "At least it was honest work."

"Now, now. There's no call to head off in a snit. Sometimes your temper reminds me of Marelda's." His hand fell on my shoulder, and when I looked, he held a clean shirt in his other hand, retrieved from I-don't-know-where. He probably had a stash in his desk for clothing emergencies such as this.

"I remind you of your sister?"

"Yes. She flies off at the least little thing. Always over-reacting."

I wanted to explode that I wasn't overreacting, but perhaps that would be an overreaction itself. "Fine." I turned around to face him, brushing his hand off my shoulder. "I am not 'heading off in a snit.' If I clean your shirt, you won't hold it against me that I surprised you by not being terrible at magic. Deal?"

"Deal." He sighed, and then to my surprise, he fidgeted with the shirt, twisting the fabric and fiddling with the buttons—almost as though he was uncomfortable. "Devil's dawn, but I'm bad at this. I wasn't meant to be a master." He stepped closer and rested his hands on my shoulders, with the clean shirt still in one hand. It tickled the side of my face.

Friar's bones, now I was closer to his bare chest than ever! Would this torture never end?

"You did well today, underwizard. I am proud of you."

That strange flush was back again, creeping up from my neck. This was the most awkward situation I had ever found myself in. "Oh," I stuttered. "Erm . . . thank you."

"And if you are able to return my shirt to its pre-perspiration state, I will be even more proud."

Just like that I was back to being annoyed again. "Of course you will be," I grumbled. "All I did was study myself to death. A shirt is much more important than that."

He gave me a blank look. "It's my favorite shirt."

"Your favorite—" I stopped myself and took a deep breath. "I'd better get started in that case, hadn't I?" I pushed his arms aside and made for the door.

In my room, I rang for water and a washbasin and got to work on the white silk shirt, now heavy with dried gray-and-brown sweat stains. And even though the master was aggravating and preposterous and confusing, as the day wore on, my thoughts turned again and again to those two simple sentences, and I couldn't stop the pleased tingle that pierced through me every time: *You did well today, underwizard. I am proud of you.*

MY RED HANDS stung from scrubbing the master's shirt by the time I went down to supper. The clean shirt lay drying by the fire in my room. It would be dry by the time I returned.

Ivan and the master were both in the dining hall already, although Oscar's regular chair stood empty. As I slipped into my seat, Ivan dunked a slice of bread in his water glass and ate it while the master watched him with an annoyed glance.

Or was it an amused glance? I had difficulty telling those two emotions apart on the master's face.

"Oscar isn't joining us?" I asked.

Master Wendyn shook his head. "He's off on one of his harebrained jaunts. Who knows when he'll return."

My stomach sank. I'd been hoping to talk to Oscar about Kurke's family and gauge how difficult it might be to get him to admit his part in their deaths. "'Harebrained jaunt'?" I repeated. "What does that mean?"

Ivan jiggled my elbow and motioned at the pot of rabbit stew. I took his bowl and filled it.

The master shrugged. "Oh, you know his little game. What does he call it? Scry and seek? Once cold weather arrives, it's a little more difficult to navigate the forests around here, so he takes himself off for warmer climes."

My mouth fell open in dismay. "For how long? He'll return before the end of winter, won't he?"

"I don't know." He raised a brow. "Is this going to be a problem?"

I forced myself to swallow a bite of stew before giving him a smile I hoped didn't appear as tight as it felt on my face. "No, curiosity. It's an odd thing for a retired PMW to do, isn't it? That game, I mean."

"Grandfather used to make more sense. Old age has addled him." He tore off a piece of bread with his long fingers but paused just before placing it in his mouth. "Although, he was always a little unorthodox as PMW. He had a reputation when he occupied that office."

It didn't surprise me to hear it. "Did he now? People knew him for being a little crazy?"

He ate the bread before answering. "No, not crazy. Just out

of the ordinary. He dealt with more drama than happens in the tenure of most that hold that position. I wouldn't say it affected him badly, but still . . . perhaps it did."

I wanted to ask what situations Oscar dealt with, but I knew that pushing the conversation further could make the master suspicious. So I fell into silence, spooning stew into my mouth and ruminating on what he'd told me. I was certain one of the hard decisions he was referring to was whatever happened with Kurke's family.

My mind turned back to my conversation with Kurke only this afternoon. The things he had said about Oscar—did it matter if they were true? If Oscar was a murderer, would it somehow acquit us of guilt when we carried out the oath? When we killed him in cold blood?

I rubbed at my head. How long had it been hurting and I hadn't noticed?

Knowing about Kurke's past gave me sympathy for the man, much as I hated to admit it. His actions were irrational, but they were driven by sorrow and anger and loss. I could understand those emotions. I could even understand the desire for revenge. I felt the same way after losing Mama and Gavin.

Perhaps I'd been going about this wrong. If I could just appeal to Kurke and let him know that I understood his viewpoint, that I'd been where he was before, then maybe I could talk him down from the extreme position he'd taken.

Maybe.

I rubbed at my head again and then poured myself a cup of water and drank it down.

"How's my shirt coming?" Master Wendyn gazed at me over the top of the pot of stew. "I don't suppose you've given up on it already?"

"Your shirt is fine. It's clean. It's better than new." The

words were a slight exaggeration, but one that felt necessary in the face of his obvious mistrust.

"I'll believe it when I see it."

"It's true," Edie spoke up as she set a bowl of something pudding-like on the table. "I saw it drying in the underwizard's room. It's as white as a snowy winter's morning." She smiled a dazzling smile at me as though her poetic description had been helpful.

Friar's bones, how often did Edie go in my room when I wasn't around? I needed to look into getting a lock on the door.

"Did you?" Master Wendyn gave both of us a measuring glance. "I'll keep that in mind."

The master's continued doubts grated on me, but I managed a smile I hoped hid my irritation. He'd eat those doubts when he saw how good his shirt looked.

That night I sent a note in the messenger to Matthias Kurke of Platten View. It contained one sentence: "Oscar is gone." Hopefully giving Kurke immediate notice of this change in circumstances would result in a hold on his revenge plan. After all, I couldn't convince Oscar to confess his crimes if I couldn't talk to him.

But Kurke never replied.

ONCE MASTER WENDYN saw his cleaned shirt, he brought me his fine fabrics to launder once a week—stacks of them. I might as well have never left Waltney. I was still taking in washing, a task I despised.

In the meantime, I watched for Oscar, hoping he'd return so I'd have a chance to get his confession and save his life. But he never appeared.

"Stupid silk stains. Why does every single shirt he owns

have to be silk? I hate cleaning silk." I wrung out a cold wet rag and dabbed at the latest shirt, a cornflower-blue color. An assortment of cleaning solutions lined the kitchen table before me. I had had Mrs. Pitts pick them up for me in Bramford.

Don't understand. Why you say you clean? Ivan gestured at me from where he crouched next to the fireplace, playing with some rocks or something. *You hate clean. Say no.*

"Hand me that bottle," I said, and when Ivan complied, I uncorked it, poured its solution onto my rag, and dabbed at the shirt. "It's my stupid fault. I'm the one who said I'd do it." I'd been grousing to Ivan for the last ten minutes.

Use spell?

I made a face at Ivan. "Believe me, I've thought of that. Cleaning spells wear out the fabric quicker. Master Wendyn doesn't want that." I chewed my lip and stared down at the stains. "Why does he like these shirts, anyway? They're so . . . frilly."

When next I looked up at Ivan, he gestured, *I like. Look nice.*

I rolled my eyes. "Not you too. Well, if you ever wear a shirt like this, don't expect me to wash it for you. Find someone else."

A gust of wind blasted in from the outside door, and a boy stepped inside, as tall as me but thicker through the chest. Not bad looking at all.

"Oh," he said, stopping short at the sight of Ivan and me. "Hullo. Didn't mean to interrupt. Cook said I could come in for some food."

"There's bread and stew in the larder." I gestured at the door in the corner, the small room where food lined the shelves.

"Many thanks." He gave a short bow and turned to go but paused and turned back. "I'm Edwin. New stable hand. You must be the underwizard."

I nodded at him. "Underwizard Mullins. Pleasure to make your acquaintance. This is Ivan."

Ivan didn't look up from his rocks.

Edwin nodded. "I'll get my food and go, then."

It took but a moment for him to complete the task, and I watched him—while trying to seem as though I wasn't watching him—the entire time.

A new stable hand, eh? And this one young and handsome. There was possibility in this. If I could interest Edie in him, would she leave me alone?

The door banged shut behind him, and in the silence of the kitchen, staring at my mound of laundry once again, I remembered I was in a foul mood. Irritable thoughts crept back in. It wasn't only the shirt that had upset me. I still hadn't heard from Kurke, which might have been good news, but under the circumstances had left me with a vaguely unsettled feeling all the time. I lived in fear of him showing his face again. Also, today marked my mother's Time. Five years ago, on a cold, cheerless day just like this one, Mama had breathed her last. Sometimes I missed her so much that my sorrow burned through my chest, an inferno waiting to consume me. On other days, it made me angry at God, the Universe, but mostly Papa, the one who caused her to work herself to death. And myself, the one who broke her heart.

Earlier in the day, I composed a letter to Mama in the traditional way, telling her about the events of the year since I last wrote to her and expressing my love. Ivan walked with me to the small chapel some distance down the highway, and I presented the letter to Mama on the altar there and burned it so the words would find their way on wings of smoke to her home among the angels.

You mother want you happy, Ivan had gestured at me afterward, apparently disturbed by the sorrow on my face. *Be happy.*

I hated the day of Mama's Time. On most days, I learned to forget my sorrow, but today it felt as fresh as the day it happened.

When next I looked Ivan's way, a few minutes had passed, and he was crouched on the ground, drawing something on the hearth with a coal from the ash bucket. I frowned and stepped closer.

A face took shape on the hearth. The distance between the eyes, the strong nose, and the confident cut of his chin made it unmistakable. It was Master Wendyn. As I watched, Ivan gave him horns and a rather wicked expression.

I was so struck by the accuracy of the simple drawing that I stood and stared. Ivan caught me looking and gestured, grinning, *Master Wendyn.*

"I can see that," I said at last, recovering myself. "The likeness is unmistakable. Ivan, I didn't know you could draw."

He shrugged before going back to the drawing, finishing it up by giving the master a forked tail and an ominous looking staff. By this time, the drawing had gotten rather large, and we both stood there staring at it, until a great bloop from the kettle on the fire reminded me I was boiling water and there was work I should be doing.

"You've captured the cunning on his face the day he tricked me into cleaning his clothes," I said, taking up the stick next to the fireplace. I stirred the great kettle with it. "I should have known he was up to no good."

Ivan added in a sinister mustache and a scar across one cheek.

"Black out some of his teeth." I edged closer again. Ivan complied, and the oddest urge broke over me—the urge to laugh. Despite the bad day and forced laundering and my mother's Time, I chuckled along with Ivan.

"And what are those?" I asked, gesturing at the scribbles

beneath the drawing. The circles and loops and lines didn't seem to be a part of the picture.

Ivan shrugged. *I write. Like you write spells.*

I felt my brow furrow. "You mean . . . you're trying to write words?"

He nodded and scribbled more loop-de-loops that meant nothing.

An idea took hold of me.

"Stay right here," I told him and took the back steps two at a time. Once in my bedroom, I rooted around in my trunk until I came up with the primer I stole from the bedroom of some rich young noble, back when Papa and I were thieving. Books had always intrigued me back then because I so wanted to read. I had slid it inside my tunic and never told Papa about it. Later I showed it to Gavin, and we hid it beneath a rock in the Midnight Forest. We would steal out to flip through the pages when we thought no one would notice our absence. But though I found the shapes fascinating and beautiful, I made no headway learning to read until Master Hapthwaite showed me the sounds the letters made. It opened the world to me.

Back in the kitchen, I showed Ivan the letters and pictures in the primer, trying to teach him their meanings by making exaggerated sounds. I was trying to get him to understand the letter C when a voice took us by surprise.

"Is that supposed to be me?"

The two of us started at Master Wendyn's voice. When had he come in? He stared critically down at the drawing.

"Er—no, no, no," I said. Beside me, Ivan gestured things that Master Wendyn might or might not understand, as he'd grasped only a few gestures in our hand language so far. "It's nobody."

"Don't be daft. Of course it's me. You've gotten a few things wrong, however. There's no scar on my cheek, and I'll have you know my teeth are all my own."

Not you, Ivan gestured again, and I translated.

"Perhaps not, but if it were, there's one thing you didn't get wrong. That tail is just about perfect."

Ivan and I both gaped at him. The master joked so rarely that it always took me by surprise. But—a pleasant surprise.

"Well, carry on," he said and left, munching on an apple and humming.

Ivan and I continued to gape, even after he was gone—that is, until we broke into relieved and nervous laughter. I went back to the kettle, dipping out boiling water, while Ivan erased the drawing on the floor with a rueful glance at the kitchen door.

It was such a happy occurrence that the master hadn't snapped at either of us, that he'd taken the joke in good fun, that some time passed before I remembered again that today was Mama's Time. But even when I remembered, some of the sting seemed to have gone out of it, and something about Ryker Hall seemed a trifle more cheerful.

Mrs. Pitts stopped in to watch me work and even paid me a compliment. "Great Hepzibah's fiddle, you're putting a lot of elbow work into cleaning those shirts. I didn't know you had it in you. I'll assume the master threatened you."

Ivan began a new drawing, and I stirred my pot. We exchanged hand gestures and laughed at nothing and everything as the evening passed.

Ivan was right. Mama would want me to find happiness.

The next day when I went to the library to take up my studying for the fourth and fifth trials—sensory and water magic —a variety of materials rested on the tables. Ivan slipped in beside me and stared in wonderment at the stacks of drawing pads, pencils, paints, canvases, and books on the craft of draw-ing, sketching, and painting.

"I'm guessing these are for you," I said, though it was unnecessary, as Ivan was already settling himself before the table and pulling out one of the drawing pads and a pencil.

I pondered on the kindness as I opened my book. How much of what the master did was for show, and how much of it was real? He was irritable and rude, and yet I remembered the kind things I'd seen him do too, like the time he handed Mrs. Pitts that fresh flower when she was in one of her foul moods or feeding stray animals when he thought no one was looking. And now these drawing supplies for Ivan. Despite his protests to the contrary, I was starting to believe there was a kind man beneath all his protests after all.

SEVENTEEN

A FEW DAYS LATER while I should have been studying in the library—but really I was helping Ivan to sight-read simple words in the primer—a commotion overtook the entrance hall. I glanced up. After a moment or two of debate, I stepped out of the room. Standing there in the main hall, back to me as he conversed with the master, was Matthias Kurke.

Blast my curiosity. I took a cautious step backward.

"—brings you by? Is this a social call or official Conclave business?"

"Social. Just wanted to stop by and see how you and the underwizard are doing. And Oscar, of course."

I eased another step backward. Bones. What was he doing here, really doing here? I had nothing new to report. I hadn't seen Oscar in at least three weeks, and the master knew as much as I did.

"Grandfather's taken flight, as he often does. Been away for several weeks now. I imagine he'll turn up soon, as he always does."

I turned around and hurried the other way.

"Several weeks? That doesn't worry you?"

"Maybe it would, if it were anyone else. Oi, underwizard."

I stopped and then turned around. Master Wendyn motioned me closer. I had no choice but to join them.

"Good day, Master Kurke." I gave a short bow. "A pleasure to see you again."

"Mullins. You're looking well. How goes the studying?"

"He's making great strides," Master Wendyn supplied. "If he can just keep from putting anyone's eyes out at the next trial, I'll count it a success."

I frowned, but when I looked at the master's face, he was smiling. Was he teasing me?

"It's water magic," I reminded him. "If you're worried about anything, it should be drowning."

"Good point. In that case, I'll think about supplying the judges with a rowboat, as a precaution."

"And what about for you?" I asked.

"Oh, I know how to swim."

I rolled my eyes.

"Well. You two seem to be getting along," Kurke observed.

"I think we understand each other better these days." Master Wendyn ran a hand over the growth of beard on his chin. "And it doesn't hurt that the underwizard can scrub stains out of any fabric."

"Stains?" Kurke repeated, and I could feel the heat creeping up my face. "Do you mean washing?"

Did he have to mention that?

"Mullins is a whiz with cleaning clothes. He's been keeping my closet in fine shape."

"You realize there are cleaning spells you can use to do that, right?"

"Nothing takes the color out of fabrics quicker than a cleaning spell. You can't replace a good washerwoman."

Kurke made a choking noise, and I glared at Master Wendyn.

"Oh, don't look at me like that, Mullins. I'm teasing. Can't I tease you?"

"I wish you wouldn't." Stiffness crept into my voice. "I'm not a washerwoman."

"Very well. You are good at what you do, though. Take pride in it." He turned to Kurke. "Will you meet me in the drawing room? I need to speak with the underwizard."

For a moment, I thought Kurke would say something else, but then he gave a shrug and shot a scrutinizing glance at me. "All right." With a nod, he left us.

Once alone, Master Wendyn gestured for me to follow. "Come to my study for a moment, Mullins. I have something to show you."

My curiosity piqued, I followed in his steps.

"I didn't know you and the librarian's daughter were so close." He came to a stop behind his desk. "She's sending you packages now?"

"I—what?" I stuttered, and then my eyes fell on the thing sitting on his desk. The brown-paper-wrapped parcel was addressed to Avery Mullins, care of Ryker Hall, from Orly Edmunns, Wizard's Library.

"Where did—" I began, but the master cut me off.

"It came in the messenger this morning," he said, motioning toward the hallway and the messenger box. I'd only ever received notes on official Conclave business via the box, confirming trial times and so forth. This was my first personal message. What could it be?

"Er . . . I asked her to look for a book for me. Something about . . ." I cast about for an appropriate topic and settled on, ". . . one of my trials."

"Let's see it, then. Open it up." He passed it over. "I've

never known the Wizard's Library to bother with home deliveries. Just how much flirting have you been doing under the guise of library research?"

My eyebrows shot upward. "It's nothing like that. She's an acquaintance."

"Yes." The master's voice said he didn't believe me. "Like Edie is just an acquaintance?"

"I've never encouraged Edie."

"I feel I should warn you, underwizard. Master wizards should be above reproach. You don't want to develop a reputation as a philanderer. Things like that get back to the Council."

"Why are you so determined to believe I'm lying about this?" I hugged the package to my chest, my grip too tight. "I'm not a mindless flirt. Edie and Orly are both just friends."

For a moment he stared at me. Then he sighed, scratched his chin, and fell into his chair. "Devil's dawn, you're right. I'm a suspicious fishwife."

"I didn't want to put it that way, but—yes."

He jerked his head in the direction we'd just come from. "Matt was always in trouble during our apprenticeships, always starting relationships and lying to his master about them. I suppose I equate the two of you as one. He used to brawl, and I first ran into you after a public brawl."

My face must have shown how aghast that statement made me, because he chuckled.

"It's not the end of the kingdoms, underwizard. Matt is a respected wizard these days. You could be compared to worse people."

"He and I are *nothing* alike."

The master's brow quirked with curiosity, and I realized my denial might have been too strong. I needed to be careful. After all, just a few walls separated us from Kurke. He might be eavesdropping on our conversation with a listening spell at this very moment.

"What I mean is, he's so . . . tall."

"I don't mean his height. I've known him since we were children. He had a difficult childhood. His family died when he was young. I think your childhood was similar."

A question lay somewhere beneath those words. I avoided answering it by asking, "How did they die?"

"That's not important," the master said with a wave of his hand. "A tragic accident. After he became an underwizard, Matt almost lost his apprenticeship for fighting, same as you. He almost killed a boy over a basket of food."

"His master didn't feed him?"

He shook his head. "It wasn't for him. Matt's always been a bit of a . . . libertine, shall we say? He had a dalliance with a certain woman. The food was for her and her child."

"Oh." My stomach sickened as I thought of the strange mix of evil and generosity that made up Master Kurke. "How . . ." I searched for the right word, ". . . heroic."

He frowned. "It wasn't heroic at all. His master would have given him food if he'd asked. But he was too proud, and his temper got the best of him. I was still an underwizard myself, and it took both Grandfather's and my intervention to convince his master to keep him."

"Maybe you shouldn't have interfered." There were signs of Kurke's unbalanced mind long ago. If he'd suffered the natural consequences of his actions back then, perhaps he wouldn't be tormenting me now.

"You may as well know it—I have a strange weakness for rescuing things. The rabbit when I was six which should have been supper. A long line of needy people when I was an underwizard. Matt when we were teenagers. Ivan. You. Should I have left you to your fate in Bramford?"

I saw his point. But still, I had a feeling that Kurke, with his heavy load of anger and resentment toward the Wendyn family, would wish for the same thing. "Maybe," I said softly. "Maybe it would have been better if you'd never rescued any of us."

He shook his head, displeased with my lack of understanding. "Matt learned to control his temper; that's what I'm saying. It's time you do too. Short tempers make for dangerous wizards." He stood and moved around the desk. I didn't know what he was about until he rested a hand on my shoulder. "You have promise, underwizard. Don't lose your way."

"Mmm." I was so embarrassed that I couldn't think of anything else to say. There was a quality to his voice I'd never heard before. It was like the pride I'd heard in his tone when he told me I did well after the second and third trials—but there was more to it, too. There was something almost like affection or friendship.

"Despite everything, you're doing well. Very well." The weight of his hand on my shoulder brought a burst of emotion to my chest and an ache to my eyes I couldn't explain. After a moment he lifted his hand and moved away.

"We've gotten off topic. Open the package. You've piqued my curiosity with this book that the librarian's daughter went to such lengths to send."

I chewed on my lip. Who knew what sort of book Orly had found for me. Still, the master didn't have to say any of that, and I couldn't say no in the face of his kindness. I took a breath and slid a finger under the parcel's paper.

Please don't let this be a book about females and magic.

The corner came undone. I performed the same procedure on the opposite corner and folded the paper open on each side.

"Devil's dawn, at this rate, I'll be old by the time it's unwrapped." Master Wendyn reached across to pull the package out of my arms and ripped the paper open with one sweeping gesture. It fell away, and he stared down at the book, consternation on his face.

"It's not what you think." I grabbed for the book, but he held it out of my reach.

"Well. Aqua Pura Enchantments and the Fourth Trial. I've never heard of this one. Is it new?"

I got a look at the cover, and relief flooded me. "Yes, it came out last week," I invented. "Orly knew I wanted to read it."

"So your sweetheart secured the first copy for you?" But this time I heard the teasing in his voice.

"We're friends. I asked her to send it when it arrived."

"She must be a good friend, then. I insist that you read it." The corner of his mouth quirked in an almost-smile. "No sense in wasting such a useful—and timely sent—book."

He swiveled and headed out of the room.

I sagged with relief.

When I was back in the library again, I opened the front cover, to find Orly had placed a note there. Thank the heavens the master never thought to open it himself.

Avery—This book came into my hands just today, and Papa knows nothing about it. I knew I'd never get this chance again, so I'm sending it to you. I can't spare it very long before its absence will be noticed, so be quick about reading it. The Belanokian dictionary I wanted to send along wouldn't fit in the messenger. If your master doesn't have one, there are several at the Wizard's Library you can borrow.

In much smaller print on the back side of the note, which I had to stand close to the window and squint to read, it said, *Superb job of magicking the cover, isn't it?*

I looked over the front of the book again, at its glossy front and gilded lettering, then flipped it open and turned to the title page.

Fancy, archaic Belanokian crawled across the page. I had a

passing familiarity with the language, thanks to the Belanokian dictionary I had found in Master Hapthwaite's library— although it disappeared once he found me studying it. It also helped I'd always been a quick hand at picking up languages.

I couldn't be certain of the exact interpretation of the title, but I believed it translated to something like Desiring Blood—A Collection of Bloody Spells.

For a moment, all I could do was stare, certain I had interpreted it incorrectly. But the longer I stared, the more certain I was that the title said exactly what I thought it did.

Orly had really done it. She'd found me a book about blood magic.

I SPENT the better part of the afternoon poring over the book, staring at its dark, swooping Belanokian characters. The longer I tried to make sense of them, the less sense they seemed to make. My feeble grasp of the language wasn't enough to interpret the complicated wizard's terminology and conjugated verbs.

A cursory examination of the master's library revealed not a single Belanokian dictionary. I combed through the books a second time with the same results.

It looked as though another trip to the Wizard's Library was in order.

I mulled over the question all afternoon and worked up the courage to ask the master at supper time.

"Go to the Conclave?" he repeated, staring at me over the top of a letter. I'd never seen the wax seal at the top before. He set it aside. "Again? What for?"

"It's Hampstone I need to visit. I need more cleaning solutions. I've had Mrs. Pitts get me every kind they have in Bramford, but they don't have what I need." It wasn't a lie, and I was counting on the master's vanity to win over any protests he might have.

But he was already shaking his head. "To Hampstone by yourself? Unwise. It's a large city, and that street outside the Conclave is lined with pickpockets."

"I've been there before," I pointed out. "Nothing happened. Besides, I was something of a pickpocket myself in my past."

He gave me a wry glance. "That's not your most appealing quality. Is that supposed to convince me?"

"I hoped it would."

"If you can't clean my clothes using what you can get in Bramford, then just use a cleaning spell. Yes, it'll wear out quicker, but under the circumstances, I can live with that." He picked up the letter again.

There went my argument. Now not only was I still stuck doing the master's washing, but I also couldn't visit the Conclave.

Which meant I had no way to read the blood magic book.

Master Wendyn went back to perusing his letter, but put it down again when he notice I was still watching him.

"Was there something else, underwizard?"

Annoyance over the blood magic book made me reckless. "I have to be honest. I don't like washing your clothes."

Confusion colored his face. "What are you talking about?"

"I loathe cleaning clothes. Detest it. I always have. The chapped hands, the monotony, the boredom. It reminds me of the bad times with my mother. I'd rather have a tooth pulled than continue washing your shirts."

His eyebrows rose. "Well. Well then. Why didn't you say so earlier?"

"Don't know." I fiddled with my napkin, just to give myself something to do and not have to stare at him any longer. "I didn't know how to say no, I guess."

He took a sip from his goblet. "Devil's dawn, underwizard, you have to tell me these things. I'm not a telepath."

"You didn't give me a chance to," I pointed out. "You assumed I'd be delighted to clean your sweat stains."

His jaw worked. "We have to learn how to communicate better if this apprenticeship is going to work. You have to tell me how you feel."

"I agree. And you have to listen better."

He rubbed at the back of his neck and then scooted his chair away from the table and stood. "I need to go." He crumpled the letter and tossed it in the fire before swiveling from the room.

I stared after him, feeling annoyed and put upon and vaguely ashamed. It wasn't my problem. I was here to become a master wizard, not a professional laundress.

But I supposed I could have been nicer about it.

I gestured at the fire. "Who do you suppose that letter was from?"

His brother, Ivan gestured from the other side of the table, one-handed, since he had an apple in his other hand. He took an enormous bite from it, set it aside, and gestured, *He beg forgiveness. I hear master talk.*

From Bastian? And the master read it? This wasn't the first time he'd received a missive from his brother. All the others went straight into the fire, unopened. It was a good sign he'd opened it. Perhaps the master was ready to forgive.

It had only taken him a few years to listen to his own brother. How long would it take him to forgive the underwizard that didn't want to clean his shirts?

———

THE NEXT DAY, the master didn't come to breakfast.

"He's out for the day," Edie said apologetically, setting a bowl of fresh fruit on the table between Ivan and me.

"Is he?" I said, only half listening. I had been up late reading the blood magic book, trying to interpret words that wouldn't make sense. My mind felt soggy, like paper dampened so that the ink ran into a cloud of color, rendering it void of meaning.

"Yes. But he said he left you a list of things to study in the library."

I nodded and stared at the pear Ivan had picked up. Edie moved toward the door which stood open. As she crossed the threshold, it occurred to me—this could be my chance. I blurted, "Do you have a moment, Edie? I'd like to talk to you, if I may. Outside."

"Oh!" Pink climbed in her cheeks, and she batted a wisp of golden hair out of her face. "Of course."

I pushed my chair back. It scraped on the stone floor. Ivan gave me a questioning look, but I shook my head. The rustle of my trousers and squeak of my boots were loud in the awkward silence. Or was it only awkward to my ears?

Nerves filled me. I hated being nervous. What if this backfired?

"Where are we going?" Edie asked when I didn't stop in the hall but continued toward the kitchen.

"To the stables," I told her. "There's someone I want you to meet."

Edwin and Edie. Two beautifully alliterative names. Handsome and unattached Edwin would be the perfect replacement for Edie's infatuation with me. Once she met him, she'd understand that too.

BY SUPPERTIME, the master had returned. I walked into the banquet hall to find him in his usual seat, as relaxed and casual as though he never left.

The meal passed quietly. Of the three of us, Ivan talked the most, in his own way. He gestured questions at me, which I answered aloud. The master offered nothing to the conversation.

The longer his silence continued, the more my irritation grew. So he just wasn't going to talk to me again, and all because I didn't want to wash his shirts?

By the time Edie brought in dessert, I'd had just about enough.

"Well," I said as Edie came in holding a tray, "If you're so mad at me over your silk shirts, I guess I can keep cleaning them. I'd rather have a master who acknowledges my existence."

He looked up from the cake Edie had just set in front of him and blinked once at me. "What are you talking about?"

"You haven't said one word during this meal. Fine. I'll keep cleaning your shirts if it's that important to you. Or better yet, I'll teach you how to do it yourself."

He blinked again. "You're making as much sense as Marelda again."

I felt less sure of myself. "Isn't this about laundry?"

He looked down at the confection in front of him. "Do you know what we're having for dessert?"

"Don't change the subject. You've been ignoring Ivan and me the whole meal. Something's bothering you, so if it's not your clothes, then what?"

Irritation tugged his brows downward. "Fine, if you're going to insist on having this unnecessary conversation. Yes. I felt sheepish over the laundry."

"I knew it. So I'll just keep doing it."

"You will not."

"Excuse me?"

His jaw worked. "Much as it pains me to admit it, your studies are more important than my silk shirts. Even if they are handmade and imported from Waldrin."

I rolled my eyes, or at least meant to. But in the process of doing so, my eyes fell on the plated creation in front of me. Ivan had already dug into his dessert with relish.

"What—where did this come from?" I asked stupidly.

"Ah," he said, his face relaxing into a pleased smile. "You do recognize it, then."

"It's a Waltney cake." My eyes rose to his face. "But . . . these are made in Waltney."

He looked rather smug. "Yes. So I'm told." He picked up his fork and inserted it into the dainty treat. "I've heard they're delicious." He lifted the fork, now filled with delicate cake and cream and the haranjes that only grew in the Midnight Forest near my old home.

"But—but—where did these come from?"

He sniffed at the bit of cake on his fork before answering, "Now, that is a silly question. You've just said they're only made in Waltney. It would stand to reason, then, that these cakes came from Waltney, wouldn't it?"

"You know that's not what I'm asking. I mean how did they come to be here?"

"Ah. That is the question, isn't it?" But he didn't answer it. Instead, he took a bite, savoring it far longer than I had patience for. "Mmm, yes, the rumors are true. Waltney cakes are delicious."

"Are you going to tell me or not?"

He smiled with a bit of the mischief and wickedness on his lips that I was only used to seeing on Kurke's face. I got the feeling he was enjoying himself immensely. "Perhaps. But not until you taste it. You've never tasted Waltney cakes before—am I right?"

I sniffed at the dessert and picked up my fork. "No," I admitted. "We couldn't afford them, though I've seen them often enough through the shop windows. We had plenty of haranjes at our disposal, but Mama was too ill to bake."

"Well, then." He nodded at my plate. "Eat."

My curiosity had fully engaged now, and he didn't have to say it again. "Very well."

I wasn't prepared for the taste of haranjes. It took me back. I was twelve years old, gathering the tangy, bittersweet fruit in the forest with Gavin. The flavor, while delicious and delicate, carried a sting that had nothing to do with the cake.

"Well?" He raised an eyebrow.

I swallowed past the ache in my throat. "It's very good."

His face relaxed into a smile. I was surprised that he even cared what I thought.

"I was in Waltney today." He stabbed the dessert with his fork, not looking at me. "I suppose it's an apology. I'm not good at that sort of thing. You've worked hard, underwizard. You've done as I asked. I'm more than a little impressed with your efforts. I wanted to reward you. And to apologize for taking advantage."

"You . . . went all the way to Waltney, just to get me some cake?"

"It wasn't that far. I have a wizard door to a fellow master wizard there." He took another bite. "He didn't remember you. But he'd heard of your father."

I choked on the bite I'd just taken and coughed. When I got control of myself, I said, "Most people would. Papa is the town drunk."

"Yes. I didn't have to ask very far before I found him."

My stomach dropped. "M-my father?" I stuttered. "You found Papa?"

He shrugged and stared at his cake. "Just thought I'd look in on him for you. I know the two of you don't seem to talk, but aren't you curious now and then whether the old fellow's still breathing?" He took a bite, then another. "Devil's dawn, these Waltney cakes are delectable, aren't they? I'm almost sorry I didn't buy all the bakery had."

"Go back," I said. "To the part about Papa. Did you . . . talk to him?"

"Ah." He put down his fork. "So you *are* curious. Well, he's alive. I found him occupying a stool in the Oak and the Cross, every bit as inebriated as you promised he'd be."

Papa was alive. And still drunk. I didn't know whether to be pleased or disgusted. "What did he say?"

"Oh, I didn't talk to him. Didn't seem much point to it, him being drunk and all and you not having a very high opinion of him. I looked him over and left him some coin."

I sat up straighter. "You gave Papa money? Are you stupid?"

"He seemed bad off. I thought you'd appreciate the gesture."

"He'll only use it for drink," I said grudgingly. And then, because I sounded so ungrateful, I added, "But . . . thank you for the kindness."

We picked at our desserts in silence, until I broke it by asking, "Who'll wash your clothes, then?"

"Same person who did it before you. Mrs. Hanson or else Mrs. Pitts, or I can send it to Bramford. You did a better job than either of them, but that doesn't matter. If you hate doing it, it can't be helped."

Perhaps I should have felt guilty, but I didn't. I took another bite of cake and beamed at Ivan.

Mrs. Pitts entered the room and handed the master a piece

of paper. I glimpsed scrawled letters as the master opened it and scanned downward. From the faint trail of magic sparking around it, it must have come from the messenger.

Abruptly the master stood. "I'm needed in Bramford."

"What is it?"

Master nodded at me. "Get your robes, underwizard. You're coming along."

I rose to my feet, surprised. The master had often been called to Bramford, but never this late in the evening. Nor had he ever taken me with him before.

The man really was softening.

Ivan looked over the Waltney cakes that remained on the table. *No worry*, he gestured at us. *I eat cakes.*

By the time the master and I were seated in the carriage and Bramford-bound, night had fallen, and the weather outside had turned thick with falling snow. I had an uneasy feeling about our mode of travel in this weather. It was unfortunate that wizard doors were only permitted between the residences of wizards. This journey would be much quicker if there were a door that spilled out, say, into the middle of Bramford's town square.

Master Wendyn summoned a light in the palm of his hand so we weren't in complete dark. "I've been summoned to care for a sick child. The physician is miles away at a difficult child-birth, and the child has worsened. The parents want me to heal her."

A healing. It was a service I longed for Gavin to receive, but one which we couldn't afford. I envied these parents their wealth and stance in the community. Both had barred Gavin from the services of a master wizard. The unfairness of it made my stomach queasy.

I wanted to become a master wizard to bring healing spells to those like Gavin, those whose station in life rendered them unable to pay the fees of a master wizard. It hurt me to think my brother would be alive today if we'd had more money, or if Papa hadn't drunk so much of our earnings away, or if I had been a better thief, or if Papa and I had never thieved to begin with.

"What do you need me for? I'll just be in the way. I haven't learned healing spells." Lie. Feeling as I did about becoming a master wizard, to help those like Gavin, I read all three of Master Hapthwaite's books on healing. But I'd hardly memorized the spells, and nor had I ever dared to use the few that I could still remember, for fear of angering the Council. Healing magic was the thirteenth trial and only to be practiced under the auspices of my master.

"You can observe, if nothing else. It's time I started to bring you along on my calls to the local folk, no matter what people say. However, I thought you might be of particular use in this case. As I recall, your brother died from the same illness. I thought you might have immunity where I don't."

I grew still, and the master's face, already dim with shadows, blurred before my eyes. "The child has the wasting sickness?"

"Yes."

Hot and cold flooded through me, sensations of uncertainty and fear. I had the sudden wild desire to leap out of the carriage and run back to Ryker Hall. I didn't want to revisit my last hours with Gavin. The panic that rushed me felt similar to the long ago day in Bramford when I fought for Ivan and lost my apprenticeship.

"But . . . there have been no outbreaks near here."

"Not yet, anyway." The grimness in his voice made his message clear: this might be the beginning of an epidemic.

I was losing control.

No. I was in control.

Thunk-a thunk-a thunk-a thudded my heart. *Run run run*.

But then I remembered. The master would heal the child. I

wouldn't have to watch the suffering and wasting away as I did with my brother. This time I would see the opposite side of the illness. I'd watch the child recover and the family rejoice. The only pain would be in remembering my loss.

I was in control.

Now that my thoughts had turned to Gavin, I couldn't turn them away. We traveled the rest of the distance in silence. I stared out the window at the passing blur of white and remembered my brother.

EIGHTEEN

THE CARRIAGE GLIDED TO a silent stop in front of the one home with lights still burning. The master and I stepped out and tromped through a world of white to reach the house.

"Your hair is white," I said to the master. Even I could hear the nerves in my voice. I was nervous to be near Gavin's sickness once again, even though I knew it couldn't best Master Wendyn.

He shook the snow out of his dark hair and raised an eyebrow at me. "I might say the same for you, underwizard."

A round, red-cheeked housekeeper led us through the house to a room at the back, where we were met by the parents. They ran at Master Wendyn when they caught sight of him. I was struck by the noisy sound of labored breathing.

"Master Wendyn. Thank you for coming." The father's eyes flitted to me and back to the master. "It came on so sudden. She was fine yesterday."

"And now she's taken a turn," the mother wailed. "I'm afraid she won't last the night."

The master and I exchanged a glance. Wasting sickness rarely moved so quickly. What version of the illness was this?

"I will do everything I can. Stand aside." The master pushed past the two of them and motioned at me. "Come along, underwizard."

I hefted the master's bag of medicines, bowed my head, and followed.

The sickbed lay against one wall. I took one look at the girl, and it was Gavin all over again—the gray face, the fine sheen of perspiration covering her face and neck, the stillness. But she was younger than Gavin, perhaps only four or five. For a moment she stirred, and her innocent, childish face turned toward me. The cloth on her forehead fell to the floor, and I retrieved it and lay it back against her hot forehead. My fingers twitched with longing to smooth back the hair at the crown of her head, to let her know she wasn't alone, but I held myself back. She stilled, her face turned up, eyes closed.

The master muttered to himself as he touched her temples, lifted her limp wrist, and held an ear to her chest to listen to her breathing. After several minutes of this, he exhaled and turned. "The bag, underwizard." He motioned, and I held his medicines bag out to him. He rifled around in it and, a moment later, came up with a bottle of brown liquid. The cork came free, and he poured a small amount into a tin cup. "Feed her this."

Carefully, as I did countless times with Gavin, I raised the girl's head with one hand and held the cup to her mouth with the other. A small amount of liquid trickled inside her mouth, while a great deal more dribbled down her front. Disappointed, I looked up at the master, but he didn't appear displeased.

"Very good." He held his hands out and launched into a spell. It took a moment to recognize it from Master Hapthwaite's healing books. It was a soothing spell, meant to ease discomfort and pain. Next he went into a breathing spell, and from there on to several more spells I wasn't quick enough to identify. The master weaved strands of magic around the child that sparked against her skin and encased her in a subtle glow.

I mopped up the liquid I'd spilled down the girl's front with a rag and freshened the cloth on her forehead by dipping it in the basin of cool water next to the bed. Then left with nothing else to do, I stood back and observed Master Wendyn.

The few opportunities I'd seen him at work were in the library and ended with him angry or upset with me for various reasons. To my surprise, I found that he was at ease here, in a way I didn't think I'd seen him before. He maintained complete control, with no anger or dissatisfaction marring his face. He closed his eyes as he weaved elegant and intricate spells, and then he leaned down to check his patient's progress before launching into further magic.

Even more surprising, I found that I enjoyed watching him work. This was healing. This was what it would have been like if Gavin had had a master wizard to spell away his sickness. A feeling built in me, and at last I recognized it for what it was—hope. I very much wanted to see the master defeat this poor girl's wasting sickness. I wanted to see her on her feet with color in her cheeks, getting into mischief like other children.

But the painful rattle that filled the room never seemed to ease. If anything, it sounded worse. A furrow appeared between the master's brows.

"What is it?" the mother asked. "Is something wrong?" She watched the master's every move like a cat poised to pounce.

Master Wendyn frowned and turned to her. "My greatest apologies, Madam, but I will ask you to leave now," he said politely, "so we can work undistracted."

The request brought protests from the mother, but the father nodded and bore her out of the room himself.

"What's the matter?" I asked once the door clicked shut.

Master Wendyn shed his robes and loosened his sleeves before rolling them up to the elbow. "The sickness may have too tight a grip on her." He held the child's wrist once again and laid the back of his other hand against her cheek.

"Then perform more healing spells. There's no sickness so great that magic can't heal it." I dabbed at the sweat beading on her face.

"Magic isn't a panacea for all ills. It has its limitations too."

I stopped what I was doing and stared at him. "But . . . but that's not true. It can save anyone from illness, apart from old age."

"Anyone who isn't beyond saving." He rummaged around in his medicines bag.

"No, you're wrong. I've seen it."

He pulled out another bottle, this one filled with a greenish mixture, thick and slogging. "What have you seen?"

"There was a boy in Waltney. He fell from a great height, breaking many bones. The physician pronounced him too far gone to help. But the parents brought in a master wizard, and the boy lived. By magic. I've seen that boy many times, playing in the street. You'd never know he almost died."

"Then the boy was lucky." The master poured out a small amount of the green mixture into the tin cup. "Here. Feed her this."

The liquid looked and smelled like swamp water. I held it to the girl's mouth, careful this time to get less down her front and more down her throat. "And another time," I continued, placing the cup aside, "I saw a wizard bring a man back from the dead, right there in the Waltney town square."

"Why was he performing healing spells for an audience? Sounds like a swindler."

"He wasn't a swindler," I said hotly. "He was a good and

generous wizard, with potions and spells he sold to poor folk, unlike most master wizards." *Potions and spells to cure everything that ails you*, had been his cry up and down the streets.

"Ah. He was a peddler."

"Of a sort," I said reluctantly. "What has that to do with anything?"

"Peddling spells in the streets is prohibited for master wizards. If the man was a master wizard, I promise you he won't be once the Council catches up with him."

If the man was a master wizard. I felt as though the ground had been pulled from beneath me. Could the peddler have been a fraud? He was an inspiration to me, of sorts. The memory of him and his healing spells had been bright in my mind after Gavin died. It had pushed me on day and night as I disguised myself as a boy and traveled across the kingdom until I found Master Hapthwaite, the fourteenth wizard I'd petitioned to accept me as his apprentice. The one who finally agreed.

And now I found out that even if I became a master wizard, my power wouldn't be absolute. I'd still have to watch people die.

Had the last three years been based on a lie?

I was shaken back to awareness by the deep rattle of the child's breathing. Gavin had trouble near the end too. It didn't bode well that she hadn't awakened once due to our ministrations. What if we couldn't save her? She might die, just as Gavin did.

I wanted to be very, very far away when that happened.

Master Wendyn must have seen something of my thoughts on my face, because he barked at me, "Get a hold of yourself, underwizard. There's work to do."

The words shook me into an awareness of the dangerous direction my thoughts had taken, and shame coursed through me. I was ready to run and hide, just as Papa did. I was nothing but a coward.

A coward who was losing control.

I forced myself to speak. "What do you want me to do?"

"We're not giving up; not yet. You know about the wasting sickness. While I'm spell-casting, I want you to do what you can for the child."

"You mean . . . doctor her?"

"Yes."

I wavered and still didn't move.

The master's brow darkened, and he continued, "Unless you want her to die."

"But my doctoring won't save her," I insisted, as earnest as I'd ever been in my life. "I couldn't save Gavin, and I won't do her any good either."

He took me by the shoulders and gave me a little shake. "Underwizard," he said, his words sharp and loud, eyes steely, "magic alone can't save this girl. Likewise, your doctoring alone couldn't save your brother. Now we'll try both together and see if we can save her this way. Pull yourself together."

He turned back to the sickbed and launched into more spellcasting.

The master wasn't giving up. I couldn't either. Not while she still had a chance.

I hurried to the door and dictated to the parents a list of herbs and other ingredients I needed from the apothecary or botanist, whoever we could rouse at this late hour. Then I set to sponging the girl down with cold water to cool her overheated body.

I would do what I could. I'd do it for Gavin.

MY HEAD DROOPED, and I caught myself and straightened. The sun floated high in the sky and spilled in the only window of the child's bedroom, warming the floor. I blinked and focused my eyes. My head leaned against the bed while the rest of me sat on the floor. I'd dozed off yet again.

"Sleep, underwizard." The master's voice sounded hoarse and strained, almost a mere whisper. Weariness reflected in every line of his body as he sat at the foot of the bed. Slumped, really. "It's all right. I will watch."

All night and morning we'd worked over the child together, he muttering hoarse spells while I administered teas and poultices and massaged oils into her limbs to promote healing.

I scrubbed at my face and slapped my cheeks to wake myself up. "No. No, you sleep. You're the one who's been spellcasting all night long. I don't know how you have any energy left. You must be flat out of magic."

A faint smile passed over his mouth. "There's always magic, remember?"

His tenacity had surprised me. No, more than surprised —astonished.

I pushed myself to my knees. "I should change her poultice." The rattle of her breathing had eased, and her cheeks had taken on a faint pink hue, but the child still hadn't awakened. At least her parents had retired to sleep a few hours ago, convinced of her improvement.

Master Wendyn resumed his hoarse spellcasting as I pulled the poultice off of her chest. Midway through its replacement, a pounding sounded somewhere below stairs. The master and I exchanged a glance. Minutes later, the door opened. The red-cheeked housekeeper poked her face in, her cap askew. "I'm very sorry—" she began, but before she could say anything more, a large man pushed his way past her into the sickroom.

His contemptuous glance took in the room. "Master Wendyn," he said. "I heard you had brought your apprentice here, but I couldn't believe you'd do it, after our agreement." The voice and face were familiar, and after staring in consternation for a moment, the man's identity came to me. He was the man from Bramford town square all those months ago, the one who knocked me down and concussed me.

Master Wendyn stepped in front of me. "Harris," he said in his hoarse voice. "We've been busy here all night, as you can see." He gestured at the bed. "Why don't we talk about this where we won't disturb the child?"

"What agreement?" I asked. But before I could get any more out, Harris threw a spell at me with a point of his fingers and muttered words. I stood frozen in place, unable to move even a muscle.

"And no words out of the likes of you. You lost the right to speak or even show your face here in Bramford," he said.

"Did you really, an amateur magician, just dare to spell my underwizard?" Master Wendyn asked, a dangerous edge to his voice that I'd never heard before.

"You know well enough that that boy and the fool aren't welcome in Bramford," Harris said, though he backed off a step in the face of the master's clear wrath. "You agreed that if either should dare to show their faces again, the town council could decide the punishment."

Was that why the master never brought me to Bramford? And not that he disliked me?

Then again, I supposed it could be both.

I struggled against the spell holding me mobile, but it was no use. This was just like that time with Kurke in the library.

"I needed the underwizard here. I wasn't about to let this child die because the Bramford Council condones the torture of children while my underwizard did not."

"So you didn't just forget—" Harris began and then broke off. "What torture?"

"That's right, torture. Even the Wizard's Council has agreed Underwizard Mullins was in the right in his defense of the fool, who was being tormented perhaps to death by local boys. Are you prepared to disagree with that decision?"

"Well, torture's a little strong . . ." Harris stuttered before trailing off.

"It's accurate. Now, if you ever dare to threaten my underwizard or the fool—his name is Ivan—again, or to spell either of them, I will not hesitate to curse you in the manner you deserve. Now get out."

The man's face had gone pale, and he looked as astonished as I felt. I knew my master and I had been getting along better than we had in the past, but I never would have expected him to stand up so thoroughly in defense of me.

Behind me an audible intake of breath sounded, and a small voice asked, "Where is Mama?"

I would turn if I could, but as it was, I couldn't even blink.

"There, see what you've done," the master said, turning to look. "You've woken her, and just when she was sleeping so soundly. Well, didn't you hear me? Leave. Now."

After a brief pause, I heard the door click shut.

"I'm Marybeth," a childish voice said behind me. "Who're you?"

Master Wendyn pointed a hand at me and muttered words, and just like that, the freezing spell ended. I sagged and then turned to find two brown eyes trained on me, inside the childish face of the girl I had been caring for nigh on to twelve hours now.

We. *We* had been caring for.

"How are you feeling?" I asked her, bending down to her level. "Does anything hurt? Are you unwell?"

"Where's Mama?" she asked again.

The master's hand fell on my shoulder, and I straightened. "You've heard the young lady, underwizard. She'd like her mother. While you're fetching her, I suggest you call the carriage too. Our charge seems much better, and I'd like to get home and rest. I think I've overspent myself. Now, if you don't mind, I'm afraid I'm going to faint."

Master Wendyn toppled to the floor.

THE CARRIAGE shimmied and swayed back and forth, throwing the master's head against my shoulder. I opened my eyes, chagrined to find I had dozed off, even for a moment, and leaned his head back against the opposite side of the carriage. The conveyance was too small and the master too tall to lay him down lengthwise. Therefore I had to ride next to him to see he didn't crumple to the floor.

I patted my cheeks and willed myself to stay awake. Just until we reached the hall so I could make sure the master arrived safely.

His hand rested against my leg. Looking at the long, limp fingers, I recalled his countless hours of spellcasting. I told him he needed to rest, but did he listen? No, he was so stubborn he kept at it until he had no strength left.

Nevertheless, I had to admit I was impressed with—and grateful for—his tenacity. Without it we might have lost the child.

Marybeth. After the master's faint, I slid a pillow under his head and fetched the child's mother. They brought food, and the little girl ate and ate and insisted on climbing out of bed to pat the sleeping "Mister Doctor" on the head. Then she ran to the window and twirled about the room.

She'd fallen into another exhausted slumber as I readied the master to leave, carrying him to the carriage with the help of two servants, since I didn't have the strength to perform a lifting spell.

Together, the master and I had defeated the wasting sickness.

A yawn took hold of me. I stretched and sat back again, my eyes growing misty with sleep, at least until the master coughed. Then I caught myself and sat up, glancing at him. Was he awake?

His eyes were closed, but his mouth moved in the next moment.

"Devil's dawn, but I'm tired," he said without opening his eyes. "I apologize for fainting. I overdid it, I suppose."

"But the child is well, or will be soon," I said, and I couldn't keep the relief and happiness out of my voice. "Thanks to you."

"Thanks to both of us." He opened his eyes and looked at me for the first time with his bloodshot eyes. A faint smile played about his mouth. "You did well, underwizard. I wasn't certain we'd be successful, but I'm glad we were."

"I was afraid it would be Gavin all over again."

His eyes closed again.

"What did Harris mean about your agreement? Am I not welcome in Bramford?"

He sighed and opened his eyes. "The town council was in favor of keeping you and Ivan imprisoned for the period of a year. They wouldn't let you come with me unless I promised neither of you would return for at least that long."

"I can't say I'm sorry to hear that. Odious town."

He chuckled. "I imagine Ivan feels the same way."

I pondered the information until Master Wendyn broke the quiet again.

"Days like today remind me why I became a master wizard.

Sometimes I grow tired of it. The monotony, the bureaucratic nonsense, the limitations. Thank you for helping me remember."

"I—you're—you're welcome. I suppose."

"Can I ask you a question?"

"Of course. You're my master."

"Most master wizards won't refuse to heal someone when a life is in danger. Why is it that your brother wasn't offered that service?"

I swallowed. It felt as though a rock had lodged in my throat. "The Mullins family didn't have a great reputation in Waltney. I visited Master Norwood several times, but his housekeeper refused to admit me. I'd beaten her son a few times, you see. She relented when she heard how sick Gavin was and sent me a note to come speak to the master wizard. But I was busy tending to Gavin by then, and when I visited, Master Norwood had left town."

"But why do you blame your father? It sounds like it was that housekeeper's fault, more than anyone else."

"I never said I blame him."

"Yes, you did. At the last trial."

Oh. That was right. Forgiveness. We had talked about many embarrassing things there on the testing dais. I was mortified to think Master Wendyn had paid attention during any of that.

"It makes as much sense to blame your mother for your brother's death," he continued.

"Mama wasn't alive when Gavin died."

"That's my point."

I blinked and stared at him as memories came. The early days after Mama's death, when I was angry and morose—angry with her for dying. "Perhaps I am too quick to blame. I used to despise my mother, you know. I felt like she sacrificed herself for my family, for Gavin and me and Papa, working herself to death when she didn't have to. There were other ways we could have filled the kitchen larder, other ways to keep shoes on our feet. And Papa just let her. No, more than that, he encouraged her."

"Listen to yourself. Do you think that makes sense? Your mother was a grown woman. She made her own decisions."

"You're right. That's what I realized after time had passed. Mama knew what she was doing. I understand the appeal of that now. I'd rather give up my life willingly for someone I care about than have it taken in a manner I have no say over."

He nodded, his eyes closed. "I'm impressed, underwizard. That's a deep idea. Deeper than I'm able to comprehend at the moment." He exhaled again, deep. "Answer me this: since the man is your father, don't you think that earns him a little respect, at least?"

"He's had his bit of respect and used up the right to have any more."

Master Wendyn ran a hand over his face. "Weren't there any good times?"

Unwillingly, I remembered the time before Mama got sick. Papa used to work hard then. We took outings to the lake. Papa played games with me and Gavin and talked about how we would go to school someday. He used to tease us and have a sense of humor.

"I suppose so," I admitted.

"Your father's lost his family too, you know."

"Why are you so determined to stick up for him?" I couldn't hide the irritation in my voice. "Since when did you become Papa's champion?"

"I don't know. He looked so lonely and lost sitting on that stool in the tavern. The man is clearly lost."

"If he's lost his family, it's his own fault. He quit working, stole every coin there was until we had nothing to eat, and ruined Mama and Gavin's health." Irritating conversation. "Anyway, you're one to talk about forgiveness. What about your brother and Cailyn?"

He laid his head back against the carriage seat and frowned. "Why bring them up?"

His nosiness about Papa had made me bold—perhaps bolder than I should have been. "You realize it's just your pride that was hurt by their marriage, right?"

Irritation quirked his brow. "You know nothing."

"Feels like you giving me advice on my father, doesn't it?"

He snorted. "Point taken."

Silence stretched between us, and I could tell the master had drifted into his own thoughts. Melancholy played about his weary eyes and mouth, and his face settled into a vulnerable expression. Something like sympathy beat through my chest. "Do you—do you still love her?"

He sighed and dropped his arm over his face, leaned back against the carriage cushions as he was. "No. I suppose not. That died a long time ago."

"So all that's left is your pride. She didn't want your heart, so you don't want to see them happy together."

"All right. You're a little bit correct. But you don't know everything about my past."

"Then tell me."

"I'd rather not. Sleep sounds too appealing at the moment."

He lapsed into silence, and I thought he had fallen asleep—until he spoke again.

"That freezing spell is a problem. An amateur magician bested you. You must learn how to fight it."

"But no one can overcome the freezing spell."

"How do you know?"

"Master Hapthwaite told me."

The master's eyes closed again, as though he couldn't find the strength to keep them open. "The laziness of the man. You can overcome almost any spell, given the right circumstances, although I doubt any book on magic will tell you so. I'm telling you this from my experience." He laughed, the sound dry and scratchy. "Devil's dawn, I shouldn't tell you this." He sat up straighter and rubbed at his eyes, looking at me again. "I used to know a boy who was fond of freezing spells. I experimented at ways to remove the spell once cast. After several failed attempts, I realized the best way is to distract whoever is casting the spell *as* they cast it."

I frowned. "What good does that do?"

He rubbed at his eyes again. "Cast a freezing spell on me, and I'll show you."

I gave him one more skeptical look and then commenced in preparations for the spell, gathering the magic to me that I could find. Just as I uttered the words to the spell, he shocked me by reaching out and tickling me in the side.

Instinct made me slap his hand away, although it was pointless—the words to the spell were out, and he sat frozen in place, his eyes staring forward blearily with their abundance of red cobwebs crisscrossing them. For the space of three breaths he didn't move an inch. But then, as I watched, his eyebrow twitched, and then his neck, until all at once he was free of the spell. He shrugged and held his hands out. "See? Simple."

"What—how did you do that?" I asked with astonishment.

"Distraction," he said with some satisfaction. "It creates weaknesses within the spell. Once the spell is cast, all you have to do is feel for the strands of magic that hold the spell together. A distracted spell will be full of holes, and you can find your way out of it."

"You mean to say you tickled a bully so you could get out of his freezing spell?"

He snorted. "Of course not. There are endless ways to distract someone. Shouting, quick movements, even pretending to faint." He yawned a giant yawn. "Yes, I'll admit I wasn't above—" yawn, "—trying that one a time or two." He exhaled and sat back, his eyes closed. "I'm sorry, underwizard, but could we cut this short? I'm afraid I—can't keep—my eyes open."

And he was asleep again.

I took a moment to look at him, really look at him, as I had never been able to when he was awake. He was not a bad looking man. Rather handsome, with his dark hair and eyes and confident air.

My insides warmed at the thought of his staunch defense of me today. Was it possible we were at last achieving the closeness I saw between so many other masters and apprentices, the tight friendship that would last a lifetime? I thought I had that once, with Master Hapthwaite, but I had been wrong about that. I yawned, leaned my head back, and took one last look at the master.

In sleep, worry and anger lines had faded from his face, leaving only a smooth and peaceful expression. He had never appeared more inviting. At another jolt from the carriage, he flopped against me, head on my shoulder once again.

Oh, what was the use. He was stable as he was, and I couldn't keep my eyes open. I'd leave him where he was and close my eyes, just for a moment—

A lurch forward threw me awake, and I caught myself. We'd rumbled to a stop, and I rubbed at my face. Where were we? I brushed the curtains aside to look out the window. Ryker Hall rose from the snowy fields, its white-capped shutters looking almost cheerful today. I turned to check on the master, and jumped when I realized he was watching me.

"Oh. You're awake."

"Yes."

"I didn't mean to sleep. How do you feel?"

His mouth worked for a moment. His expression was not quite what it should be, and a ribbon of unease worked its way through me.

"Mullins," he said at last, clearing his throat. "How long have you been a girl?"

NINETEEN

I SLUMPED IN MY chair, hands covering my face. The sound of Master Wendyn's pacing brought me no comfort. From one side of his study to the other, his boots tapped a furious rhythm across the floor. He muttered a spell.

The worst had happened. Why, oh why, had I fallen asleep?

"There." Barely controlled fury filled the master's voice. "I've finished with the privacy spell. Now—*now* you're going to explain yourself."

I rubbed at my eyes where exhaustion lingered and tried to dull my senses. Then, as I couldn't seem to look him full in the face, I settled for staring at the ground while I tried to come up with a plan.

"Well?" he barked. "Speak. And please, just try lying. I've cast a deception defense spell, and you'll be rather uncomfortable every time more false words come out of your mouth. I'm not a vindictive man on the whole, but I think I'd enjoy inflicting a little pain right now."

"What do you want me to say? I'm—I'm a girl." I had to push the words out. Admitting to three and a half years of subterfuge did not come easy. I couldn't deny that a part of me was relieved. The truth was out. There would be no more lies of my making between us.

Except for the whole killing Oscar thing.

"Sit up and look at me when I'm talking to you." His voice sounded harsher than I'd heard it—maybe ever.

I straightened and raised my eyes to meet his. The anger there made me quake, but I forced myself to hold his gaze.

His jaw ticked. "Let loose your hair."

"What?"

"Your hair, underwi—girl. Loose it."

With fingers that fumbled, I unwound the tie that held my hair back. Brown waves tumbled around my face.

He peered at me, scrutinizing me in a way that caused me to blush. After several seconds he backed away, fingers shoved into his hair. "Devil's dawn. You must be mad to think you can get away with this. You *look* like a girl."

"It's only because of my hair. Even boys look feminine with long hair."

He snorted. "No boys look like *that* with their hair down. Perhaps it escaped my notice for a time, but that was before the —before the carriage." His expression turned uncomfortable. Was he blushing?

"The carriage?" What had happened while I was asleep? And did I even want to know? Judging by the odd expression he had taken on, maybe not.

He saw something of what I was thinking. "Nothing inappropriate took place." His voice was sharp as tacks. "At least, it wouldn't have been inappropriate if you were a boy. You were supposed to be a boy."

This was maddening. "Tell me what happened."

He ran a hand over his eyes. "You leaned into me. Or maybe I leaned into you. Or both of us together. I just wanted to push you against the other side of the carriage. But I noticed when I took hold of you that—your form is more feminine than it ought to be."

"Feminine?" I would die of embarrassment. No need to imagine where he grabbed me.

I wanted to rail against him, but I didn't have any legs to stand on in this argument. I didn't know where to look. My face flamed with fire. I became very absorbed in tying my hair back once again.

After another moment of awkward silence, he pivoted and walked to his desk, whisking an item into his hands. He seated himself in his high-backed chair, turning the thing over and over. Light caught and gleamed along the sleek rounded metal: a trammel.

"And your voice?" He tilted an eyebrow at me. "You must be doing something to make yourself sound so male. Is it a spell, or have you always spoken at such a low pitch?"

Would he make me reveal all my secrets? Would I have to tell him about the soiling spell for the monthly bleeding and the binding that made my bosom lie flat? I cleared my throat. "It's just a little magic."

"End it."

I regarded him uneasily. "Are you gathering evidence to report to the Council?"

"Perhaps. I don't see where you have room to object." The trammel clicked open in his hands and then closed again.

He was right, and what was more, I knew a threat when I heard it. "Very well." I muttered the words to cease the voice-modulating spell. The thick, deep feeling in my throat lightened.

"Say something. I want to hear your true voice."

"I don't know what you want me to say." My voice had returned to its regular soft huskiness.

He cursed, and the trammel clunked against the desk as he

pushed to his feet. "I knew it. I knew you sounded different on the testing dais, but I put it down to nerves." He pushed fingers into his hair and paced behind the desk. "I'm a fool. Of epic proportions."

Guilt crept in as I watched him. My lies had brought my confident, unshakable master to this. I should apologize, but was an apology enough? It seemed such a paltry nothing when faced with all the lies I had told. Still, it was all I had.

I opened my mouth. "I'm sor—"

He turned his angry glare in my direction. "Don't say it. I know you don't mean it, and you'll regret it. Deception defense is quite painful."

Hurt flooded me that he thought I wasn't sincere, but I forged ahead anyway. "I *am* sorry. I'll admit that when I began this charade, I was only thinking of myself. All I knew was I wanted to be a master wizard. For my brother. Gavin never got his chance at wizardry, or even life. I couldn't bear the thought of that happening to anyone else."

He shook his head. "The Council doesn't care about your motives. When they find out, you'll be Punished just like Ingerman."

A desert spell headache had begun, and I rubbed at the ache in my forehead. "I know. I knew the risks from the beginning."

"And you still did it? Are you a fool?"

I shrugged. There seemed nothing more to be said.

"What about Master Hapthwaite? Did he know you're a girl?"

I didn't like his expression, the suspicion mingled with disgust. "Of course he didn't. He would have—" I broke off, because I didn't want to say it. Master Hapthwaite would have turned me in to the Council if he'd known. But I didn't want to put voice to those words and remind the master that was just what he should do.

But he had caught on anyway. "He would have turned you in, am I right? Just as I should." He fell into his chair, head in his hands.

The words of the oblivion were beyond my reach, knocked loose by the unexpectedness of the situation. But I wasn't fool-hardy enough to attempt such a spell while he was this angry. At my first chance, I had to escape from this house and flee, or risk the Punishment.

We sat there in silence for what seemed an eternity. Nothing I said could make this right, and I knew it. At last the master raised his head and stared at me. "I must be a fool too." His voice no longer held anger, just weariness. "A stupid fool."

Well, at least he'd stopped shouting. Perhaps now was a good time to beg for mercy. My lips felt like rubber, but I forced them to move. "Please," I said, and I hated the pleading I heard in my voice. "I know I have no place asking anything, but I'm asking just the same. Please let me leave here before you tell the Council. Give me a day or two head start before you turn me in."

He shook his head, and my stomach sank to my toes. "Mullins," he said, pushing to his feet to walk closer to the window. Quiet suffused his tone, and the half of his face I could see was bathed in brilliant white light from the sun reflecting off the snow outside. "What makes you think I'll turn you in at all?"

It was the last thing I expected him to say. "Wh—what?" I squeaked. "But why wouldn't you?"

He walked fully into the light, as though reaching for its warmth. "Do you realize how much of a fool I would look? We make up a small community, master wizards. Word would get out. I would be a laughingstock."

His self-serving reasoning surprised me. "So you won't tell?"

"I've said as much." Irritation laced his tone. "I won't bother asking the same of you, as I've seen how you value promises."

The words stung. I responded hotly, "That's not fair. I've been honest in every way, except—"

"Except the most basic thing you could have lied about. And if you lied about this, what other secrets are you keeping?"

I opened my mouth and realized I couldn't claim there was nothing else. I had pledged to kill his grandfather.

"I see." He turned his head at my silence, to look me full in the face. "You have nothing to say to that, so I can only assume there are so many lies you've told that you don't even know where to begin."

Just as we were establishing a real friendship, I had lost it. I didn't know if it mattered that I had his trust, in the grand scheme of my web of lies, but losing it hurt. "I will never tell anyone I am a girl. All I want is to become a master wizard."

"So you've said. Do you think the Council will accept that excuse when faced with all the lies you've told them?"

I swallowed, hating that he was right. "No," I said in a tiny voice. I scratched my nose.

He wiped a hand across his eyes. "Does anyone else know?"

"Uh . . . well, Orly."

"That librarian's daughter? Oh, I see now. All this time I thought you were flirting, you were just sharing your secrets. I suppose that means Edie knows too."

"Edie doesn't know anything," I said stoutly. "I never shared any secrets. Orly guessed."

He pinched the bridge of his nose. "Fine. Anyone else?"

I pressed my lips together and tried to think. "Mmm . . . I don't think I've ever said as much to Ivan, but I'm pretty sure he knows."

"So Orly and Ivan. An oblivion spell would take care of both of them."

My mouth opened. "That's not necessary. Orly's known for

several years and hasn't told anyone. And Ivan's no danger to me."

He raised an eyebrow. "You want them to know?"

There had been something nice in knowing my secret was safe with Orly and Ivan, in knowing that I had two people on my side, come what may. For so long I had been on my own, and now I didn't have to be. I squared my shoulders. "Yes, I do. I trust them both."

He shook his head, as though he couldn't understand my reasoning. "Fine. That's everyone that knows?"

Here it was, my chance to come clean. "Well," I said carefully. "There's also . . ." But it was no use. I could feel that blasted forgetfulness hovering, waiting to hammer down on me if I so much as tried to say *Matt*.

"Yes?" Master Wendyn tapped his foot. "There's also who?"

"M—" I started, and blank fog descended on my brain. I blinked and blinked and looked around me. The master stood before me, a shrewd look on his face. We were in his study. My eyes felt dry and scratchy, and an unutterable weariness rested along my tense shoulders.

I rubbed at my nose.

"Well?" Master Wendyn folded his arms. "Is there anyone else who knows or isn't there?"

Bits of our conversation came back to me. I'd tried, once again, to tell him about Kurke. But I couldn't force the words out. I'd need to try a different tack.

"Master Wendyn, who do you consider your closest friend?"

He frowned. "No games. I've had enough of those from you."

"This isn't a game, I promise. Just answer me who is your closest friend." Confidence surged within me. I knew how he'd answer this question: Matthias Kurke. And then I'd tell him he'd just answered his own question.

His jaw tightened, and all at once he turned and kicked viciously at the desk leg. Books and paper scattered across it and onto the floor. "Blast it all, Mullins, stop treating this apprenticeship like a game. Fine, you want to know who my closest friend is? At this point in our apprenticeship, it should have been *you*. But come to find out you're just a liar with an agenda."

"But—"

"No." He held up a hand and didn't look at me, as he moved behind the desk straightening things that had tumbled with his kick. "We'll discuss this no further. You will continue your training, at least until I figure a way out of this mess. That's the only concession I'm willing to make for today. Now I'd like to be alone." He didn't look up, not even once, and from the formidable frown on his face I knew he needed time to cool off.

I stood there for a moment. We'd lost something in our relationship, and I felt it keenly in that moment. I opened my mouth to say something—what?—but there was nothing to say. I closed my mouth and left the room.

In the hallway, I leaned my head against the closed door and breathed out. I should be relieved. I was still an apprentice, at least for now.

But somehow it didn't feel like a victory.

TWENTY

IN THE WEEK THAT followed, Master Wendyn kept to himself and avoided mealtime and the library. He didn't even bother leaving me any instructions, such as spells to work on or books to read to prepare myself for the fourth and fifth trials. It was as though, despite his words, he thought of himself as without an apprentice.

For a time I tried to study and wandered around the library whenever I got bored, looking over Ivan's shoulder at his drawings. It got quiet there in the library, with only an occasional hand-conversation to interrupt. At one point I looked out the window and saw Edie and Edwin near the stables, conversing in the chilly air. Small puffs of steam came from each of their mouths as they talked, and Edwin put a hand to Edie's arm. Their relationship had deepened since I first introduced them, and Edie had been far less smothering of late.

My plan had worked.

When I could distract Ivan from drawing, I asked him how his unknotting spell was coming. He pulled out the bit of rope—at least he was carrying it around—and stared at the knot in concentration. It didn't move.

"You'll get it," I encouraged. "Just keep trying."

Maybe, he gestured. *Look this.*

He retrieved his drawing pad and flipped through the pages, drawings of cows in the meadow, snow in the forest, the library shelves. At last he stopped on a drawing of a boy with bound hands. It resembled Ivan.

"But . . . why did you draw this?"

You look, he gestured. He held a hand over the drawing. After a moment of clear concentration, he stopped and looked at me, as though he expected a reaction.

"What? What do you want me to—" But I broke off when I glimpsed the sketch again. The picture of Ivan no longer had bound hands. He stood unbound, loose rope dangling from his fingers.

"What in the—" I said.

Ivan grinned.

I didn't know how he did it or what it meant, but I made him show it to me three more times. *Just think spell,* he told me when I demanded how he did it. *Think spell and hands untie.*

"The unknotting spell?" I clarified, just to be certain. He nodded.

But I tried it and couldn't reproduce his results.

It might be the oddest thing I'd ever seen. I would ask Master Wendyn about it when I got a chance, if he ever spoke to me again.

With Ivan absorbed in his drawing, the master angry at me, and no trials to prepare for now that Orly had shown me the secret to unlocking my magic, I made my way to my room to find an occupation. I found it when I glimpsed Orly's blood magic book on my desk.

She'd be expecting it returned soon, so I should use it while I could.

I flipped through a few pages of the book before I remembered that I needed a Belanokian dictionary. Tomorrow would be a trial day. If I could get away from the master long enough, perhaps I could borrow a dictionary from the library. But how would I smuggle it home?

Don't borrow trouble. I'd worry about that when the time came.

When I left my room at noon to go downstairs for the meal, I encountered Edie dusting knickknacks halfheartedly. She brightened when she saw me.

"Avery. I need to talk to you."

"Oh?"

"It's—it's about us," she said in a hushed voice, looking around as though afraid of being overheard.

I didn't like the sound of that word 'us.'

"All right. What do you mean, 'us'?"

Her face sank into a frown, eyes large and mournful and beautiful. I thought she might cry.

"I've found someone else," she said all at once, in a loud whisper. "Someone wonderful. I didn't mean to. It sort of . . . happened."

Relief rushed me. "Oh. That's—that's—" But I couldn't say what I really wanted to say: *That's wonderful!* And: *Thank the heavens!* Instead, I inserted into the silence, "I'm glad you're happy, Edie."

She put a hand to my arm. "You're a good friend, Avery Mullins. I'll never forget you."

I had to own I'd never forget her either. She turned and hurried away, her dusting brush swinging from one hand as though she'd just shed a giant weight from her shoulders.

I certainly felt as though I had.

"HAVE YOU SEEN MASTER WENDYN?" I asked Ivan at breakfast the next morning.

In study. Ivan barely looked up from his heavily buttered biscuit.

"I hope he's eaten something in there. It's a trial day. Do you think he's forgotten?"

Ivan shrugged.

I knocked on the door to the master's study fifteen minutes later.

"What do you want?" Through the door, the master's voice didn't sound inviting. Nevertheless, I took it as an invitation to enter, turning the knob and pushing the heavy door open. The master sat at his desk in one of his foppish shirts, lace tangled at his throat and sleeves pushed up to his elbows, looking as casually handsome as usual. He didn't look at me.

"Er," I said, standing there in the doorway. "It's a trial day. I'm taking the fourth and fifth trials. Have you forgotten?"

"No. Go ahead." He waved at the tapestry without looking at me. His eyes fixed on the paper upon which he scrawled.

"But . . . aren't you coming?" I squeaked.

"No."

He didn't even care enough to come to my trial. He'd abandoned his responsibility.

But on the bright side, at least I'd be able to visit the library uninhibited.

I hesitated for a moment, waiting for him to say something, anything. Maybe bark at me to take Ivan along or something. When he said nothing, I inserted into the silence, "Can you at least tell me if there have been any more cases?"

He looked at me for the first time. "Cases of what?"

"The wasting sickness. Does anyone else need healing?"

"That's not for you to worry about any longer."

"But—"

"There haven't been." He bent to the paper again.

"Ivan's drawing in the library."

He grunted in response.

"Do you want me to take him with me?"

He put his pen down and looked at me. "Do whatever you like, Mullins. Just get out of my study. I have work to do."

It grated on me that he called me Mullins rather than under-wizard. He hadn't called me by my official title once since he discovered my gender.

I stepped to the tapestry, pushing it aside with one hand. The wizard door shimmered beyond, beckoning me to the Conclave. Behind me, the master's gaze pushed against my back. I couldn't stop myself from looking over my shoulder. Our eyes met.

"Well? Are you going or not?"

I licked my lips, which suddenly seemed parched, as though all the air had been sucked out of the room in preparation for what I was about to say. "You'll have to pay attention to me eventually, you know. I'm your apprentice."

His lips thinned.

I took courage from the fact he hadn't launched into a lecture. "I am trustworthy," I said, and though I could tell my voice was too eager, I couldn't stop myself from pleading my case. "Give me another chance, and I'll show you. Please, you must."

His jaw ticked. "The only thing I must do is see you're no longer my responsibility as soon as possible. Now get out."

My stomach sank, and I turned my eyes back to the tapestry. I'd been hurt far worse than this. Words said by my father, master wizards who chased me from their property with various unpleasant spells, or the jailer in Bramford who kicked me in the head. The master's words shouldn't hurt me any worse than any of those times, but they did. It felt like a strike to the face, and my throat ached.

I'd grown soft toward Master Wendyn. I'd given him the power to hurt me. When did I do that? And why?

The spell to open the door came through my stiff lips, a bare whisper. I hoped he wasn't watching as my shaking fingers took hold of the doorknob and turned.

IT WAS different waiting for my name to be called without my master by my side. I felt conspicuous, as though everyone was staring. When my name was called, at long last, the proctor stared at me as though I'd grown a second head when I announced my master wasn't with me.

"He isn't strictly required to be present, but still . . ." he trailed off, and what he'd left unspoken was clear. It was unusual.

During the fourth trial, I had to explain all the times I'd experienced humiliation. It was an embarrassingly long list. Then I created a small spring bubbling up from the center of the dais. It was a shame the master wasn't there to see how well I'd done, and that his joked-about rowboat wasn't even needed. I passed with minimal discussion from the judges.

During the fifth trial, we discussed mastery over self, and I confessed the times when I'd lost control over my own emotions. Then I reported what a man several rooms away whispered to himself. This time there were no missteps or out-of-control magic. I felt a singular sense of satisfaction as the test proctor announced that I had passed.

The satisfaction slipped away when I remembered I had arrived back where I began before Master Wendyn stripped me of all my levels. I'd done as he asked and passed all five trials in three months. But with what had happened, would he keep me as his apprentice, or was it too late?

ORLY'S FACE broke into a beatific smile when she saw me cross the library's foyer, and she balanced the stack of books she held on one arm to wave at me. The ache in my throat eased, and I managed a smile back. I headed in her direction, listening to the soft lull of library sounds: the hushed murmur of lowered voices, the whisper of turning pages, the tap of my own footsteps as I crossed the floor. The ordinariness of the noises soothed my mind so I could almost forget the look of repulsion on Master Wendyn's face when he looked at me. Almost.

"How did the trials go?" She deposited her stack of books behind the counter, then leaned down to sweep another stack into her arms. "I set these aside for you days ago. Perhaps we can go somewhere quiet and discuss the finer points of—" she looked at the top book and continued, "—summertide demilunes." She hoisted the books higher in her arms and gestured with her chin toward the back of the library and our customary empty room. "Follow me." We weaved through mazes of tables and bookshelves, through narrow aisles with stacks of books looming on either side. She dumped her armload of books on the table and closed the door.

"Here, sit." She pushed me into a chair and pulled out another for herself so that we sat across the table from one another. "I can see you're upset. Did you fail the trials?"

I looked at her miserably, then waved my hand, muttering the words of the privacy spell. Better that no one should overhear this. "I passed. But he didn't even come. He knows."

"Knows what? Who knows?"

"Master Wendyn. He knows I'm a girl."

Her eyes widened. "How?"

The whole story spilled out of me: the carriage ride, the silent past days, his extraordinary talent at shunning. How he wanted me gone.

"Wait. So he's not turning you in to the Council? He didn't want you Punished?" She leaned back in her chair and folded her arms.

I threw my hands in the air. "I don't know what he wants. Pretty sure *he* doesn't even know what he wants, other than not having to look at me anymore. I don't know what to do."

She pursed her lips. "Show him you're an honest person. Prove to him your ability and don't lie to him ever again. I'm sure you can regain his trust."

"How do I prove anything to him? He won't even spend five seconds in the same room with me if he can help it. He wants to be rid of me."

"I don't know." She played with a lock of her hair as she mulled over that problem. "Maybe you should just do as he asks, then. Maybe you should just leave. Find another master."

"Oh, sure. Because it was so easy to find the first one."

A smile played across her mouth. "Admit it. It's kind of romantic he doesn't want you Punished. Is it possible he has feelings for you?"

I choked. "Feelings?" I sputtered. "Don't be ridiculous. The only feeling he has for me is contempt. Until two weeks ago, he thought I was a boy."

"Yes, but he wants you gone, not dead. It's a little romantic, at least."

"Romantic that he stops short of murder? Yes, the man is obviously besotted. I myself am wildly in love with everyone I don't want to kill." I pushed my chair back and paced the room, agitated at the idea of romance between myself and the master.

A giggle escaped her. "Wouldn't that be something, though?

A master in love with his apprentice? Or an apprentice with . . . her master?"

I glared at her. "I assure you, there is no danger of that happening."

"Well, of course. You wouldn't fall in love on purpose, would you? That sort of thing happens by accident, before you even know it." She clasped her hands together. "By the time you realize it, there's nothing you can do about it. You're in love."

I made a noise of frustration in the back of my throat. "Stop acting like a child, Orly. This isn't some romance novel. Not everything ends with true love and a happy ending." I knew my tone had been too harsh when I saw the hurt in her eyes, but I was too irked to stop myself now. "Have you even seen Ingerman's shattered barrel out there? This is my life and death we're talking about here, not some lark."

"I know it's not a romance novel." Hurt shone in her eyes. "I understand what's involved. I'd have to, wouldn't I? Do you think I wouldn't learn all about the risks before I become an apprentice myself?"

"*What?*"

She drew backward. "You heard me. I'm going to be an apprentice too. I'll run away and disguise myself as a boy and find a master, just like you."

I rose without even realizing it. "You will not."

"Oh, so it's all very well for you to do it, but no one else? You're just afraid I'll be a better apprentice than you."

I laughed, but without humor. "Better than me? Don't be ridiculous—of course you would be. That's not the point, though, is it? You have a father who loves you, Orly."

She came to her feet too. "So do you. I read your record. I know your father's still alive."

I shook my head. "My father is the most selfish person I know. I despise him. Do you think if I had a family who cared for me that I would just leave them? Tell them nothing about where I was going and just disappear? It's cruel. It's unnecessary."

"That shows your lack of dedication," she said with a determined lift of her chin. "*I* would."

I closed my eyes and then opened them to pin her with a look. "Orly. Be reasonable. I would trade everything I have right now just to have a family who cares for me again. Don't give up your father so easily."

"Papa will still be here when I'm done with my training." Her mouth had a stubborn set to it, and from the defiance in her eyes, I could see she wasn't about to change her mind.

"Very well." I folded my arms. "If you persist in this, then I'm going out there right now to tell your father your plan."

Her eyes widened. "You wouldn't."

"Oh?" I took a step toward the door, but she held up her hand.

"Fine. If you tell him about me, then I'll tell him the truth about you. How you're a girl."

I rubbed at my forehead. "You may as well. This whole thing is falling apart. What's one more person knowing the truth?"

Silence stretched out, and then she stamped her foot. "This isn't fair," she cried. "You're nothing but a hypocrite, Avery Mullins. Telling me I can't do something you've done yourself?"

I heaved a sigh. "I never said I was a good person, Orly. In fact, I'm one of the worst people I know. Now, are you going to give up this plan, or do I need to go have a talk with your father?"

She glared. "If you stop me from doing this, I'll hate you for the rest of my life."

"So hate me. Just as long as you give up this foolish plan. I want your word. Swear it."

Redness and anger rimmed her eyes, and it gave my gut a twist. It had been a pleasant thought to have Orly's trust and friendship this little while. To have lost it hurt more than I thought it would.

"Fine." She spat the word. "I swear I won't do it. I'll stay here and work in this stupid library with Papa for the rest of my boring existence."

I leaned over the table, reaching out to her. "Come on, Orly, don't be angry."

She flounced toward the door. "If you need help again, find someone else to be your minion."

But losing Orly's friendship along with Master Wendyn's trust was too much for me. For a moment panic rose within me, so that I blurted out my first thought. "Just wait a little, all right? I'll be a master wizard in a year or less, if I keep up this rate of passing the trials. I'm going to need an apprentice."

She stopped, her hand on the doorknob, then slowly turned to face me. "Really?"

"Yes, really."

The anger on her face faded. "You're not just saying that? What about my father?"

"If the Council implements their new apprentice rule, I'll have to have an apprentice. I'd be thrilled if it were you. I'll help you keep in touch with your father without revealing your secret, so you'll never need to cut ties with him like I have with mine."

Her face broke into a tentative smile.

A tapping at the door made us both freeze. We exchanged a look before she reached for the doorknob. I waved a hand, dismissing the privacy spell.

Maximo stood there, Orly's librarian father. "There you are. You're needed at the checkout desk."

"Of course."

She gave me a backward glance, then disappeared through the doorway. I heard her father admonishing her in quiet tones, "You shouldn't have been in there alone with him . . ." Their voices faded.

My eyes fell on the stack of books on the table. Orly had said she set these aside for me. The book on top had a shiny new cover and barely cracked spine. *Labyrinthine Enchantments for Summertide Demilunes*, the spine read. Confused, I opened the cover and flipped several pages before I encountered the real title: *Magic and the Female Mind*. The shiny new book bore no resemblance to the ancient leather-bound volume I recalled.

The second book was as tall as one hand and appeared to be a Belanokian dictionary.

I shook my head and stared at the books. Orly was a study in contrasts. On the one hand, she was delighted at the thought of romance and adventure, and on the other, she could develop complex spells that many master wizards were unaware of. She deserved the chance to develop her magic just as much as I did. But the truth was, I couldn't guarantee I'd still be apprenticed in a month, let alone that I'd be a master wizard in a year.

At least the promise had made Orly happy. I hoped that I'd be able to keep it.

The dictionary had the approximate weight of a small child. I left the library with my armload, tottering toward the wizard door at the head of the cathedral hall.

Not until I hefted the door open did Orly's words come back to me.

Show him you're an honest person . . . I'm sure you can regain his trust.

The master wanted me gone, and not only because I was female. It was because I betrayed his trust, the same as Cailyn did.

What if I could prove to him I was trustworthy? What if I

could do the one thing I hadn't been able to do yet: tell him about the blood oath with Kurke and put to rest the last false-hood between us? I didn't even know if it was possible. Every time I'd tried it felt like my thoughts were trickling out my ears like water through a leaky cauldron. But if I was successful, it would make it evident to the master I was trustworthy. Perhaps he'd even be grateful to me for trying to save Oscar's life. Grateful enough to keep me on as his apprentice.

I stepped the rest of the way through the wizard door, the tapestry pushing aside easily. The tether gave a great twang. I stopped where I stood and stared at the master's desk.

Matthias Kurke sat there, smiling at me.

TWENTY-ONE

THE TAPESTRY FELL FROM my fingers. For a moment I drowned in the weight of its heavy fabric across my face and shoulders. I fought my way out, and Kurke's face bore an amused smirk when I emerged.

"Hello, Avery."

A hundred questions wanted to jump out of my mouth all at once. The one I settled on was, "Where's Master Wendyn?"

"Out. Superb timing, isn't it?" He nodded at the chair on the other side of the desk. "Take a seat, if you like. Edie will be in with tea shortly. Charming girl."

I hefted the books. "Superb timing for what?"

He didn't answer that question, only pushed to his feet and squinted at me. "You're studying Belanokian?"

I flushed. "It's an assignment. From Master Wendyn." I set the books down on the nearest chair and straightened. "Is it time for murder already?"

He smiled. "Flippancy. I like it. But no, it's not time. Not just yet."

"That's good, because I haven't seen Oscar in weeks."

"Yes." He rubbed his hands together. "His whereabouts are

a problem. I've been working on a theory for where he might have gone and how to get him back here."

"And?" I asked, though I didn't really care about the answer. I was wondering how best to talk him out of it.

"He'd come back if his favorite grandson were in trouble."

Nerves moved through my midsection at the words. "Leave Master Wendyn out of it."

He frowned. "I warned you not to get close to the Wendyns, Avery. You can't trust them."

"I never said I trust them," I retorted. "I just trust them more than you."

"Pity. It's why I had to send the wasting sickness to that child in Bramford, you know."

I gaped at him. "What do you mean?"

"That girl. I gave her the wasting sickness to drive you and Garrick apart. I knew you'd come to pieces and Garrick would be disgusted by it. From what I can tell, my plan worked. I hear Garrick has been storming around here like a thundercloud and spent a good deal of time yelling at you after coming back from Bramford."

My mouth opened and closed, overcome by the gall of the man. "You might have killed her. She's an innocent child!"

He waved away my protests. "Calm down. She didn't die. Didn't you ever wonder why it never became an epidemic?"

"I . . . I guess I thought we were lucky."

He chortled as though I'd said something ridiculous. "You should know better than most how improbable that is. Now, getting back to Garrick. I have no plans to put him in actual danger—just to make Oscar think he is. That's where you come in. I want you to send him a letter via the messenger."

"I've told you, I don't know where he is."

"Doesn't matter. You'll just write a nice believable little letter saying something about how Garrick's taken ill and refuses to send for a doctor or family to tend to him. That sounds like something he'd do. Say you're worried about him. Address it to Oscar Wendyn, address unknown. If he's anywhere near a messenger, the magic will find him."

I frowned at him. "No."

He sighed heavily. "Do you really think I've made all of this up?" His tone was light, but I could feel the anger underlying it.

"No. I understand why you feel the way you do about Oscar. I didn't lose my family in the same traumatic way you did, but I lost them just the same. That's not something you get over."

He frowned, his good mood unraveling. "You don't have the slightest notion what it's like to lose your family in such a violent way. Do you know Oscar lied to me about it? He said it was a buggy accident. That they died on a pleasure ride in the country when their horse got spooked." He laughed, a mirthless noise. "I thought he was bigger than life, the most important and kindest man in the three kingdoms. Why should he lie to a ten-year-old child if he had nothing to hide?"

"To spare your feelings?" I held my hands up, a barrier against his angry expression. "It's just that if they died as you say, what benefit could there be in telling a child such gory details?"

"Yes. Telling me their buggy rolled off a cliff is so much better."

I grimaced. "Very well. But how do you know it didn't happen that way?"

"Never mind that. I just know. Oscar's gone too far, and he has to die."

"But he doesn't. Listen to me. When my mother and brother died, it felt like my heart had fractured. I would have done anything to bring them back." His magnetic eyes warmed at my words, becoming deep and fathomless and impossible to look away from. I reached out, laid my fingers on his forearm, and looked up at him, as earnest as I'd ever been in my life. "But you must see—you must—that this plan of yours is madness. You can't murder a man without making yourself as evil as you feel he is."

The warmth retreated from his face so swiftly that I moved to draw my hand back. He grabbed my wrist and held me in place. "Madness, is it? I've never claimed to be sane. I *am* mad, driven to it."

"You're not. You're as sane as anyone else. The problem is, you hide behind your grief."

His grip tightened on my wrist, and then he advanced on me, pushing me up against the tapestry with one forearm pressed to my throat before I even knew what he was doing. His other arm pressed my midsection and both arms into the wall. "I am hiding nothing. I am evil, and I admit it." He smiled down at me and leaned forward, his arm pushing into my windpipe.

He was just trying to frighten me. He wouldn't really kill me.

"Tell me what the Belanokian dictionary is for, Avery."

My mouth opened, but only gasps came out. Through the tapestry, the wizard door felt solid and heavy at my back with Kurke's weight pressing against me. I couldn't move. Couldn't breathe. Couldn't escape.

"You must take me for a fool," he continued, almost conversationally. "Did you think I wouldn't know? Belanok's only known for three things, after all: their abundance of ore, their talent at cheese-making, and blood magic. You haven't taken an interest in Belanokian cheese, have you?"

"It's the . . . ore . . . actually," I gasped out, my voice raspy and hoarse. "I'm looking . . . into their . . . mining methods."

He made a disgusted noise and leaned forward further, cutting off my air.

Spots appeared in my vision. I struggled against his hold, until finally Kurke dropped his arms. I collapsed against the wall, breathing hard with both hands to my throat.

"You've been a help, but your protests irritate me. Keep it up, and I'll have no choice but to get rid of you. Or even better, those close to you. I've never been all that attached to Garrick. There are blood spells that could take him out in an instant." He reached toward me, and I flinched. But all he did was trace a finger down the side of my face and bent his head a little closer. "It's nothing personal. You understand, don't you?"

I gazed up at him, at the man whose beautiful face had charmed me for three years. A man with a beautiful face and a cankered soul.

"You really are mad," I said, my voice faint in my own ears. A lifetime away, there was a whisk of unidentifiable noise.

He smiled at me, and a low rumble of a chuckle moved through him. His hand dropped to my shoulder, and he gave it an almost affectionate squeeze. "Yes," he said. "Yes, I told you that."

Behind him, the door slammed shut with such force that the walls rattled. Kurke and I leaped apart.

"Well," Master Wendyn said, glowering at the two of us with something past fury coloring his face. "I apologize for interrupting."

With a thunk, my stomach dropped to my feet.

Kurke's hand rested on his midsection. "Good God, Garrick. Are you trying to give me an attack of the heart?"

"Oh, I'm sorry. Did I startle you?" The master's voice was thick with sarcasm. "My sincerest apologies. Please, go back to kissing my apprentice."

"We weren't—"

Kurke held up a hand to silence me. "Don't be dramatic." He betrayed no hint of discomposure. "Why in the three kingdoms would I kiss your apprentice? He's a boy. You know that doesn't interest me."

"I see." The master's voice contained all the warmth of a glacier. "Then what were you doing?"

"He had something in his eye. I was trying to help him get it out."

They both looked at me. "That's not—" I began, and stopped myself when I noticed Kurke's hand twitch. *There are blood spells that could take him out in an instant.* If I didn't agree with Kurke, would he kill the master right now?

I swallowed past a lump in my throat. "All right," I said. "Yes, that's all it was." I rubbed at my eye for good measure. "I can honestly say if I were to kiss a man, he'd be the last one I'd choose."

Master Wendyn looked back and forth between the two of us. "Underwizard, I'd like you to wait in the hall."

I rubbed at my eye a moment longer, then nodded and edged toward the door, pausing only long enough to swoop my books into my arms. The two men were too busy staring each other down to spare me another glance. Once I closed the door behind me, I ran the books upstairs to my room. By the time I returned and tried to listen through the heavy wood door, the master must have cast a privacy spell, for it was no use listening; I couldn't hear a thing, not even when I cast a spell.

The weariness really hit me then, and I let myself plop into a sitting position against the door, my knees drawn into my chest and my head in my hands.

All at once the door opened, and I fell into the study, flat on my back, staring up at Master Wendyn.

"Get up, Mullins." His voice was short. "I'm ready to speak to you."

I scrambled to my feet and into the room. But though I

peered into every corner, I could find no sign of Kurke. He must have exited via the wizard door.

Master Wendyn closed the door behind me and then took the chair behind his desk. "Sit," he said without even looking up at me. "Depending on your answers, this will either be a very short or very long interview."

I took the chair across from his desk uneasily, wondering how much the master knew.

He ran a hand over his face. "Devil's dawn, Mullins." He looked me in the eye. "You know how to complicate matters."

I chewed on my lip, hating all of this. Knowing there was a lie between us and I couldn't even speak of it felt like torture. I hated not having the master's trust.

He slumped back, his face resigned. His eyes, dark and disappointed, bored into mine. "I know Matt well enough to see he's not being honest. It's plain as plain he knows you're a girl."

I cleared my throat. "Yes," I admitted.

Master Wendyn sat forward. "I'll be honest. I'd expect this deceit from you, but not Matt. How long has this been going on between the two of you?"

"He's known for quite some time," I admitted. "From the first time I met him."

"I see." His jaw worked, and he fiddled with one of the magical devices on his desk, the one with the spinning arrow on the top. "You realize that as your master, I can't allow this to continue."

"Allow what to continue?"

"Your relationship with Matt, I mean. I know him well enough to realize when he takes an interest in a woman, it's for one reason. You two have been meeting secretly, haven't you? Having some secret affair, perhaps?"

My mouth fell open. "That's not true!" I said hotly, coming

to my feet. "We never—I would never—I despise the man. I would never meet him in secret!"

Pain like a hammer slammed into the base of my skull. My vision splintered, and I collapsed in the chair, whimpering.

From far away, the master's voice came to me. "I should have warned you I worked another deception defense. I told you it was painful, didn't I?"

A moan bubbled up from my throat, and I rubbed at my thumping head. I should have chosen my words more carefully. I *had* met Master Kurke in secret, though it was always against my will.

"You don't understand," I managed, peering up at him. "There are things you don't know, things I have to tell you about Ku—" But I'd gone too far, and blank fog descended on my thoughts.

Master Wendyn sat before me, bitterness in the lines of his face. "You don't need to tell me anything," he said. "I figured out what I need to know already, that Matt can't be trusted, and neither can you."

I blinked and the immediate blank hole in my memory filled in. The master had caught Kurke and me together.

"I've been trying to decide what to do with you, Mullins, and this . . . situation . . . clarifies things. I won't turn you in to the Council, but I want nothing more to do with you. You'll need to find another master. Or better yet, give up this madness altogether." He ran a hand over his face. "I don't care what you do. You're not my problem any longer; that's all."

"No," I whispered, rubbing at my temples, trying to will away the thumping pain that made it hard to think. "Please don't."

"I've decided. I'd like you gone within the week, although sooner is better. Now, please leave. I have work to do."

My mouth opened. I had to keep talking. There was more to

say—but my head hurt so much that I couldn't even think what. Pain thumped through my skull with an insistent pounding, like my father's fist on the door when he came home drunk and couldn't figure out how to get inside the house. *Thumpity thumpity thump thump thump*.

This conversation would have to wait. I'd convince the master to talk to me tomorrow, when my head was clearer.

"Yes," I said. "Very well. Goodbye."

And then I stumbled to the door and left.

IT WAS A REASONABLE PLAN, made more difficult by one little detail. Next morning, the master had left.

"What do you mean, 'he's not here'?" I asked Mrs. Pitts over the breakfast table.

She set the tray down. "Just what I said. Master Wendyn is not here."

"But—but—where's he gone?"

With practiced hands, she poured the tea. "I'm not sure. He took his fishing pole and enough clothes to last for a week or two."

"I didn't know he fished." My voice seemed to be coming from far away.

"He goes all the time," she offered. "Not sure which fishing hole. He's never told me. He could be anywhere in the three kingdoms."

What a nightmare. Then again, something about the way she said it made me doubt that it was true. More likely Mrs. Pitts did know where the master had gone—but she'd promised not to reveal it.

I chewed on my lip for a moment, until resolve came over me and I squared my shoulders. Fine. If that was the way he wanted it, I'd wait right here until he returned. No matter what he said about leaving within the week.

She gave me a stern look. "He mentioned that you would be leaving. Before he gets back, he said."

My mouth opened and then closed again. So this was how Master Wendyn won arguments. He retreated so there was no possibility of further conversation.

"I have a lot of packing to do," I said. "I can't promise it'll be done by then."

"Then I'll help you. You won't be here when the master returns; I can promise you that. Do you understand?" She frowned at me. Either she'd retrieved some of her memories from the oblivion spell—which was impossible—or she had developed a dislike for me anew.

"Very well," I said. "No need to help. I can do it on my own."

Ivan slipped into the room just then, delight crossing his face as he took in the hot food on the table.

Mrs. Pitts nodded at Ivan, gave me one last stern look, and limped out of the room with her empty tray.

So much for my plan.

I SPENT several days packing and trying to come up with a strategy. When that grew tedious, I turned to translating the book Orly sent me. There seemed to be a section on blood oaths, judging by my sketchy translations. Following the words with one finger and flipping through the dictionary with the other, I made slow progress, recording my translations onto a piece of parchment as I tried to muddle through the meanings of each sentence. When I finished an hour or more later, I'd come up with the following translation:

Blood oaths are always forged using the blood of two or more parties. It is optimal if all parties are consenting, as each person must say the incantation. It is possible (but not recommended) to force a party to say the incantation by means of magic. The more people sworn into the oath, the higher risk of oath failure. Consequences of unfulfilled blood oaths are more permanent and damaging than any other oath, save for life bonds. Blood oaths should never be undertaken lightly. See fine print for dangers of unfulfilled or failed oaths.

The incantation was written below, though I couldn't find meaning in the translation.

I chewed on my lip as I stared at the words I'd written, reading through it one more time. None of it seemed to give me any new information, although the bit about oath consequences being "more permanent and damaging than any other oath" didn't comfort me. Oscar had alluded to something along the same lines—but just what sort of consequences did he mean?

I traced the words of the footnote as I flipped through the dictionary to translate it.

As with all blood spells, the magic ties one life to another, blood to blood.

That explained the twinge in my chest whenever Kurke was nearby. We were literally tied together, my blood to his.

I shuddered and continued with my translating.

For the duration of the oath, all parties to the oath are tied together as though their hearts beat as one, symbolizing that blood oaths must be fulfilled, or the consequence to all parties is death.

I stared at that sentence and then read it again.

Blood oaths must be fulfilled, or the consequence to all parties is death.

The weight of the words settled on me, until I felt as though I couldn't breathe. I moved to the window and pushed it open.

The cold wind moving past revived me, and I tried to think what I must do.

It couldn't mean what it said. It wasn't meant literally.

Yes, that must be it. Perhaps it was a metaphor. The consequence to both parties was death, it said. It could refer to all sorts of deaths. The death of reason, for example. Or the death of one's magical abilities. Inconvenient, but preferable to being dead, I suppose.

But the longer I stared out the window, growing chilled and restless, the more I doubted this assessment. Spell books, as a rule, didn't speak in hyperbole. And I'd heard Belanokians were known for being a quite literal people—besides being sociopaths. I returned to the book and read the words one more time.

Blood oaths must be fulfilled, or the consequence to both parties is death.

If Matthias Kurke and I didn't kill Oscar Wendyn, both of us would die.

TWENTY-TWO

I SAT ON THE floor of my room, surrounded by open spell books, when a tapping sounded at the door in the usual pattern that Ivan used.

"Go away, Ivan." If I didn't memorize all the spells in these books before Kurke turned up again, I'd have lost already.

The door opened, and Ivan strode into the room, mouth twisted into a scowl.

You leave? he gestured at me, movements so frenzied that I almost couldn't understand him.

I frowned. "I have no choice. Who told you?"

Heard Mrs. Pitts talk Edie.

I sat down in a chair, facing the window so I didn't have to see him. I purposely hadn't told Ivan because I knew he'd take it hard. We'd become as close as Gavin and I were, my own brother. But wherever I was going, I couldn't take Ivan with me.

"Master Wendyn wants me gone within a week. Well, I suppose I'm down to five days now." I ran a hand over my face.

A weight dropped on my shoulder, and I glanced up. Ivan stood beside me, his face covered with determination, hand on my shoulder. *I come.*

"No. You're staying here. You don't know half of what's going on. You could wind up—" Dead, though I couldn't bring myself to say it. As dead as I might. I shook my head. "Never mind. But you're not coming. It's better for you to stay with someone who can take care of you."

Ivan's jaw tightened in a show of determination and anger I'd never seen from him before. *Don't care better me. Us together.*

"Listen, Ivan. It's for your own good."

You good?

I understood what he meant by it—what about what was good for me? But I couldn't take it, this extra worry about Ivan on top of everything else. My fist came down hard on the table, and everything jumped. "Blast it, Ivan! You're not my brother, all right? You know nothing about me. Stop pretending you do! You're some kid I ran into in Bramford one day, and you've been tagging after me ever since. Will you stop being such a bother and leave me alone?"

Ivan stared at me with a tightness in his mouth and jaw. His eyes turned hard and angry, and he stomped out of the room.

When he was gone, I stared at my ink-splattered hands and desk. It must have happened when I pounded on the table. I had made a mess of everything.

I washed my hands, scrubbing and scrubbing at the ink. It wouldn't come off. At last I gave up and went back to packing my trunk.

LUNCHTIME CAME AROUND, and though I had nearly finished my packing, I couldn't bring myself to face Ivan or anyone else. My stomach growled, and I pondered whether to go down to the kitchen to grab a bite to eat. I didn't want to run into anyone, but I was also tired of being cooped up in my room.

Maybe if I took the back stairs.

I emerged into the kitchen a short while later, to find it void of company but for Cook. She dished me some stew without comment. I enjoyed the solitary meal and was close to finishing, when voices from the hall alerted me to visitors. I peeked out from the kitchen door.

"When do you expect him back?" asked a deep voice coming from a broad-shouldered man. A woman stood beside him. Both shook snow from their over-things.

"I don't expect him back anytime soon," Edie said. "He's gone fishing."

"Fishing?" the man repeated, slapping a snow-encrusted glove against his thigh. "Garrick likes to fish?" He looked to the woman as if for confirmation, but she only shrugged. I saw the man in profile now. Something about the set of his jaw reminded me of . . . someone.

I cleared my throat as I stepped into the hallway. The three of them turned toward me, and I saw the swelling at the woman's midsection.

"Ah . . . hello. I'm Underwizard Mullins. Are you, by any chance, the master's brother?"

The man strode forward, hand outstretched. "Ah, the underwizard. I've heard about you. Bastian Wendyn. Pleased to meet you. This is the one that saved Vito," he told the woman, who could only be Cailyn.

I shook his hand. "I'll take care of this," I told Edie.

She frowned before turning to head for the kitchen.

"Can you tell us where Garrick is?" Cailyn asked. Delicate tendrils of honey blond hair wisped against her jawline, falling from a smooth bun at the nape of her neck. Her comeliness left me feeling frumpy and outlandish in my underwizard's robes.

"No." I fussed at straightening my already-straight sleeves, then settled on folding my arms. "He left rather abruptly."

Bastian gave me an appraising look. "Two of you quarrel?"

I opened my mouth in surprise. "I—how did you know?"

"He ran out on me after we fought too. The temper on that kid . . ."

A memory came back to me of the master in that carriage ride home from Bramford when we spoke of Bastian and Cailyn. I remembered the melancholy on his face in that moment of weakness. "He's hardly a kid," I said. "And anyway, it's not like you didn't do anything to deserve his anger." I stopped then, surprised at my indignation on the master's behalf. But I couldn't take the words back now.

Bastian and Cailyn exchanged a glance.

"He told you about what happened?" Cailyn asked.

I wondered how much I should say to this couple who had brought such sadness to the master's face. After a moment of chewing on my lip, I shook my head. "Not really. I've heard things. What I know for sure is one of you jilted him and both of you betrayed him."

"I wouldn't put it like that," Bastian said. "He's the one who threw us together, asking me to watch after Cailyn while she was in Hutterland. I mean, what did he think would happen? If you look at it that way, this is actually his fault."

So that was how this had all come about.

Cailyn laid a hand on his arm. "Let's just go, Bastian. Garrick isn't here."

Bastian glanced at his wife. "We're settling this, Cay. It's been a year now that I can't show my face at family functions. Well no more."

She sighed. "You're not going to let this go, are you."

"Nope."

"You're welcome to wait in the sitting room," I said. "But it seems unlikely that he'll come back today. He's gone fishing to nobody-knows-where."

"So be it. We've come all this way. It's time to settle this once and for all," Bastian snapped.

"But . . . it could be days before he returns," I said.

"So find him," Bastian said. "You're his underwizard. It would seem to me if anyone can get him here, you can."

"But Bastian—" Cailyn began. She broke off when he fixed her with a look.

"We're staying. Even if it takes days."

She settled one hand on her belly. "You'd better show us to the kitchen, underwizard."

"What for?" I asked, startled.

"I'm hungry. Besides that, if we're going to foist ourselves on Garrick, I'd like to see that his favorite meal is on the table when he arrives." She tugged at Bastian, and he followed her, a pleased smile on his face. "Stop looking so smug," she told him. "You're making dessert."

I sighed and led them toward the kitchen, passing Edie on the way carrying a tray of tea. She was already frowning, apparently as put off by the unannounced visitors as I. She even muttered and glared when I held the door open for her to pass me into the kitchen.

These unannounced Wendyns had thrown everyone off.

MRS. PITTS and I held a whispered discussion in the hall outside the kitchen, while Cook's objections and exclamations of dismay carried from the kitchen over the noise of Bastian and Cailyn's conversation.

"How long are they planning on being here?" Mrs. Pitts demanded in a hiss.

"Until the master returns. Maybe days."

"Cook will be furious."

As though to illustrate the point, Cook's voice carried to the hallway: "I told you, don't touch that!" Something large and heavy clanged against the floor.

"You have to tell me where to find Master Wendyn."

Her mouth turned obstinate. "Great Hepzibah's fiddle, I will not. He gave me that information for emergencies only."

"Are you prepared to make them wait days for him to return? If her childbirth begins, they could take up permanent residence here."

"They also might get tired and leave," she reasoned. "The master doesn't like when his family shows up unannounced. He'll thank me if he misses their visit."

I massaged my temples. "Fine. Then you get to take care of them. I want no more to do with this drama."

"Very well. I will."

"I have packing to finish." And with that, I retreated up the stairs.

NOT A QUARTER of an hour passed before a tap sounded on my door. Feeling a little smug—so Mrs. Pitts had already relented, had she?—I set a stack of books inside my trunk and turned toward the door. "Come in."

But once the door swung open, the figure standing there bore no resemblance to Mrs. Pitts.

"Oscar?" The man whose life hung in the balance as precariously as my own at the moment.

"Ah. Hello there, Mullins." He took a few steps into the room. "What's the idea, sending me a letter saying Garrick's ill? Mrs. Pitts says he's fine—at least to her knowledge."

"A letter? I never sent a letter." Friar's bones. Kurke must have written it and signed my name.

He pinched the bridge of his nose. "To be clear, my grandson is not ill or dying? And I've rushed back here for no reason?"

"I—I guess I exaggerated," I improvised. "When did you arrive?"

He wore a homespun wool shirt and broadcloth trousers, looking rather haggard. "A few minutes ago. Now out with it. What's going on around here? My grandson and his wife are in the kitchen cooking up a feast, Ivan is sulking, and Mrs. Pitts says Garrick's gone fishing? He hates fishing. What's happened?"

I bit my lip and then straightened my shoulders. Best to come out with it, I suppose. "The master and I had a misunderstanding."

His gaze sharpened on me. "About what?"

I shrugged and evaded his eyes. I couldn't tell Oscar the truth. "Why does Master Wendyn do anything? He's an unreasonable man."

"At times. But he doesn't go running away from just any situation. In fact, the last time . . . yes, it must have been Cailyn."

"I assure you, I had no idea he was going. He just . . . went."

"Ah. But you know *why* he left, don't you?"

My eyes flashed to his face.

"I was an underwizard once too. Whatever you've done, just apologize and move on. Garrick's a reasonable man. He'll understand."

I shook my head. "How can he understand? He won't even talk to me." I turned toward the window. "Anyway, an apology isn't going to help. He's asked me to leave. I'm going tomorrow."

"Tomorrow? Has your oath been invalidated, then? Do you have a new master?"

I shrugged as if I didn't care. "Wizardry isn't for me, and I've accepted it. I'll go back to . . ." I trailed off and pondered the possibilities, things I hadn't even allowed myself to dwell on yet. Would I take in washing again? Perhaps sewing as well? Or would I go back on my promise to Mama and go to thieving? Or would I try something new, such as amateur magician? "I'm not sure what I'll do," I said at last, turning back. "Something. It doesn't matter what, does it?"

He folded his arms and regarded me with a frown and a furrow between his eyes. "So you're giving up, just like that? After all the work you've put into it? Come now. Garrick's been hard on you, yes, but I thought you two had come to an accord."

"So did I. But he changed his mind. It's over." I paced across the room and stopped before my trunk, throwing haphazard things into it.

"Miranda's cutlass, underwizard. You mean to tell me that —" He broke off, and after a moment of silence I stopped what I was doing and looked over at him.

He was staring at my desk, at the books and papers scattered across it.

"Mullins, where did that book come from?" His quiet voice held an edge of danger. I'd never heard such a tone come from Oscar before.

"What book?" I glanced over the desk and realized with a start that all my books from the Wizard's Library sprawled across it, from the two books Orly had disguised to the large Belanokian dictionary.

"Oh, that. That's nothing." I arrived at the desk in two strides, stacking the books and papers. "Just some books from the library."

"Stop!" His thunderous voice echoed in the small room.

That alone stunned me into compliance, but before I could obey of my own volition, a spell pinned me in place. Oscar pushed past me and unstacked the books and papers. He flipped through them, staring at me after each one.

"I thought this book looked familiar. Not bad work at disguising it, but I recognize the trail of magic this sort of book leaves." He held the blood magic spell book up. "Where did you get this?" He flicked a finger, and my head broke free from the freezing spell.

"It's not what you think." Stupid words to say in any situation, but in the immediacy of the moment, nothing else came to mind.

"This is a blood magic spell book. *Bloodlust*, I believe is the proper title, not this *Aqua Pura* nonsense. This should be in the Conclave's vault, and yet here it is in your bedroom. Explain."

I'd never heard Oscar's voice sound so hard. For a moment I could only stare at him, trying to formulate an explanation. "I—I want to tell you," I stuttered. "I do."

"So tell me, then."

Orly. I couldn't let her part in this come to light. If it became known she stole a book from the vault, what would her punishment be?

I shook my head. "I can't."

He slammed the book down on the desk, and I flinched. "Do not toy with me, underwizard. I am not the fool you seem to think."

"I don't think you're a fool." But I suppose I did. I seemed to recall terming him "nutty as a fruitcake." This backboned version of Oscar had me completely flummoxed.

"How did this book come to be in your possession?"

"I bought it," I lied glibly, thanking the heavens he hadn't had time to cast a deception defense.

"Bought it?" he echoed. "Where? What bookseller would

dare to sell this sort of book?" His voice thundered throughout the room, and I wished I had the use of my limbs so I could shrink away from him.

Perhaps it was an ill-chosen lie. I didn't expect him to react so angrily. "A stall in Hampstone," I improvised. "A few weeks ago."

"Give me the bookseller's name and location."

"Why? What are you going to do to them?"

Oscar stepped closer. He didn't touch me, but his face was so close that I squirmed—at least, everything from the neck up, which were the only parts of me able to move. "Give me the bookseller's name and location."

"He's not there any longer. I only saw him the one time."

He gave me a shrewd glance. "It's just as well your relationship with Garrick is over. I could have overlooked your being female, even helped you patch things up with Garrick, but I can't let this go. Dabbling in blood magic is going too far."

My mouth opened in shock. "You knew I was a girl? And you never said?"

"A girl wizard is one thing, but practicing banned magic is different."

"I never dabbled in blood magic. At least, not—"

I meant to say not me personally. But the words evaporated, replaced with a familiar stupor that reminded me of . . . something. Something I couldn't remember.

"Yes, you didn't dabble in blood magic," Oscar said gravely. "You just purchased an illegal book on blood magic from a questionable seller. Perhaps to satisfy your own curiosity?"

I took precious moments to catch on to what we were talking about, and I realized why the stupor was familiar. It had happened to me before. It was the stupor that came whenever I tried to talk about the cursed blood oath. "Yes, that's right, curiosity." I grabbed onto the excuse that Oscar had offered me for whatever question he'd asked—I couldn't remember what it was. "I ask too many questions. Master Wendyn will tell you."

He sighed and rubbed at his forehead. "This is just what I need. Now I either have to turn you over to the Council or clean up this problem myself. Which would you prefer?"

The Council meant Punishment, and from the look on Oscar's face, I couldn't expect much better from him. "I would prefer neither. I'm leaving tomorrow. No, wait—I can leave tonight! You'll never see me again."

"Yes, and you could spread your blood magic to who-knows-where all over the three kingdoms."

"I would never—"

He silenced me with a spell that stilled my mouth and head. A freezing spell. "Enough. I'm well aware of blood spells that twist lies into sounding like truth. I don't want to hear it from you."

His footsteps tapped across the floor, out of my line of vision. Whispers of noise made me itch to turn my head, if only I could: the swish of fabric, a clink of metal against metal, the thump of something heavy landing on the floor. From the direction he went, he must be rooting through my trunk. At last he moved back into my line of vision. "Garrick found out you're a girl, didn't he. That's why he's turning you out. I could have told you he wouldn't respond well to being lied to. Not with his history."

I couldn't reply, though I wanted to ask him who he thought *would* respond well to being lied to.

"An oblivion might do," he said, halfway to himself.

I didn't want anyone tampering with my memories. Poor oblivion spells could remove entire lifetimes, and while Oscar had the skill to perform one, when it came right down to it, I didn't wish to forget anything in my past. Even the bad things bore remembering, for the sake of protecting myself.

Not to mention that forgetting things such as blood magic and Matthias Kurke could be very, very dangerous—for Oscar.

I struggled against the freezing spell, trying to find a hole in its structure, as Master Wendyn had told me was possible. I wished now I'd had the foresight to practice it.

The spell Oscar had cast felt like steel mesh against my skin. I knew he was a powerful magician—he'd have to be, wouldn't he? The Council wouldn't just make any old master wizard the PMW—but the tensile strength in the structure of his spell was further proof. No matter where I poked or prodded at the magic holding me captive, I couldn't find a weakness.

"Yes, I think oblivion is going to be the best choice," Oscar went on, coming to a stop in front of me. "And then I will release you, Mullins, to go back to whatever life you want. But I think it'll be best for all parties if you have no memories of magic after this."

He might as well have just kicked me in the gut, for the way the words hit me in the stomach. Take my memories of magic? It would render the last three years of my life meaningless.

"It isn't anything personal," he went on, looking me in the eye. "But I've been fighting blood magic for a long while, since before my tenure as PMW, and I'm not about to let an upstart of a young girl change that."

A picture formed in my head. I was in Waltney, working as a barmaid at the Oak and the Cross, Papa's favorite tavern. I served the boys—now strapping young men—who once pronounced me too stupid for book learning. The me in my imagination had no recollection of any attempt to break free from such a life.

It was a sad picture, but the alternative depressed me equally. I could either be Oblivioned Avery, with no memories of magic and no memories of Oscar Wendyn, who had been murdered by Master Kurke. Or I could be Dead Avery.

I deserved Oscar's oblivion spell and more, but if he performed it I couldn't stop Kurke from killing him.

Master Wendyn said distraction was a wizard's best option in any fight. If Oscar would just release me from this blasted freezing spell, I could try it.

Oscar took a step back. "Perhaps I'm being too hasty. Let's converse, you and I. But first—" He turned his back on me as he performed a long spell I didn't recognize. And then another shorter spell which I did—deception defense.

Hope rose in me as I watched him work. Had he had second thoughts about taking my memories?

"Before the oblivion, I'd like answers. I will release you now, but I do so with a warning. If you lie, I will know it and so will you. Deception defense is like a kick to the head from an angry mule."

The hope died within me. If I had the power to talk, I'd tell him his warning was unnecessary. I knew the pain. But I couldn't help wondering why he would release me when moments ago he didn't trust me not to blood-spell him.

Dust clouded up from his trousers as he seated himself in the chair next to the fireplace and crossed his legs, leaning back as though he didn't have a care in the world. Although, from the way his fingers were tensed against his legs, perhaps he wasn't as relaxed as he looked. "Now, speak. Tell me what your connection is to blood magic." And with those words, he waved a hand, and I came free of the freezing spell.

I looked down at my fingers, stretching them, and then I looked at Oscar accusingly. "I hate that spell."

An eyebrow rose. "You've had it performed on you before?"

I frowned. "More often than you'd think. First Kurke, then that great oaf from Bramford." I froze, staring at my fingers curled up in a fist, as I realized what I'd said. Shouldn't I be swooning in confusion right now?

Bemusement flitted across Oscar's face. "Kurke? Matthias Kurke? He cast a freezing spell on you?"

My mouth opened and closed. Shock and hope crawled through me. "I—yes, he did." My words came tentatively as I waited for the swoon—and still nothing happened. My thoughts remained my own.

"Why ever did he do that? Helping Garrick during a lesson, I suppose?"

"No."

Oscar looked at me closer, perhaps drawn by the strange tone my voice had taken on.

I gulped and plunged ahead. "He cast it the day he forced me to swear a blood oath."

TWENTY-THREE

I TENSED, WAITING FOR something awful to happen—I didn't know what. But nothing did.

Oscar stared while I blinked and wondered if I were dreaming. Had I just said that?

"Blood oath?" Oscar repeated, coming to his feet. "Matthias Kurke has been practicing blood magic?" Confusion colored his face. "But how did he—"

I snapped my fingers. "That first spell you cast. It's some kind of blocking spell, isn't it? Something to stop blood magic? You wanted me to try casting a blood spell. You *wanted* to catch me in the act."

He put his hands on his hips and stared at me, as though trying to make sense of a riddle impossible to unravel. "It was a neutralizing spell. It renders blood spells useless."

"But this is—this is tremendous." I paced to the window in excitement and swung around. "I've been trying to speak of the oath for months!"

"It's Matthias." Oscar stared at some spot on the floor beyond me. "He's the one causing all of this chaos. He's following in the footsteps of his father. But how did he know?"

His sharp glance darted to me. "The attack on the vault. Were you involved too?"

"Attack?" I echoed. "What attack?" But then I remembered. "Friar's bones, that explosion? Was that Kurke?"

It made sense. That was where Kurke got the blood spells he'd been using. Where else would he have learned them?

Oscar snapped his fingers with impatience. "I need you to come straight out and tell me. Were you involved in the attack on the vault?"

"Of course not."

He gave me a hard look, and then apparently satisfied that the deception defense spell hadn't knocked me silly, he gave a tight nod. "Very well. Then tell me what you know of his doings these past months. Have you been helping him?"

One wrong word would earn me a blow to the head from the deception spell. I chose my words carefully. "I helped him, but only because he forced me to with the oath. He wants to kill you."

"Sweet carrot sticks." He sank into his chair. "I've been wrong all the way around, haven't I. About you. About Kurke." He ran a hand over his face, looking unutterably weary. "I thought the best way to prevent Matthias from becoming like his father was to keep the truth from him. And I've always regretted what happened with Ingerman. She shouldn't have had to die. I thought I could correct things with you. But all I did was give Matthias someone to assist him in his experiments." He leaned forward, head in his hands. "What a fool I am."

"It's not your fault. Kurke's crazy, that's all."

"No, I should have caught this sooner." Oscar shook his head. "What a slip-up. Maybe it's time to retire."

His words confused me. "I thought you *were* retired."

"Hardly. Oh, I suppose it doesn't matter what I tell you. You're in too deep now. I take scrying assignments from PMW

Robenhurst these days. My latest was to track down the perpe-
trator of the explosion in the Conclave's vault."

I stared at him. "So *that's* where you've been all this time."

"Scrying can be a slow business. It took a while to track him
to Hutterland, but I always seemed to be a step behind."

"You know, it's not too late," I said, taking an eager step
forward. "We can still stop Kurke. He hasn't carried out his plan
yet. With your knowledge of blood magic, we can stop whatever
he has planned."

Something like disbelief flitted across Oscar's face, his stiff
lips and wide eyes. "You mean there's more to the plan than the
dozens dead in Hutterland?"

Cold rushed me. "Dozens dead?" I sputtered. "What are
you talking about?"

"He's killed an entire family," Oscar continued, "using an
unknown blood magic spell. Forty-two people."

My mouth hung open. I felt sweat beading along my
upper lip, the hairs prickling at the back of my neck and my
face flushing hot. "Forty-two?" I choked out. "Are you
certain?"

"We've tried to keep it quiet. It was a little known family in
Hutterland. He killed four generations, from little babies to an
elderly grandparent—although he left spouses alone, killing only
along the bloodline."

"But why would he—why should he—" I sputtered, until I
understood. Kurke didn't mean to kill only Oscar. He meant to
kill his entire family. His children, grandchildren, and great-
grandchildren. Everyone I met at the master's natalis—anni-
hilated.

And Kurke had been in Hutterland all this time, perfecting
the spell. Practicing on innocent people. With my help.

I was an idiot. All this time I assumed it was only about
killing Oscar. It was about much more than that.

Those deaths in Hutterland were on my head just as much as Kurke's.

"I'm going to be sick," I croaked, as nausea moved up my throat. I stumbled to the window and shoved it open, but the cool air against my skin helped the burning in my throat to recede so that, after a moment, I merely felt ill. I turned back to Oscar.

His eyes rested on me, watching me, until he shook his head. "I can't let you go now. This has gone too far. I need you to relay what you know to the Council."

"But . . . they'll find out I'm a girl. It's a vital part of my story with Kurke, that he discovered my gender and blackmailed me. How can I keep from telling them?"

"Forty-two people have died, underwizard." His voice rang through the room. "Do you care anything for them? Or will you persist in thinking only of yourself?"

Kurke had described me with similar words, saying that I didn't care about who would become collateral in the wake of my plan to become a master wizard.

Perhaps they were both right. Yes, I wanted to live. But I also wanted no more unnecessary deaths on my conscience. "You must see, Oscar, how he plans to use this spell on you and your family. He'll kill all of you. You need my help to stop him. I'm connected to him, blood to blood. I can help you find him. Take me to the Council and I'll be Punished before being able to do that."

His face softened. "I'm well aware of the danger to my family. But I'm also aware of the danger of facing him alone. There are those with experience fighting blood magicians who sit on the Council. The sooner we alert them to this danger, the better I'll feel about it."

"He said he'd let you go free if you'd just acknowledge your part in his family's deaths publicly. That's all he wants."

He held up a hand. "Don't be stupid. If he said that it was just to placate you. The Council is well aware of my part in his father's death, and Matthias knows that. Come now, don't worry. I won't let the Council Punish you. My opinion still holds sway at the Conclave."

But he couldn't control that, not anymore, and I could tell he knew it from the way he avoided my eyes.

I rubbed at my nose.

Oscar's finger twitched, a familiar movement that triggered a warning in the back of my head. He was about to shoot another spell at me. Panic pushed me into action, the knowledge that I couldn't let him freeze me again, because that would be the last stop before the Council. If I could just get free and find the master, perhaps between the two of us we could save Oscar without involving the Conclave.

The first spell that came to mind was also my best. I held my hand out at Oscar, hoping to take him off balance with a powerful burst of fire. But the flame that roared to life had more power than I planned. It shot in Oscar's direction, a plume as long as I was tall. He scrambled sideways, and the shaft of flame encountered the brick of the fireplace, leaving it smoking. Surprised by the enormity of the thing, I reeled backward.

Oscar's freezing spell hit me, and I finished the stumble I began, falling flat on my back, unable to move.

Lights sparked through my vision with the blow to the back of my head, but I could do nothing but lay there, staring at the wooden beams above me.

Oscar came closer to look down at me. "You're overwrought, underwizard, and so I won't mention to the Council you tried to kill me." He wiped his palms on his trouser legs and stepped out of my line of vision. "Now, enough of this. We're going to the Conclave."

One more muttered spell, and I levitated off the ground, floating toward the door.

Unbidden, the image of Ingerman's barrel came to my mind. I wondered if they'd put mine next to hers with another plaque explaining my demise. *Here lies the barrel of Avery Mullins, a girl. She was a terrible underwizard.*

I cursed myself. But when I poked at the structure of the spell, I discovered something surprising. Master Wendyn had been right. My fire spell must have taken Oscar off his guard at least a little, because weaknesses had woven themselves throughout the strands of magic, holes that weren't present in the last freezing spell.

I could find my way out of this spell.

"I admit, underwizard. I'm disappointed in you, but I'm more disappointed in myself. Scrying my way halfway across the kingdoms while the answer was right in my home."

I expected the door to open at any moment, but it didn't. Instead, I floated lower as Oscar looked down at me.

"I'm not looking to expose you to ridicule." He gave a great sigh. "I won't take you through Garrick's door to the Conclave. This is an undertaking best kept private, in my estimation. Be patient while I build another wizard door, one that will take us straight to PMW Robenhurst's office."

He raised his hands and, in a commanding voice, uttered the incantation for a spell. On the edge of my vision, the outline of a door shimmered to life.

The freezing spell loosened as I worked at the holes in the lines of magic. I worked part of the way out of its hold and even felt the smallest finger on my left hand wiggle. Then the spell tightened, pushing me back within its confines.

At last Oscar lowered his hands and wiped a hand across his brow. "This might seem like an overreaction to you, but you never knew Matthias's father. Nox was ambitious, but with a skewed sense of right and wrong. He also had an affinity for blood magic. Despite my precautions, Matthias may have turned out just as dangerous as his father. It's funny . . ."

He trailed off, deep in thought. I pushed at the magic that bound me, and this time I had it. The holes in the spell widened as I pushed at them, until I could move all of my right hand.

Oscar, apparently oblivious, continued, "Matthias has always had a quick temper. Almost killed a boy when he was an underwizard. And I vouched for him. I *vouched* for him." Frustration leaked out of his voice. "I can't figure out how he learned of Nox's connection to blood magic. I was so careful."

All at once the freezing spell fell, and I had the use of my limbs again. But the levitation spell still had me floating off the ground, and I held still so Oscar wouldn't guess before I was ready. This time I chose my spell carefully.

I didn't want to harm Oscar, just stop him. But I didn't have confidence that my freezing spell would hold him. I needed him unconscious.

A throwing spell.

It took only a quick pull of magic in my direction and then muttered words. A book flew off my desk—*Magic and the Female Mind*. But Oscar must have heard its approach because he turned before it could reach him. It knocked into his shoulder and fell to the ground with a thud.

"Wha—" he said, and the break in his concentration dropped me to the ground. I rolled away and tossed another book via spell at him. It crashed into the wall behind him.

Blast my terrible aim.

He sent a freezing spell my way, but I scrambled behind my desk so that the spell just missed me, the magic bouncing off the wall behind me, dissipating into sparking tendrils.

"You said you wanted to stop Kurke." Oscar's voice vibrated with disapproval. "Stop this foolishness. I command you."

"If you think the Council won't vote to Punish me, then you're the foolish one. I can't help you if I'm dead."

"Very well. You leave me no choice."

I heard footsteps and scrambled backward, deeper behind the desk. Then—the sound of an impact and a thud. The room went silent.

After a few moments of quiet, I risked a peek out. That mound of homespun fabric on the floor must be Oscar, and standing over him, patting his cheek—Ivan?

"What did you do?"

He looked up at me. *Pull rug.* He pointed at the rumpled runner beneath Oscar's feet. *Hit chin on desk.*

"Is he . . ." I couldn't seem to bring myself to say dead, as unlikely as it was that Ivan could kill anyone.

No dead. Sleep.

I crept from behind the desk. "But why—why did you do that?"

Help you. Hurt?

"I'm all right." I stopped beside him and looked down at Oscar. A line of blood trickled down his jaw. His face had gone paler than I liked.

I hoped he wasn't too badly injured. I was, after all, trying to save his life.

The irony of the situation didn't escape me.

Why he do that?

I sighed. I didn't want to involve Ivan in this, but perhaps it was inevitable. "Look, I'm in some trouble, Ivan. I have to find the master. You don't know where he is, do you?"

Ivan gestured in the negative.

"I'm going to go find him. But I need you to do something for me while I'm gone."

He gave a firm nod and squared his shoulders. *Yes.*

I hoped this wasn't a mistake.

Together we moved Oscar to his room, using the same lifting spell Oscar had just used on me. Ivan kept an eye on him while I snuck down to the master's study and found a bottle marked "sleep" mixed in with a variety of other glass bottles in his medicines bag, the one he took to heal the child in Bramford. Back in my room, I fed it to Oscar. Then, reasonably certain he wouldn't wake up anytime soon, I healed the head wound using the spells I learned from Master Hapthwaite's healing books.

Finally, Oscar rested quietly, color in his cheeks.

"Keep an eye on him," I instructed Ivan. "If anyone asks, tell them he was exhausted from his travel. I'll be back in a few hours."

At least, I hoped.

Ivan nodded in acknowledgment.

I patted him on the back. "Thank you, Ivan. And I—I'm sorry for what I said earlier. You're not a bother. You're a good friend."

His face flamed red, and he looked away. But a pleased smile lit his face.

Oscar's collection of scrying sticks still leaned in the corner. I looked through them and selected a sturdy looking specimen. "I shall call you Xalvador," I announced, since I couldn't tell if it was Forthwind or not, and it was heresy for one of Oscar's mallets to go nameless. A trunk rested next to the sticks, hidden from view by the desk. It stood open, stacked to the top with Oscar's various dessert boxes. Just how many of these things did he need? It took seconds to magic a few sweet rolls into existence, fuel for the journey.

I uttered the scrying spell I'd heard Oscar say dozens of times, this time inserting the master's name, and the stick gave a tug in my hand. I followed its pull.

TWENTY-FOUR

WHITE LIGHT GLINTED OFF the knee-deep snow, and ominous trees reached for me with white-laden branches. I shivered and pulled my thin cloak tighter around myself. It had been foolish to put myself at the mercy of late winter unprepared, but I hadn't given myself time to think. It hadn't occurred to me that I would be in for a two-hour hike through deep snow when I went in search of Master Wendyn. He had never struck me as a woodsman.

The hand holding the scrying stick felt like a block of ice, even though every few minutes I switched hands to warm one up beneath my cloak. I cast another warming spell, hands shaking, as I stood in a circle of thick brown trees. The spell settled with a flood of heat, warmth coursing through my fingers, toes, to the end of my nose. It even melted the snow caked to my cloak, trousers, and boots. But then the immediate effects of the spell dissipated, and I felt the bite of winter air pushing against my face moments later. I had five minutes until the warmth from the spell would fade completely.

I heaved a sigh, gathered my energy, and plunged ahead into the snow.

Who went fishing in the middle of winter, anyway? Back home in Waltney, I remembered hearing about fishermen who cut holes in Lake Kyria in the winter to catch fish. While we could have used the food, we hadn't lived near enough to the lake to try it. I couldn't imagine that Master Wendyn felt so passionate about fishing that he was out on a frozen lake somewhere, cutting holes through solid ice.

I had probably cast twenty warming spells over the past two hours. I would run out of strength soon—strength I needed just to keep placing one foot in front of the other. And now the sun had dipped below the horizon. If I didn't find the master soon, I'd be at the mercy of the wild animals of the wood. He could be in Waldrin or Hutterland, for all I knew. What if I'd embarked on a days-long journey when I only had hours to complete it?

What a stupid idea.

For about the hundredth time, I worried the scrying stick had pointed me in the wrong direction. I checked the lines of the magic, and while the scrying stick's spell held, its strength appeared to be waning. But it wasn't the spell that was losing strength; it was me.

I should conserve my energy. Given the weakness I could already feel settling into my legs, I couldn't afford to cast any more warming spells.

Quiet permeated the forest. The whisk of my footsteps in soft snow, my own heavy breathing, and the occasional cry of a bird or call of a forest animal were the only sounds to pierce the stillness. Chill pulled into me, numbing my extremities once again. Daylight dimmed, the glimmer of the setting sun disappearing below the horizon.

My thoughts turned to the steam springs in the Midnight Wood. We had brought Mama there often during the duration of her ill health, hoping it would bring improvement. If nothing else, it always relaxed her and lifted her spirits for a few days after. Papa refused to take us there after she died.

I imagined the steam rising from the pool, the intense heat when I first stepped into the water, the way I became overheated if I stayed too long.

Overheated. If only I could remember what being overheated felt like right now.

In the winter, the snow around the pool melted in a wide circle around the lapping water. If I concentrated hard enough, I could almost imagine the steam wafting upward, engulfing my face in its hot breath.

Perhaps my imagination was helping me to feel warmer, because I felt a change in the air. Something seemed different.

I pushed through the trees and snow and stumbled into a clearing. Blooming flowers nodded their heads in preparation for sleep, and ground bare of snow remained solid and real beneath my feet. I looked back to the ground behind me, with its thick white coat, and then ahead of me to the bare, blooming dirt, trying to reconcile the two conflicting images. Perhaps a dozen paces away, a tiny one-story cottage lit up from within, light spilling from its windows into the half-lit gloom of twilight.

I no longer felt a pull from the scrying stick.

But if I needed further proof that I had found the right place, the cottage door swung wide, and Master Wendyn stepped outside in a foppish ivory shirt, the sleeves pushed halfway up his arms.

"Devil's dawn, not you again." Exhaustion ran through his voice like a ribbon. His scowl showed a man pushed to his limit by the mere sight of me. "I told Mrs. Pitts—"

"W-we have to talk," I stuttered through my numb lips. "And you have t-to listen. There's t-trouble."

He raised an eyebrow, unimpressed, and for a moment, I

thought he would toss me out of his warm clearing. "We settled this, Mullins. Your troubles aren't my troubles any longer."

"No, not m-me. Your f-f-family!" I felt myself thawing in the clearing's warmth. Still, violent shakes settled over me, perhaps the result of nerves, and I grasped the cloak tighter around me.

Master Wendyn seemed to notice my condition for the first time. His glance moved over me, head to toe. His expression didn't change. "My family? That sounds rather dramatic."

"M-maybe it is dram-matic, b-but this is im-im-important."

He closed his eyes and heaved a sigh. "Fine. I don't have much confidence in your ability to be sincere, but I'll listen. And then you're leaving, understood?" He stood aside and held the door open.

"Understood," I croaked and passed him into the warm cottage.

THE INSIDE of the tiny house contained a handful of furnishings and the occasional ostentatious decorative accent, such as the giant chandelier hanging from the center of the ceiling. From the outside the building looked like a rough, humble structure, but from the inside, the walls seem to expand and climb before my eyes. It was three times larger inside than I would have guessed. A staircase in one corner showed a second level, which the outside view of the cottage would render an impossibility.

An empty fireplace sat against one wall, but it sprang to life as the master spelled a burning blaze into existence. A yellow and lavender settee perched in the corner, a contrast to the bare, rough-hewn walls surrounding it. The other side of the cottage contained a kitchen area with a round table for sitting, a sink, and a heavy worktable bearing a kettle, a few wooden bowls, and some colored pottery.

I shivered, and my eyes swung back to the fire. Then I stopped, staring at the tapestry hanging along the back wall, embroidered with various shades of green. Light shimmered and flickered from behind it.

"Y-you have a w-w-wizard door?" I demanded, my voice holding as much outrage as a voice could when the speaker still couldn't feel their lips.

The master looked up from the fire he had woven. "I have no interest in traipsing through the woods for hours to get here." His glance at me carried the barest hint of amusement. He was laughing at me. Laughing at how I'd been near to freezing to death for the past few hours.

"B-but why—"

"Only a handful of people know the door exists." His tone made it clear I was not one of those people. "This is where I come for solitude. That wouldn't work if I made it easy for people to get here."

I swallowed my indignation and reminded myself I had a higher purpose in being here—and it wasn't to rage at the master. I pushed past him to get nearer the fire. "You W-Wendyns are the m-most exasperating people—" I trailed off as the warmth from the blaze sank into me. It felt so heavenly that for a moment I stood there, letting the heat thaw me, my eyes closed.

"I'll assume Grandfather's not back yet."

His voice was so close it surprised me. My eyes popped open. He stood to one side of me, looking down at me with those inscrutable dark eyes.

"What makes you say that?"

He reached for the scrying stick, which I still held. "He

rarely lends these out. I can only conclude you took it without asking. Here, let's have it."

I let him twist it out of my hand, glad to free up my icy fingers. "It was an emergency. I didn't know how else to find you."

He raised an eyebrow as he examined the scrying stick. "Grandfather will be furious if you damaged Forthwind."

"I don't think that's Forthwind. And anyway, didn't you hear me?" I stuttered in a voice that sounded shrill to my ears. "It's an emergency."

He slipped past me to lay the stick on the table. "You could be right. I can't tell the difference between any of his sticks. And yes, I heard you," he tossed over his shoulder as he continued toward the kitchen area. "Has anyone died?"

"No, but—"

"Is anyone close to dying?"

"Well . . . not yet."

"Is my family at the Hall?"

I paused and then answered, "Sort of."

He gave a snort as he set about pulling two mugs from a shelf and then filled them from the kettle. "That explains it. Definitely not going back there, then."

I should have argued more and made him listen, but instead, I closed my eyes and leaned into the warmth of the fire, letting it thaw the last remnants of cold out of me. I'd argue in a minute.

"Look, this is all very interesting, but let's get on to the real reason you're here, with none of the false drama," Master Wendyn said from across the room.

My eyes flashed open. "What do you mean?"

He approached, two mugs in hand, and extended one toward me. "Do you think I'm a fool? You expect me to believe you hiked all the way out here because of some benevolent wish to save my family from an ambiguous danger? I know why you're here, Mullins. You want me back as your master."

I blinked in surprise. "There's nothing wrong with your ego, is there."

"Fine then." His tone turned mocking. "My family's in danger. Well, go on then. Tell me about the danger." He gestured with the mug again, which I had yet to take. "And drink this while you're at it. You'll need the warmth when you walk back through all that snow to the Hall."

I took the mug and resisted the urge to fling the drink in his self-satisfied face. Instead I took a sip of the steaming brown liquid, which had a nutty, sweet flavor. Warmth coursed through me. I looked up at the master.

"What runs in your veins, Master Wendyn?"

His brow furrowed. "Blood, obviously."

At the word blood, the tether stirred in my chest, as though waiting to spring. "And what is it you and I have sworn between the two of us?"

He scowled. "Look, Mullins, if you've dropped in on my solitude to play some childish guessing game—"

I held up one hand. "It's not a game. I swear."

"Oh, you swear. Your promises don't mean much, though, do they?"

"Please. Just bear with me a little longer. What have we sworn?"

For a moment I thought he wouldn't answer, but at last he did. "An apprentice oath, of course."

"Just one more question now. Your friend, the one you suspected me of having an—an improper relationship with." With the fall of dark, shadows crowded the edges of the master's face, so that I couldn't read his expression.

"What about him?"

"There is something—" I began, and I felt it coming, the

swoon of forgetfulness. I cut myself off before it could hit me. The feeling subsided. "There is . . . something," I said again. "To those three things I said. Something to think about."

There. It was vague, but the forgetfulness hadn't come. That, too, was something.

The master stared at me and took a sip from his own mug. Then he turned, walked back toward the round kitchen table, and placed his mug on it. "Mullins," he said without turning. "I'm tired of your games. All you need to know is that I'm not taking you back. I will never take you back." He turned to look at me. "I think it's time you left."

"The three questions. Think about those three questions," I said, gritting my teeth and wondering if I had the patience for this.

He made a noise of impatience and then raised a hand, three fingers out. "Very well." He ticked them off. "We two swore an oath, you've been trysting with Kurke, and I have blood running in my veins. How enlightening. You forgot number four: you're desperate to keep your master."

"I didn't tryst with Kurke, and you've got the order wrong," I snapped. "Besides, why should I want you back as my master? How desperate do you think I am? You're incapable of trust, and more often than not, you're in a foul mood. Are you under the mistaken impression that there's a line of underwizards hoping you'll deign to become their master? There's not."

His back had gone stiff. "And that's what you came to say?"

"Of course not, you bumblehead!" I bellowed. "I came to tell you that Kurke fo—"

I meant to say *forced me to swear*, but instead I blinked, my head swimming. Master Wendyn stood a few paces off, glaring at me. I couldn't remember why. I couldn't even remember what we were talking about—if we were talking about anything at all.

"Very well, out with it if it's so important to you to say it," he growled. "Kurke what?"

My mouth opened. "I . . . don't remember."

"But you—" The anger on his face evaporated, and he stood in front of me in four strides, his hands gripping my upper arms, dragging me closer to peer into my face. "Mullins, have you sworn something with Matt? An oath?"

Hope rushed through me, and the tether gave a yank in my chest. "Ye—"

Again I blinked. A dull pain thumped at the base of my head. Master Wendyn had me by the arms, peering into my face so I had to stand on the tips of my toes.

"Devil's dawn," he said and released me.

———

I BLINKED, trying to clear the fog in my head.

"You've sworn a blood oath." The master's face had gone ashy as snow. He staggered backward, latching onto a chair with one hand for support. "Just how big a fool are you?"

Ah, now I understood—at least a little, anyway. "I'm a fool? I didn't have a ch—" I blinked and wondered what I was saying. The master stood a few steps in front of me, leaning on the back of a chair pushed up against the meal table. He looked as though he might collapse with the weight of some heavy thing.

What had I been saying? I exhaled, breath leaking out of me in a stream of long, slow confusion. It took words with it, things I meant to say.

He wiped an arm across his forehead, his fine sleeves dragging across pallid skin. "Choice? Is that what you were going to say? How could you not have had a choice?"

The room felt like a spinning top, and his confusing words didn't help matters at all. "A choice about what?"

He shook his head and muttered something about this oath being a thorn in his heel. "I'm speaking of you and Matt. Does the oath you swore have anything to do with the romantic involvement you keep denying?" He raised his eyebrows. "Perhaps Matt discovered your gender and swore an oath to protect your secret? It's more chivalrous than I give him credit for, but maybe for the sake of true love . . ."

"For the last time, there's no romance. Never in a million years would I even consider it. Friar's bones, I'd fall for you before I'd look twice at that slimy eel!"

With a thump from the chair—two legs meeting floor—Master Wendyn straightened. A tinge of color had crept back into his face. "Why would Matt have become involved in blood magic, anyway? Under duress, perhaps? And what did you swear? And if he needed help, why didn't he come to me or Grandfather?"

I held up my hands. "Give me a chance to answer, will you?"

"Fine, answer. Start at the beginning. And leave nothing out."

From what I could remember, that was what I'd been trying to do. "All right. You want to know if he was under duress? Not even a lit—"

My voice stuttered to a halt. What was I saying? I stared at my hands, held before me, two strangers whose actions I didn't recognize or understand. After a moment of silent consideration, I dropped them to my sides.

Master Wendyn rubbed at his forehead. "This is getting ridiculous."

"What is?" I rubbed at my head too, near the back. A dull pain had commenced near the base of my skull.

He shook his head. "We have to figure out a way to talk about this without you getting forgetful every other sentence."

Oh. It had happened again. "This would be so much easier if you knew the spell Oscar used."

His gaze shot up to meet mine. "Grandfather used a spell? What are you talking about?"

Perhaps I shouldn't have mentioned that. Now he'd ask questions, and I couldn't afford for him to find out the state I had left Oscar in.

Maybe I could skirt the truth.

"Oscar knows a spell that makes it possible for me to speak of the—" But I could feel it this time, the cloud of forgetfulness waiting to descend on my thoughts, and I stopped myself short of speaking the words that would bring it on. "It makes it possible for me to speak of . . . what we're speaking of. Without the side effects, understand."

"Grandfather knows about all this? The oath and everything else?"

"Yes."

"So he is back. And, what, he sent you out here?"

"Something like that."

He folded his arms. "Was it something like that, or was it *that*?"

I scratched my nose. "The details aren't important." And then, because I couldn't think of any other way to distract him, I asked, "Have you heard about the deaths in Hutterland?"

His eyes narrowed at the change of subject. "What deaths?"

"Forty-two." It took only a moment for me to explain the things Oscar had told me a few hours ago.

The master's face went grim again. "Matt had a part in something as heinous as that?"

I shook my head. "Not a part. He had the only role."

He eyed me. Then all at once he straightened from the chair he leaned on and gave it a swift kick in the leg. It crashed into the table and teetered sideways, clattering against the wooden-planked floor. He paced the length of the room and then swung around before the rough-hewn timber of the south window. "There's still something I don't understand. What you've sworn. It wasn't to kill all those people in Hutterland, or else you wouldn't be able to speak of it. Just what did you swear then?"

It would be useless to try and force the words out, but then again—shouldn't I at least try? I opened my mouth. "It has to do with O—"

I blinked and looked around me. This place seemed familiar. The longer I stared at it, the more I remembered. Ah, yes. Master Wendyn's secret cottage.

"Blast it all!"

I jumped at the sound of the master's angry voice, which brought to my attention a dull pain thumping at the base of my skull. He strode toward me.

"Why are you in such a foul mood?" I asked.

"You said the oath has to do with aw. Aw-what? What's the next sound?"

Oh. I had probably tried to say Oscar. "Sc—" I broke off into blinking confusion.

The master stood before me. His expression turned from bewilderment to dread to horror. "Oscar? The oath has something to do with Grandfather?"

"Who told you that?" I rubbed at my neck. "My head hurts."

"He's hoping to wipe out my entire family," he said slowly. "Starting with Grandfather. You swore to help him kill Grandfather."

Surprise lit up my face. But I could feel the blankness waiting to spring on me, depending on what I said next. "I—I'm sure I can't say anything in response to that."

"Never mind." He wiped a hand over his eyes. "You just did. It's written all over your face. Matt's spell can't regulate your expressions, at least. So he wants to kill my entire family? He's lost his mind."

I didn't disagree with that. "Thank you. I've been trying to tell you that for months."

"Months?" He fixed me with a look and strode closer to grab my arm. "How long do we have? When is he planning on putting this little genocide into motion?"

Before the winter solstice, that's what Kurke said that day in the library. Still more than a month away, but that was a large window of time. "He said before the wi—" Black foggy forgetfulness descended on me.

"Before the what? Is it soon?"

I blinked and stared and wondered why Master Wendyn had hold of my arm. "Is what soon?"

He made a noise of exasperation and dropped my arm. "This is impossible," he growled. "Can you at least tell me if it's happening at this moment? Is that why you rushed out here through two feet of snow?"

Ah. Now I remembered what we were talking about. "Everything is fine back at the Hall." Not counting an unconscious Oscar, but I wasn't about to mention that. "When I discovered what had been going on in Hutterland, I knew I had to find a way to tell you. Especially since I'm leaving tomorrow."

A part of me hoped he'd ask me not to leave so soon, now that all this was out in the open. That part gave a twinge of disappointment when he said, "And you couldn't have just written me a letter before you left?"

"I've tried that," I informed him. "Writing letters is no good. Anything I write disappears."

He strode across the room, past the south window, past the staircase, past the wizard door. A small table stood against the wall, stacked with papers and parchments, which he rifled through. "If we could only speak of this, Matt and me. Is it possible I could get him to see reason?"

I made a noise between a laugh and a snort. "See reason? You'd have more luck convincing a rock it was a tree."

He stared at me before dropping the papers and rubbing at his eyes. "What am I saying? He's decided. There's no going back from this." He went back to rifling through the papers. "Devil's dawn!" he ground out in frustration. "Is there no calendar in this place? What is the date?"

I blinked at him. "The date? What does that matter?"

"Ah, never mind. Here it is." He pulled out a sheet of parchment and held it closer to the candle on the table.

"What are you looking for?"

He shook his head, and then all at once his body relaxed, the parchment dropping to his side. "Well, that's a relief," he said, halfway to himself. "It *is* this week. He'll be too busy to try anything until next week, at the earliest."

"What's this week?" I asked.

Again he shook his head. "Not important. We've got to come up with a plan of action, you and I. I'd like to go back to the hall and get Grandfather's thoughts on this. He has more experience with blood magic than I do—and more connections at the Conclave. I suppose he's researching, and that's why he sent you on alone?"

Blast it all. He wasn't supposed to ask that. And here I was trying not to lie to him anymore. "Yeah, research." The untruth tasted like dust in my mouth.

"Good." He gave a decisive nod. "I'll grab a few of my things, and we can take the door back to the Hall. If we're lucky, we'll have this mess figured out before midnight. Then you can still be on your way in the morning." He headed for the staircase in the corner and took the steps up two at a time. I stared at the empty stairs and gathered my thoughts.

No. It wouldn't happen like that at all. Oscar would turn me over to the Council and I'd be Punished before suppertime tomorrow.

I needed a better plan. One that didn't involve the Council.

Once we got back, I'd wake Oscar from the sleeping potion. Then I'd slip away while he was still groggy. After all, with both the Masters Wendyn aware of the truth, they didn't need me any longer. I'd be more of a hindrance than a help in this situation.

Yes, that was true.

I stared at the staircase and listened to the master moving around upstairs.

Then why did I feel so guilty?

TWENTY-FIVE

I HAD SPENT A long time silencing my conscience. Thieving with Papa, becoming a boy, lying to my masters. With this new desire to be honest with Master Wendyn, it felt like my conscience had awoken for the first time in a long time. When the master came down the staircase a few minutes later, the weight of guilt upon my shoulders for the lies I had told—or, to be more precise, not told—felt like a boulder on my back.

"I'm ready." Master Wendyn carried a bundle of things tied up in a knapsack.

"What's all that?" I eyed the bundle.

"Just a few things. Clothes."

I knew they were his silly silk shirts, but I didn't criticize. Where did a lying murderess-to-be get off criticizing a man's silk-shirt obsession? "We'd better get back." I held the tapestry aside for him. Nerves ran through me as I thought about everything waiting for us at the Hall. When should I confess that Bastian and Cailyn were there?

He said the spell that opened the wizard door and then turned the handle and swung it inward. Musty smells floated on chilled air. I followed him through, unable to make out much in the dark room, and swung the door closed behind me.

Dim light flickered and shimmered from door-shaped rectangles lining three walls, casting strange shadows on the stone floor. Wizard doors. I counted seven of them, including the one we had just come through.

We had arrived somewhere, but I couldn't say where. It was too dark to see much of anything. Damp crawled along my skin, and I shivered.

Master Wendyn muttered an illumination spell, and several candles ensconced in wall holders flickered to life, throwing the room into focus. Wooden crates and casks lined the one wall void of doors. "We're in the cellars." He strode across the room, toward the only door that didn't glow. "That's why it's so cold."

"So this is where you hide your wizard doors? Master Hapthwaite kept most of his in the attic."

"Yes, I remember."

I gave him a questioning glance which he didn't see. "What do you mean, you remember?"

"Hmmm?" He didn't even seem aware of what he had said. "Oh. Never mind that."

He opened the non-glowing door, revealing a dingy hallway. He muttered another illumination spell, and the hall brightened to a less dingy version of dingy.

"You can't say something like that and just expect me to forget it. Besides, you've been talking Master Hapthwaite down ever since I first came here. What's your connection to him, anyway?"

He gave a short burst of a sigh and stopped in the middle of the hallway. "This isn't the time—"

"I'm leaving tomorrow, doomed to spend the rest of my life wondering why you hate him so much. Just take five seconds and answer the question."

Another short sigh. "Fine. I'll tell you—if only to stop you from going back there to beg him to become your master again." He swung around to face me. "When I say he's a baboon, I'm speaking from personal experience. Hapthwaite was my first master."

My mouth opened, closed, and then opened again. "But I thought Uphammer was your master. You had two?"

"Unfortunately. I spent four years with Hapthwaite, the idiot."

"Did he disapprentice you too?"

He laughed, a dry, mirthless sound. "I wish I'd been that lucky. If he'd disapprenticed me, I might've gotten somewhere with my training sooner."

I could feel my brow puckering. "What did he do that was so awful?"

"It's what he didn't do. Didn't teach me, didn't let me sit for trials, didn't give me access to spell books. I was only eight years old when I was first apprenticed, a child. Hapthwaite was up for a position on the Council that year. When he didn't get it, he blamed Grandfather and took it out on me."

He became absorbed in straightening a candle that had gone askew in its holder. "Whenever I tried to tell my parents what was going on, they put it off as homesickness and told me apprenticeships weren't meant to be easy. Grandfather warned me not to disgrace him. I thought the problem must be me. So I stayed—for four years." He hefted the knapsack higher under his arm, and something made a clanking noise. There was something more than shirts in there. "Things didn't get better."

"What happened?"

"We grew more antagonistic toward each other. I began calling him 'the baboon,' which always got a rise out of him, and he'd rage at me for being an imbecile. At last he agreed to let me sit for the first trial, even though he'd taught me nothing, not in four years. I think he believed it would humiliate grandfather, the PMW, for his grandson to fail so publicly. And that's pretty much how it happened."

"So how did you end up with Uphammer?"

"Hapthwaite's plan backfired. While it made Grandfather look bad, for the first time he listened and realized I'd been telling the truth. My apprenticeship ended, and he found me a new master."

I stared at him in fascination. "This is why you brought me home from Bramford that day, isn't it? Did you think you were saving me from Hapthwaite?"

He sighed and ran a hand over his face. "I suppose, yes. I wasn't thrilled to have you foisted on me, but I knew I couldn't send you back to Hapthwaite. Your lack of self-control seemed like further proof he wasn't giving you the attention he should have—just as he did with me."

I shook my head. "Master Hapthwaite wasn't like that. He was boring and concerned about appearances, but never vindictive. Not with me."

He nodded. "Then you were lucky."

I couldn't stop myself from asking one further question. "Did you try to get Hapthwaite to disapprentice me, hoping it would bring scandal on him?"

After a pause he answered, "Don't think it didn't cross my mind. But it didn't take encouraging at all. Once he knew you'd been brawling in the streets, he was through with you." He pushed off the wall and straightened. "Underwi—I mean, Mullins. I—I feel I should say this now, since you'll be leaving. I've been hard on you, and I know it. Thank you for trying to help my family, despite my . . . prickliness, shall we say?"

Heat suffused my face. "Oh. You're welcome." I felt worse than ever about my lies.

"Now. Let's go find grandfather and take care of Matt." He

continued down the hall and tossed over his shoulder at me, "I'll try his bedroom, and you check his other favorite places—the library and the kitchen."

"Er . . . maybe we should do it the other way around, because . . ." I followed him up a winding stair. "Because Master Wendyn, there's something I have to say too."

He glanced over his shoulder at me and then continued the climb. "I don't like that tone in your voice. That's your I'm-about-to-confess-something-bad voice."

"It's not bad, exactly—well, all right, maybe it is . . ." Maybe I should start slow, with the least bad confession.

"Well, tell me already. Get it over with."

I chewed on my lip. "Listen. Remember the carriage ride home from Bramford? After we saved that girl?"

"You mean when I found out—" He cleared his throat.

"Yes, that one. Before that we got to talking. You said you weren't in love with Cailyn anymore. Remember that?"

He looked back at me again, his mouth turned downward in a scowl. "That's none of your business. I never should have—"

"Yes, well, you said it, and you can't unsay it now." We reached the main floor and rounded a corner into the front hall.

"Well, please just forget it. It's none of your business. Why bring it up now, of all times?"

"It's just that . . . well, if you were telling the truth in the carriage that day, you'll want to remember what you said. It's about to become very pertinent."

Master Wendyn came to an abrupt halt and swiveled to stare at me. "What did you do?"

I held my hands out in front of me. "Nothing! I'm innocent here."

The kitchen door swung open. Bastian strode into the hallway and stopped when he saw us.

"They came here all on their own," I blurted, my voice low. "Nothing to do with me at all."

"They?" he repeated, staring at Bastian.

"Ah, Garrick. You're back." Bastian's voice sounded very like Father Wendyn in that moment. "I knew you could track him down for us, underwizard." Bastian strode forward and clapped Master Wendyn on the back, apparently oblivious to the master's stiff shoulders and frozen expression.

Master Wendyn fixed me with an accusing expression. "'Track him down'?" he repeated.

"Don't be too mad at the boy, Garrick. We asked him to find you." Behind him the kitchen door swung again, and Cailyn emerged. She stopped short when she saw us, one hand on her belly. "But since we are here, maybe you'd consent to talk? Just for a few minutes?"

Master Wendyn's jaw worked, but his expression turned from anger to resignation. "Ah. Talk. How nice." Once more his eyes flashed to my face, his jaw worked, and then he looked back to his brother. He sighed. "Fine. I'll just say this now, then. I've forgiven you. Truth is, I just . . . never found the right time to say it."

"Truly, Garrick?" Cailyn asked, stepping closer.

"Yes, truly."

I couldn't seem to hold back my smile. A feeling I couldn't quite put a name to worked its way up the back of my throat. Was this . . . pride?

When the master looked back at me, his expression turned annoyed. "Mullins, go find Grandfather. I'd like the three of us to meet in my study in ten minutes, and don't forget that what we have to talk about is time sensitive. In the meantime, I'll have a chat with my brother and sister-of-the-law."

"All right." I backed away and then turned and headed up the stairs.

It touched my heart to see the master soften toward his brother. He'd learned to forgive, and just in time. He'd need that skill when I was gone and Oscar told him what I'd done.

BY THE TIME I reached the landing at the top of the stairs, the plan had solidified in my mind. I'd wake Oscar, grab what belongings I could, and then take the door to the Conclave. I didn't think they locked the entrance there until midnight, so I should be able to pass through into the city of Hampstone without difficulty. There in the big city I would begin my new life.

I turned the corner and saw Oscar's door ahead—and then paused.

Could I really just leave? Flee the scene of all the trouble I'd caused, like a coward? Hope that everything would somehow right itself?

I reminded myself of someone I despised—Papa. Fleeing the scene of Gavin's impending death, because it was too much to take. How was that any different from what I was about to do?

If only I knew how much time I had, really had, before Kurke put his plan in motion. But then, even if I knew how much time I had, what could I do about it?

My fingers grasped the doorknob.

Time.

I froze again, staring at the door but not really seeing it.

When the time is right.

That's what Kurke said when I asked him about the timing of his revenge. When the time is right. Or was it . . . when the Time is right?

Master Wendyn had seemed very certain that Kurke would be otherwise occupied for a few days. Could it be possible that today was the anniversary of his family's death? Their Time?

It would make sense for Kurke to carry out his revenge now.

I withdrew my hand from the doorknob. This question couldn't wait. No matter how rude, I'd have to interrupt the master and his brother to find out the answer.

But before I could even step back, a yank pulled me backward by the collar. I collided with something solid and man-sized. When I craned my neck up and back to look, I met magnetic blue eyes.

"I hear Oscar's returned. Five whole hours he's been back, and yet I didn't hear it from you." Kurke jerked on my collar again so it cut into my windpipe.

My fingers scrabbled at my neck, trying to loosen the fabric there. "Been . . . busy," I said, my voice little more than a grunt as I struggled to speak.

He loosened his grip, and my choking eased. "Well, no matter. You're here now. You know I couldn't do this without you."

"Do what?"

"Carry out our oath, of course. It's time."

Cold dread rushed through me.

TWENTY-SIX

NOT A SINGLE DEFENSE spell came to my mind. I stood paralyzed by fear.

Kurke propelled me forward with one hand and then reached past me to jerk the door handle and shove it open.

Ivan looked up. He sat next to a still Oscar on the bed, holding a spell book in his hands. He smiled, and then his glance went beyond me. The smile slid south.

"Ah. The fool." Kurke rested a hand on my shoulder. "He's no use to me. What do you suggest I do with him, Avery?"

"With Ivan?" I clarified. "Nothing. He's harmless." I stood with my back to Kurke, so it was a simple matter to gesture at Ivan. *Run.*

But Ivan didn't run, although I could tell he understood, judging by the concerned quirk his brow took on. He came to his feet, the book falling to the floor.

"Harmless or not—" Kurke said and raised one hand, sending a spell at him. Ivan tried to duck too late. The spell tumbled him into the chair, which then tipped backward to the floor. He sprawled on his back in the alcove, half on the chair and half out of it, unmoving.

"Why did you do that?" I scrambled closer to Ivan and knelt, looking him over for injuries. He lay pale and still, despite the lack of any visible blood.

Kurke didn't apologize or explain or even anything close to it. He took several steps forward, surveying the room and Oscar snoring in the bed. "You gave him a sleeping potion," he said, delighted. "For me?"

I frowned. "It was an unfortunate coincidence."

He chuckled. "Either way, your timing couldn't be better. Come over here and help me."

I pushed to my knees, slow and stiff, my thoughts racing as I tried to come up with a plan. I'd like to snap him in half for hurting Ivan, if only I knew a spell for that. Stupid of me to just now realize Kurke meant to carry this out on the anniversary of his family's death. Of course that would be when he'd want to do it, blaming Oscar as he did.

No one would die today. No one would die today. I repeated it to myself over and over, a mantra I hoped upon hope would come true.

All I had to do was get away from Kurke long enough to alert the others in the house what was going on. Then Master Wendyn would take care of the rest.

Yes, I was certain it would be that easy.

Unless it wasn't.

"What do you want me to do?" My voice sounded far more compliant than I felt.

He fished in his knapsack and handed me a trammel. "Put this on Oscar."

I stared down at the metal device he'd left in my hands, while Kurke fished in the bag and moved away from me.

Bones. He meant to incapacitate Oscar completely.

But I had a better idea for the trammel. Either I was about to do the dumbest thing I'd ever done or the bravest.

Kurke turned his back to me. Quickly, before I could think better of it, I sent a freezing spell at him. He stopped where he stood, leaned over the knapsack he kept fishing in. Stuck in place.

I stepped nearer and circled the trammel around his neck. It shut with a click, and I moved in front of him to insert the key.

Kurke's foot moved.

Blast it all, he was unweaving my spell! I fumbled with the key, haste making me clumsy. I shoved it into the locking mechanism at the same moment Kurke's knapsack dropped to the ground with a thunk. His arm darted out and knocked me aside before I could finish with the lock. I stumbled backward and fell on my backside.

Dumbest thing I'd ever done. Definitely.

He reached up and plucked the key from the lock around his neck, then clicked the trammel open. "Maybe I didn't make myself clear, Avery. You can help me kill Oscar, or you can die. Those are the only two options."

The ground fell away beneath me, and a choking pressure crushed my throat. Kurke held me in place with the point of one finger, floating above the ground, touching nothing, clawing at the invisible hand around my neck. "You and I are supposed to be in this together. You swore the oath, and might I remind you, willingly. Now what's your choice? Will you help me, or shall I kill you now?"

"I'll . . . help . . ." I choked out. All at once I dropped to the ground in a heap.

"Good," Kurke said, his voice filled with disgust. "Now go put that trammel on Oscar like I asked you to. And if you dare to spell me again, I *will* kill you." He tossed the metal mechanism at me, and it clanked at my feet.

I retrieved the trammel and rubbed at my neck. It took

everything in me not to spell Oscar awake as I stepped closer to him. But I'd drawn enough ire from Kurke for the moment.

"Now," Kurke muttered halfway to himself, "to tie him up."

My hands trembled as I lifted Oscar's head, his snowy white hair tickling my fingers. I circled the trammel around his neck. The key turned in the lock, and I slipped it into my pocket. "You'll need rope," I offered. "There's some in the stables. Shall I get it?" I hugged my arms around myself, trying to stop myself from trembling.

"No need." He pulled his hand out of the bag, rope clutched in his fist. "Hand me the key and then go get rid of the staff."

I pulled the key out of my pocket and handed it to him. "Get rid of them?"

"Yes. Tell them they're not needed today. I'd hate for them to get in my way." He tossed the key in the air and threw a spell at it. It exploded into nothing, leaving behind an ashy, sooty smudge on the wooden-planked floor.

It didn't take much imagination to know what happened when people got in his way. "That's a big job. It will take me more than a few minutes."

"This isn't that difficult, Avery. Tell them they're dismissed and say it with authority."

I moved toward the door.

"And bring Garrick back with you," Kurke continued. "But don't tell him I'm here. I'd like to surprise him."

Yes. I could just imagine the surprise he'd have in store.

"If I find out you've gone against any of my instructions, you can say goodbye to the fool."

My fist clenched, but I forced myself to relax. No. I must remain calm. Now would be the absolute worst time to lose control. "His name is Ivan."

"Noted. Poor, sweet little Ivan's life is on the line, so get moving." He tapped his ear. "I'll be listening. Watching too."

"Watching?" I repeated stupidly. "There's no spell for that."

"Wasn't till now. I developed one in recent months." He pointed a finger at me and uttered an incantation. I felt magic settle around me, the close, warm feeling of a cocoon. "There. Now it will show me everything you see. Get going."

I took one last look at Ivan, lying in the corner limp and helpless. Visions of Mrs. Pitts with her broken legs moved through my memory. I hurried out of the room.

What if Kurke killed Oscar while I was gone? What if this was all a ploy to get Oscar alone so he could perform his killing spell?

No, he wouldn't kill him, not yet. He wouldn't have trammeled Oscar if he didn't plan on waking him up first. Besides, if I knew Kurke, he'd want an audience for his killing spell. Me and Master Wendyn, at the least.

Halfway down the stairs, I met the master coming up.

"What's taking you so long? Where's grandfather?"

I couldn't let the master go into Oscar's room. Who knew what would happen? I had to keep him out of there for as long as possible. "Perhaps he's in the library?" I said, too brightly. "Or scrying outside?"

Master Wendyn gave me a strange look. "In the snow?"

"Yes, well, you never know with Oscar, do you? He's done some strange things," I said briskly.

He nodded and seemed to accept that. "True enough. Very well, I'll go check the library. If you find him before I do, tell him that Bastian and Cailyn are determined we're sitting down for a meal together before they go, and it's just about ready." He huffed out a quick sigh. "I understand why they want to, but still, it's blasted inconvenient right now."

"Yes. Well, I'll look in the sitting room. He may be reading."

"Wherever he is, he must be with Ivan. I haven't seen him either."

"Yes. Nor I." I continued down the stairs and promised myself if we made it through this alive, I'd never lie to the master again. Not that it meant much, seeing how I was supposed to leave Ryker Hall tomorrow.

Behind me, I heard Master Wendyn turn and follow me down the steps. At the bottom of the staircase, I veered to the left toward the sitting room while he went to the right toward the library. The front hallway stood empty, and I continued right on past the sitting room and through the servant's hall to the kitchen. On the way, I passed Edwin and Peck and another stable hand and told them they were dismissed for the day, per the master's order. Their faces brightened, and they beat a quick path to the side door.

In the kitchen, Cailyn and Edie looked up from something that must be a soufflé.

I didn't waste words. "Edie, Master Wendyn has dismissed you for the day."

She looked up, a frown on her face.

"If you hurry, you can catch up with Edwin and the others on their way back to town."

"Edwin?" she repeated. "But—" She looked at Cailyn, and her face smoothed out. "Right. I'll just be going." She wiped her hands and left.

I turned my attention to Cailyn, who had leaned herself over a bowl in order to spoon something velvety white and smooth into it. Tendrils of golden hair fell around her face. "And you, Ms. Wendyn—"

"Call me Cailyn."

"Yes, well, you'll have to go too. Oscar's not feeling well, so supper together is out of the question."

"Not feeling well?" Concern dotted her brow. "Is this Garrick's doing? He's backing out of what he said earlier, isn't he? He hasn't forgiven anything."

"No, of course not. He doesn't say things he doesn't mean."

She tilted her head and looked at me. "True, but this illness seems to have come on quickly."

"Many illnesses do." My eyes dropped to her swollen belly. "Think of your baby."

That ought to be a hard enough push.

I couldn't stop my next thought. If Kurke's spell succeeded, Cailyn's husband and baby would both die.

Her eyes followed mine, and she rested a hand on her belly. "Yes, I suppose you're right. I'd better find Bastian."

"No," I told her. "Just go. I'll send you through the wizard door to the Conclave. Don't you live in Hampstone? It'll be quicker, and I'll send your husband through as soon as I locate him."

"But we brought our carriage, and the footman—"

"I'll send him through too," I told her as the flash of an idea came to me. "It's too dangerous to stay here. The wasting sickness is quite contagious."

"Wasting sickness?" she repeated. "Oscar has the wasting sickness?"

I lowered my voice and looked around. "Maybe. It's too dangerous for you to be here. Just wait for your husband at the Conclave."

After a moment's hesitation, she nodded. I motioned for her to follow me, and in less than a minute, I'd sent her through to Hampstone.

One more Wendyn to go.

I FOUND Cook sulking in the larder, as if the tiny room was the last domain she could still lay claim to. Dismissing her took more work. "I will see Master Wendyn fed, come what may," she insisted, when I told her she'd been dismissed. But when I explained to her that Oscar's "illness" might be the wasting sickness, she exclaimed about her children and fled the kitchen.

Master Wendyn must be making a thorough examination of the library, because I didn't see him as I investigated the lower level of the house, dismissing the last remaining servants as I ran into them. I sent three more manservants and a serving maid off into the night and then Bastian's footman through the wizard door. I argued with Mrs. Pitts for at least five minutes, and when she still refused to leave, regardless of what illness might have swept the household, I shoved her into a closet off the breakfast room and cast a privacy spell around her so no one would hear her shouting or knocking.

Even though I did it for her own safety, I couldn't say I didn't take satisfaction in it.

I stuck an ear to the library door minutes later and discovered voices emanating from within. A quick turn of the door handle and I looked inside the room.

"—funny how it all happened. Both of us in Hutterland and the same city, even. We never meant—"

"Never mind that." I could hear the weariness in Master Wendyn's voice. Whatever generosity pushed him to proclaim his forgiveness to his brother, it had worn thin. "Why don't we go eat? It must be ready by now."

I cleared my throat. "I apologize for interrupting, but I have bad news. Ms. Wendyn—that is, Cailyn—felt unwell. I sent her to the Conclave with the footman. I thought it would be the quickest way back to your home."

These lies were coming easier and easier.

Bastian came to his feet. "What? What's the matter?"

"She wasn't looking well. Not at all. Said something about . . . headache. And . . . nausea. And bleeding." Yes. That sounded dire enough.

Alarm colored his face. "I must join her."

"Calm yourself, Bastian. I'm sure everything will be fine." The master arose and gestured for his brother to follow him. "It sounds like we'll need to postpone our supper for now."

I tailed after the two of them, out the library door, down the hall, around the corner. I waited outside as they entered the study.

The whole house felt empty, devoid as it was of servants. The extreme quiet struck me as odd and rather obvious. Hopefully Master Wendyn would notice, because with all the restrictions Kurke had put on me, I couldn't think of any other warning I could give.

A few minutes later the master came back alone, hand to his forehead. "What a relief. Good work, Mullins."

"What do you mean?"

"Coming up with that lie. Whatever you said to get Cailyn to go, you have my thanks. There are more important things to think about at the moment."

My mouth opened in surprise. "How did you know I made it up?"

His head tilted as he considered. "I don't know. Something about your expression, but it was mostly a guess. And now you've confirmed it. Did you locate Oscar?"

I bit my lip. "He's in his room. Did you . . . see anyone in the hallway?"

"Like who?"

I shrugged. "Just anyone."

"No. Only Edie.

"That's unusual, isn't it?" That would have to be enough of a hint to the master that all was not well, because I couldn't risk saying more. I continued brusquely, "Oscar thought the best place for the three of us to meet would be his room. So that's where he is." I didn't look at the master to see his reaction to my words. If he caught on to what I was trying so obliquely to hint at, I didn't want Kurke to see it happen.

The master's voice came after a moment. "Very well. Let's get this over with. Come along."

I followed him back up the staircase, planning what to do next all the while. Defense spells, those were what I needed. The fire spell would be an ill-advised choice for the indoors. But there was always the freezing spell, although I obviously couldn't trust my own to hold Kurke for long. I'd learned a couple of killing spells in that forbidden book of Hapthwaite's which I memorized. Oh, and also the dry as desert spell, with which I dried up my own tears. Master Wendyn had said it was a killing spell.

He stopped at the top of the landing. "Was he outside?"

The question took me off guard. "Hmmm? Was who outside?"

"Oscar. Was he out with his scrying stick?"

"Oh. No. No, he was in the sitting room."

"Ah. Well then. At least he won't be chilled."

Something about the way he looked at me gave me pause, but then he turned and headed for Oscar's room. Perhaps I had imagined it. As he took the door handle and turned it, something shifted in the surrounding air. Not until I followed him through the door did I realize the magic had shifted. Master Wendyn had cast a spell.

A blinding blast of magic exploded just in front of the master as we walked into the room.

Bones, what had he done? He shoved me further behind him. "Get down, Mullins!"

I crouched, wondering what in the three kingdoms that spell was, when another blinding flash of magic rushed toward us.

Wait. That explosion hadn't been the master's doing. That was Kurke, the slimy toad. He'd moved Oscar's bed so it stood parallel to the door, and the fuzzy edges of the messy hair on his head peeked up from behind it every now and then as he used the man's unconscious body as a shield. The master, meanwhile, had performed a shielding spell that kept Kurke's magic from hitting us. That must be the power I felt him gathering.

He had known I lied.

Another blast of magic hit the master's shield spell. Kurke had him pinned down, and he couldn't send a spell back at him because he might hit Oscar.

I peeked around the master, toward the corner of the alcove where I last saw Ivan. The corner stood empty. "What did you do with Ivan?"

"Got rid of him. Don't feel so bad, either, now that I know you double-crossed me."

"I double-crossed you?" I came to my feet without thinking about it. "If you've so much as left a scratch on him—"

"Mullins, get back!" Master Wendyn shoved me to the side, and magic bounced off the spot I had just stood in, with a hiss and crackle that sounded as though we stood in the middle of a flaming fire.

Was this it? Was Kurke finally going to kill me as he'd been promising to do, longing to do, even?

But no, he wasn't trying to kill me. That hadn't been a killing spell. He wasn't trying to kill Master Wendyn either. He wasn't through with us yet. He hadn't gotten from either of us what he wanted, just yet.

Once he did, *then* he'd kill us.

"What's this all about, Matt? Why are you doing this?"

Kurke came to his feet. "It's simple, Garrick. You Wendyns killed my family. Today, I'll kill yours." He let loose another spell, one that sizzled across the master's shield spell like butter on a hot pan. It licked the back of my hand, the only part of me unfortunate enough to be sticking out past the edge of the spell, which didn't encompass me. The flesh burned like it had been dipped in liquid fire. I hissed and slunk back further behind the master, hand clutched to my chest.

Bones. I was out of my depth here. What sort of spell was that?

"Nobody's killed anyone. Your family died in an accident." Master Wendyn's tone was placating, like he spoke to a confused child.

"Stop being so smug and sure about how right you are. That's one thing I hate about you." Another spell flew at us. This one set the master back on his heels, but his shield spell held.

Now with Kurke more exposed, Master Wendyn dared to throw a spell his way. Magic exploded toward Kurke like a vacuum of energy, a spell that knocked into his shield like a giant fist. He fell back two steps and then gave a wheezy laugh. "A pummeling spell? That's the best you can do?"

"I don't want to fight you, Matt. None of this is necessary." Frustration laced the master's voice.

"But it is. Oscar killed my family—no, don't argue with me; it's true. You don't know how long I've been waiting for this day, when I'd be able to tell you and your grandfather how much I despise you."

"So tell us. Both of us. Wake grandfather—or are you afraid that you won't be able to handle him, even bound and trammeled?"

Kurke's brow darkened, and then, all at once, he disappeared.

I blinked and looked around. I crouched behind the master, hand still stinging like I stuck it in the fireplace, and I couldn't think of a healing spell to make it stop. I looked left, then right. No Kurke.

He must have used a transporting spell. He couldn't have

gone far as they only worked for short distances. I scrambled to the overturned chair Ivan was lying in when last I saw him. "He's done something with Ivan." My voice shook, and I swallowed against it, trying to push down the rush of something I couldn't name. "He was here. Kurke said he'd hurt him—"

"Calm down. We'll find him." Master Wendyn approached the bed and looked Oscar over.

I straightened, hand to my chest where I could feel the racing of my heart. "How did you know Kurke would be here? You had that shield spell in place before you even opened the door."

He looked up from Oscar. "Your left eye squints when you lie."

My mouth opened. "Is that true?"

"Believe it or not. How long ago did he give grandfather a sleeping potion?"

Oscar still slept as peacefully as when I left him earlier. I chewed on my lip. "That was me. I gave it to him before I went on that stupid expedition to find you."

His face stiffened. "Because Matt forced you to?"

My gut twisted, and I looked away. "No. Because Oscar wanted to take me to the Conclave to explain myself to the Council. I wanted to avoid the Punishment."

When I looked again, the master's jaw had clenched. "Mullins, later you and I are going to have a long talk about your aversion to telling the truth."

He flicked a waking spell at Oscar. After a moment the form on the bed shifted and made signs of waking. Master Wendyn put a hand to his face and tapped him on the cheek. "Grandfather?"

"What if he's dead?" I tapped my chest, against my beating heart. "Not Oscar. I mean Ivan."

He didn't look up. "He's not dead."

I wished he sounded surer. "But—"

"Garrick?" Oscar said sleepily. "What's . . . going on? S'this a . . . trammel?" He ran a hand over the metal contraption around his neck and then yawned and closed his eyes again.

"How much sleeping potion did you give him?"

"Only . . . maybe half a bottle."

"Devil's dawn, Mullins, that'd take down an elephant!"

I dropped my hand. "Well . . . how was I supposed to know? It's not like you label the bottles with instructions!"

"That's because it didn't occur to me anyone would use them other than me." His clipped tone signaled to me just how he felt about it.

I sighed. "All right. I'm sorry. I shouldn't have done it, but I was in a bind."

He ran a hand over his face. "This isn't productive. We need to get this trammel off him."

"We can't. See that smudge on the floor over there? That's the key. There's not even enough left of it to do an unbroken spell."

Master Wendyn cursed. "We need another trammel, then. One for Matt."

"Where do you suppose he's gone? Is he off preparing his bloodlines spell?"

"I don't know, but I'm sure he'll be back. I want you to promise to stay out of the fight, Mullins, whatever happens." Master Wendyn held his hands out before him. He built a spell, drawing magic inward. "No stupid heroics."

"What makes you think my heroics would be stupid?"

"I haven't forgotten how you became my apprentice—running into a fight you couldn't win. A lot of lives are at stake here, and I understand oaths. Let me handle this."

I swallowed. "Fine. What's your plan? Is there a way to get

rid of the—" Nope, couldn't say blood oath. "—the . . . you know. What I swore."

"Not unless you're keen on dying."

"Excuse me?"

"Blood oaths are, as a rule, pretty straightforward. Either you do what you swore to do, or you die. It forces swearers to stay dedicated to a cause, rather than losing their nerve. Blood oaths always have a deadline and a consequence—death."

My collar suddenly felt too tight and the room too close. "But there's a way to remove it, right?"

A frown tugged his mouth downward. I knew I was drawing his concentration from whatever spell he was weaving, but this was my future we were talking about here.

"I see I wasn't clear enough. If you want to end the oath without killing Oscar, your options are few. There's just one, really—you or Kurke has to die."

I swallowed. "You're saying either of our deaths would end the oath?"

"Render it null and void, more like."

More death. Would I never escape it?

"But what if—"

Kurke appeared in the alcove, mere steps from Master Wendyn. His bloodless fingers clutched an ebony-handled dagger, and stuffed under the other arm he held a sheaf of papers.

"I've brought some reading for you, Garrick. Thought you might find it interesting before I send you to the underworld."

Master Wendyn let loose the spell he'd woven. It crashed into Kurke, bounced off his still-intact shield spell, and then—to my astonishment—broke through it. Something— another pummeling spell?—knocked Kurke back. He crashed into the window seat and tumbled to the floor, the dagger knocked loose from his limp fingers. The master followed it up with a quick freezing spell while papers fluttered to the ground.

"Mullins." He didn't take his eyes from Kurke. "Freezing spell. Now."

"It won't work."

"*Now.*"

Why Kurke needed to be held by two freezing spells was beyond my comprehension, and I knew my spell was practically useless, but I performed it without further protest. Master Wendyn moved closer, kicking the dagger away from Kurke's hand.

He retrieved the papers, which had scattered about the floor. His ruffled white shirt showed signs of perspiration. "What is this, Matt? A file? I realize this week is your family's Time, but I think you're letting the sorrow of the day affect you for the worse."

One of Kurke's fingers moved. Master Wendyn straightened and cast another freezing spell.

"Again, Mullins." He waved at me, and I recast my spell as well.

Now I understood. As Kurke dismantled the spells, we cast them again. Even my freezing spell—which was sure to be weaker than the master's—was of some use in this situation, because it slowed Kurke down at least a little.

"What do you think he's done with Ivan?" I stepped past Kurke and turned the handle to the alcove's little door, which led out to the balcony. Outside, I looked to the ground below, almost afraid to. What if I saw Ivan's broken body lying down there? But only the blank snow stared back at me.

"Wherever he is, we'll find him." The master's voice drifted out the door, and I went back inside, away from the cold. He leaned against the desk, looking over Kurke's sheaf of papers. I crowded next to him, trying to read over his shoulder. He gave me an annoyed glance. "Do you mind?"

"What's it say?"

He moved away. "It's a file from the vault. Not meant for your eyes."

"Yours either," I pointed out.

"Yes, well, one of us has to look at it."

I made a face.

For a moment all was quiet, and then the master cursed.

"What? What is it?"

He looked up. "Freezing spell. Now."

We both sent our freezing spells at Kurke again.

"It's a file from the vault kept on Nox."

Nox. I knew that name. "His father?"

"Yes. By the Council."

"Does it say—"

He put the papers down. "They didn't die in a buggy accident." His voice was quiet, and he looked at Kurke, frozen on the floor as he was, and then to me. "I need you to go to my study, Mullins. I left my knapsack on the desk there. Bring it."

"This isn't the time to worry about a little perspiration on your silk shirt."

He scrubbed a hand down his face. "I don't care about the shirts; just bring the bag. And then it might be best if you left. Grandfather and I can handle Matt. Go hide somewhere for a day. When you come back, we can find Ivan together, if he hasn't turned up yet."

The words tempted me. A part of me wanted to do just as he said, and I despised that part of myself.

I wasn't my father. I wouldn't run off into the night at the first hint of trouble. "Your grandfather is incoherent. You need a conscious person's help. You need me."

"It'll be safer for all of us if you're not here."

"Safer how?"

Movement from the ground behind us. "Freezing spell—" Master Wendyn said, but that was all he got out. A blinding blast of magic hit him in the back. He stumbled forward, smashed into a chair, and sprawled.

I whirled and sent a freezing spell toward Kurke. He'd already come to his feet, and my spell froze him mid-stride. I turned, scanning for a weapon.

No, what I needed was a trammel. I needed the trammel from the master's study.

I took three steps toward the door and then Kurke moved again, tossing a spell at me that threw me backward into the wall. I slithered to the ground, head spinning and blackness before my eyes.

It took several minutes for me to gain control of myself again. I opened my eyes and watched Kurke clamp a trammel around Master Wendyn's neck. He must have had another one in that little knapsack he'd been poking around in. The master's head lolled sideways, eyelids fluttering, and he sagged back to the ground in a heap when Kurke released him. Kurke tossed the key in the air and hit it with a spell that exploded it.

My ears rang with the noise, and nausea rose in my throat. Friar's bones, I wasn't concussed, was I? I blinked and tried to clear my blurry vision. Must help Master Wendyn.

I opened my eyes again. Kurke bound the master's hands and feet. I was still trying to push myself up off the ground when Kurke dragged Master Wendyn across the floor to the middle of the room. Then he muttered a spell that sounded familiar—oh yes, that was a revealing spell—and a wizard door shimmered into existence just in front of him. He turned the handle, pushed it open, and dragged the master inside, wherever inside was.

Kurke emerged and slammed the door with a bang of finality. It shimmered into nothing.

Wherever he'd sent Master Wendyn, there was no way for him to get back. He was bound, trammeled, and who knew how hurt.

My arms shook as I pushed myself up. "Why did you—where did you—"

"On your feet." Kurke ran a hand over his face.

When I didn't comply as fast as he would have liked, he pointed a finger in my direction. Magic yanked me to my feet and rushed me toward him. He took hold of me by the front of my shirt and pulled me closer, too close, his face inches from mine. I could see the stubble on his chin. The bruise forming beneath the stubble on his chin. The spittle on his lips as he hissed at me.

"If you ever dare to defy me again—" He pulled back and slapped me across the face, so hard my teeth rattled in my head. "I thought I'd let you live once we're done with this, Avery. Don't make me change my mind."

Something in me snapped. "Do it then," I told him. "I *will* defy you again, so you might as well just kill me now. I won't help you do this."

My words must have surprised him, because for a moment he stared at me, blinked, and then his face relaxed into a smile. "If that's what you want, then that's your choice, I suppose. But you're wrong. You *will* help me. In fact, you'll have the privilege of performing the killing spell, Avery."

He tossed his head back and laughed.

And laughed and laughed.

TWENTY-SEVEN

HIS LAUGHTER MADE ME nervous, but more than that—angry. "Where's Ivan? What've you done with Master Wendyn?"

Kurke wiped his eyes. "They're gone. If we're lucky, never to return."

The words brought a heaviness to me. "Friar's bones, you're mad." I didn't mean to say the words; they sort of slipped out. "You really are. You're insane."

He let go of my shirt and stepped away to straighten his mussed robes. "Why do you always say that as though it's a bad thing? Mad just means I'm willing to do what is necessary without feeling bad about it." He ran his hands over his hair as though it was important to make sure one looked presentable before one killed an entire bloodline. "Oscar's life has been far longer than it should have been. Much longer than my own father had."

From the bed, Oscar made a sputtering noise. "Wasss . . . going on?"

Four steps and Kurke slapped his face. "Wake up, old man."

Oscar attempted to open his eyes, but they slid closed again a moment later.

"Oscar should have died on Garrick's natalis, that day in the library. But you outwitted me with that little boy, using him to manipulate me. I realized later it was the wrong day for it to happen, anyway. It had to happen during my family's Time in order for it to mean something." He sighed. "I suppose that's the poetic side of me."

"It's a little extreme to kill the entire family, isn't it? Even little Vito and the other children? They've nothing to do with this."

"They'll grow up to be big Wendyns one day, and they'll leave their rotten imprint on the world, same as Oscar. I'm doing you a favor. I'm doing all of Faronna a favor."

"And what about that family in Hutterland?"

"So you figured that out, did you?" Pride threaded his tone.

"Oscar did."

"Good. I'm glad it was him. Their patriarch wronged me once. Don't worry—they got what they deserved. Come help me." He retrieved his knapsack and dug within. After pulling out a few more lengths of rope, another trammel, a small cup, and another knife, he set them in a neat row on Oscar's desk.

"The Council won't let this stand. Murdering a former PMW and his family? You'll never outrun them."

"You mean *we'll* never outrun them. Don't forget you'll be performing the spell. I'll just sort of be your assistant. But how are they going to know it was us? By the time they figure it out, we'll be gone. There are places we can go that they'll never find us."

"If you think I'm going anywhere with you—" I broke off. I was going to say "then you're mad," but it seemed redundant at this point.

He eyed me. "There's a place for you there, Avery. Think about it."

The offer made my skin crawl. "Have you ever given Oscar a chance to tell his side of the story? There could be a reasonable explanation for all of this."

The knapsack appeared to have outlived its usefulness. He tossed it to the side and went to retrieve the dagger from the floor where Master Wendyn kicked it. He hefted it in one hand and frowned at me, eyebrows pushing south. "I don't need to hear his side of the story. I've read all about it in the file."

"Wha—?" I blinked. "You've only read about this on paper? When you could hear about it firsthand?"

"I could hear lies about it firsthand, you mean." He offered me the knife, handle out. "Here. You're going to do this."

"I am not."

He moved toward me, and I retreated. We hadn't sparred yet, and I wasn't eager to throw out the first spell and escalate the conflict.

"You're bleeding, Avery." Kurke lowered the knife and reached toward me. His hand touched my face, somewhere near my temple. I flinched, surprised to find that the spot felt tender. He drew his hand back, showing me blood on the ends of his fingers. "You need to be more careful."

"*I* need to be careful? You're the one who—"

He uttered a spell, blood-stained fingers pointed at me.

I backed off a few steps and cast a shield spell—one I memorized among those first hundred spells from the master. I felt its protection settle around me.

Kurke's spell built. The magic climbed and weaved and pulled and pushed against the shield I'd erected around myself. It prodded and poked, and I scrambled backward, as though I could get away from it. I had to get away from it.

My back ran into the wall.

I felt the moment my spell fell. Kurke's magic reached through the barrier and took hold of me in a way I'd never felt before. It felt as though it anchored itself to my insides. To my blood.

This was like the blood oath . . . only different.

Kurke wiped his fingers on his robes, came closer, and held the knife out to me once again. "Take it, Avery."

I wouldn't. I opened my mouth to say so, but the words didn't come. Instead, my hand reached out and took hold of the ebony handle. It felt foreign and wrong and comfortable and familiar.

"Follow me." Kurke made his way to Oscar's side, where he fiddled with Oscar's left sleeve—made more difficult because Oscar's hands were bound in front of his body. He loosened the sleeve and rolled it above the elbow. I stood next to him, my entire body clenched as I tried to move away from his side or drop the knife or say something or do anything but what he wanted me to do.

But I couldn't. My body remained unable to obey my own commands.

I'd never heard of a spell like this before, one that took away a person's free will.

Kurke pointed at Oscar's arm, lying on top of the quilt, bare to the elbow. "Cut him open right here." He pointed to a spot above the wrist and then walked closer to the desk and picked up the cup. "You can collect the blood in this."

No.

My lips wouldn't form the word.

I'd kill myself before I'd harm Oscar. My fingers clenched tighter around the knife, and I tried to direct it at myself. My muscles bunched and strained, but the knife refused to budge. I couldn't seem to do anything but what Kurke told me to.

I reached a hand out to take the cup.

"I'll hold him down in case he wakes. Be quick about it."

I bent to my task. The knife sliced into Oscar's arm, and blood flowed. I let the knife fall to the floor. Oscar twitched once and then fell back into his slumber. I gathered blood in the cup, until Kurke said, "Very well. That's enough. Now leave five drops of blood in each corner of the room and recite this incantation each time." He said the spell, syllables long and unfamiliar. The flavor of the words struck me as Belanokian.

I shouldn't do this. I couldn't do this.

My body moved to the first corner of the room, the one nearest the bed. My movements came lurching and uncontrolled as I tried to fight against the spell.

I was doing this.

Five drops of blood fell to the floor. I said the incantation.

I moved to the next corner, fighting against my body the whole way.

Oscar's scrying sticks leaned behind the desk. I pushed them aside, and they clattered to the floor. *Drip drip drip drip drip.* Five drops of scarlet stark against the wood. The incantation, now feeling less foreign, came from my lips.

The trunk stood next to the bookcase. It was full of Oscar's dessert box collection. Maybe I could use it as a weapon, unleash the power of strawberry fizzes or something. If I could just—overcome this spell—enough to grab one—

But I only succeeded in slowing my jerking movements to a crawl, and I still found myself in the next corner of the room, drip drip dripping blood onto the floor behind the table. I uttered the incantation for a third time.

"You're just making this harder on yourself, Avery." Kurke's voice drew me, and my body allowed me to turn my head and look at him—perhaps because his voice was my master now. He had settled in next to Oscar, having righted the chair that Ivan once occupied. He had the knife in his hand, touching the bloody tip as though he enjoyed the slippery feel of Oscar's blood on his fingers. "You'll exhaust yourself with all this resisting. How will you enjoy the celebrations after?"

I'd kill him when I got free of this spell. I would rip Matthias Kurke to pieces with the vilest, most inhumane curses I could remember from Hapthwaite's forbidden book.

Step, step, step. I moved toward the final corner.

I couldn't let myself complete the spell. Oscar, Master Wendyn, Cailyn's baby, Vito, Maud. They'd all be dead.

"Ah, Matthias," Oscar's voice wheezed from the bed. From the corner of my vision, I saw him struggle to push himself up on one elbow. My captive body wouldn't let me turn and look at him. "I understand you've decided to kill me? Oh. I'm bleeding."

At last, he was awake! Was it too late to help me?

"Seems only fitting, since you murdered my family."

"The term murder's a bit strong, and it was your father, not the entire family," Oscar said. "What does Mullins have to do with it? Whom did he kill?"

"Not important," Kurke said. "Avery is mine now."

My feet continued moving. I resisted the whole way, my movements slow and painful. At last I stood in the final corner.

"I think you underestimate Underwizard Mullins, Matthias. He's quite resourceful."

"You mean she."

Drip.

"Ah. You're aware of that, are you? Very well. She. For example, she escaped from a freezing spell I cast on her earlier today. I mean, I think it was today. What day is it?"

"That's enough talking," Kurke growled.

"Don't you even want to know what happened to your family that day?"

The freezing spell. Friar's bones, I was a fool. I hadn't even examined the lines of this spell to attempt an escape.

Drip, drip.

I could get out of this spell. All I had to do was find a weakness within its structure.

But when I examined the magic tying it together, the spell was different somehow. It seemed to reach right inside of me with its weavings. I pushed against its structure, testing its strength and searching for weaknesses. There was a thinness to it, but it was tight and strong.

"I know what happened. It wasn't a buggy accident, either. How does it feel to be so helpless, Oscar? I imagine this is how my father felt when you murdered him."

Drip, drip. I couldn't stop my hand from pouring out the last two drops of blood, even as I worked on the spell's structure, seeking for the tiniest hole. My mouth formed the words of the incantation.

"Ah. So you retrieved his file from the vault. We weren't sure if you destroyed it with your explosion or not. The story of the buggy accident was meant to protect you. But I doubt Nox felt helpless before he died. He had me pinned on the floor while I almost bled to death from a knife wound to the gut."

"Yes, I'm aware of your version of events. Interesting how you went from being incapacitated to killing him in the matter of a few seconds."

"Nothing interesting about it. It was luck."

The incantation came out of my mouth. I ripped at the spell holding me captive, desperate to destroy it.

"Yes, let's call it luck. But I'm more interested in what happened to my mother and Cynthia. That wasn't in the file."

"It won't do you any good to know it, Matthias. Leave it alone."

"Tell me."

I fell to my hands and knees. Pain burned through me like the blade of a razor, ripping along every part of me. When I looked at the lines of the spell holding me captive, its structure remained unchanged.

I hadn't broken it.

My voice stopped. Had I finished the blood spell? Were the Wendyns all dead? I lifted my head and looked up. Magic flashed, and I stared at the ceiling. Lines of the spell I had just cast crisscrossed the room above me, taut, interwoven links humming and thrumming with energy.

Horror and sickness burned through me—and a deep, unending anger. I felt as helpless as the day Gavin died. A sucking tide of fury waited to pull me under, and I knew once I was in it, I wouldn't emerge the same person. If I emerged at all.

"Well," Kurke said. "That was stupid, Avery. Blood spells tie to your blood, you fool. Try to find your way out of them, and it's like pulling yourself apart. You won't get out of that spell, I can assure you."

I had to calm myself, or I'd do something I'd regret, as I did that day in Bramford.

But I didn't regret what I did in Bramford. It had brought me here—with Ivan and Master Wendyn.

I was a fifth level underwizard. Calm and in control.

Having completed Kurke's orders, my body's autonomy reverted to me again—at least for the moment. I looked toward the bed. Was Oscar—was he dead? I couldn't look. I had to look.

He still sat up, eyes open, face contorted in a frown. "Very well, Matthias. You're sure you want to know the truth?"

"There's just one more step to complete this spell, old man. Tell me about my mother and sister, and maybe it'll change what I do with you."

A pause. Then Oscar spoke. "It was your mother, Felina," he said. "Nox had been schooling her in the practice of magic. He must have told her what to do if Council members ever came asking questions. She was prepared to hurt them. To kill them." He paused, as though searching for the right words. At last he said, "I'm certain she never meant to hurt Cynthia."

"Don't you dare lie about my mother!" Kurke lunged, but Oscar ducked and swung. He connected with Kurke's jaw. More pushing and shoving and swinging, and I couldn't tell who had the upper hand. Kurke swore, and Oscar grunted with a landed blow. I lunged to my feet. Kurke had Oscar by the throat above the trammel, rattling him back and forth.

I couldn't freeze him, not while he had hands around Oscar's throat. So I did the only other thing I could think of—I rushed at Kurke.

TWENTY-EIGHT

I LANDED A FEW blows, pounding on Kurke's back and wrenching at his arms. He batted me away like a pesky fly, and I stumbled backward, tripping over the rug in front of the fireplace and landing on my backside.

"It was . . . your mother's . . . actions . . . that killed . . . Cynthia," Oscar choked out. Crimson stained his abdomen, caused by the furrow I left in his arm. Kurke must have loosened his fingers then, because Oscar's words came easier. "Your mother was wielding magic . . . that she didn't understand. When the Council members tried to stop her, she sent a curse so powerful, so ugly . . . its effects harmed everyone within its reach. Your mother died first, the next day. Cynthia the day after that. Three grown men, wizards, standing within reach of the spell, died the day after that."

"I don't believe you." But Kurke's voice held no conviction. He dropped his hands and backed away.

This was my chance. I pushed to my feet and sent two spells in quick succession at Oscar, unknotting the rope around his hands and feet. He swung his legs over the side of the bed. Kurke didn't even react, apparently too affected by Oscar's revelation. He stumbled back another step, and his thighs hit the table against the wall.

"I tried my best to protect you from it. I've done everything I could to make your life whole, Matthias." Oscar reached a hand toward Kurke, his tone filled with as much earnestness as I'd ever heard coming from him before.

A pause stretched long. Kurke pressed fingers against his eyes. At last he shook his head. "No. No no no. Don't pretend you're some kind of humanitarian." He leaned down, and the dagger flew into his hand. He held it out toward Oscar. "Anything you did for me was to make yourself feel better."

Oscar came to his feet. "I hid the truth to protect you. It was safer to keep your father's blood magic connections from you."

"Safer in whose opinion? You and the Council have always been close-minded about blood magic. Never willing to accept the benefits it would bring Faronna."

"What sort of *benefit* leaves forty-two innocent people dead?"

Kurke's fingers tightened around the dagger. "Fortunately I don't need the permission of a murderer to carry out my plan." He jerked a finger at me. "Come here now, Avery. I've had enough of your defiance." The compelling spell still had a hold on me, and my feet moved toward him of their own accord.

There must be some way to defeat him. Yes, he was a stronger wizard than I, but I had learned long ago that when faced with a larger opponent, creative thinking could weight a fight in anyone's favor.

I won't help you, I wanted to say but couldn't. My feet dragged me closer to him.

"That's enough, Matthias," Oscar said from somewhere behind me. "Leave Mullins out of this. Your quarrel is with me, remember?"

"That's one thing I'm unlikely to forget." Kurke twitched a

finger, and magic buzzed past me. Somewhere to my rear, Oscar cried out. Something thumped to the floor.

If only I could turn and look. But Kurke's order to "come here now" must be obeyed. Oscar's wheezy breathing filled the space behind me.

"I've just broken Oscar's ankle," Kurke said conversationally to me. He rested his hands on my shoulders and leaned down to look me in the eye. The butt of the knife, still held in his hand, scratched against my neck. "And that's your fault, Avery. His death might have been quick and painless, but the more you fight against me, the more painful I will make it. Did you know there's two hundred and six bones in the human body? That leaves two hundred and five more at my disposal."

Oscar moaned.

Healing spells. I knew some from Master Hapthwaite's library. There was one for bruises—no, stupid, Avery. That was no good here. One for cuts. One for fevers and congestion and aching. One for pain.

Why, oh why, didn't I know a spell for broken bones?

Now that I'd obeyed Kurke's order, my autonomy returned —and with it, the ability to speak. "Fine. I'm sorry. I won't do it again. Now heal him." I tried to twist out of his grip, but his hands tightened on my shoulders. "Or let me try to. You have no right to torment him."

"I have the right to do whatever I want, especially to Oscar. Now, are you ready to carry out the rest of the spell, or would you like me to maim him some more?"

I scowled. "What do you need me for? Why don't you perform this stupid spell yourself?"

A frown crossed his mouth, and his hands dropped from my shoulders. "Blame the Belanokians."

My brow furrowed, until all at once understanding came to

me. "You can't do it. You can't perform this spell. *That's* why you need me."

"Of course it is." Irritation threaded his tone. "Why else would I have tied myself to a lowly underwizard? This spell has to be performed by a woman to work. I had a devil of a time digging up a female magician in Hutterland to perform it for me the last time. If I'd known you were going to be so difficult about this, I would have kept her around a little longer before sending her on to Belanok."

My mouth fell open in astonishment, and I searched for a response. Finally I settled on, "But why . . . why a woman?"

He waved a hand in frustration toward Oscar. "You see? *This* is what the trade ban with Belanok has brought about, Oscar. It's an information embargo, more than anything. She should know about Belanok's witches."

"You know there are reasons far beyond information . . . that we banned trade and travel with Belanok. It has nothing to do with . . . those women." Oscar's strained voice came from behind the bed.

"What are you talking about? What witches?" I looked back and forth from Kurke to the white tuft of Oscar's hair, just peeking above the back side of the bed.

"This is a Belanokian spell." Kurke swiped a hand over his eyes. "They're the real reason women can't do magic in the three kingdoms. In Belanok, only women perform magic. The Belanokian witches."

"What? But how—why—"

"They'll tell you all about it when this is over. That's where we're going, to Belanok. You can practice whatever magic you want there, in the open. You won't have to hide anymore."

I took a step back. "And what about you?"

"Oh, I won't be staying. I'll transact a little business and be on my way."

Something about his tone gave me pause. "Business having to do with me? What are you doing, selling me to them? Is that what you did to that other female magician?"

He frowned. "It's more like a trade. Don't worry. They just want to examine you. And maybe perform a few experiments. They're interested in the females of the three kingdoms, especially those with an inclination for magic."

Knowing what I knew of Belanok, this felt like a fate worse than death. I clasped arms around myself. "I won't be going with you. I'd rather die here with Oscar."

He made a noise of disgust. "Hear that, Oscar? She wants to die here with you. How appropriate."

No reply.

Kurke's eyes moved past me. He swore and pushed me out of the way as he strode across the room. "You can't hide for long, Oscar!" he bellowed.

I swiveled and ran quick eyes over the room. Oscar had vanished. Thank the heavens, but how in the three kingdoms had he accomplished it?

Out of the corner of my eye, I saw a small form dart out the bedroom door. Was that—Ivan? But that was impossible. He couldn't have been hiding in here the whole time. There was nowhere for him to hide. I turned, and there, shimmering out of existence in the middle of the room, stood Kurke's wizard door. I looked past it and found Master Wendyn standing at the corner of the desk.

Impossible.

"Murk and shadow, are you back already?" Kurke's growling voice came from the alcove. Magic zinged across the room, and he fell back several steps.

The trammel had disappeared from around the master's neck. But no one could remove trammels without the key. Only Ladarius the Heroic.

I gave myself a shake. Master Wendyn was a clever master wizard, but he was no Ladarius.

"Turns out Ivan's not a bad hand at unknotting spells." Master Wendyn nodded at me. "Someone's been teaching him."

I blinked in surprise.

Whatever spell Kurke sent in return, it whooshed across the room like a rippling flame and tumbled Master Wendyn back into the wall. Kurke swiveled and skirted the bed, heading in my direction.

Bones, what now? I backed toward the fireplace and sent a fire spell at him. His shield spell absorbed it easily.

"Hold still," he commanded me tersely. With the words I stood pinned in place by the compelling spell. He shoved the dagger into my hand. "You will plunge this knife into Oscar Wendyn's heart. And then you will say these words." He repeated the incantation for me, Belanokian words that felt heavy and black.

He bent closer so his eyes filled my view, his breath hot on my face.

"Enjoy this, Avery. Take pleasure in killing Oscar for me, as I can't."

The order took hold of me. The bed was the last place I saw Oscar, and my body pulled me to it. I moved around the alcove behind the bed, but it stood empty, with no explanation of Oscar's current whereabouts.

Master Wendyn struggled back to his feet and erected another shield spell.

"A fine dagger, Mullins." He straightened the sleeves of his shirt. "I suggest you put it down before you hurt someone."

I tried to open my mouth to explain that I couldn't, but instead I tightened my grip on the dagger and asked, "Where's Oscar?"

Master Wendyn's eyes narrowed. "I see you're bleeding."

"You should have stayed where I put you, Garrick." Kurke pointed at a pile of books and sent them careening toward the master.

Master Wendyn's spell held, at least until the last book broke through and battered him on the side of the head. He stumbled backward a few steps and then sent a spell back at Kurke. The sparkling trail of magic burst through Kurke's shield spell and exploded, all sizzling magic and sparking rays of light. Kurke staggered backward, blood streaking the side of his face.

"We're not . . . doing this again, Garrick." He lurched on the fireplace rug to regain his balance.

"It looks to me like we are."

Kurke touched the side of his face and winced. "You'll be sorry for that. Anyway, you're too late. Avery's already performed most of the bloodlines spell. As soon as she says the last incantation, we'll be free of you Wendyns forever."

Master Wendyn didn't look at me. "Well, then. I'll make sure she doesn't finish it, that's all." He hit Kurke with another spell, one that ripped the sleeve of his robe and left a bloody gash along his arm.

"Come, Avery," Kurke wheezed.

Four steps, and I stood in front of Kurke on the rug, almost before I realized what I had done.

"There you are. Good girl." Kurke turned me around, hands on my shoulders, so that I was a human shield standing in front of him. Master Wendyn couldn't send a spell at Kurke now without hitting me.

Hoarse panting in my ear. Warm breath against my cheek. "I'm tired of this, Gare," Kurke said. "Your interruptions are, frankly, stupid and tedious."

"Master Kurke?" The voice came from the doorway, Edie's voice.

"Leave, Edie," Master Wendyn barked. "It's not safe."

She didn't pay him any mind. "I thought you should know, Matt—I caught the fool here trying to go through a wizard door." She pushed Ivan into the room. He looked mutinous but unharmed.

I stared at Edie. What was going on here? Why was she helping Kurke? She needed to get out of here, to go find Edwin.

"Oh, Edie," Master Wendyn said heavily. "You let him turn your head, did you?"

Her face flushed. "Turn my head?" she repeated. "Matt loves me. He told me so himself."

I tried to make sense of the words. Matt? Could she mean the madman standing behind me? But what about Edwin?

"And do you know what I like best about him?" She turned to me. "He never tried to pretend to be something he's not. Like a girl pretending to be a boy. Making other girls fall in love with her."

Once again I tried to open my mouth to say anything, but I couldn't. Kurke gave a soft chuckle. "Yes, you heard Edie. I love her deeply."

Even I could hear the false note in his voice. Why couldn't Edie?

"Now, here's your job, sweetling. Make certain the fool doesn't run off again." He jerked a finger at the second dagger on the desk, and it flew at her, handle-first. She caught it and shoved Ivan against the wall nearest the door.

"So you were trying to go through a wizard door?" Kurke put a hand to his mouth and surveyed Ivan. "Can you do magic, little fool?"

Ivan stared at him with a blank expression.

"No matter. I'll deal with you once the Wendyns are dead."

I wished I could get my mouth to move. If I could, I'd tell Master Wendyn to kill me before I finished Kurke's spell.

"You're let go, Edie," the master said. "When this is all over, I suggest you get your things and get out."

"When this is over, you'll be dead." Kurke flicked a finger, and a chair from the table flew at Master Wendyn. It bounced off the shield spell and clattered to the floor, but the master still stumbled backward and had to rebuild his spell once again.

"I want you to look, Avery." Kurke pressed his head against mine, speaking into my ear in an intimate manner that made my skin crawl. I couldn't move away. "Can you see the magic woven throughout this room?"

I blinked and let my eyes adjust. The spell woven around myself and Kurke, Master Wendyn's shield spell, the first part of the bloodlines spell, which had a canopy of magic arching over our heads. And there, in the alcove, a large spell woven around an unidentifiable shape.

What *was* that?

I heard the smile in Kurke's voice when he noted the direction I stared. "An illusion spell," he whispered against my ear. "Oscar is hidden in plain sight."

He called out a revealing spell, and the illusion fell. Oscar knelt on the far side of his bed, crawling toward the alcove, at least until Kurke's next spell crashed into him. He tumbled into a very still heap.

"Go," Kurke urged. "Complete the spell. Then I'll take you to Belanok, where you'll be free to do whatever magic you want."

The words brought no comfort, none at all. And yet my feet dragged me toward Oscar, intent on completing my mission.

"FIGHT IT, MULLINS!" Master Wendyn stood closer to me than Kurke now. He stepped nearer and reached for my arm.

My body reacted all on its own, swiping at him with the dagger and nicking his arm. He swore and stepped back.

He was wrong. I'd looked at the lines of the magic. I couldn't find a weakness.

Behind me, a volley of magic sounded, sparks and pops and sizzles of sound. Master Wendyn and Kurke shouted various spells, their voices at times gasping and hoarse. Undeterred. Just like me.

In the alcove, Oscar lay on his back. His right leg twisted at the ankle, turned in a direction ankles shouldn't turn. Blood trailed the side of his head, and he moaned, only half coherent. I moved toward him.

"Overcome it, Mullins! Avery! You can do this!" Master Wendyn shouted at me.

What did he *think* I was trying to do? My footsteps slowed, every muscle in me burning as I tried to keep myself from moving toward Oscar. I fought so hard my muscles shivered and shook with the effort to hold myself back. But even with all that, I still reached Oscar's side and knelt, oh-so-slowly, dagger outstretched. I raised it, the dagger held tight and high in two hands.

I must not do this.

My hands and arms shook like leaves on a windy day, the blade jerking up and down.

Ready to plunge the knife into Oscar's chest.

Can't lower the knife. Don't lower it.

Arms circled me, trying to hold me back.

For a moment, it seemed as though the arms would succeed, but then my traitorous body ruined it by grabbing one of the hands and giving a yank. Ivan tumbled across Oscar's knees.

But—how—I thought Edie was guarding Ivan.

Stop, he gestured. *Not you. Stop now.*

"Avery!" Kurke yelled in a commanding tone.

I managed a look over my shoulder, compelled by Kurke's voice. He and Master Wendyn grappled, locked in intense conflict. Blood dripped down the side of the master's face, and red slicked down Kurke's fingers. Beyond them, Edie sat motionless by the wall, dagger still gripped in her hand. Frozen.

Hit by a freezing spell?

"Finish this, Avery!" Kurke ground out. "Do it now!"

And in that moment, Ivan did the worst thing he could have possibly done. He tried to grab the dagger out of my hands.

We struggled for control. My fingers closed around the dagger's handle, and I wrenched it away from Ivan. And then, before I could stop myself, stop whatever horrible thing had control of me, my hands thrust the dagger toward him.

Time slowed. I blinked and stared stupidly at my hands, trying to comprehend what they'd done. They still held the dagger's handle, but the blade had disappeared. It seemed to be buried deep in Ivan's chest.

My hands pulled the blade back toward me, and blood spilled over Ivan's white shirt. His mouth rounded with shock or horror or something incomprehensible, and his eyelids fluttered.

What had I done?

So much blood. The knife clattered to the floor.

"No. Oh no. Oh no no no no no . . ." I tried to cover the wound with my hands, but there was blood, so much blood. I couldn't make it stop, and it kept coming and coming. "I'm sorry, I'm sorry, I'm so sorry, Ivan . . ."

His mouth formed words, almost as though he thought he could speak, but no sound came out. He blinked and blinked again.

"You'll be all right. You'll be all right," I told him. "I won't let anything happen to you."

I had said the same words to my brother. False words. Lies.

Ivan would die, and it would be my fault. Come morning,

I'd have to dig a grave for him out on the hill, same as I did for Gavin. I leaned forward and babbled the only healing spell I could think of, one for cuts, over and over. If the blood leaking from his chest lessened to any degree, I couldn't tell.

"Finish it!" Kurke's voice. "Finish the spell now, Avery!"

I stared at Ivan dully. Horror sang through me. I wouldn't. But my body moved of its own accord. My fingers, slick with Ivan's blood, picked up the dagger and shoved his feet out of the way. I scooted closer to Oscar, knees touching his arm.

Think, Avery.

Somehow I had freed myself from the compelling spell, if only for a moment. If I could break free for a moment, I could break free altogether. Couldn't I?

The lines of the spell wavered before my eyes as though in flux. The magic remained woven as strong as ever, and yet—something had affected it.

I was losing control. Maybe even my mind. Stay calm, Avery. Stay in control.

But too much had happened for me to believe that I could do that any longer. I had fallen over a cliff, and I couldn't come back. I'd killed Ivan, and in another moment I would kill Oscar too.

Sorry, Gavin, for not becoming a master wizard like we dreamed of all those years ago. Sorry, Master Wendyn, for disappointing you yet again. Sorry, Orly, for not becoming your master as I promised.

Orly.

"We girls can't just tamp down our emotions and pretend we don't have them," she said to me that day in the Conclave. "That's not how we work. We have to work *with* our emotions. Feel them. Don't suppress them."

Three months now I'd been trying to work with my emotions, but I'd also been trying to stay in control, to stay calm.

I felt emotion pushing at me now, everything I didn't want to feel—panic, fear, sorrow, and a hundred more. The logical part of me said I couldn't let them take control, or I'd lose any chance to stop Kurke.

I raised the dagger above Oscar's chest. No one remained who could stop me.

Only myself. Only the voice of reason telling me to stay in control.

But I didn't stay in control. I closed my eyes and sank into the emotions. Terror washed me. Anxiety crawled through me. Grief like I'd never felt rushed at me.

Magic came, without my even reaching for it, pulled like a magnet. Power filled me, magic I couldn't hold, more than I'd ever known. When I looked at the spell that held me, I saw woven magic that shivered and pulsed before my eyes. I reached for it with my mind, reached for the lines shimmery with flexing magic.

The spell shattered like brittle glass.

I threw the knife against the wall and turned back to Ivan. His sallow skin resembled parchment, and blood smeared dark across his chest. As I watched, his eyes fluttered and his chest rose with breath.

Thank the heavens he still lived.

Kurke.

I spun, but couldn't tell who had the upper hand in the battle between Kurke and Master Wendyn. Both bore wounds of a hard-fought battle. Kurke tried to wrench the dagger from Edie's frozen grip and failed. Instead, he settled for tossing the fireplace poker at the master with such force that, after the master dodged it, its tip stuck in the wall. The master fired back with a spell that collapsed Kurke where he stood, though he sprang back to his feet in a breath. Moments later, the poker clattered to the ground.

Find a person's weakness, and you control them. Papa's favorite saying. But what was Kurke's weakness? His family? Women? His desire for control?

I couldn't think how to make those things help me.

"Kill him, Avery!" Kurke shouted at me.

"I won't. I'm not performing this spell for you. You're out of options."

He cursed and shoved the master into the wall with a spell. "Fine." He stalked toward me, hand outstretched. The dagger flew into it. "I'll take care of this myself. I can still kill Oscar, anyway." He tossed a spell at me, and I stumbled back and fell to my knees. He knelt beside Oscar and raised the dagger.

The only way I really had to get at Kurke was through our connection. The tether. Could the tether, the strength that tied us together, also become a weakness?

Only if I also used it against myself.

I rose to my feet on shaky legs, opened my mouth, and uttered the words of the dry as desert spell. The words came easily, almost as though I'd spent weeks practicing it. In reality, I hadn't said the incantation aloud in at least two years.

Kurke's arms lowered. The dagger clattered to the ground, useless. His hand reached for his throat, and he crumbled to the floor like ash on a breeze.

Moments later, heat overtook me. It washed in waves of fever, a desert wind pushing its way through my skin. I wavered in place, the room spinning.

Kurke's shoulders shook. Was he seizing? Were these the last throes of his life, of my life?

He sputtered and coughed and jerked, and I realized he shook with mirth, not death. "You've killed yourself." His voice came like sandpaper, rough words scratching against the walls of his throat. "We're inseparable, you and I, remember? My heart's blood is your heart's blood." More rough chuckling. "And I thought you were . . . intelligent."

Hands rested on my shoulders, and my knees gave out. Somebody bore me to the ground. "Look at me," Master Wendyn's voice commanded. "Mullins, look at me." How many times had he said it? I stared up at him, at his shirt, ruined by perspiration and blood. My head seemed to be lying in his lap. "What spell did you cast?" he asked.

I stared at him, struggling for breath, as heat and thirst and an awful aching in my head bore down on me. "Ivan," I said. "Ivan is dying." My voice sounded scratchy.

"Avery!" he said sharply. "The spell. What was it?"

I blinked and forced my thoughts together. "Desert. So thirsty."

Then Master Wendyn did the last thing I expected him to do. He laughed. The short, sharp, bark of a laugh rumbled through his whole body, jostling me. He took my face in his hands and peered down at me. "Mullins, I do believe you're brilliant."

The words made little sense. Having just uttered the words that would kill me, nothing about it felt brilliant.

I blinked and blinked and blinked. By the third blink, Master Wendyn and Kurke had disappeared. Everything about Oscar's room had vanished, replaced with a brilliant white and two people: Gavin and Mama. I almost couldn't look at them straight on, they were so bright.

"Darling, what have I always told you?" Mama said, rubbing at her nose in that way she always did when worried. "Think before you jump."

"You're being headstrong again, she means." Gavin leaned closer and squinted at me. "This time might even be worse than when you jumped over the waterfall."

"Didn't . . . jump," I rasped. "You pushed."

"Regardless," Mama said. "Think. You're not a child anymore."

I blinked, and they disappeared. The master looked down at me. Concern overwrote his features.

"Waterfall," I rasped. "Gavin pushed."

Somewhere nearby someone wheezed in and out, in and out.

Kurke.

No, me.

Both of us together.

Master Wendyn launched into a spell. Healing magic, maybe. The ache in my head eased, and the pressure in my lungs lightened. But it took only moments for the aching pressure to return to its former severity. I wanted to tell him it was no use. But that would use up energy and words, and there were so many of them I wanted to say right now.

My last farewell to the master. This was it. I'd cry if I could. If I had tears. If I could breathe. If I weren't dying.

"Thank you," I rasped. "For being . . . my master."

"Don't talk," he said tersely.

Nearby, Kurke made a choking noise. No, not just Kurke. Me too. My windpipe was closing.

The master's face, anxious, hovered above my own. He'd given up the spellcasting. I could see he didn't know what to do. For once, he appeared at a loss. I wanted to tell him it was all right, that I had made this decision.

I blinked, and Mama took his place.

"He means well," she said. "Even if he has been hurt. I like this Garrick Wendyn."

"Doesn't laugh enough," Gavin said. "Can he do a fire-breathing spell? Ask him to do a fire breathing spell."

"Gavin," Mama scolded. "This isn't the time for that." She

put a hand to my cheek. "Be happy, sweet one. Trust again. Someday find your father."

"Papa." I choked on the word. "I can't—"

"He is your father." Her voice sounded stern.

I wheezed in response.

"Underwizard!" a voice shouted at me. It was clove and fire in my nostrils. "You must stay with me."

The lights turned brighter, pulling at me. Master Wendyn's hot breath touched my face, and I looked at Gavin and Mama and wondered which was the dream world, the one they were from or the one where the master didn't make any sense.

I could take only one more rattling breath. Air pulled into my lungs and stuck there. I stared at Mama and Gavin and felt the lights pulling.

"Blast it, underwizard!" The master's voice pulled at me harder. "Find the magic! Fight!"

I blinked, and his dark eyes were still there, right in front of me, fierce in their intensity.

Even in death, he was pestering me about finding the magic.

But when I stopped to consider it, I felt it along my skin, the one cool thing in this hot, dry ocean around me. I pulled it inward, and for one moment, total clarity filled me.

The loud wheezing nearby came to an abrupt halt. Then white light surrounded me, and I blinked and fluttered to the ground in a million pieces.

TWENTY-NINE

MY EYES WOULDN'T OPEN.

I meant to rub at my lids, but my arms had turned into bricks. Halfway lifted from the bed, they fell back against the fabric beneath them.

"Mmph." I tried again to open my eyes. At last I worked the seal over them apart, and the room around me came into focus.

I lay in my bed at Ryker Hall. Somehow, impossibly, I seemed to be alive. A quilt covered me up to my armpits. I attempted to readjust myself in the bed, but I hurt everywhere. My body was a heavy weight unused to obeying commands. Further across the room, an occupied chair sat near the window.

"I'm reading," Master Wendyn said from the chair. He held a book in front of his face so that I couldn't see his expression. "Any chance you'll fall back asleep again?"

Again? I didn't remember waking before now.

I eyed my arms lying across the bedclothes. With effort, I lifted them further than my first attempt. The action exhausted me.

Memories returned to me. Kurke came to kill Oscar. Ivan, covered in blood.

If I was alive, that meant Oscar was dead. Maybe Ivan too.

We killed Oscar. Me or Kurke; I couldn't really remember. No wonder the master wouldn't even talk to me.

Shame flooded me. My heart pounded, and my eyes burned. I wished the floor would open and swallow me whole. I didn't deserve to be alive while he lay dead somewhere—

"Stop that." Master Wendyn's irritated voice cut into my thoughts. He snapped the book shut and stared at me, scowling. He wore one of his outlandish shirts, looking as normal as ever. It might have been the most beautiful thing I'd seen in my whole life.

I sniffled. "Stop what?"

"Crying."

My breath hitched. "What do you mean? I can't cry."

He raised a brow. "What's that on your face?"

I swiped at my eyes—this time lifting my arm all the way—and my hand came away wet. "W-what? How—" I stared at him, trying to make sense of things. He had several days of beard growth on his chin, a deep purple bruise across one side of his face, and a puckered red cut across his forehead. "You're hurt. Is that from—did Kurke do that?" Tears pricked at my eyes again. "This is all my fault."

His face darkened. "It's your own self you should worry about. You've been unconscious for three days. And please stop crying." He grimaced and waved the book. "I should have let that desert spell take you. Do you always cry this much?"

I scrubbed at my eyes, wanting to cry now more than ever. "I'm sorry," I whispered, even as my tears overflowed. Friar's bones, but this was embarrassing. I scrubbed harder at my face and then gave up, wailing, "I never cry. I'm just . . . so . . . ashamed!"

"Sweet carrot sticks, Garrick, what have you done?"

The voice brought me up short because it was so very

Oscar-like. In fact, I'd put money on the fact that it *was* Oscar. I took in, through the blur of my tears, the wavy form of a round man standing in the doorway to my room, floppy hat on his head.

"Oscar?" I whispered, unwilling to trust my eyes. "You're not dead?"

"Nope. Still as alive as ever. So, might I add, is Ivan."

"He's . . . alive?" I whispered. More treacherous tears gushed out.

"Didn't you tell her anything?" Oscar asked, and the wavy form moved closer, swinging something by his side. I scrubbed at my eyes, and his form came clearer.

"I've hardly spoken," Master Wendyn said. "She woke up and went straight into hysterics. I'll never understand females," he added, halfway to himself. He pushed himself to a standing position, working a spell as he went. By the time he reached me, he'd plucked a handkerchief out of the air. He held it out to me and pushed my feet aside to perch on the edge of my bed. "Here, clean yourself up. I suppose we should talk if it will prevent an uncomfortable crying episode. Hold on." He pulled several more handkerchiefs out of air and dropped them in a pile on my lap. "In case. Although, I'd prefer if you didn't need them."

I sniffled and wiped my eyes and thanked him. "But why aren't you dead?" I said to Oscar, who stood at the end of the bed, swinging Forthwind and looking for all the world the same as always. "Or why aren't I dead?" I sucked in a breath. "Wait. It's not over yet. The blood oath isn't finished. Kurke's still out there somewhere."

Oh. I had spoken of the blood oath without a single clouded thought or drift in concentration.

"Wrong on three counts, underwizard," Oscar said. "Look, I've had my fill of talking about Matthias to the Council, so you're on your own on this one, Garrick. Not to mention that misguided maid is back again. I'll go get rid of her."

"Edie? Try another oblivion," Master Wendyn suggested.

"Edie?" I repeated, as more memories came back to me. "She was . . . helping Kurke, wasn't she? I thought you let her go."

"So he did," Oscar said. "I cast the oblivion spell myself, making her forget everything about Matt and your gender and that unpleasant scene in my bedroom. But she still had to be let go. The girl has proven herself untrustworthy. So I told her her knick-knack dusting was shoddy. Trouble is, she keeps coming back to apologize and beg for her old job back. Persistent little thing."

That sounded like Edie.

"Oh, before I forget, Ivan says hello," Oscar continued.

"He does?" Flashes of terrible memories came to me. Ivan's bloodstained chest. The knife in my hand. "He's—he's not mad at me?"

"Couldn't help it, could you? Nice work at those healing spells. They worked pretty well to patch up that hole you put in him. He needed a few more spells, and he's still mending, but he'll be all right."

A thumping sounded through the wall.

Oscar rolled his eyes. "That'll be him. Have your talk first, and I'll send him over."

"Ivan . . . did magic, didn't he? A freezing spell."

"Among others," Oscar agreed. "An unknotting spell and an unbroken spell too. Wordless magic, at that." He and the master exchanged a glance. "We'll decide what to do with him before too long." He shuffled closer and placed a hand on my shoulder. "I thank you for stopping Matthias, Avery Mullins, and at your own peril. I don't like to speak ill of the dead, but anger crawled through that boy's soul, enough to send him teetering into madness. And I never saw it." He shook his head and shuffled out, closing the door.

I watched him go, mystified. "Kurke is dead, then? How is that possible? I should be dead too because of our connection."

"Are you being honest right now?"

I blinked at the heat in the master's voice. "Why . . . why wouldn't I be?"

"Just answer me this question, Mullins—and I won't be casting a deception defense to ensure your honesty. I'm going to trust you." Tightness lined his face. Whatever the question was, it seemed very important to him.

"Fair enough." Trust. New territory for us.

"What did you think the outcome would be when you cast the desert spell?"

His earnest expression demanded honesty, and I found I couldn't do anything but answer with the truth, even if I'd wanted to lie, which I didn't. "You told me yourself it was a killing spell. I knew what would happen. I was trying to kill Kurke."

"And what did you expect would happen to you?"

I looked down at my hands resting on the bedspread even though my body should be stiffening in a cold December grave. "I wasn't really sure. I thought maybe I might die. Why didn't I?"

His chin jutted out in a displeased frown. "What you're saying is it was a suicide. How stupid can you be?"

I pushed myself up a little straighter. "Oscar's alive, isn't he? So are you and the rest of your family. I don't suppose you're complaining about that?" My lungs ached with leftover weakness from the desert spell. I pressed a hand to the throbbing and continued, "If he were dead, and we were sitting here having this discussion, I suppose you'd thank me for not doing the spell?"

"It was foolhardy to take such a risk, that's all." He wiped a hand across his eyes. "And yes, thank you just the same."

Moments passed while we stared at each other. At last I said, "I don't understand you. First you're angry with me because I'm dumber than a box of insects, and now you're grateful? Can you say what you mean?"

"I'm not mad at you. I'm annoyed. There's a difference."

"Kurke is dead. We're alive. Why are you annoyed?"

He dropped his head in his hands. Then he stood and paced the length of the room. At last he turned to face me. "Mullins, I've misjudged you."

I swallowed. "Oh?"

The corners of his mouth tilted downward. "When I found out you were a girl, I was so furious I'd been lied to that I couldn't focus on anything else. It was a heavy blow to my pride, which was already smarting from—well, other things. I may not have been fair to you in the things I said and the way I treated you."

My mouth opened, but I couldn't come up with an intelligent response, I was so surprised. "Oh," I managed. "I—oh."

He sighed, deep and heavy, and ran a hand over his face. "You're a problem; one I don't know quite how to handle. I don't even think the Council is ready to deal with you."

The Council? He couldn't be considering Punishment now, not after talking about how unfair he'd been. Could he? I frowned and stared at my lap. "Must anyone . . . deal with me? I'm leaving, remember?" The mere suggestion of the Council had me worried, and I slid my feet off the bed so that I sat sideways, facing him. My bare feet poked out from beneath the dressing gown I wore, which struck me as vaguely indecent. "I can leave this place in an hour. As soon as I regain a little of my strength."

"Absolutely not."

"Forty-five minutes?"

He made a noise of exasperation. "This isn't a negotiation, Mullins." He grabbed my feet and swung them back under the bedding again before pulling the blanket up to my chin. "You're not going anywhere. At least, not unless you want to."

Well, that was somewhat reassuring, anyway. I settled back against the pillow behind me. "You still haven't explained to me how I'm still alive. Or why I can cry."

"So I haven't." Five striding steps, and he picked up his chair at the window and brought it back to the bed, where he seated himself. "If you'd chosen any other killing spell, you'd be dead along with Matt, as it would have leaked over to you through your connection. But the desert spell—well, it was a good choice. You've already cast it on yourself once, so your body's been fighting off that spell for years. You've adapted, for lack of a better word. When I said you were brilliant, I thought you'd done it on purpose."

"I've adapted?" I rubbed at the pain in my chest. "This is adapting? Are you sure?"

"Yes. But I was wrong that you'd fight it off easily. For a while there, it looked like you might just die right along with Matt. But your resistance to the desert spell—combined with my healing spells and your magic—saved you at the end."

I shook my head. "But the consequence for unfulfilled blood oaths is death."

"The oath dissolved with Matt's death. If he'd lived, and you reached the—what was the agreed upon day? The winter solstice?—you'd both have died."

I mulled this information over. "I still don't understand."

His body shifted in the chair. "It's not that complicated. You didn't die."

I chewed on my lip. "No, not that. I understand that. But . . .

why would it matter to you if I died? Why try to save me at all? Wouldn't it be simpler if I were out of the way?"

His brows pushed together. "You think I'm that heartless?"

"Well . . . no. Not exactly."

"Devil's dawn, you think I'm that heartless." He pinched the bridge of his nose as though to stave off an aching head.

"No. Maybe sometimes."

When he didn't speak, I wondered if I'd gone too far. "But it's not as though I have room to complain. I mean, I'm a liar. I'm so used to being dishonest that I don't know how to tell the truth anymore."

The side of his mouth twitched, and he dropped his hand. "Liar. You know how to tell the truth. It's just easier not to."

My mouth opened to disagree, but then I closed it and, after a moment, nodded. "I suppose you're right."

"So we've established that neither one of us is perfect. In fact, we're far from it. Having said that . . ." he trailed off and then took what looked like a fortifying breath and tried again. "How would you feel about staying at Ryker Hall?"

It took a moment for me to understand the full meaning of the words. My eyes widened.

"I could use help around here, I mean," he continued.

Oh, I understood now. "You've just lost a serving maid, is that it? You need a replacement for Edie. Even better if they're good with washing."

"No, not as a serving maid. I need an apprentice. Yesterday the Council declared it mandatory for able-bodied wizards to have an apprentice. And I've gotten used to having you around."

My eyes flashed to his. "This isn't funny." In fact, it bordered on cruel.

"I'm not joking."

"But . . . I'm a girl."

"Are you? I hadn't noticed. The fact is, you can perform complicated spells better than many boys."

"I'm also a liar and a former thief. And my father's the town drunk."

"This isn't a marriage proposal, Mullins. I don't care about your family or your past. You have the ability to be a talented master wizard; that's all."

I bit my lip because it didn't feel right. There were too many reasons he shouldn't be saying this. "But . . . why? It would put everything you've accomplished at risk."

He gave an aggravated sigh. "Because you were willing to give your life to save my family's. Because we work well together. And because I'd like to believe I can trust you."

The deep ache returned to my throat, the one brought on not by the desert spell but by tears. I blinked them back and looked at the master. I could see he could sense my emotion too, although his face hadn't gone into full panic mode at the hint of tears yet. No, for the moment his eyes were dark and warm and full of compassion.

"What about my gender? If it's found out, you'd be in danger. Oscar too."

"Maybe it's time for a revolution. If girls can do magic at the same level as boys, something needs to change."

I raised an eyebrow. "And you're willing to be the face of that movement?"

His eyes flashed to me in surprise. "Me? I was thinking of you."

I blinked. "Well. Let's make leading a revolution a secondary plan. For now, I want to be a master wizard."

He sat back with a self-satisfied air. "Very well. Then we're a team again."

Something like excitement rushed me, and I struggled to sit

up. "I won't cause you any trouble," I said. "At least, I'll try not to."

"That would be boring. Trouble is what you excel at." He handed me another handkerchief, and I dabbed at my eyes, at the leftover tears there.

"Now explain why I can cry."

"That was Grandfather. He did some digging yesterday and found out how to undo your unfinished desert spell. Your first one, I mean. The one that took away your ability to cry. He performed the counter-spell this morning." His face turned sheepish. "I suppose I should have asked for his help earlier."

"I'm just glad it's gone." I rubbed at my head. "No more headaches? No more endless thirst? I'll bake him a Waltney cake later as thanks. But first I'll learn how. Now last question, I promise. How did you get the trammel off?"

A smile tugged at his mouth. "Dumb luck. When I was a boy, I opened one using only a dip pen. At the time, it seemed like a fluke, but come to find out, it worked again."

My mouth opened in surprise. "I wonder if that's how Ladarius the Heroic did it too."

"Legend says Ladarius got his off within a few seconds of its placement. Took me a lot longer. I kept snapping the pen in half. Good thing Ivan was there to perform an unbroken spell so I could keep working at it." He shrugged. "They'll never call me Garrick the Heroic, but it did the trick."

"Garrick the Lockpick, maybe?" I suggested.

He snorted. "I suppose there are worse things to be known for."

I couldn't keep myself from smiling. "My title would be less favorable. They'll call me Avery the Counterfeit. Or the Counterfeit Apprentice, Accomplished in All Forms of Deception."

His head tilted as he looked at me. "I suppose that's technically true. You *are* a counterfeit apprentice. But you're a real wizard, and that matters more."

I flushed, embarrassed at the compliment. We stood on new ground, the master and I, and the change in our relationship would take getting used to.

But I couldn't wait to see what it brought.

THIRTY

I PICKED MY WAY over the bare cobblestones of a Bramford path. Snow blanketed the trees, but the warm day had cleared the roads, so that the master had consented to a trip to town. My wizard's robes swung around my legs, edged with red at the hem and collar and sleeves—red, for the novitiate underwizard that I was.

Ivan tapped me on the arm and gestured at a cow that had slogged closer through the snow to gaze at us over a sturdy fence. Ivan uncovered some grass buried in the snow and pulled it up in patches to feed to the mournful-looking animal.

"Come on," I said when he had finished. "We don't have much time." I turned back to the path and took several steps before I realized he hadn't followed. I looked back to where he stood next to the fence. "What's the matter? Aren't you coming to the botanist's?"

I stay here, he gestured.

The thought of leaving him there in the streets of Bramford cut through me, there in the town that used to torment him. But things had changed since his days of being Bramford's whipping post. He had changed, as had I.

"Don't wander off," I told him. "Wait right here for me."

I wait, he gestured in agreement.

It was funny to think we met here in Bramford less than six months ago. It seemed so much longer.

William the Botanist greeted me, a plant in each hand. He looked the same as I remembered, large and good-natured with dirt beneath his fingernails. His smile turned to puzzlement as he looked at me. Then all at once his eyebrows lowered, and his pleasant expression morphed into a frown.

"You're Master Wendyn's apprentice."

It was a statement, not a question, but I still smiled and said, "Yes, you're correct."

His frown didn't subside. "The one what beat my John."

I nodded again.

He put the mugwort and lavender down on the counter. Then he planted his hands and leaned toward me. "The Council banned you from Bramford."

"Yes. But they rescinded that order." Just a few days ago, after Master Wendyn and I took our personal appeal to the council meeting.

He nodded. "So I've heard. But that doesn't mean I'm willing to do business with you."

My chin lifted. "Are you refusing me service? Master Wendyn can take his business elsewhere, you know. We have a wizard door to Dunsby, and the botanist there has the same inventory you have."

"I don't mean that," he said. "I only meant—" But he seemed to understand that he was in no position to turn business away, and master wizard business least of all. His lips thinned, and he nodded. "Very well. What do you need?"

I handed him my list and watched as he busied himself gathering herbs and plants.

But I couldn't leave things like this. Trying to work with a botanist who didn't trust or like me would get me nowhere. This was a man I could have a working relationship with for many years to come.

I cleared my throat. "I'm sorry for fighting with your son all those months ago. But he was mistreating a boy who couldn't defend himself. I couldn't stand by and do nothing."

His gaze flicked toward me, and he grunted in response. "All those boys have had a talking to since then," he said. "Including my John. He's a different boy these days."

"I'm glad of it," I said, even though I doubted any of the boys had really changed. At least the townsfolk were aware of the problem, if nothing else.

William's chin dipped as he stared at me, his gaze curious. "It was a good thing you did for that fool. Not many would have taken up for him. I think you're different from other under-wizards."

"Yes," I agreed, "I am."

I left William the Botanist's storefront with heavy laden arms. Calendula and basil and a dozen other varieties of plants and herbs weighed down a crate I carried in my arms.

Back at the fence, the spot Ivan had previously occupied stood empty. The realization tripped my heart.

Had he run into those boys? How much could they really have changed after all? Was he being beaten and bullied this very moment?

I shouldn't have left him alone. Stupid, stupid, stupid, Avery.

I hurried through the city, down alleys and streets I'd never been down before. No sign of Ivan. I hefted the crate in my arms and cast a listening spell, seeking for any noise that might identify itself as Ivan. After several long moments, I heard something familiar.

Laughter. "What's he doing? Hey, Ivan. Get up off the ground! You're not a farm animal."

"Or maybe he is," another voice said, and laughter flickered from one male voice to the next.

My fists clenched in anger. If those boys were tormenting Ivan again, I wouldn't answer for the consequences.

From the trickling sound of water, they might be near the river. Or I thought I remembered a fountain in the town square.

I hurried in the direction that I thought might lead me to the center of the village, and by dumb luck I happened to be right. A few people milled about the square, going about their normal daytime business.

I adjusted the crate in my arms and looked around. Where had Ivan gotten to?

Someone shouted with laughter. "Ivan, do another!" My gaze swung around, and I still couldn't find them, not until I moved around the stone fountain. There a group of teenage boys crouched around a smaller boy in the middle of the circle— Ivan. He knelt and scratched at the ground.

For a moment my heart picked up speed. Had he been beaten again? Was bringing him to Bramford a bad idea? The master seemed to think the townsfolk would treat him better now, but he had been wrong.

As I watched, Ivan looked up at the boys, excitement and enjoyment etched across his features. He scrambled to his feet, and the boys made room for him to move backward. He pointed at the drawing he had made on the ground. He sent a silent, wordless spell at the sketch of a mountain cat about to pounce, and it sprang to life, appearing to jump at the boy closest to it. They all jumped back amid a babble of laughter and chatter.

"Next draw me!" a boy demanded.

"No, me!"

"That's not fair; I've been waiting!"

I stepped to Ivan's side. "Friar's bones, boys, give Ivan some room to breathe. We have to be leaving, anyway."

A groan moved through the group. "When will you be coming back?" one demanded.

I shook my head. "Next time we're in need of herbs. Watch for us."

The boys dispersed, with slaps on the back for Ivan and calls that he should "practice drawing me, all right?"

"Well, that was unexpected," I said, as we moved away across the cobblestoned streets.

Ivan nodded and grinned, gesturing, *They not hate me.*

I shook my head. "They never hated you. They only—they had to remember you were a person, just like them, I suppose."

We walked toward the bridge that passed over the river. In the middle of the structure, he stopped me with a hand to my arm, motioning at the water. I set the crate down, and we watched the roiling liquid as the water tumbled over and over itself.

"How did you end up in Bramford, anyway?" I asked. "Did you have family here once?"

He shrugged. *No family. Yours?*

"My father is still alive somewhere."

He nodded and then pointed at the water. *Rough,* he gestured. *Water rough. Life rough sometimes too.*

"Yes." I stared at the water and thought of Ivan, abandoned and alone on the streets of Bramford, with no family or friends. At least I had the good years with Gavin and Mama to look back on.

Ivan reached for my hand. *Not rough now. Now you my family,* he gestured with his free hand. *Master Wendyn and Oscar too.*

"Yes. I suppose we are a family," I said. "But don't tell Master Wendyn that."

Boots thudded on the bridge behind us. "And why not?" Master Wendyn came to a stop beside the two of us. "Family, are we now? I can agree to that, even if it is more sentimental than I care for."

"Really?" I turned a questioning gaze on him.

"An unorthodox family," he said, "But I suppose we're family just the same." He nodded at the crate. "How's William?"

"A little hesitant, but willing."

"Good." Master Wendyn turned to the east. "Come along, little family. The carriage is waiting. It's time to go home."

Home. How nice that sounded. I picked up the crate, blinking at the moisture in my eyes.

Ivan broke into a run when he saw the carriage.

"Stop that," the master growled at me, taking the crate in one arm. "No crying unless you're dying or maimed. And maybe not even then."

I swiped at my eyes. "Yes, yes. I know."

He fished in his pocket and handed me a handkerchief. "I'm going to need more of these," he muttered to himself. I took the handkerchief and put it in my pocket for later. For now, I didn't need it. My tears had disappeared.

From Bramford on this sunny winter day, the future looked bright.

KEEP READING

Thank you for reading *Tethered by Blood*, the first book in The Counterfeit Apprentice Series. If you'd like to find out about new releases or anything else Jane finds awesome and interesting enough to tell you about, you can sign up for her newsletter at janebeckstead.com.

Did you love Tethered by Blood? You can ascend to Rockstar Reader status by leaving a review on Amazon or Goodreads. And haven't you always wanted to be a rockstar?

Avery's adventures continue in *Hunted by Shadow*, book two in The Counterfeit Apprentice Series.

ACKNOWLEDGMENTS

I owe a lot of people a lot of thank yous. The list is intimidating. But I've always enjoyed a good challenge, so here goes.

First off, my siblings and parents, who enjoyed the first stories I wrote when I was a child (or at least pretended to; thanks, guys). Thanks to Auntie M., who always asked how my book was coming, even twenty years ago (little did she know how long it would take me). Thanks to Judge C., who always, ALWAYS asked about my writing, and Judge H., who gave me the sweetest pep talk ever when I left my job to pursue writing.

Thanks to Mugsy, who's been my sounding board and beta reader and idea person, and who once gave me twenty bucks to reserve a copy of my book, long before it was even close to being published. Thanks to my roommates and friends Shelly and Jenay, who both shared my interest in writing and believed in my dream. Thanks to my writing group, Annette, Caryn, Dyany, Jessica, Lisa, and Pania, who made my writing hobby into something serious and whipped my prose into shape (or tried to).

Thanks to my traveling buddy Heater (misspelling intentional), who never commented when I brought my laptop on various trips and spent hours perfecting scenes, even though we were supposed to be on vacation.

Huge thanks to Alyson Misseldine, my genius cover designer, and to Christina Schrunk, editor extraordinaire.

And a huge thank you to you, for reading! None of this would be possible without your support, so thank you for joining me for Avery's adventures. The only thing better than writing something I love is hearing from readers, so feel free to connect with me at janebeckstead.com, Facebook, Instagram, Pinterest, and/or Goodreads.

See you soon!

ABOUT THE AUTHOR

Jane Beckstead is a confirmed notebook addict (the doctors say it's incurable) since every blank notebook represents a story that needs telling. For years she has jotted down tales of every sort, most with a liberal dusting of magic. She loves writing strong female characters who grow into strong women.

Jane is a busy aunt to forty-three nieces and nephews and lives in the Pacific Northwest or Intermountain West, depending on who you ask. She thinks heaven on earth can be found at the Oregon Coast, with her family, or both at the same time. Her first masterpiece, entitled "The Biggest Pumpkin in the World," was written in crayon shortly after she learned how to make words into sentences, and is her greatest literary work to date. It is, unfortunately, not in print.

Read more at janebeckstead.com.